MW01272986

ᛒLOOD
ᕼAMMER

BLACK HAND RISES

Book Two of the Blood Hammer Trilogy

For Chris Foulds-Chanilyah
for all the ink.

C.S. KEMPLING

Tellwell Talent
www.tellwell.ca

ISBN
978-0-2288-5752-5 (Paperback)
978-0-2288-5753-2 (eBook)

ACKNOWLEDGEMENTS

I am grateful for the editing assistance and feedback of my daughter Adrienne Yates. The team at Tellwell was amazing—thanks to all of you. To my grade six school teacher, Mr. Kondrat of Maquinna Elementary School in Port Alberni, British Columbia, I have truly valued your encouragement of my story-telling. Thank you as well to Chief Stanley Boyd of the Nazko First Nation, Dr. Bill Poser, and the Ootsa Lake elder (who must remain anonymous) for teaching me the meanings of Carrier/Dakelh words. Any usage errors are mine alone. To Tamba Kemoh of Sierra Leone, whose impressive physique inspired a character, thank you. To Kaelina Hascarl, thanks for bringing my map to life. And finally, many thanks to Li Sheng Mei of Taiwan for her wonderful cover art.

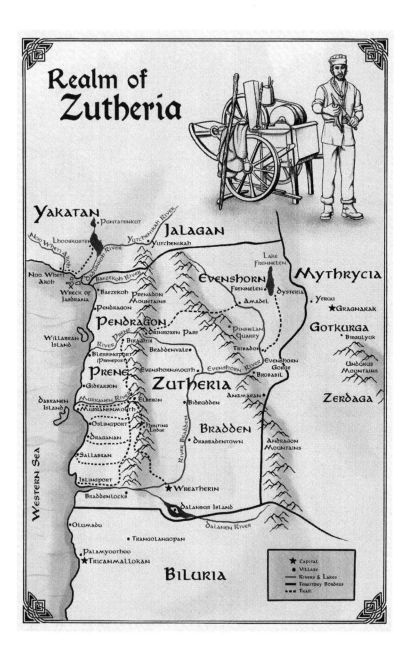

Realm of Zutheria

Yakatan

Puntatenkut

Noo Whet Joongh

Lhooskasten

Noo Whet Akoh

Wreck of Jasdrana

Baezekoh

Pendragon

Jalagan

Yutchenikah River

Yutchenikah

Salangon River

Baezekoh River

Prenadon Mountains

Evenshorn

Lake Frennelen

Frennelen

Amadel

Mythrycia

Oysteria

Yeruu

★ Gragnarak

Pendragon

Orinroxen Pass

Willabran Island

Prene River

Biraghir

Braddenvale

Gotkurga

Biraglyuk

Pinnelan Quarry

Tribadon

Prene

Blessingport/Preneport

Gidearson

Sabranen Island

Murranen River

Prene

Evenshornmouth

Evenshorn River

Evenshorn Gorge

Brobabil

Undurus Mountains

Zutheria

Elberon

Bidrudden

Angmaran

Zerdaga

Murranenmouth

Oslingport

Draganan

Hunting Lodge

River Bradden

Bradden

Drabbadentown

Andragon Mountains

Sallabran

Islimaport

Western Sea

Braddenlocks

★ Wreatherin

Dalanbar Island

Olumadu

Dalanen River

Trangolangopan

Palamyoothoo

★ Tricanmallokan

Biluria

★	Capital
●	Village
—	Rivers & Lakes
▬	Territory Borders
‧‧‧	Trail

iv

LIST OF CHARACTERS

Zutherians

Amathea the elder (Thea), oldest half-sister of the Set brothers, herbalist

Amathea (Ammy), oldest daughter of Genneset

Ambera, daughter of Futt

Ambrogran, Admiral, Zutherian navy

Ambrosin, Lieutenant, Zutherian army, Preneport barracks

Ardenfoyl, stick-maker of Biraghir

Astaran, Zaharbat of the Laguntzaileas of Zutheria

Bahnuran, cousin of Bahomet, Zutherian merchant, Tricanmallokan

Bahomet/Karpukkai, Valikatti and Myanpur of Biluria, husband to Elomir

Bahramin, uncle of Bahomet, Zutherian merchant, Tricanmallokan

Bandonnen, trooper, Zutherian army, Preneport barracks

Baragin, King Zuth XXIII of Zutheria

Baragran, Baragin's son

Barnagel, cook, Dabranen Island garrison

Baskar, blacksmith, Linkman of Tribadon

Bellawin, maid to Queen Amathea

Berendell, Equerry to Baragin, son of Chancellor Berenfromm

Berenfromm, Chancellor to Baragin

Bidnarin, marine supply merchant, Blessingport

Bilanna, daughter of Donneset

Bobbingran, barman, Prenadon Inn, Braddenlocks
Bradnarin, son of Bidnarin, friend of Futtsam
Branderron, Accusatim, County of Prene
Brandonwill, Governor of Prene
Cranadan, Linkman of Braddenlocks
Darrabee, barge captain of the *Lazy Bee*
Damagal, Laguntzailea of Bradden
Danaquill, son of Doroquill
Danstorin, Ambassador to Mythrycia
Darrabin, son of Sennabin
Demmenbel, Protocol Master, court of King Baragin
Demmerdran, Captain, Selvenhall Palace Guard
Dobberan, Corporal, Zutherian Army, Bidrudden barracks
Donbidden, merchant, Iblingport
Donneset, older brother of Genneset, tin merchant
Donnarin, son of Bidnarin, twin of Bradnarin
Doralaine, wife of Futt
Doralee, daughter of Donneset
Doroquill, Mayor of Blessingport
Drellabin, Judge of the County of Prene
Drezzerell, Governor of Prene
Dulgert, cook's helper, Dabranen Island garrison
Durrenbar, avocatim, Wreatherin
Ebba, wife of Sennabin
Elomir, Marquesa of Bradden, wife of Bahomet
Erenbil, Zutherian Ambassador to Biluria
Ferrelaine, twin sister of Berendell
Filden, Chamberlain to Duke Robagrin, Elberon
Futt, Harbourmaster of Blessingport
Futtsam, son of Futt
Ganabir, Linkman of Brobabil, bookseller
Gella, nursemaid to Robduran
Genneset, youngest of the Set brothers, travelling tinker
Germilda, wife of Genneset, washerwoman

Gibberast, trooper, Zutherian army, Preneport barracks
Gormanen, Head Customs Inspector, Braddenlocks
Grandabin, nephew of Filden, merchant, Iblingport
Gryn, Major, Commander of BLK Guards, Zutherian Army
Hanraddin, Selvenhall palace guard
Ibbingrin, Harbourmaster of Preneport, owner
of the *Alladonna*
Joya/Nooshtal/Nooshta, Khokhgui warrior, youngest
daughter of Genneset
Krindellin, Captain, Zutherian Army, Bidrudden barracks
Milla, daughter of Baragin and Amathea
Pendramon, Captain of the *Amathea*
Pharigon, Captain/Major of the Zutherian Army
Philabin, son of Sennabin
Plinweggin, hardware merchant, Evenshornmouth
Ringforin, Judge, High Court of Zutheria, Wreatherin
Robagrin, Duke of Bradden, Prene and Pendragon
Robduran, son of Bahomet and Elomir
Sabah, daughter of Sennabin
Saragon, apprentice Laguntzailea to Astaran
Sennabin, Pendragon miner
Stornowin, Laguntzailea of Prene
Suberon the Blind, Laguntzailea of Pendragon
Timbraset, oldest of the Set brothers, tin merchant,
mayor of Preneport
Trillabon, General-in-Chief, Zutherian Army
Trinrudden, cider merchant, Braddenvale
Umbraset, son of Donneset
Wilmund, older brother of Germilda, tinworks foreman
Wranbeddin, blacksmith of Brobabil
Yanneron, sergeant, Selvenhall palace guard
Zerdunlee, Selvenhall palace guard
Zolenfan, Laguntzailea of Evenshorn

Mythrycians
Aruzhan, daughter of Ulugan, Khokhgui warrior
Batzorig, Sasag Darga of Mythrycia
Enkhtura, father of Batzorig, previous Sasag Darga
Muunokoi, Ambassador to Biluria
Onghul, Captain, Mythrycian Army
Ulugan, travelling tin trader, father of Aruzhan
Zythramin, Mythrycian Ambassador to Zutheria

Gotkurgans
Aikorkam, daughter of Aklach Saaral Chono
Aizat, Khokhgui warrior, squad leader
Alinur, Sogis Bassisi (war chief) of the Gotkurgans
Arayu, Khokhgui warrior
Arsen, blacksmith, Birgulyuk
Ayana, Khokhgui warrior
Ayaulym, Khokhgui warrior
Aylin, Khokhgui warrior
Ayzera, Khokhgui warrior
Bakhtiar, son of Aklach Saaral Chono
Bergara, Khokhgui warrior
Booshchoo, a Jalag, Kaskir Ana (Wolf Mother) of the Khokhguis
Enkhara, Khokhgui warrior, squad leader
Inkar, Khokhgui warrior
Inzhu, Khokhgui warrior
Kashkara, Khokhgui warrior
Medara, Khokhgui warrior
Nurasyl, son of Arsen
Oyunchumai, Mongomaa (Silver Mother) of the Khokhguis
Saaral Chono, Aklach of the Gotkurgans
Sanzhar, village simpleton, Birgulyuk

Yakats
Dzulhcho, Yakat warrior
K'uidlih, daughter of Tsis Dunecho of Lhooskustenkut
Naudnil Ujun, duyun of the Lhooskustenkut Yakats
Noostel, Dunecho of Puntatenkut Yakats
Tsis, Dunecho of Lhooskustenkut Yakats
Yat'ahna/Balyan, son of Baragin and K'uidlih

Dwarves
Druzganan, goldsmith of Amadel
Gernzedden, Captain, Dwarvish Regiment
Graznibur, Master of the Goldsmiths' Guild
Grodminan, Dordran of the Miners' Guild, General,
Dwarvish Regiments
Gymradraz, Head Miner, Brazinan Mine
Zerribil, Dashgran of the Andragon Dwarves

Bilurians
Agan, stonecutter, Elberon marble quarry
Anasamang Prin, Bilurian soldier
Arashbilan, wife of Darabindoo
Bandeenmanash Asan, Captain, Bulankayan ship
Bansundalang Boyan, Captain of the Aranmanai
Guard, Tricanmallokan
Baroneeloman Dran, Patolukai Kumpal (training
master) Karuppsertai assassins
Besh, Governor of Tricanmallokan province
Bilanguree, great-aunt to Bahomet
Bishnannam Brin, Karuppsertai torturer
Brandeeshpuran Fayan, Grand Vizier of Biluria
Danputmanan Saran, Kiritam Ilavaracar (Crown
Prince) of Biluria
Darabindoo, cousin of Bahomet

Dasalimpanong Trin, Uyam Picari (high priest)
of Balongupong,
Daragoonbalai Dra, Valikatti, great-grandfather
of Bahomet
Dareeshput Aban, close friend of Danputmanan
Dormandesh Kiran, General-in-Chief, Bilurian Army
Dringmanan Saran, Myanpur, great-grandfather
of Bahomet
Gandaman Abin, Karuppsertai assassin
Gampreeshdalan Saran, brother to Myanpur Geelanguran
Gandrapreen Oban, Bilurian Ambassador to Zutherian
Geelanguran Saran, Myanpur (Sultan) of Biluria
Paradaman, Chief Valikatti of Biluria
Sriwalloban Ohn, Karuppsertai assassin

CHAPTER ONE

Bahomet lay on his cot in the drafty cell of the Dabranen Island prison, staring at the mold-mottled ceiling. He ran the fingers of his good hand over the red scar that decorated his left brow—the scar that Blood Hammer had left. The day that was supposed to be the day he was crowned King of Zutheria became the day of his greatest humiliation. Beaten by an Astaran-spelled stick, then having his right hand turned black and withered with a blast from Zolenfan's dragon staff. But the physical scars were nothing compared to the devastation to his aspirations.

He grabbed the wrist of his flame-charred hand to move his arm into a more comfortable position. It didn't do much good. The pain in his hand was unrelenting, a constant reminder of the Amadel square disaster. The skin was hideous, black, with weeping sores that never healed. Bahomet had had over six years to dream of his revenge, though. It was almost time.

Dulgert the cook's helper was the one who was tasked with bringing Bahomet his food and removing his waste bucket. He was pudgy and rather simple-minded, with a ready smile. He had come with the new rotation of guards from the Iblingport garrison who rotated through Dabranen Island once every month. The guards weren't permitted to speak to him, but

Bahomet was allowed simple communications with the cook's helper.

"Well, what have you brought today, Dulgert?" asked Bahomet in a friendly tone.

"It's a fish stew, sir. I added a few herbs myself, so I think you'll like it," replied Dulgert slowly.

His speech was as slow as his mind.

"A few herbs? Yourself, you say? Let me taste," said Bahomet, dipping a wooden spoon into the large bowl. He made some exaggerated 'Ohs!' saying, "That—is truly delicious. I'll reckon they'll be promoting you to cook on the next rotation. You've got real talent, my boy."

Dulgert beamed. It was rare he got a compliment about anything. Cook Barnagel was a gruff and impatient man and was not averse to giving Dulgert a cuff if he didn't move fast enough.

"Uh, I don't think so, sir. Cook Barnagel almost never lets me do a meal on my own," drawled Dulgert.

"Well, he's a dullard for not recognizing your genuine gift. I'll bet he'd change his tune if you put some Dabranen truffle into the next stew," rejoined Bahomet.

"Dabranen truffle? What's that? Never heard of it," said Dulgert.

"Never heard of it?" said Bahomet, acting astonished.

Leaning in close, he whispered conspiratorially, "I spotted some the other day, on the north ridge. Very rare, and absolutely delicious. They have little dark purple flowers. You dig up the root—you can tell it's Dabranen truffle by the three-lobed root. You grate it like garlic into a stew, and you'll have the whole crew singing your praises. But hush—you can't tell anyone. Real chefs have their own secret ingredients, and this can be yours. You'll be famous because it only grows here," said Bahomet.

Dulgert's eyes got big with anticipation.

"The north ridge, you say? Purple flowers? Would it be alright if I showed you the truffle if I manage to find it?" he asked.

"Of course, of course, my boy. I tell you, you're going to be the most famous cook in all of Zutheria," said Bahomet, clapping Dulgert's shoulder with his good hand.

Three days later, Dulgert looked over his shoulder at the waiting guards, but they were chatting with one another and paying no attention to him or Bahomet.

"I think it found it, sir. The truffle!" said Dulgert, pulling a dirt-stained rag out of his coat pocket.

He unwrapped the rag revealing a large three-lobed root. Gallarderian—the most deadly poison in all of Zutheria.

Bahomet hissed, "Wrap it up! Wrap it up! You lucky boy, you found it. Clever lad! But you can't let anyone know you have it—chef's secret. I can hardly wait to taste it. When do you think you can add it to a stew?"

"Well, Barnagel has me do the base broth for the stew. It'll be tomorrow," answered Dulgert.

"Excellent!" beamed Bahomet. "Remember, mum's the word. Real chefs never tell their secret ingredients."

Dulgert smiled at the "real chefs" label.

"I can't thank you enough, sir. This could be my way to being master of my own kitchen one day."

"Absolutely, absolutely," smiled Bahomet. "Looking forward to your masterpiece."

Dulgert lumbered off to the kitchen after stuffing the galladerian "truffle" back into his pocket.

Bahomet knew that dried galladerian was beneficial as a soporific in small quantities. But fresh, it was absolutely lethal, even in tiny amounts. An entire root grated into a stew would be enough to dispatch the entire garrison.

Bahomet had seen a ship's boat pulled up onto the only beach on the island during his daily walks. He also knew that Dulgert never ate until after he had returned from serving the prisoner. A cook tasting a broth would only ingest enough galladerian to put him into a peaceful slumber for a few hours. With only one good hand, Bahomet would need Dulgert to launch the boat and get to a safe harbour—Tricanmallokan in Biluria was the only place he would be able to stay out of Baragin's—and Astaran's—clutches.

Bahomet lay back on his cot, thinking furiously. He finally fell asleep, dreaming of his black hand around Baragin's throat.

CHAPTER TWO

Amathea sat bolt upright in bed, screaming, "No!"

Her chest was heaving and her brow was beaded with sweat. It was the same dream she had had many years ago in the dungeon at Amadel Castle. She had started embracing a shirtless Baragin but felt a mole on his back—a mole with three lobes and a tuft of hair. Her forehead touched a black beard and when she looked up, she was staring into Bahomet's dark, cruel eyes.

A groggy Baragin stirred beside her.

"What? What is it Ammy?" he slurred.

"He's coming. He's coming for us," whispered Amathea, shaking with fear.

Baragin, fully awake now, pulled her into an embrace.

"Who, darling? Who's coming? My goodness, you're shivering." Baragin held her tightly until he calmed her down, but only slightly.

Amathea was chewing on her fingernail, something she hardly ever did anymore. Baragin pulled back and looked at her intently.

"You've had a dream. One of those dreams. I know you. Things have been going so well, I'd almost forgotten your gift. Who did you dream of, Ammy?" asked Baragin, staring intently into her eyes.

"Him."

She didn't have to say his name. Baragin knew immediately of whom she spoke.

"Darling, I do not take your dreams lightly. But Bahomet is no threat to us or anyone. He is moldering away on Dabranen Island. I get a pigeon every week telling me all is well. I just had one yesterday. He will never get off that island. His final resting place will be an unmarked grave there," said Baragin firmly.

Amathea pulled back and looked at Baragin.

"He's already left," she said with a tone of finality.

Baragin's jaw dropped. Amathea swung her legs off the bed and went to check on Baragran in the next room.

Baragin followed her. She was sitting on the edge of Baragran's bed, stroking the hair of the sleeping lad.

"I will send Berendell personally to Dabranen tomorrow. I hope you're wrong."

Amathea turned slowly and fixed her grey eyes on Baragin, her mouth tightened into a grin line. She didn't have to say anything. Baragin's heart sank within him. She was never wrong with her "danger dreams".

He couldn't sleep now. He opened the door to his chambers and headed towards his personal office. The night guard outside the door snapped to attention at his sudden appearance. A second guard was caught snoozing until Baragin roused him with a kick.

"You! Wake the Captain of the Guard immediately. Send him to me at my office. Go!" ordered Baragin.

Baragin strode purposively towards Berendell's chambers at the far end of the corridor in the Selvenhall palace. He knocked twice then walked through the door. Berendell was entangled with his latest young woman in a dishevelled bed.

"Up, Berendell. There is evil afoot. Join me in my office as soon as you're decent," he ordered.

He waited until Berendell gave a muffled response then headed out the door to his office.

When a rumpled Berendell joined him a few minutes later Baragin was pacing nervously. Berendell eyed him carefully, knowing from experience to wait until he was ready to speak. He couldn't remember when he had seen Baragin this agitated.

"Amathea has had a dream. A dream that Bahomet has escaped. Escaped! How is that remotely possible? Did you not tell me only yesterday the Dabranen pigeon said all was well? Didn't you?" said Baragin putting his nose close to Berendell's.

Before he could reply, Baragin fired another question.

"Who is the captain in charge there now?"

"I'd have to check, I...," faltered Berendell.

"Well check! Now! Damnation!"

A knock at door interrupted them.

"Who is it?" yelled Baragin.

"Captain Demmerdran, sir," answered the Selvenhall Captain of the Guard.

"Enter!"

Demmerdran stood before Baragin nervously. The king was nornally very courteous towards him, but this was an entirely different Baragin.

"The guard I sent to summon you—what is his name?" demanded Baragin.

"Zerdunlee, sir," responded Demmerdran.

"He was asleep at his post. Take care of his discipline," ordered Baragin.

"Yes, Your Majesty. I..." started Demmerdran.

"That's not why I summoned you in the middle of the night, Captain," interrupted Baragin. "I want the palace night guards doubled. Immediately."

"Is there some specific...?" began Demmerdran.

"Double the guards! Now!" yelled Baragin.

"Yes, Your Majesty."

Demmerdran snapped a crisp salute and made a hasty retreat out the door of Baragin's office.

"Well, what are you waiting for? Get me that captain's name!" snapped Baragin.

Berendell paused a moment, fixing his friend of many years with a gaze. "Calm yourself, Baragin. Easy. It's not like you to fly off in all directions like this. We'll get the facts and deal with them," said Berenfromm soothingly.

Baragin slumped into his chair.

"You're right, you're right. But you know Amathea is never wrong with *those* dreams. What if it's true?" he asked, his face taking on a pained expression.

Berendell didn't answer.

"I should have taken his head at Amadel Square," said Baragin ruefully.

Berendell put his hand on Baragin's shoulder.

"If he is on the loose, we'll catch him and remedy that mistake," he said confidently.

Baragin looked up at him, with a doubtful expression.

"I be back with that information shortly," said Berendell as he headed towards his own office.

Chapter Three

Bahomet pricked up his ears as he heard one of the guards saying, "Well, it's about time you showed up, Dulgert. What's for dinner tonight?"

"Stew. Dab...." Dulgert stopped.

He was about to say Dabranen truffle stew, but remembered he was supposed to keep his secret ingredient secret.

"Stew tonight, boys. I think you'll like it. I made the broth for it."

Dulgert spooned out two bowls for the guards and another for Bahomet. One of the guards unlocked the cell and sat down to gobble the stew.

"Great Zuth, that is tasty! Tell Barnagel he can do this one again," said the guard, shovelling in spoonful after spoonful.

Dulgert glanced at Bahomet, who gave him an 'I told you so' smile and a nod.

"Just put the bowl over there if you wouldn't mind. I'm in the middle of washing my hands," said Bahomet, bending over a wash basin.

As Dulgert moved in behind him, Bahomet suddenly moved his heel backwards, causing Dulgert to stumble. The bowl of stew went flying and Dulgert along with it.

"Oh no! My stew!" said Bahomet, as Dulgert picked himself and the cracked wooden bowl up off the floor of the cell.

"I'm so sorry, sir, so sorry. I'm just a clumsy oaf. I...I didn't see your foot. It won't take me but a minute to go get another bowl for you," said Dulgert apologetically.

"We should lock you in there with him for the crime of wasting good stew. Get a move on and get him another bowl, you great tangled-footed ox," laughed the guard.

"Right away, sir, right away," answered Dulgert.

The guard re-locked the door and sat down with his mate to finish off their bowls.

Dulgert never made it to the kitchen. He started feeling extremely drowsy on his way back and stopped to hang onto a nearby tree as the entire island began spinning rapidly. He slumped down against the tree and was soon unconscious.

When he awoke, it was dark, and his head was throbbing. Confused, he headed for the kitchen. Barnagel was there, seated at the small table he and Dulgert used to eat their own meals. His head was on the table next to a near empty bowl with the remains of the stew in the bottom.

"Barnagel. Barnagel!" shouted Dulgert.

Alarmed, he shook the cook's shoulder, but he just rolled sideways onto the floor. Dead. Dulgert covered his mouth in horror. "Help!" he yelled.

"Help! Help!" he yelled.

Hearing nothing, he went through the doorway into the mess hall. A grim sight greeted him. The entire garrison—fourteen soldiers, the sergeant, and the captain—were all slumped over their bowls. Dead.

Dulgert let out a long, low moan and sank down with his back against the wall of the mess hall, hands to his head.

He stumbled back down the trail to Bahomet's cell block. Both guards were motionless, one with the remains of vomited stew staining the front of his tunic.

"Bahomet?" Dulgert peered in through the cell door.

"Are you back with my stew, boy? Took you long enough," answered Bahomet.

"They're dead. They're all dead, sir." said Dulgert. He started crying.

"What? What are you saying?" asked Bahomet, feigning incredulity.

"Everyone's dead, sir. I...it must have been the stew. I only had a taste and it knocked me out. But it killed everyone else. You...you tricked me! That wasn't truffle! It was some kind of poison, wasn't it?" said Dulgert accusingly. He dabbed at his eyes.

Bahomet smiled.

"Of course, it was. Galladerian, especially fresh galladerian, is extremely dangerous. Now you know. But the question is, what are you going to do now? Eventually, someone is going to come here to see why no one has sent a pigeon. Then you'll have to tell them that you were the one who poisoned nineteen soldiers of the Zutherian army. They are going to think you are in league with me and execute you in the most horrible way. They'll probably start with the rack, then red-hot pokers, then..."

"Stop! Stop! Stop talking! I...I...Nooooo!"

Dulgert started sobbing, inconsolable.

Bahomet let him sob for a while. Then in a soothing voice, he said, "Your life is over. I doubt you will survive the interrogation. But perhaps we can help each other out."

Dulgert gave a hiccough, wiped his eyes, then looked up at Bahomet.

"What do you mean?" he asked, suspiciously.

"There's a boat on the beach. I know how to sail one, but I would need your help. I have friends in Biluria. Tricanmallokan is only two days sail from here. I'll make sure you are set up in a safe place. You can't go back to Zutheria—ever. It's your only option," said Bahomet.

Dulgert just moaned again and grabbed his head.

"No, no, no. I can't, I....noooo," he moaned.

"You think about it. Me? I have nothing to lose. I'm here for life no matter what. But you...."

Bahomet let the comment hang in the air.

"Have you ever heard the screams of someone on the rack?" asked Bahomet.

"Noooo!" howled Dulgert.

He jumped up and ran towards the cliff edge. He stopped suddenly as he looked down at the roiling sea crashing against the rocks at the base of the cliff. He plopped himself down, grabbed his hair with both hands and started sobbing again, rocking back and forth.

It was morning when Bahomet heard a key grating in the lock of his cell door. Dulgert was there, eyes still red and puffy from weeping. He looked defeated.

"Just get me away from this cursed island," was all he said.

CHAPTER FOUR

Genneset gently cradled the pigeon he had just retrieved from the rooftop coop he had installed on the Silver Dolphin pub. He could have moved into Selvenhall after Amathea's marriage to the king, but he liked his independence and running his own show. He and Germilda actually made a good team. He handled the bar and dealt with customers and suppliers, while Germilda managed the kitchen and the financial end of things. Along with Joya, a cook and a kitchen helper, they produced all the meals as well. Their nephew Umbraset tended bar and doubled as a bouncer when needed. Joya occasionally served as a bar maid, but she had such a wicked temper she caused more trouble than she was worth. Usually, it was due to a drunken fisherman trying to steal a pinch or a kiss, for Joya had turned into a real beauty. More than once Genneset and Umbraset had to toss a tipsy flirter out on his ear (but usually after Joya had gotten in a punch or a knee to the groin herself). For serious brawlers Genneset always had Blood Hammer as an option, but he'd only had to use it twice in the last six years.

As he read the note from the canister he frowned. Amathea had had another dream, a dream of Bahomet's escape from Dabranen. Baragin asked him to come to Selvenhall in Wreatherin as soon as possible—and bring Blood Hammer with him. Genneset had no idea how a one-armed prisoner guarded by twenty soldiers could escape from the storm-tossed Dabranan Island, but if Amathea dreamed it, he knew it had happened. The note asked him to meet Berendell in Iblingport in three days time.

Genneset stuffed the note into his pocket and went downstairs to talk with Germilda. She wouldn't be happy about his leaving, but if it was to protect Amathea from a serious threat, she would agree it was necessary. Besides, Genneset was anxious to see his grandson Baragran again. Germilda would likely ask her brother Wilmund to fill in at the bar, something he had time to do now that he had retired from active work at the tin shop. Wilmund would only agree to such a request if Genneset was not around—he still didn't like him, even if he was the king's father-in-law.

After talking things over with Germilda, Genneset wandered down to the docks to see if there was a boat sailing south. He spotted the *Alladonna* at the second wharf and strolled over to see if Ibbingrin was aboard. They had gotten friendly since he had helped Baragin with his return from Yakatan.

Ibbingrin wasn't in sight, but he heard some thumping below deck.

"Halloo, Ibbingrin! Permission to come aboard," yelled Genneset.

Ibbingrin poked his head through an open hatch to see who was hailing him.

"Genneset, it's you, is it? I said I'd pay my tab at the Dolphin after this next catch," started Ibbingrin.

"I know, I know. That's not why I'm here. Just wondering if you were heading to Iblingport," asked Genneset.

"As soon as I have this gear stowed. I need some tackle and a new net before I head north to Pendragon. Why do you ask?" queried Ibbingrin.

Genneset paused, wondering how much he should tell him. But he remembered his discretion when Baragin used him as a secret transport to the Midsummer's Day ball in Blessingport.

He looked around to see if anyone was within earshot, then said, "There's a rumor Bahomet has escaped. The king has asked me to meet Berendell in Iblingport then head to Wreatherin. Amathea's a wreck and he wants me there while he takes care of this nasty business."

Ibbingrin's face turned serious.

"Great Zuth! Now that's news nobody wants to hear. How on earth could he have gotten away?" he asked, incredulous.

"No idea. We don't have any details yet, and don't even know for sure if it's true. But my Ammy has had one of her dreams, and that's enough for me. Can you give me a lift to Iblingport?" asked Genneset.

"Not a problem. I'm just waiting for my boy to arrive with some fresh vegetables for the galley, then we'll cast off. You have everything ready?" asked Ibbingrin.

"Give me half an hour to grab my things and say good-bye to Joya and the missus. I'll be right back. And don't worry about your tab," said Genneset with a smile.

The next morning the *Alladonna* was slicing through the dappled seas near Dabranen Island. Genneset was in the bow and spotted a large ship anchored in the small cove next to the only beach on the island. It was the *Amathea*, the king's personal ship. Genneset shouted at Ibbingrin to change course.

As they pulled alongside, the captain, with Berendell beside him, peered over the side wondering who was approaching. Berendell recognized Genneset and Ibbingrin immediately and spoke quickly into the captain's ear. He gave an order, and several sailors grabbed the lines that Genneset threw them and fastened them. Genneset clambered up the rope ladder the sailors threw over the siderail.

Ibbingrin shouted up at him.

"Let me know if you still need a ride to Iblingport. If you don't, I don't want to miss the tide."

Genneset looked over at Berendell, who said, "We'll get you to Iblingport."

Genneset retrieved his pack and Blood Hammer from the *Alladonna* and joined Berendell on the main deck. He waved good-bye to Ibbingrin as he cast off.

Berendell put his hand on Genneset's arm, and with a serious expression said, "Come aft. There's something you need to see."

As they walked to the rear of the ship, a smell of putrefaction assailed Genneset's nose. Then a chilling sight came into view—nineteen canvas-wrapped bodies lay in a row.

The captain, who Berendell had introduced as Pendramon, joined them.

"We've just finished gathering them all and sewing them up. We couldn't leave them to rot on that island, or even bury them there. The place is cursed. Balleramin will take them all at sunset," said Pendramon.

Genneset was speechless at the ghastly sight.

Finally, he said, "But how....?"

"Poison, probably galladerian. We spotted one or two plants when we searched the island. Somehow Bahomet got hold of some and talked, or tricked, the cook's helper into spiking the stew. He's missing along with Bahomet and the ship's boat. My guess is that he's headed to Biluria. He's fluent in the language and has some family there from the old days. He's out of our reach now. But one thing's for sure—Baragin won't be safe until that snake is impaled on a pike," concluded Berendell grimly.

CHAPTER FIVE

Bahomet pulled the hooded cloak close about his face with his good hand as he guided the small boat towards a creek mouth on the northern outskirts of Tricanmallokan. He was alone. Bahomet had retrieved a Bilurian blade from the body of one the dead guards before he and Dulgert fled Dabranen Island. When Dulgert fell asleep after two long days of sailing, Bahomet had slit his throat and rolled him over the gunwales into the foam-tipped waves. The blood running freely from his throat soon attracted three large sharks.

They had been close to shore at the time. The winds were favorable and Bahomet was able to manage the boat on his own for the last stretch to the Bilurian coast. He nosed the boat towards the beach, hopped over the side into waist deep water, then waded ashore. He watched the boat drift away with the tide until it faded into the twilight. It was completely dark when he reached the village of Palamyoothoo, just north of Tricanmallokan.

The last time he was here was almost twenty-five years ago, visiting his grandmother, his pattam. It was his pattam who had introduced him to the knowledge of herbs and potions—and magic.

Bahomet's father had taken a Bilurian girl as a mistress, but she had died giving birth to him.

Bahomet's grandmother had found him a wet-nurse, her own much younger half-sister Bilanguree, and the two of them raised him until he was a teenager.

When Bahomet was fifteen, his father had been swept overboard in a storm. His uncle Bahramin had taken him in and apprenticed him to the Tricanmallokan trading house where Zutherian goods were marketed to Bilurian customers. Bahomet had spent much of his non-working time with his pattam, though, and she taught him much. His skill at making potions and casting spells caught the attention of Damagal, the Laguntzailea of Prene, during an extended visit to at Iblingport. Aladrash had taken him on as an apprentice. Lat, he was awarded the bailiwick of Amadel after he developed a successful spell to thwart the Mythrycian cavalry. He had come within a cat's whisker of becoming king of all Zutheria, but Baragin and Astaran—and that blasted tinker with the magic stick—had ruined everything. Bahomet vowed that was about to change.

He stood outside his pattam's house, watching. Someone was carrying a lamp past a window. It wasn't his pattam—she was likely long in her grave. It was an old woman. Bahomet stared at her as she sat at a table, sipping some tea. He recognized her. It was Bilanguree, his pattam's half-sister, Bahomet's great aunt, the one who had been his wet nurse after his mother died. He didn't see anyone else in the house.

Bahomet waited until she went to the outdoor privy to relieve herself, then slipped into the house. When she re-entered, he clapped his good hand around her mouth and hissed in Bilurian, "Quiet, Attam (auntie). It's Bahomet."

Bilanguree struggled briefly in fright, then relaxed and turned slowly towards him as she recognized his voice.

"Anapay," she said, using the Bilurian word for "dear one". She put both hands on his cheeks and kissed him.

"Anapay, anapay. It's been so long. Where have you been? Did I not hear you were going to be king of the Zutherians? What happened, anapay? And what happened to your hand, anapay?" asked Bilanguree, piling question upon question.

"Too many questions, Attam Gurgoo," said Bahomet, using his pet name for her from years ago.

"First of all, do you live alone?" asked Bahomet.

"Yes, these past three years, since your pattam died. But my grandnephew, your cousin Darabindoo and his wife Arashbilan, look after me. They live three houses away. Shall I call them? Let me make you some tea first," said Bilanguree.

"Tea, please. But let's wait until tomorrow to see Darabindoo. I need to sleep," said Bahomet.

"Of course, of course, Bah-bah," said Bilanguree, using her old pet name for him while fussing over him.

While he drank his tea, his attam put together a cot for him with a soft pillow and warm blanket. The sun was high in the morning sky when he finally awoke.

Bilanguree placed a basin of warm water on the table for Bahomet to wash his face and handed him a towel to dry himself. Bahomet looked around at the simple two-room hut with its plain furnishings and undecorated walls. Bilanguree poured tea for him, then served him a plate of sliced mangoes and warm flat bread. She gazed at him with a smile as he ate, one-handed.

She reached out to touch his black, withered hand, but he pulled it back with an annoyed grunt.

"Don't be angry, Bah-bah. It looks sore. Let your attam put some salve on it for you. Come, let attam help you," she said soothingly.

Bahomet grudgingly let her apply some ointment. He had to admit it felt much better. Clearly, his attam had taken over his pattam's herbalist business, which included making healing salves.

"I have something for you. While you slept, I made a glove for your hand, with a sling to hold it up," said Bilanguree with a shy smile.

She brought out a well-made black glove in soft kid leather and laid it on the table.

Bahomet smiled.

"Thank-you, Attam Gurgoo. It's been a long, long time since anyone pampered me like this," he said as he planted a peck on her cheek.

He slipped the glove over his blackened hand and lifted the sling over his head. It fit perfectly. Bilanguree beamed. Then she jumped up and quickly shuffled to the other room.

"There's something your pattam left for you, in case you ever came back," she said.

Bilanguree came back with a dark wooden box, inlaid with multi-hued shell pieces.

Bahomet looked at it, intrigued. He slowly opened the box. Bahomet recognized what it was immediately and let out a gasp of pleasure. It was a mantirakolai, a Bilurian magic wand. It was similar to the one Bahomet had used in Amadel square, but more ornate.

"Where did this come from, Attam Gurgoo?" asked Bahomet.

"It belonged to your perraya tattam, your pattam's father. His name was Daragoonbalai Dra. He was a great valikatti, like your Zutherian Laguntzailea. Your pattam thought you would be a valikatti like him, but you left to be a Laguntzailea in Zutheria. So she kept this for you. She said you would know what to do when the time came, anapay," said Bilanguree simply.

Bahomet let his fingers hover over the mantirakolai. A small blue flame-like tongue of light sprang from it, curling around his fingers. Bilanguree's eyes widened in wonder.

"Oh, Bah-bah. It knows who you are," she said in a whisper.

This was a stroke of luck. A real mantirakolai, probably even more powerful than the one he had lost in Amadel. But he would need to conduct the ceremony of sassamandolanoo to bind it to himself—and that could only be done at the holy mountain of Trangolangopan.

Bahomet had been there twice before. Once was to bind the wand he had purchased when he lived in Tricanmallokan. The other time was to visit the stronghold of the Bilurian assassins' guild. It was a secret visit shortly after he became Regent of Evenshorn. He went there to recruit four Bilurian assassins for his service. Their training base was at the foot of the mountain overlooking Trangolangopan. Bahomet wondered if the same training master, the Patolukai Kumpal, was still in charge of the assassins' guild. What was his name? Bahomet wracked his memory. Dran. Boroneeloman Dran.

He would need Dran's help if he was to succeed in his plan of revenge. But he couldn't go there as a beggar. A man of the Patolukai Kumpal's stature needed a gift, even if Bahomet had already rewarded him richly for the services of his assassins. Unfortunately, all four of the assassins he had recruited didn't come back, victims of Baragin, that Yakat giant, that old customs officer in Brobabil, and the tinker's magic stick. He would need a substantial gift to compensate the master for his losses. Those kinds of funds were not easily found. But Bahomet knew a possible source—the money counting room of the Zutherian trading house on the harbour at Tricanmallokan. He decided tomorrow would be a good day to get acquainted with his cousin Darabindoo. He would need an assistant with two working hands.

CHAPTER SIX

Chancellor Berenfromm stood uneasily in Baragin's personal office, waiting for him to read the pigeon's message from Berendell at Dabranen Island. Baragin had kept him on as chancellor when he became king, acknowledging that Berenfromm's extensive experience would help offset his youth and lack of knowledge of the affairs of the kingdom. It had been a wise choice.

Baragin looked up grimly from the note and slowly crumpled it in his fist. He let out a roar of frustration as he flung it into the nearby fireplace. Nineteen dead soldiers and Bahomet on the loose, likely in Biluria. Amathea had said he was coming for them. There was no doubt in his mind that Bahomet's thirst for revenge would consume his every waking thought. He had probably spent the last six years on Dabranen Island dreaming of this very moment.

"Amathea thinks Bahomet will waste no time coming for us. I think she's right. The man is evil incarnate. He will not stop striving for our deaths. He will want the kingdom he thinks I stole from him. His marriage to Elomir is still valid and that makes him a legitimate contender if I were out of the picture. What are your thoughts, Berenfromm?" asked Baragin.

"Berendell thinks Bahomet is in Biluria, most likely Tricanmallokan where he grew up at his uncle's trading house. We need to get a message to our spies in Biluria through our Ambassador Erenbil to locate him if possible. The reward needs to be great. We should also pursue him through official channels. He is Zutheria's most notorious escaped prisoner. I don't think the Myanpur of Biluria will want to risk our good relationship by harboring such a despicable criminal. We need to summon Ambassador Guranpandrinath Adan immediately to let him know we expect the myanpur's full cooperation in finding Bahomet and turning him over to us. There are many ways we can apply pressure in this matter. I'll send a message to Erenbil to request an audience with the myanpur on this matter. We also need to consult with Laguntzailea Damagal and Zaharbat Astaran as soon as possible," continued Berenfromm.

Astaran had transferred Damagal to the Bailiwick of Bradden after he became Zaharbat. It was Zutheria's largest bailiwick, and he wanted a very experienced Laguntzailea handling the Council of Five's business there. Stornowin had finished his apprenticeship and had been assigned to the bailiwick of Prene.

"There's one other thing—Bahomet will likely soon find out that he has a son," continued Berenfromm.

Elomir's wedding night encounter with Bahomet had resulted in a pregnancy. He had been named Robduran and was being raised in the duke's villa in Elberon. The knowledge of his existence had been deliberately kept from Bahomet.

"Discovering that will give him an even greater motivation to regain the crown. Under Zutherian law, young Robduran has as valid a claim to the throne as

Prince Baragran. Astaran would never agree, but the threat, even though remote, is still real," concluded Berenfromm.

Baragin mulled over what Berenfromm had said for a moment.

"Tell Ambassador Adan I want to see him immediately. And get a pigeon to Ambassador Erenbil in Tricanmallokan—you know what to say. I'll wait until Berendell and Genneset return here before I meet with Astaran, but let Damagal know I wish to see him as well. I also want all Bilurians in Wreatherin checked— assign Major Gryn at the Wreatherin garrison to handle it. I want to make sure every Bilurian has a valid reason for being here. And put extra border guards at Iblingport and the land border crossings with Biluria," said Baragin.

"As you wish, Your Majesty," said Berenfromm with a bow.

He exited the room to carry out Baragin's directions.

The Bilurian ambassador bowed low as he entered Baragin's formal reception room in Selvenhall. He had just seen the king two days before on a minor matter, so the call to another meeting so soon was a little surprising.

"You wished to see me, Majesty? I hope all is well," began Adan politely.

Baragin fixed him with a steely gaze.

"No. All is not well, Ambassador Adan. Bahomet has escaped from Dabranen Island, poisoning nineteen of my soldiers. We believe he is in Biluria now," stated Baragin grimly.

Adan paled. That was not good news. The crown prince, the kiritam ilavaracar, had been an eyewitness to the debacle at Amadel Square over six years ago. He expressed his amazement to his father, the myanpur, that Bahomet had not been executed immediately. But the myanpur was secretly relieved he would not have to deal with Bahomet as ruler of Zutheria—Baragin was much more reasonable and lacked Bahomet's ruthlessness. The mypanpur was well aware of Bahomet's prior use of Bilurian assassins from Trangolangopan.

There was something else that was even more problematic. Bahomet was half Bilurian, but he was unaware that he had royal Bilurian blood in his veins. His mother was a result of an unpleasant liaison between the current myanpur's uncle and Bahomet's pattam. He had gone to her to get a love potion made and forced himself on her. The myanpur's uncle wasn't told about the pregnancy, but when the girl had grown, she had tried to get a royal allowance. The myanpur refused but did give her a substantial gift and passed her along to Bahomet's father at the Zutherian trading house.

If Bahomet were to discover these facts, he could make trouble for the myanpur as well. Bahomet's friendship with Boroneeloman Dran, the Patolukai Kumpal of the assassins' guild at Trangolangopan, was sure to be renewed if Bahomet was indeed in Biluria. He would have to consult with the myanpur, though, before he could respond to whatever Baragin might request.

"That is concerning news, Majesty. And what would you have us do, sire?" asked Adan.

"I want him arrested and turned over to me as soon as his whereabouts are discovered. Should Biluria choose to harbour such a dangerous criminal, I can assure you relations between our two countries will be seriously affected. I have directed officials to check the status of every Bilurian currently in Wreatherin and doubled our guards at the border and at Iblingport. We will be taking extra care with our cargo inspections there," stated Baragin firmly.

This was concerning. Lubricating the palms of a few border officials allowed many Bilurian goods to escape the import duties. Extra scrutiny at the borders would be sure to send the merchants complaining to the myanpur's Grand Vizer Fayan.

"I will be sure to consult my master as soon as possible, Majesty. There is no doubt in my mind, though, that the myanpur will respond favorably to your requests," said Adan with a bow.

"Be sure to be persuasive, Ambassador Adan. There will be consequences if Bahomet is not surrendered," Baragin concluded.

"I will bring the myanpur's response as quickly as the pigeon flies, Majesty," said Adan, bowing more deeply this time.

CHAPTER SEVEN

Bahomet looked intently at his younger cousin, his uravinam, Darabindoo. He had never met him before. He was lithe and dark, like most Bilurians. He pulled a wheeled passenger cart, a vanti, for a living, ferrying some of the wealthier citizens to their various shopping excursions.

Bilanguree fussed about, pouring their tea. She was the closest thing to a mother Bahomet had had, and the only one for whom he had any real affection.

"Attam, stop," said Bahomet, putting his good hand on her arm.

"I need you both to listen to me," he said with a dark look.

Darabindoo looked worried. He had heard stories of Bahomet's ruthlessness when he was Regent of Evenshorn. He also knew he was a fearsome valikatti, capable of inflicting horrible deaths on anyone who displeased him.

"Only two people know that I am here."

Bahomet looked at Bilanguree, then at Darabindoo.

"No one else must know. No one. And no one must hear my name spoken. But I will need your help," he said, fixing his gaze on Darabindoo.

Darabindoo just nodded, eyes wide with a combination of fear and admiration.

Bahomet reached over and opened the lid of wooden box holding the Bilurian magic wand.

"Do you know what this is?" he asked Darabindoo as the blue flame-like light curled around his fingers.

"Yes, Karpukkai. It is a mantirakolai. It..."

"What did you call me?" interrupted Bahomet.

"Karpukkai—Black Hand. You said we could not use your name. Please don't be offended, uravinam," said Darabindoo worriedly.

Bahomet sat back, thinking. *Karpukkai. Valikatti Karpukkai. That might be a useful alias, one that could inspire fear.*

"Just use uravinam. No names for now. I need to take this mantirakolai to Trangolangopan, but first I need to relieve my Zutherian uravinam of his gold. Do you have curtains on your vanti?"

"Yes, uravinam. Some ladies don't like strange men to look at them when they are riding in my vanti, or when the rain is blowing hard," said Darabindoo.

"I need you to take me down to the harbour, to the Zutherian trading house. You know the one?" asked Bahomet.

"Yes, uravinam. I know it. I have regular customers who want to go there after the ship arrives from Iblingport," answered Darabindoo.

"When is the ship due to arrive next?" asked Bahomet.

"In two days. They bring many new supplies each time," responded Darabindoo.

Bahomet mulled his responses. This was fortunate news. The trading house spent a month selling Zutherian goods and accumulating payments in the walk-in money counting room in the back of the warehouse in the factor's office. Bahomet knew it would most likely be his cousin Bahnuran. He was a few years older than Bahomet and had treated him with constant disdain when he was growing up. When his father, Bahomet's uncle Bahramin, was out of earshot, he referred to Bahomet as "that half-breed bastard". When Bahomet left for Iblingport, Bahnuran had left a pile of excrement in the middle of his cot with a note saying, "Farewell, cousin".

"Just take me down there today but keep the curtains down. We will go back tomorrow night. There will be much gold for you after tomorrow, uravinam," said Bahomet with a slight smile.

Darabindoo grinned in anticipation.

Bahomet wracked his memory as he bumped along inside Darabindoo's vanti. The money counting room in the back of the trading house was locked, but Bahomet had secretly had another key made when his uncle had entrusted him with it for an afternoon. Both Bahramin and Bahnuran had been out of town on business, but his uncle had needed a large payment from a purchase of Zutherian specialty foods from the myanpur's personal chef deposited in the money counting room. Bahomet, taking advantage of the situation, pressed the key head into a wad of sealing wax, then paid a locksmith to fashion a duplicate key. There was a loose brick under the loading dock in the alley behind the trading house. Bahomet had stashed it there years ago.

There was usually a night guard who would have to be eliminated. He asked Bilanguree if she had any sea snake venom, which sent her scurrying to her small storeroom of vials and bottles. She emerged with a dusty vial and a quizzical look.

"Someone needs to be napping," was all he said as he fitted two needles into a cork.

Bilanguree gave a nod and knew not to ask any further questions.

Darabindoo arrived at the Zutherian trading house late in the day with Bahomet behind the curtains of the vanti. Bahomet signalled him to stop at the fishmonger stalls across the narrow street where his vanti did not look out of place with those of the other shoppers. After a short time, he saw three Bilurian clerks leave the front door. Then a Zutherian—it was definitely Bahnuran—exited the door and locked it, speaking briefly with the night guard who was standing to the left of the entrance.

Bahomet called out to Darabindoo to take him down to the wharf, turn around, then return to Palamyoothoo.

As they returned from the wharf, Bahomet noted the night guard turn down the alleyway behind the trading house, obviously doing his rounds. It was a perfect spot for him to become acquainted with sea snake venom.

CHAPTER EIGHT

Baragin, Berendell, and Damagal sat in Astaran's office at Elberon. Baragin had left for Elberon shortly after Genneset had arrived in Wreatherin. He really didn't want to leave Amathea and Baragran alone for a moment with Bahomet on the loose, even with a palace full of Zutherian soldiers. But with Genneset in Selvenhall, Baragin knew Blood Hammer would be an additional defense weapon until he could arrange for more protection from Damagal and Astaran.

"It seems your dear wife has given us yet another prescient warning, Baragin. Taking her as a bride was a very wise decision," commented Astaran.

"Well, that wasn't the only reason. She's an amazing woman and a wonderful mother to Baragran. And another is on the way," he added, much to Berendell's surprise.

Noting his expression, Baragin said, "It's a very recent bit of happy news. You are the first to hear about it. Actually, the second, because I let Genneset know he was to be a grandfather again."

"Congratulations to you both. That makes our current discussion even more important. We all know it would be a serious mistake to underestimate Bahomet.

He is on the run and without an entourage, but if he somehow is able to acquire a mantirakolai, a Bilurian magic wand like the one he had in Amadel, there is no limit to what he might do. Whatever he might get would be no match for the staff of Elbron, though," noted Astaran.

Damagal tapped his finger on his cheek and pursed his lips, indicating he wanted to speak. Astaran gave him a nod.

"I believe Amathea still has the amulet I gave her. That should keep her and the little one safe from conventional threats. Selvenhall is much too large for a spell like the one I put on Genneset's house in Blessingport. Should the king wish it, I can provide a protection amulet for him as well. Of course, it would not be an effective defense against a mantirakolai should Bahomet manage to get close," said Damagal.

"I'll accept an amulet, at least until Bahomet is captured. But I don't think he'll risk crossing the border until he becomes much stronger and establishes a base in Biluria. Where is that place where the Bilurian assassins train?" Baragin asked, turning to Berendell.

"Trangolangopan. It is quite remote, and most Bilurians are quite fearful of getting anywhere near it. Even the myanpur treats the patolukai kumpal, the master of the assassins' guild, with considerable respect. Given Bahomet's previous relationship with the patolukai kumpal, I suspect he will try to garner his support. I think our best option is to pressure the myanpur to intercept Bahomet either in Tricanmallokan, or on the road to Trangolangopan," offered Berendell.

"That's sound advice. I'll also ensure that Stornowin is on high alert in Iblingport. Are we agreed, then?" concluded Astaran.

As they all nodded, Astaran said, "Baragin, a word?"

The two remained in the room as the others left for some refreshments.

"Your son in Yakatan, Yat'ahna is it? Suberon tells me he has the gift. I had heard you were planning a trip to retrieve him," said Astaran.

"Yes, but I've had to put that trip on hold repeatedly due to the pressures of running Zutheria. And now the Bahomet situation and Amathea's pregnancy are interfering again. He is safe with Dzulhcho. He's still quite young, nine summers, but Ghost Singer is providing him with training in the ways of Yakat duyuns, their name for shamans. I would appreciate it if Suberon would offer him some guidance from time to time until I can arrange for him to come here," said Baragin.

"Certainly. I'll send a pigeon, but I think Suberon already has things well in hand."

Astaran paused.

"Don't let Bahomet trouble your sleep. The Council of Five exists precisely for threats like these. Come. Let us join the others," said Astaran, putting a friendly hand on Baragin's shoulder.

CHAPTER NINE

Joya balanced a tray with six steins of beer as she navigated through the tables of the crowded Silver Dolphin in Blessingport. She was fifteen summers old now, strong and lithe, with long blonde hair cascading halfway down her back. She had it braided to keep it out of the way while she worked. Her green eyes, full red lips and a pert upturned nose attracted a lot of attention, even more so now that she was nearing marriageable age. Not only did her looks turn heads, but the fact that she was the king's sister-in-law made her even more desirable.

She rebuffed any suitors who tried, most with bruised egos, but some with actual bruises. And her "nose-puncher of the king" status added to her notoriety. Joya simply wasn't interested in boys. But she was interested in doing what boys did—hunting, wrestling, staff-fighting, riding horses, archery. In her spare time, she often did these activities with her cousin Umbraset. He was a talented wrestler and had taught her quite a few moves he had developed to bounce rowdy customers. Joya had already brought down her first deer and was an excellent shot with the Zutherian hunting bow.

One of the advantages of being related to the king was her access to fine Mythrycian horses—she kept a fast, golden-coated gelding at her aunt Amathea's place on the outskirts of Blessingport and rode him as often as she could. Baragin had given her a beautifully embossed saddle, the kind used by the female warriors of the Gotkurgan tribe, the Khokhgui. The Gotkurgans spoke a similar language to the Mythrycians. Gotkurga was part of Mythrycian territory, but they had subjugated them with great difficulty.

One of the reasons for their fighting prowess was their use of distinct units of women warriors. In Gotkurgan culture, a small number of young women committed themselves for light cavalry duty for seven years, usually from fifteen to twenty-two summers in age. They excelled in archery using rams' horn bows, which were small and light but more powerful than wooden bows. In addition to a personal dagger, they wielded small-bladed battle axes with a pyramid-shaped hammer on the back side for hand-to-hand combat.

The Khokhgui were mainly responsible for defending the tent camps when the Gotkurgan men went to battle. If the risk of attack on the home camp was low, however, they were sometimes used as scouting units and skirmishers alongside the men.

Joya was absolutely fascinated when she heard of the Khokhgui and peppered any Mythrycians who happened to pass through Blessingport with questions about them. She had asked one trader, a Mythrycian named Ulugan who was a sales agent for her uncle, what the name Khokhgui meant. He had blushed and stammered, but Joya insisted he tell her. Finally, he said it meant "without a breast" because the Khokhgui bound their right breasts tightly so it did not get in the way when pulling back the bowstring of their horn bows. To everyone's surprise in the Silver Dolphin, she gave the

Mythrycian trader a rare smile and a kiss on the cheek by way of thanks for that bit of special information. She made him promise to bring her a Khokhgui horn bow the next time he came through town.

Business was brisk in the Silver Dolphin. Joya had been pressed into serving tables as her father Genneset was down in Wreatherin with Blood Hammer dealing with the Bahomet threat. She lowered her tray of steins onto a table of Pendragon fishermen, then turned to deal with a foursome of locals shouting at her for more beer.

They were already drunk. There was Danaquill, the son of Mayor Doroquill, Futtsam, the son of Harbourmaster Futt, as well as two twin brothers, Bradnarin and Donnarin, the sons of Bidnarin, the marine supply merchant in Blessingport. All of them had been quite cruel to her sister Amathea when they were younger, teasing her about her birthmark.

Futtsam, who would be the next to inherit the title of Linkman of Blessingport, was the most obnoxious of the four.

"Hey darling! We're thirsty here. How be you bring that pretty face over here for a little kiss when you bring the beer," he yelled.

His three companions joined him in raucous laughter.

Joya scowled and bit her lip. Both Genneset and Germilda had warned her severely about over-reacting to lecherous customers. But Genneset wasn't here to intervene and Umbraset was up to his eyebrows in customers himself.

She set her mouth in a grim line and poured four steins for their table.

"This is the last round for you. Time to move along when you're done," said Joya firmly as she lowered the tray.

"Oh, darling, you don't mean that. Now tell me, how is it you turned out so beautiful when your sister has the face of a burlap sack?" slurred Futtsam.

Joya's eyes blazed, and she swung her tin tray at Futtsam's head with a howl of rage. Futtsam blocked the tray with a brawny arm and grabbed Joya around the waist.

"Now calm down, calm down, my little bearcat. Perhaps I can introduce myself to you face-to-face after you close. I sure won't be coming at you from the rear like I'm sure the king has to do with your dog-faced sister," he said with a drunken leer.

Umbraset saw that Joya was beset and vaulted over the bar to help. But the crowded pub slowed his progress.

Joya grabbed one of Futtsam's fingers and bent it back sharply, breaking it. As he released her, howling in pain, she pulled the Bilurian dagger from her hip sheath and swung it at Futtsam's cheek. He pulled back to avoid the blade, but it caught him just under his left ear.

"That's the last time you'll speak that way about my sister, you shite-eating swine!" she shouted as Umbraset grabbed her from behind with both arms.

Futtsam clutched his bleeding throat, eyes wide in fright. He fell against Danaquill, gurgling and choking. The two collapsed on the floor as a stunned silence enveloped the noisy pub.

Danaquill squirmed out from underneath Futtsam and bent over him, shouting frantically, "Give me a towel! Bring a towel to stop the bleeding! Great Zuth! Somebody help!"

A large pool of blood spread out underneath Futtsam and the spurting from his neck gradually abated. He gave one last rattled breath, then fell still, eyes wide and mouth agape.

"He...he's dead. You killed him. You killed my best friend, you murderer!" yelled Danaquill as he lunged at Joya.

Umbraset moved to block him and hissed, "Go!" to Joya.

Stunned, realizing what she had just done, Joya dropped her blood-stained dagger and ran for the door.

CHAPTER TEN

Joya's Aunt Amathea, returning from herb gathering, found her in the stable combing the mane of her gelding Swiftfoot. She still had Futtsam's blood staining the front of her serving frock.

"Oh, my goodness, Jo-jo! Are you hurt? What is all this blood?" asked Amathea as Joya collapsed into her arms, sobbing.

Amathea just held her tightly, kissing the top of her head and whispering soothing words into her ear. After a few minutes the tears stopped, and Joya pulled back and looked at her aunt.

"I killed him, Auntie! I killed that pig Futtsam! And I'm not sorry I did," said Joya defiantly after she had calmed down a bit.

"Oh, no, Joya, no. This is not good, not good at all. Tell auntie what happened," encouraged Amathea.

Joya told the whole story, relating Futtsam's manhandling of her and his extremely vulgar insults about her sister Amathea.

"So I broke his finger, then slashed at him with my dagger to give him a scar to remember me by. I…I….I didn't really intend to kill him, Auntie. He just made me so mad! I just wanted to give him a scar!" said Joya, talking rapidly.

"Hush, girl, hush. This is very serious, Joya. Very serious. You've killed a man, and not just anyone. Futtsam is Harbourmaster Futt's only son and due to inherit the Linkmanship. He will be absolutely devastated and wanting revenge. It's very bad timing since your father is in Wreatherin, but I'm going to send for your uncles. Timbraset will know what we should do," concluded Amathea.

She brought Joya into the house to make her some tea and find some clean clothes for her.

It wasn't long afterward that Timbraset and Donneset showed up, but they weren't alone. After not finding Joya at home, the Blessingport barracks commander, Lieutenant Ambrosin, had stopped at the tinworks to alert the brothers of the incident. Mayor Doroquill, his son Danaquill, Harbourmaster Futt and the Narin twins were also in the group. Danaquill still had Futtsam's blood staining his clothes.

When they arrived at the door, Harbourmaster Futt shouted, "Send that murdering bitch out!"

Lieutenant Ambrosin turned and said, "I only allowed you to come along to see that we took her into custody. Now I know you're extremely upset, but I have a job to do and I will do it."

Turning to the house, he mounted the steps to the porch, his four soldiers in step behind him.

"Bring her out, Amathea. Don't make this difficult," he called out loudly.

He saw Joya peeking out from behind a curtain.

Amathea opened the door to the house and surveyed the scene in her front yard. The angry faces of Futt and the others were ominous.

"Why would you bring everyone out here like this? It's clear they mean to do Joya harm. She is still a child, not yet sixteen summers, so she cannot be treated like a common criminal," said Amathea determinedly.

"She is a criminal! She is a criminal!" shouted Futt.

Amathea raised an eyebrow at Ambrosin, challenging him to prove he was in control of the situation. Timbraset and Donneset moved a step closer to the front door, ready to prevent anyone from charging the house.

Ambrosin sighed deeply. After a moment he turned and said, "Trooper Bandonnen, Trooper Gibberast— escort Harbormaster Futt back to town."

"What? Who do think you are telling me what do? I want to see that murdering bitch in irons. Do your job!" yelled Futt, his face mottling with rage.

"Who I am is the person charged with enforcing Zutherian law. And I will do that. But your outbursts are interfering with my job. Troopers..." said Ambrosin, giving his men a nod.

As the troopers moved to obey the lieutenant's orders, Mayor Doroquill grabbed his friend's arm and said, "Come on, Futt. The girl is obviously here. Ambrosin will take care of the matter, I'm sure of it," he said, glaring in the lieutenant's direction.

Doroquill and his son each took an arm and propelled Futt back out onto the road into Blessingport.

"I'll see you with a rope around your neck!" roared Futt over his shoulder as they retreated down the road with the Narin twins trailing behind.

The two troopers looked at Ambrosin questioningly, and he motioned with his head for them to return towards the house. They took up positions on either side of the front door.

"Alright if I bring her out, lieutenant?" asked Timbraset.

"Fine. But make it quick. I need to get her back to the barracks brig before Futt organizes a bigger mob," said Ambrosin.

Timbraset exchanged a serious look with his sister as he entered the house. Joya threw herself into his arms, crying.

"Oh, Uncle Timba! I was so scared they were going to hurt me! What is going to happen to me?" asked Joya, tears staining her cheeks.

Timbraset held his niece close, his own eyes tearing up. He and his wife were childless, and he had been a second father to both Joya and the younger Amathea when Genneset was on the road with his grinding cart.

"Now, now, Jo-jo, my pet. Uncle Timba is here and so is Uncle Donny. We'll make sure nobody lays a hand on you. But you have to go with Lieutenant Ambrosin and the soldiers. They will make sure you're safe at the barracks. No one will harm you. But you will have to stay there a bit until we get this all sorted out," said Timbraset soothingly.

"But Uncle Timba, I didn't really mean to kill him! He was so horrible to me and said such mean things about Ammy. But I'm glad he's dead," she said through clenched teeth.

"Hush, Joya, hush. Let's go with the lieutenant and get things straightened out."

He gave Joya another big hug, but the glance he exchanged with his older sister showed how worried he was.

At the barracks, Lieutenant Ambrosin allowed Timbraset and Germilda to join Joya in the small cell that served as a brig and the town jail. It was rarely used. The whole town was in an uproar, and quite

44

a crowd had assembled outside of the barracks, all talking at once. No one could remember when a girl had killed someone. And it wasn't just any girl—it was the king's sister-in-law. The gossip mill was in high gear and anyone with a pigeon to anywhere had sent it out. Ambrosin sent one to his captain in Iblingport, as that was the administrative centre for Prene where all serious cases were heard.

Joya was sitting slumped against the wall, arms crossed and frowning. Germilda was beside her stroking her long hair. Timbraset sat down on the bench next to her, then reached out and took her other hand. Joya managed a weak smile and squeezed her uncle's hand.

"What will happen to me, Uncle Timba?" she asked quietly.

Timbraset paused for a moment.

"Well, I'm no judge, or avocatim, but I do have an idea of what comes next. The governor in Iblingport will send a ship here to collect you. All serious cases like this one must be dealt with there. You are not yet of age so any penalty you might receive will not be as severe. It's likely you will be charged with manslaughter as you did not plan to kill Futtsam. But your father will have to pay the blood price to Futt—and that will be a lot of money. He'll probably have to sell the Silver Dolphin to raise the funds," said Timbraset.

"Sell the Dolphin? But he loves that place. And Momma really likes working there, too," protested Joya, looking at her mother.

"No, Uncle Timba, no. Can't Baragin do something? He's the king. He's my brother-in-law. He'll be furious when he finds out what Futtsam said. He should give me a medal," declared Joya.

"Joya, Joya, don't be talking nonsense now. Futtsam deserved to be beaten within in an inch of his life for what he did to you and what he said about Ammy. And if your father had been there, Blood Hammer would have done just that. But 'within an inch of his life' and someone's entire life are very different. I know it wasn't intentional Joya, but you went too far. And there are going to be serious consequences. It could be up to five years," said Timbraset.

"Five years? Five years? No one's taking my Joya away for five years!" yelled Germilda.

Joya's emotional reserve finally broke. She burst into tears and buried her face in her mother's neck, sobbing.

Lieutenant Ambrosin appeared at the door of the cell.

"Time to go, Timbraset. I'm going to let Germilda stay until night. It should be a few days before the ship comes to retrieve her, but I've posted extra guards to make sure no one tries anything," said Ambrosin.

Timbraset nodded and stood up to leave.

"Don't lose hope, Joya," said Timbraset.

CHAPTER ELEVEN

Bahomet affixed a second small cork over the points of the two needles he had inserted into a larger cork. He had just finished drizzling sea snake venom over the needles but wanted to make sure he didn't accidentally prick himself.

"Are you ready?" he asked his cousin Darabindoo.

"Yes, uravinam. I have my black clothes on as you said," replied Darabindoo.

"Good. Now, when we get down to the Zutherian trading house, pull the vanti to the far end of the alley. As soon as the night guard passes by and turns the corner, we'll slip by and go to the rear loading dock. I'll roll under the edge of the loading dock, while you pretend to settle down for a sleep. The guard will certainly try to make you leave. While he is rousting you, he will feel a little snake bite on his leg. Sea snake venom is very fast-acting so get ready to catch him. Just roll him under the loading dock. That's where my uravinam Bahnuran will find him in the morning," said Bahomet, smiling.

"Yes, uravinam. Do you know where the money is?" asked Darabindoo.

"I can find my way in the dark in that place. But I will need your help to carry the money chests out.

There will be three of them if they still do things the way they used to. One will be the profits for the month. One will be to pay the captain for the supplies the ship from Iblingport has brought. The last one is the chest they use for day-to-day business."

Bahomet paused, looking intently at Darabindoo.

"If you do well tonight, uravinam, there is a place for you—with me. Don't fail me and you will be rewarded beyond what you can imagine," said Bahomet.

Darabindoo returned his gaze with a serious expression.

"You are my uravinam. You are family and you need my help. I am with you forever, uravinam. But uravinam, whatever you must do, you must do it quickly. I have heard talk in the marketplace that the myanpur's soldiers are looking for you, the Zutherian man with the black hand. It will not be safe for you here," answered Darabindoo.

Bahomet reflected a moment on what Darabindoo had said. Baragin must have found out about his escape, but it was sooner than he expected. Perhaps his dreaming wife had warned him. Baragin had obviously put pressure on the myanpur to arrest him and turn him over. He would have to get to Trangolangopan as soon as possible.

"We will leave tomorrow, after we have what we need from my Zutherian uravinam."

Bahomet paused, then said, "Let's go. I hope you are strong. Those chests will be heavy."

Darabindoo laughed.

"Don't worry uravinam. I pull fat ladies around all day long."

Darabindoo had doused his clothes with arickmatu, the potent Bilurian rice wine. As soon as the night guard passed, he and Bahomet moved into position. Darabindoo stretched out on the loading dock and prepared to start snoring loudly as soon as he heard the guard's footsteps on his return around the building.

Bahomet crawled under the dock. He couldn't remember exactly which brick he had stashed the money counting room key behind. It was pitch black under the dock platform, so he ran the fingers of his good hand rapidly over the bricks, feeling for the loose one. The area under the loading dock was full of cobwebs and stank of cat excrement. Bahomet ingored the smell and kept on feeling.

Suddenly, Darabindoo started snoring loudly—the guard was coming! Bahomet stopped looking for the key and grabbed his snake venom cork. He removed the small protective cork and crouched in the gloom under the loading dock. He heard steps approaching, but Darabindoo was doing a pretty convincing job of imitating an arickmatu-sodden drunk bedding down for the night.

"Hey! Kutkaran!" shouted the guard using the Bilurian word for drunkard. "Hey, hey! Kutkaran! You can't sleep here! Kutkaran! Wake up! You can't sleep here!" he shouted giving Darabindoo's shoulder a shake.

Then he shouted, "Oweeee!" as Bahomet stabbed his leg with the sea snake venom-coated needles.

Darabindoo sat up quickly and grabbed the slumping guard. He lowered him to the ground and rolled him under the loading dock.

The guard had been carrying a small lantern on his rounds. Bahomet picked it up and quickly located the brick with a tiny amount of mortar missing around it. He loosened the brick and pulled it out—a cloth-wrapped key lay behind it.

"Quickly, take the guard's keys. Hold them up for me," hissed Bahomet.

As Darabindoo held up the key ring, Bahomet found the key to the loading dock door. They clambered up onto the dock, opened the door, and slipped inside the rear warehouse.

Bahomet held the lantern higher. The smells brought back a flood of memories. There were multiple crates of Milredden Pink and Sweetsap apples, racks of cider and Bradden liquor in earthenware jugs, stacks of Blessingport tinware, iron tools from the Pendragon foundry, as well as a variety of Mythrycian leather goods. How hard Bahomet had worked when he was younger, stacking all those crates, racks and boxes. But he was never paid much, and his cousin Bahnuran had made his life miserable with his constant bullying.

The money counting room was off to the side. Passing the lantern to Darabindoo, Bahomet took the counting room key and fit it into the lock. It didn't move at first and Bahomet struggled. Finally, he told Darabindoo to give him the lantern and let him try the lock. Darabindoo struggled as well, but as he had two hands, the lock mechanism finally gave way.

"Hold the lantern high," he directed Darabindoo, as he passed it back to him.

He spotted the three strong boxes immediately, right where his uncle had always stored them. The two of them dragged the boxes to the loading dock door.

"Go get the vanti. Make sure there is no one around. If there is, wait. When you come back, give two knocks, wait, then give two more knocks," said Bahomet.

Darabindoo peeked out the door, and seeing no one, scampered down the alley to retrieve the vanti.

Bahomet went back into the money counting room. There was one more thing he had to do. He found the ledger book and tore out the last page. Then he loosened the waist tie to his trousers and squatted over the open ledger book. It was a very large deposit. He used the ripped page to wipe himself and stuck the money counting room key into the middle of the pile. Then he stood back to admire his handiwork. Oh, to be there the next morning to see Bahnuran's face!

"A little present from the half-breed bastard," said Bahomet aloud.

Bahomet returned to the loading dock door and waited for Darabindoo's knock. Instead, he heard voices. Two men, obviously drunk, were trying to hire Darabindoo's vanti for a ride home. He was trying to dissuade them, but they were blocking his way and trying to clamber into the vanti.

Thinking quickly, Bahomet opened the loading dock door. He shouted at the two drunks using a combination of Zutherian and Bilurian,

"Hey! Kutkarani! Get away from my vanti. I hired this vanti. Off with you!" he shouted.

Bahomet was quite a bit taller than most Bilurians and he knew how to intimidate from his long years as Regent of Evenshorn.

"So sorry, kuram," slurred one of them, using the Bilurian term of respect. "We did not know this vanti was already hired. So sorry, kuram," he said as he pulled his even drunker companion by the sleeve.

Bahomet watched them until they staggered around the corner. "Quickly! Grab the money chests," he directed Darabindoo.

While Darabindoo stowed the first chest, he dragged another to the edge of the dock with his good hand. Darabindoo loaded that one into the vanti and grabbed the last one. Bahomet then locked the door and put the key ring back on the unconscious guard's belt. He did not envy his fate.

Despite Darabindoo's bragging about being able to handle heavy loads, he struggled with the weight of both Bahomet and the money chests. It was nearing dawn when they finally rolled into Palamyoothoo.

Chapter Twelve

"**G**reat Zuth! This is the last thing I need!" groaned Baragin as he read the note from Governor Drezzerell in Iblingport.

He had been focusing all his attention on pressuring the Bilurians to hand over Bahomet, but they claimed he had yet to be located. Now Amathea's sister, not even sixteen summers old, had gotten herself charged with manslaughter. Manslaughter! What a mess that nose-puncher had created!

Despite his annoyance, Baragin smiled at the memory. He had laughed uproariously when Genneset had told him the "Poppa, what's a king?" line Joya had asked after she walloped him in the nose in front of everybody.

His smile faded quickly, though. He wanted to help Joya. What Futtsam had said about Amathea—his wife, the queen of all Zutheria, was absolutely outrageous. Baragin would have strangled him personally if he had been there. He had the authority to pardon Joya and absolve her from all responsibility. After all, she was a minor who had acted hastily and without pre-meditated malice. Yet he knew the eyes of the kingdom were on him. Would he honour the law? Or would he make an exception for a relative?

Baragin asked Berenfromm to send him the most respected avocatim in Wreatherin, and have Genneset join them.

Avocatim Durrenbar was clean-shaven, with a halo of white hair below a bald pate. He was slightly hunched and had rheumy blue eyes from years of pouring over law books. He could have been appointed a judge—Duke Robagrin had offered him a judgeship more than once. But he knew he would miss the cut and parry of the courtroom—and the hefty fees he commanded.

"Well, Your Highness. Your sister-in-law is the talk of the kingdom. How might I be of assistance?" asked Durrenbar.

Baragin nodded toward Genneset.

"My father-in-law, and Joya of course, need good legal counsel. I'm hoping you will take them on. Perhaps you could offer some ideas on how to deal with this mess," began Baragin.

"Hmmm," said Durrenbar, making a tent of his fingers.

"You are in somewhat of a pickle, Majesty. Your sister-in-law has killed someone, a Linkman-in-waiting, so to speak. That is a serious matter indeed. From what I understand, there were extreme provocations, yet most would agree punishments should match crimes—and death is too severe for what Futtsam did. The people are watching to see if their king will honour Zutherian law, the law that must apply to everyone equally—including the queen's sister," said Durrenbar.

"Yes, yes, I know all that. But what can I do? I can't let her spend the rest of her teenage years in a cell. And I can't let her off scot-free, though there are some who wouldn't blame me if I did, given Futtsam's outrageous insults. What would you advise?" asked Baragin.

He glanced over at Genneset while waiting for Durrenbar to respond.

"She's fascinated with the Khokhguis," interrupted Genneset.

Baragin and Durrenbar looked at him, puzzled.

"They're female warriors of the Gotkurgan tribe in southern Mythrycia. I encountered a few of them in the marketplace when I was at the embassy in Gragnarak," interjected Berendell.

All eyes turned back to Genneset.

"Is banishment an option? Maybe a stay with the Khohkguis could help tame that wild side of Joya, or at least channel it with some discipline. And I could still see her from time to time. Please, Baragin, don't let my baby girl rot in a cell," pleaded Genneset.

Baragin exchanged glances with Durrenbar.

"It's actually an elegant solution, Majesty. If Genneset pays the blood price and Joya serves a term of banishment, the whole kingdom will see that justice is served, that they have a king who honours Zutherian law. And you do always have the option to grant a full pardon later on, no matter what sentence is imposed," said Durrenbar.

Baragin paused, mulling over all that had been said.

"Berenfromm, I want to see the Mythrycian ambassador. Take Durrenbar with you and see to his fee. I'm sure Harbourmaster Futt will not say no to the deed for the Silver Dolphin as the blood price for his son. Let the Iblingport judge know that we may have a solution that will see justice done. He will have to decide on the length of any banishment—I will not interfere with that," said Baragin to Genneset.

"I understand. Thank you. Now I just have to figure out what Germilda and I are going to do without a pub to run," said Genneset, running his fingers through his hair.

Chapter Thirteen

Bilanguree shook Bahomet's shoulder.

"Wake up, anapay, wake up. You said you wanted to wake up early," she said.

Bahomet snapped awake. The theft would probably have been discovered by now, and his cousin Bahnuran would have been screaming and tearing his hair out. It wouldn't take long for him to contact the authorities, who would put two and two together to figure out it was Bahomet's doing. Then they would start asking questions of the long-term employees to see where Bahomet's relatives might live. It would only be a matter of hours before they arrived in Palamyoothoo.

"Pack for a trip, Attam Gurgoo. You must go immediately with Darabindoo's wife. Somewhere safe. Soldiers will be here soon, and you must leave. They are looking for me, here, and on the road to Trangolangopan. I must think of a disguise," said Bahomet.

Bilanguree looked at him.

"They are looking for a Zutherian man, bald, with a beard and a black hand. You stand out, anapay."

Suddenly, her eyes brightened. She turned and went rummaging through a box on a high shelf.

"Your pattam was almost bald near the end. She had a wig. I think I put it up here. I should have thrown it out, but I keep things," said Bilanguree.

"Hah! Here it is," she said, holding up a gray-haired wig.

"This should work. But you must take off your beard, Bah-bah," said Bilanguree.

Bahomet sighed. He had had his beard for over twenty years, but he knew she was right. He sat still while Bilanguree removed his whiskers and was soon looking at his chin for the first time in two decades.

His aunt then brought him a large gown with flowing sleeves, long enough to hide his damaged arm. She looked at him with the wig on and giggled.

"You are a very ugly pattam, Bah-bah!" she laughed out loud.

There was a noise at the door, and Darabindoo entered, his young wife standing shyly behind him.

"My uravinam," he said by way of introduction. He remembered not to use Bahomet's name.

"My wife, Arashbilan."

Arashbilan looked briefly at Bahomet in his wig, then back down at the floor, eyes wide.

"Uravinam. Arashbilan must take Bilanguree away from here. Now. Somewhere safe. Here is some money for them," said Bahomet, handing a sack of coins from one of the chests to Darabindoo.

"Arashbilan's uncle lives one day's walk from here. They can go there. It is a village north of here called Olumadu. They will be safe there," said Darabindoo.

Handing her the money, Darabindoo said, "Take attam to Olumadu. Do not talk to anyone or say anything about our uravinam. Nothing! You understand?"

Arashbilan nodded quickly, looking scared.

"Stay there until you hear from me. Go now," said Darabindoo, giving her a kiss and a quick hug.

Bilanguree quickly gathered her things and went up to Bahomet to kiss him good-bye.

"Farewell, anapay. I'm so glad you came back to me. Please come and find us as soon as you can, Bah-bah," said Bilanguree.

"I will never forget what you did for me, Attam Gurgoo. I will come for you when it is safe," said Bahomet.

He gave her a hug and was surprised to feel moisture in his eyes.

Then Arashbilan took Bilanguree's arm and the two quickly left.

After they had gone, Darabindoo looked at Bahomet and giggled. "You're a very ugly pattam, uravinam."

"Yes, yes, I know. Attam already told me that. I've hidden two of the chests under the woodpile and moved all of the gold coins into one chest. Put the chest in the vanti. We need to get on the road to Trangolangopan right away," said Bahomet.

"Your disguise is good, uravinam, but it may not be enough. We need something more in case they stop us on the road," said Darabindoo.

He looked thoughtful for a moment.

"They won't search a vanti with a tolunoyali in it," said Darabindoo, thoughtfully.

Bahomet looked puzzled. He had forgotten many Bilurian words during his time in Zutheria.

"What was that word?" he asked.

"Skin disease. Easy to catch. Very dangerous. Eats away at your nose, your fingers," said Darabindoo.

"Oh. Leper. We call that disease leprosy in Zutherian," said Bahomet.

"If we tie a red flag on the vanti, they will know I am carrying a tolunoyali in it. I will say a rich tolunoyali has hired me to take her to the shrine in Trangolangopan to pray for healing and make an offering to Balangupong. If you wear a red scarf on your face, they won't look any further," concluded Darabindoo.

"Excellent. You are proving to be a very capable assistant, uravinam," said Bahomet.

Darabindoo grinned.

Chapter Fourteen

The Iblingport courtroom was packed. There was no trial as Genneset and Joya had accepted Avocatim Durrenbar's advice to plead guilty to manslaughter in return for banishment. Genneset and Germilda were in the front row behind Durrenbar and Joya. Genneset held the deed for the Silver Dolphin in his hands and looked down at it ruefully from time to time. Durrenbar, in his dark green avocatim robe, turned around and gave him a reassuring look. This was the sentencing hearing and the whole kingdom was agog with speculation as to what penalty Judge Drellabin would impose on the king's sister-in-law. There was a large crowd outside the Iblingport courthouse—those who weren't privileged enough to get a seat inside.

Harbourmaster Futt and his wife Doralaine, along with their three daughters, were on the other side of the room behind Accusatim Branderron. Doralaine just looked down at her hands which were clutching an already moist kerchief. Futt had a dark frown and pursed lips. He was staring straight ahead at the back of Accusatim Branderron in his grey robe.

A buzz of excitement and whisperings suddenly erupted. Some said, "It's the queen. Queen Amathea is here!"

Necks craned as Amathea entered the courtroom accompanied by two soldiers in palace guard uniforms. Her expectant condition was clearly visible under her dress.

Baragin had argued strenuously against Amathea's travel to Iblingport, citing her pregnancy and the fact that Bahomet still had not been apprehended. But Amathea had quietly and repeatedly insisted that she needed to be by her sister's side in her darkest hour. She also pointed out that she had had no dream at all about immediate danger. Finally, Baragin relented, but only if Damagal accompanied her. He accepted Berenfromm and Durrenbar's advice that it would be very inappropriate for the king to attend the sentencing hearing in person.

Amathea made her way to the one seat available next to her very surprised father and sat down.

"I just had to come," she whispered as she put her hand on his arm and kissed his cheek.

"I'm so glad you did, poppet," said Genneset.

Amathea reached across him and put her hand on her mother's arm with a smile. Germilda suddenly put her hands to her face and started crying. Genneset quickly stood up and motioned Amathea to move in beside her mother to comfort her.

Genneset had just sat down again when the low hum of conversations in the courtroom fizzled as a side door opened. A clerk entered and announced in a loud voice, "All rise for Judge Drellabin. The Zutherian Court of the County of Prene is now in session."

At first, no one appeared at the open side door and necks craned to see when he would appear.

After a short pause, Judge Drellabin walked through the door in a measured pace. His black robe had the blue trim used only by Prene judges (Bradden, Evenshorn and Pendragon had their own distinctive trim colours for their judges' robes). Drellabin was a tall, thin man with close-cropped grey hair and a long grey beard, but with no mustache. His nose was quite prominent, almost hawk-like. As he reached the raised platform with the judgment seat, he turned slowly and faced the crowd. He frowned at no one in particular, bushy eyebrows knitted together. He was an imposing figure. Then he swept back his robe and took his seat, nodding to clerk.

In a loud voice, the clerk intoned, "Judge Drellabin is now presiding in the Zutherian Court of the County of Prene. Please be seated."

There was volley of murmurings and rustling as the audience took their seats. Someone coughed loudly and another blew his nose.

Drellabin waited until it was completely silent.

"I don't usually say this, but this is not a usual situation," began Drellabin. "It's been three hundred and forty years since we've had a king, and this is the first time that a close relative of a king has been called to justice in the history of Zutherian law. I am not unaware of the gossip that has been flying about, speculating as to whether the king would direct my judgment. I am telling all of you, here and now, that King Baragin has not spoken to me, or given me a message through a third party, or directed me to judge this case in a direction favorable to the queen's sister in any way. The sentence I am about to deliver is my sentence, and mine alone, based entirely on the circumstances of this case and the precedents in the past judgments of Zutheria," he said, looking pointedly at Futt.

Drellabin paused, letting the import of his words diffuse through the room.

"Accusatim Branderron, do you have the details of the settlement agreement in hand?" asked Drellabin.

Branderron stood quickly and said, "Yes, Your Honour."

"Avocatim Durrenbar. Is your client ready to plead formally to the charge against her?" asked Drellabin.

Durrenbar rose, saying, "Yes, Your Honour."

"Joya, daughter of Genneset of Blessingport in the County of Prene, stand for judgment," Drellabin directed.

Joya stood, but quickly turned her head to look at Amathea, who had covered her mouth with both hands.

"Joya of Blessingport, you are charged with the manslaughter death of Futtsam of Blessingport, son of Harbourmaster Futt, Linkman of Blessingport. What is your plea?" asked Drellabin.

"I am guilty, Your Honour," answered Joya. Her chin was up and her voice was strong.

"That's for sure," said Futt, not quite under his breath.

"I'll thank you to keep your comments to yourself in my courtroom, Harbourmaster Futt," said Drellabin sternly.

Futt scowled but said nothing more.

"Joya of Blessingport. You have pled guilty to manslaughter in the presence of all these witnesses. Are you ready to receive your sentence?"

"Yes, Your Honour," answered Joya in a loud clear voice.

"Manslaughter is a serious crime. It is apparent the death of Futtsam was not premeditated, and there is a certain element of self-defense in what occurred. That self-defense should have ended after you broke his finger. I can understand that you wished to defend the honour of the queen, your sister. That did not require the use of deadly force. That type of behaviour must be deterred by the courts of Zutheria.

"Therefore, this is your sentence. You must pay the blood-guilt price to Futtsam's family. As you are not yet of age, it is your father's obligation to pay that on your behalf. I have determined that the value of the Silver Dolphin public house in Blessingport owned by your father Genneset meets the standard required to satisfy the blood-guilt price. Do you have the deed?" asked Drellabin looking at Genneset.

Genneset stood, holding out the deed.

"Yes, Your Honour."

Drellabin motioned for the clerk to retrieve the document. He placed it in front of Accusatim Branderron.

"Accusatim Branderron. You will register this deed as blood-guilt payment for the death of Futtsam of Blessingport and surrender it to Harbourmaster Futt afterward," stated Drellabin in a formal tone.

"As you order, Judge Drellabin," replied Branderron.

"Joya of Blessingport. The penalty for manslaughter is imprisonment or banishment. Your avocatim has stated that you have agreed to banishment. Is this your wish? State loudly so all can hear," said Drellabin.

"I accept banishment as punishment for my crime," said Joya clearly.

"You have committed the crime of manslaughter. You have deprived a worthy family, a Linkman, of their only son. You are banished from the town of Blessingport for no less than ten years. You are banished from the Kingdom of Zutheria for four years and nine months. It would have been five years, but it has been three months since your arrest. Should you be found anywhere in the kingdom of Zutheria before your banishment ends, for any reason whatsoever, you will be arrested and serve the balance of your sentence in Iblingport jail. I call on all the citizens of Zutheria to ensure this banishment is completely fulfilled.

You will be escorted to the border of your choice by a detachment of Zutherian soldiers. You have two weeks from today to leave Zutheria. The Court of Zutheria of the County of Prene has spoken. Now, is there anything you wish to say?"

As Joya hesitated, Durrenbar stepped on her toe under the table and shook his head at her.

"No, Your Honour," said Joya, in a resigned voice.

"Captain Pharigon. I understand you have been tasked with escorting the prisoner to the border. Take her into your custody," ordered Drellabin.

Pharigon, standing in the back of the room next to the queen's guards, nodded and moved closer to the front of the court. Pharigon had recently been promoted and transferred from his post in Evenshornmouth to an aide-de-camp's role at the Zutherian Army Headquarters in Wreatherin. Baragin himself had selected him to escort Joya into Mythrycia.

Drellabin glanced at his clerk, who shouted, "Court is adjourned! All rise!"

Those assembled stood in respectful silence until Drellabin exited the side door. As soon as the door closed, they began chatting animatedly with one another. Joya turned and ran to her father's embrace while Germilda and Amathea joined them.

Futt stood and glared at the family.

"The first thing I'm going to do when I get back to Blessingport, tinkerman, is burn that damned pub to the ground. And ten years isn't long enough. I don't want to see any of you Sets in my town ever again."

And he turned and headed for the door, wife and daughters in tow.

"Come on, poppets. Let's get out of here," was all Genneset said.

CHAPTER FIFTEEN

The road to Trangolangopan was busy with freight wagons, carts, carriages, vantis, travellers on foot, and an occasional rider on horseback. As Bahomet and Darabindoo neared a bridge, they could see an army checkpoint at the far end. They were waving people through who obviously did not match Bahomet's description.

As their turn came, the soldier took note of the red tolunoy flag. He shrunk back, but his commanding officer shouted, "Check inside!"

The soldier approached gingerly using his lance to pull the vanti's curtain aside. Bahomet stared back at him from behind his red face covering, his wig's hair hanging loose under another head scarf.

"I am taking this tolunoyali to pray at the shrine at Trangolangopan. Perhaps Balangupong will have mercy on her," said Darabindoo.

The soldier wrinkled up his nose in disgust.

"Just a very ugly tolunoyali," he shouted back at his commander.

The commander gave a swish of his riding crop, motioning Darabindoo to proceed. Bahomet breathed a sigh of relief.

They trundled along until dusk. Tolunoyalis were not permitted at inns, so Darabindoo set up a makeshift bed underneath the vanti for Bahomet. He went off to a nearby roadside inn to purchase some flat bread and a container of arickmatu.

As they ate, Darabindoo said, "There is a fork in the road up ahead. We will reach it before noon tomorrow. The right fork goes to Trangolangopan and the shrine. The left fork goes to the camp of the assassins' guild. No one goes there, uravinam. There are sure to be guards. No one is permitted near it. What shall we do?" he asked, with a worried expression.

"Take the right fork. We need to go to the shrine first. When I have bound my mantirakolai, we will fear nothing," said Bahomet.

Darabindoo nodded. His uravinam was a fearsome valikatti after all. He pulled his coat around himself and fell asleep against the wheel of his vanti.

Bahomet stretched in the pale light of dawn. He was stiff and sore from sleeping on the ground. People were already moving on the road but gave the cart with the tolunoy flag a wide berth. Bahomet gave Darabindoo a nudge with his foot.

"Up. Time to go. Go straight to the shrine. Don't stop for anything," said Bahomet.

Darabindoo stuffed a flat bread into his mouth while he put his shoulder strap on. Bahomet clambered into the vanti and settled in. Bahomet didn't eat. Fasting before the valikatti ceremony of sassamandolanoo was required.

It was almost noon when they reached Trangolangopan. Darabindoo kept going as Bahomet had directed but stopped near the base of the mountain road to the shrine of Balangupong.

"Why have you stopped?" demanded Bahomet.

"Uravinam. Please. I need to rest a bit before the road to the shrine. It is very steep. Please, uravinam," begged Darabindoo.

Bahomet cursed in annoyance, but reluctantly agreed. He needed to be at the shrine before sunset. He could not use his mantirakolai until it was bound to him, and until that happened, he was vulnerable to being captured.

"Pull in behind those trees. Keep it short. We must make it to the shrine well before sunset," ordered Bahomet.

Darabindoo smiled in gratitude, squatted down on his haunches, and took a long draught from his water flask.

As Darabindoo rested, Bahomet thought ahead to his next move. Boroneeloman Dran, the Patolukai Kumpal (training master) of the assassin's guild would likely be expecting him. He made it his business to know about everything of import that happened, not only in Biluria, but also in Zutheria and beyond. His spies were everywhere. Knowledge was a powerful force, even more so than his assassins' snake venom darts. He would have already heard of Bahomet's escape from Dabranen Island and would assume he would make his way to Trangolangopan.

Bahomet needed his support. He would find a way to defeat Astaran, rid Zutheria of Baragin and everyone connected to him, and take Selvenhall for himself. But he could not do that alone, even with a mantirakolai. With Dran as an ally, though, he would be sitting on the throne at Wreatherin.

CHAPTER SIXTEEN

"**H**e actually said, 'my town'? He doesn't want to see you, my queen, in 'his town' ever again?" asked Baragin, incredulously.

"Yes, right after he said he was going to burn down the Silver Dolphin as soon as he got back to Blessingport," said Amathea

Amathea was back on the royal barge *Elomir* relating the events of the courtroom drama that day. She was putting Baragran into a new change of clothes while she talked.

"That pub was my gift to your father, the man who gave me you, who helped rescue me from Bahomet, who saved my life from the Bilurians, and who helped me get my crown and my kingdom. The gall of that man!" said Baragin, fuming.

"The Futts have played a leading role in Blessingport for generations. He helped Doroquill become mayor— he never makes a big decision without asking Futt. But the harbourmaster never treated my father well, and his son..."

Amathea started chewing a fingernail.

"I don't want to speak ill of the dead, but he was often at the centre of those who were cruel to me. The way he spoke of me in the Dolphin does not surprise me at all. But losing the Linkmanship for his family, which they've held since King Zuth the First, must be a terrible blow for Futt. Please don't be too harsh on him, Baragin. He's lost his only son," concluded Amathea.

Baragin enveloped her in a bear hug from behind, cradling her burgeoning belly with both hands.

"That's why I love you so much. You don't have a mean bone in your body, even for those who mistreat you. But there must be consequences for disloyalty, and for dishonouring the 'Poppet of Blessingport'. A Linkman has higher standards to live up to. Don't worry, my response will be appropriate," said Baragin, giving her a kiss on the nape of her neck.

Baragin left their suite and went onto the deck. Berendell was chatting with the bargemen but excused himself when Baragin caught his eye.

"I was just telling the crew that their king is an experienced poleman," said Berendell with a smile.

Baragin smiled at the memory of his time aboard Darrabee's barge. Then his face got serious.

"Bring Governor Drezzerell here at once. We have an important matter to discuss," said Baragin.

He glanced over at Genneset, who was tickling Baragran, making him laugh in delight. It would be good to have Baragran's grandparents closer to Wreatherin. Germilda had barely let the little one out of her sight—becoming a grandmother had softened her considerably. She had her ear to Amathea's belly and giggled like a little girl when the baby inside kicked her cheek.

Further up the deck, Pharigon was trying to speak with Joya, but it was clear she was intentionally ignoring him. Baragin smiled. She was as ferocious as a noostel, the Yakatan wolverine, and it would not be easy for any man to win her heart. Baragin had appointed Pharigon as military attache to the embassy at Gragnarak, specifically tasked with keeping an eye on Joya.

Baragin had had to pay a heavy price for having the Mythrycians accept Joya for the term of her banishment. Batzorig was the Sasag Darga of Mythrycian, who had replaced his father Enkhtura. He had agreed to place Joya with the Khokhgui in the Gotkurgan settlement of Birgulyuk two days ride south of the capital, but only if Baragin would accept Zythramin as the Mythrycian ambassador to Wreatherin.

Baragin had earlier rejected the proposed appointment outright. Zythramin had worked for Bahomet and had been the one to give the order to burn his old caretaker Dellabur alive. Baragin simply could not imagine having to meet with him on affairs of state.

But the Sasag Darga had insisted. Zythramin was fluent in Zutherian, knew the country well, and most of all, was trusted by Batzorig. Besides, Batzorig had given his personal guarantee that Joya would be very well taken care of with the Gotkurgan tribe. Baragin swallowed his pride and agreed but told Berenfromm he never wanted to deal directly with Zythramin.

After taking a meal with Amathea and the others, Baragin saw that Berendell had returned with Governor Drezzerell in the governor's carriage. Drezzerell was a short, stout man with a ready laugh. He was a fairly astute administrator, however, and had served Baragin well, as he had Duke Robagrin beforehand.

"Your Majesty wished to see me?" asked Drezzerell, bowing low.

"Yes, Drezzerell. Let's meet in my stateroom. Berendell, come along as well," said Baragin.

After an aide had brought Milredden Pink cider for the three of them, Baragin began.

"I'm sure you are aware of the situation with my wife's sister," said Baragin.

"Indeed, sire. Quite the tragedy—for both families," said Drezzerell, diplomatically.

"My sister-in-law reacted disproportionately to great provocation. The sentence she was given was fair. But I am not at all happy about the behaviour of Futtsam towards Joya, or with his outrageous comments about my wife—that is a poor reflection on Harbourmaster Futt. Futt has declared he is going to burn down the Silver Dolphin pub and publicly stated that he does not wish to see anyone from Genneset's family, and that includes Queen Amathea, in 'his town' ever again. 'His town'," said Baragin with emphasis.

Drezzerell frowned. He could see where this was going.

"An intemperate comment, to be sure, Your Highness. What would you have me do?" asked Drezzerell.

"You appoint harbourmasters, do you not?" asked Baragin.

"Yes. Appointments of longstanding positions occur every Midsummer's Day, but are generally routinely renewed for those who have done their jobs well..."

"And supplied the required 'gift'," interrupted Baragin.

"Well," said Drezzerell, with a wry smile, "it is the custom of the country—not only for harbourmasters, but also for mayors, customs agents, barrack commanders and the like. It's how things are done."

"And have you received the customary 'gifts' from Futt and Doroquill?" asked Baragin.

"They have been generous as usual, sire," said Drezzerell, squirming a bit.

"I am only going to say this once, Drezzerell, so listen carefully. You will be going to Blessingport this Midsummer—it's five days away now. You are going to make three important announcements. First of all, Blessingport is to resume its old name—Preneport. Ensure all the maps and official documents reflect that change, effective five days from now. Secondly, Timbraset will be appointed the new mayor of Preneport. And thirdly, Harbourmaster Futt will no longer be Harbourmaster Futt. You will appoint Ibbingrin to that job. You will say that this is a direct command from the king. Are we clear?" asked Baragin.

Drezzerell's jaw dropped, and at first, he was speechless.

"Yeh...yes, Your Highness," he stuttered.

"And if Futt asks why, you can tell him that Preneport is not 'his town', that he cannot ban anyone from it, especially the queen of Zutheria. You can tell him that Linkmen have a duty to train their sons to be gentlemen and he failed miserably at it. He and his good friend Doroquill are welcome to drown their sorrows in the ashes of the Silver Dolphin. Tell him that. You'd best return home to pack for your voyage to Preneport," concluded Baragin, dismissing him with a wave of his hand.

As Drezzerell scurried out the door, Berendell commented, "Well, that was a bit harsh."

Baragin fixed his friend with a steady gaze.

"I want all Zutheria to know nobody dishonours my wife. Nobody."

He paused.

"Did you find another pub?"

"Yes, but there weren't any for sale in Wreatherin. The closest was the one in Braddenlocks, the Prenadon Inn. It's less than a day's ride away from Wreatherin, though. I think both Genneset and Germilda will be pleased," said Berendell.

"Good. It's time for some good news for all of them. Let's wait until we get to Braddenlocks to surprise them," said Baragin with a smile.

CHAPTER SEVENTEEN

Bahomet and Darabindoo rolled through the town of Trangolangopan towards the gates of the shrine of Balangupong. He was the principal god in the Bilurian pantheon of deities, associated with creation, new birth, and health. Trangolangopan was always crowded with those hoping for healing for themselves or family members, barren women, or anyone seeking a blessing for a risky enterprise. The merchants of the town did a rousing business housing and feeding pilgrims, selling charms and amulets, as well as supplying the sacrificial animals offered to Balangupong.

There were many priests of Balangupong, the pucarim, all headed by a high priest, the Uyam Pucari, Dassalimpanong Trin.

It was also the place any valikatti had to go for the binding ceremony of sassamandolanoo. No mantirakolai was usable by any Bilurian wizard until that ceremony was complete. It was Trin Bahomet needed to see, for only he could supervise sassamandolanoo. He was the one who had overseen the binding of his other mantirakolai many years ago. Although he was very old now, he was still the Uyam Pucari of the shrine.

There was one other vanti with the red tolunoy flag in the line-up of people waiting to enter the gates of the shrine. People gave those vantis a wide berth, both in front and behind. As their turn came, Darabindoo handed the gatekeeper a coin and bowed deeply to him. The gatekeeper pointed to a separate area reserved for tolunoyalis.

Darabindoo gasped as the temple of Balangupong came into view. It was an enormous building, built of pure white Prenadon marble from the quarry at Elberon. But the roof was sheeted with pure gold and shone brilliantly in the declining sun. Dozens of pilgrims and priests were milling about in the wide plaza directly in front of the temple.

After parking the vanti, Bahomet called to Darabindoo to the side curtain.

"Here, take this empty mantirakolai box and this bag of coins to the main doorway of the temple. Give them to the doorman and say 'sassamandolanoo'. Then wait, however long it takes, for an answer from inside. I will stay here until you return," said Bahomet.

Darabindoo did as Bahomet directed and squatted down to wait. It was a long wait. The sun was low on the horizon and most of the pilgrims were heading for the exit gate to their accommodations in the town. Darabindoo wondered if he should knock on the door and ask how much longer it would be. He was hungry, and he had to relieve himself.

He stood and began to look around for a private place he could urinate. He had just stepped down off the colonnaded porch when the door creaked open.

"Rejoin your master and wheel your vanti around to the back of the temple," said the doorkeeper.

Then he closed the door.

Darabindoo ran back to the tolunoyali area but stopped behind a bush on the way to empty his bladder.

"Uravinam! We must go behind the temple now," said Darabindoo.

"Take the tolunoy flag off first," directed Bahomet.

Darabindoo complied and began wheeling the vanti to the rear of the temple. At the exact moment when the sun slipped below the horizon, the rear door of the temple opened. Two guards, in very ornate uniforms, armed with swords and long lances, exited and took their place on either side of the doorway.

A very old man with a staff in his right hand, slowly walked through the doorway. He was slightly bent, with a wispy white beard contrasting his dark, wizened face. He had the white and gold robe of the high priest of Balangupong draped about his frail body.

Bahomet stepped down from the vanti, and whispered to Darabindoo, "Go back to the tolunoyali place. Stay there until morning. Someone will bring you something to eat. Go."

Dassalimpanong Trin fixed his gaze on Bahomet and motioned for the guards to go inside.

"Come closer, Karpukkai," said Trin.

Bahomet started. He did not expect to be greeted as "Black Hand".

"Your old name, your Zutherian name, no long fits, Karpukkai. A valikatti with a new mantirakolai needs a new name. It has been a long time, Karpukkai, since you left for the land of the godless," said Trin.

"Land of the godless." That's what Bilurians sometimes referred to Zutheria as, as they did not appear to worship or give reverence to anything, other than a deep respect for the ancient wizard Elbron.

Bahomet bowed deeply.

"You honour me with a new name, Uyam Pucari. I am here for sassamandolanoo," said Bahomet.

"Yes. We should take care of that," said Trin.

He paused.

"I'm sure you know the myanpur wants you. And the Zutherian king wants you very badly. They reward he has offered is very large. But after sassamandolanoo, no one will be able to take you. Please tell me that if you return to rule, you will build a temple for Balangupong in Zutheria for the Bilurians who live and work there," said Trin, fixing Bahomet with an intense gaze.

Bahomet returned the gaze. He recognized this was a pivotal moment. Trin would not bind his mantirakolai without a price, especially given the huge reward Baragin had offered for his capture. With a word, his guards would take him captive and hand him over to the myanpur. Despite the repcated requests of the small Bilurian merchant community in Iblingport and Wreatherin, the dukes of Bradden and the Laguntzaileas of Elberon had adamantly refused to allow a temple to be built anywhere in Zutheria. King Baragin was merely the last ruler to say no. It was a long road from Trangolangopan to regaining rule in Wreatherin and building a temple to Balangupong in Zutheria. But he didn't have much choice.

Bahomet pulled out his dagger, stuck out his tongue, and gave it a nick, the blood-speaking oath of the Bilurians.

"I swear, by the blood of my mouth, that when I rule in Zutheria, I will build a temple to Balangupong," said Bahomet.

Trin smiled.

"Come. Let us begin."

CHAPTER EIGHTEEN

The royal barge *Elomir* nosed into a berth at Braddenlocks. Genneset, standing on the prow, recognized the barge ahead of them in line for the locks—it was Darrabee's *Lazy Bee*.

"I'm going to go have a chin wag with an old friend," he said to Germilda and Amathea, who were trying to calm down an irritated Baragran.

Amathea gathered Baragran in her arms and said, "He needs a nap. Come below with me, Momma, while I put him down."

She tried laying him in his cot, but he continued fussing.

"Here, give him to me. Nana will sing him to sleep," said Germilda, taking the squirming toddler.

"You? Sing? I don't remember you singing, Momma," said Amathea, her eyebrows raising slightly.

"Well, I haven't had much to sing about for many years. But when you were a baby, you fussed a lot, too. But you always fell asleep when I sang to you," reminisced Germilda.

"But I don't remember you singing for Joya," said Amathea.

"Hmph. It's strange. You were the fussy one, but now you're calm. Joya's a wildcat now, but when she was little, she was the sweetest thing—fell asleep in a minute. I'm sure you'll notice quite a few differences when your second one comes along. You sometimes wonder how two siblings have the same parents," said Germilda, musing.

Then she started singing in a surprisingly melodic voice:

In the green meadow
Where waldenflowers grow
A soughing wind
Soothes my cares away

And smoothly flows
The laughing River Prene
That takes my love
Out to the Western Sea

I miss him so, I miss him so
Each day I stand and long for him
I miss him so, I miss him so
O setting sun, send him back to me
O setting sun, please send him back to me

In the green meadow
Where waldenflowers grow
A soughing wind
Soothes my cares away

He'll come for me
My own true love
He'll come for me
And hold me to his heart

I miss him so, I miss him so
Each day I stand and long for him
I miss him so, I miss him so
O setting sun, send him back to me
O setting sun, please send him home to me.

Joya was standing in the doorway, listening. Tears were streaming down her cheeks. She rushed to Germilda's side.

"Oh, Momma, that was so pretty. Why didn't you ever sing that for me?"

Germilda paused and turned to lay the now sound asleep Baragran down in his cot.

"I don't know. I'm a grandmother now, so now I want to sing. I never had time for singing in Blessingport. Your father was away so much, and it was work, work, work all the time to keep food on the table. I guess I was just too tired to sing," said Germilda.

"What's that song called, Momma?" asked Amathea.

"*Setting Sun*. It's a song from long ago, when Blessingport was Preneport, and so many young men went out to fish, sometimes for weeks. Some never came back, storms and such," said Germilda.

"It's a pretty song, but I'll never let a man make my heart feel like that," said Joya.

Amathea and Germilda exchanged a glance.

"Just you wait. It hits you when you don't expect it, when the right one comes along. You're so pretty, I'm sure there'll be many who'll try. And I can tell you it's so wonderful to be loved, to be held, to be cherished," said Amathea.

"Hmph," snorted Joya.

"You forget I grew up seeing how boys treated you. And I worked in a pub. You think Futtsam was an exception? I had to fight them off all the time. Men are pigs and I'm never giving them the time of day. I'm happy for you Ammy, that you found your true love. But you won't hear me singing a song like that—ever," she said with finality.

"We'll see," said Amathea.

Changing the subject, she said, "Midsummer's Day is four days away. You'll be turning sixteen summers, Joya. Even though you're on your way to banishment, you should be a part of the ball at Selvenhall," said Amathea.

"The ball? You mean wear a dress so all the men can ogle me? Haven't you been listening to me?" asked Joya, bristling.

Germilda's eyes began brimming with tears. She held out her arms for Joya and embraced her.

"Oh, Joya, Joya. I won't see you for five years. I don't know how I'll ever bear it. Please, please give your momma the joy of seeing you come of age. Please let me have that memory of you. Please, Joya, please..." and she began sobbing, her face buried in Joya's shoulder.

Amathea moved in to hug her mother from the other side, giving Joya a "big sisterly" look.

Joya sighed, then said, "Momma, Momma, hush. I didn't realize it was so important for you. I always knew Poppa wanted it, but not you. Hush, stop crying. I'll wear the silly dress, just for you and Poppa. But I won't dance!"

Germilda gave Joya a tear-stained kiss on her cheek and wiped her eyes with both hands. Then she gave a little laugh and said, "Holy Elbron, what a sight I must be."

And the three of them broke into laughter.

CHAPTER NINETEEN

Bahomet emerged from the sweat room, dripping. A servant dowsed him with cool water and towelled him dry. Bahomet got down on his knees and began the slow crawl to the sassamandoloo chamber. The cool of the night pervaded the hallway and his naked skin reacted.

Trin stood at the doorway to the chamber, facing away from Bahomet. When the naked Bahomet reached him, he raised the mantirakolai box high over his head, and whispered an incantation. The door opened of its own accord.

Trin entered. It was a small room with a high ceiling. Two torches guttered in wall sconces, but did very little to illuminate the room. A statue of Zazzamin, the god of magic and spells, was at the far end, with his trademark mantirakolai in his raised left hand. Trangolangopan was the only place for the shrine of Zazzamin, inside the temple of Balangupong, for it was thought only Balangupong could contain him. There was another very old shrine on Dalanbur Island, but the Zutherians had captured that years ago and it was no longer in use. Zazzamin had a fearsome face, with pointed ears, glaring eyes and a snarling mouth filled with sharpened teeth.

Trin stopped before the altar just in front of the statue of Zazzamin, bowing low. Bahomet stopped as well, shifting from his raw and bleeding knees to his haunches. After he had crossed his legs, he placed his hands by his side, palms up. He used his good hand to place his blackened right hand in his lap. Now he would wait. All night he would sit in this position.

Trin removed a large brass bowl from below the altar, and held it up high in front of Zazzamin, murmuring another incantation. He lowered the bowl, filled with the blood of a freshly slaughtered goat, and turned.

"May this offering to Zazzamin be pleasing to him, and bind this mantirakolai to his servant, Karpukkai," said Trin.

With that, he poured the blood over Bahomet's head, drenching him completely. Bahomet blinked, but otherwise did not move.

Trin replaced the empty bowl under the altar and went over to the mantirakolai box. Bahomet had given him the wand when he entered the temple. Trin opened the box and lifted the mantirakolai high over his head to the statue of Zazzamin, muttering another incantation. Then he waited, listening for some sort of signal.

A bell tolled, marking the beginning of midnight prayers in the rest of the temple complex. Trin turned to Bahomet and knelt down beside him. He pulled a razor-sharp Bilurian dagger from its sheath and held it in front of Bahomet's eyes.

"Are you ready for sassamandoloo, Karpukkai?" he whispered.

Bahomet gave the briefest of nods.

Positioning himself behind Bahoment, Trin moved one hand down to the skin just above Bahomet's hips and pinched his flesh. He jabbed the dagger into the pinched skin a finger's width. Bahomet did not flinch. The wound was right beside the scar from his previous sassamandoloo binding ceremony.

Trin picked up the mantirakolai and pushed it horizontally into the wound. The end of the wand poked against the skin three fingers width from the knife wound. With a sharp slap of the palm of his hand, Trin pushed the mantirakolai hard until the point emerged through the skin of Bahomet's side. Bahomet winced slightly but did not cry out. Trin rose, bowed to Zazzamin, and walked backward out of the chamber.

Bahomet heard the door close but did not turn. Blood—his blood and the goat's blood—was starting to congeal all over his body. He did not move. He could feel the mantirakolai inside him, unnaturally warm. He closed his eyes and practised the mind-numbing meditation Aladrash had taught him during his apprenticeship at Elberon. With it, a wizard could withstand any pain, any discomfort.

Three hours passed. Three bells tolled, indicating the third hour of the morning, the darkest hour of night. The chamber door opened and Trin re-appeared. He bowed to Zazzamin, then turned towards Bahomet.

"Are you ready to complete sassamandoloo, Karpukkai?" asked Trin.

Bahomet nodded again.

Trin knelt in front of him, grasped the front point of the mantirakolai, and pulled sharply. He rose with the bloody wand and knelt down on Bahomet's left side. Trin took his dagger again, grabbed a pinch of skin on Bahomet's opposite side and made another slash wound. He inserted the mantirakolai, waited, then pushed sharply until the point emerged from the opposite side.

Trin rose, bowed to Zazzamin, then backed out of the room. Again, Bahomet forced his mind towards calm and painlessness. It was only with extreme effort that Bahomet withstood the next three hours. The mantirakolai felt like it was burning a large hole in Bahomet's side.

Finally, a ray of light appeared under the edge of the door—dawn. The door opened with a slight creak, and Trin re-entered. He bowed to Zazzamin and turned to face Bahomet.

He knelt behind him. He grasped the point end of the wand and pulled sharply. He held the wand high and shouted, "Zazzamin sassamondoloo!"

He moved in front of Bahomet and placed the mantirakolai sideways into his mouth. Then he grasped his left arm and helped him to his feet.

"Now you and your mantirakolai are bound, Karpukkai. Wield it with power," said Trin.

Bahomet bowed low to Zazzamin, then took the mantirakolai from his mouth and raised it high. "Sassamandoloo Zazzamin," he cried in a loud voice. A small blue flame erupted from the end of Zazzamin's mantirakolai arcing to the tip of Bahamet's wand, enveloping the entire room in a flash of light.

Bahomet smiled.

Chapter Twenty

Genneset and Darrabee chatted animatedly for some time, catching up on all the news. Finally, Genneset said, "All this blathering has given me a powerful thirst. How be we wander up to the Prenadon Inn for a pint or two?"

"That sounds wonderful. I'm awfully parched, too. It'll be a couple of hours before it's our turn to go through the locks," replied Darrabee.

"Berendell? Baragin? You thirsty? Germilda? The Prenadon has an excellent stout if I recall."

"Not for me. You go ahead, Berendell," said Baragin with a wink.

Germilda hemmed and hawed, and finally said, "Oh, why not? I could use a good stout."

The Prenadon was only a short walk from the wharf. When the four of them entered, the place was fairly crowded. They found a table, but it took them a while to get the waiter's attention.

"Great Zuth, the service is slow in here. That wouldn't happen if I were running this place," complained Genneset.

Germilda cast a disapproving eye around the place.

"It could use a good cleaning. And those pictures on the wall would have to go. Something brighter, I think."

The four chatted for a while, but due to the slower service, they weren't able to order another round. Finally, Darrabee said it was time to go as their turn for the locks was coming up.

Genneset said, "It was my idea to come here. The round's on me."

He motioned the waiter to bring their tab. Berendell caught his eye and gave him a pre-arranged signal. The waiter brought over a tray with a document on it.

Puzzled, Genneset asked, "What's this, my good man?"

"Compliments of the house, sir," answered the waiter.

Genneset and Germilda exchanged a bewildered glance. As former pub owners, they knew that type of courtesy was never offered to strangers.

"What do you mean, 'compliments of the house'? Tell me what we owe. We need to get back to the locks," said Genneset getting annoyed.

"Owners don't pay for their drinks, sir," said the waiter.

"Owners? Owners? What are you talking about?" asked Genneset.

The waiter set the tray down in front of Germilda and Genneset. Genneset looked at it, totally bewildered. It was a deed. It was the deed for the Prenadon Inn. And on the deed were their names, with the official stamp of the Governor of Prene certifying them as the legal owners.

Genneset looked up, first at the waiter, then at Darrabee, then at Berendell, who gave them a smile.

"You lost the Silver Dolphin, the king's own gift to you, through no fault of your own. The Prenadon is its replacement. Besides, both Baragin and Amathea want you closer to Wreatherin—Baragran and the one that's on the way need their grandparents nearby. It's yours," said Berendell.

After letting that stunning news sink in for a moment, Germilda let out a scream that turned heads throughout the pub. She jumped up and started hugging Genneset. Then she grabbed a very surprised Darrabee and gave him a big kiss, then did the same with Berendell. Then she hugged Genneset again. Finally, she called out to the waiter.

"You! What is your name?"

"Bobbingran, ma'am," he answered.

"Well, Bobbingran, I want this place scrubbed from top to bottom before you open tomorrow, do you hear me? Top to bottom! It had better be clean when I get back here, or you'll be wishing you were poling a barge instead of slinging steins. I want to see…"

Genneset interrupted her.

"Sweetsap. Please. We need to get back to the barge. We'll come back after Midsummer's Day and see to all the details. Just let Bobbingran manage things until then. Besides, we have to give our thanks to Baragin in person. What a marvellous surprise," he said, turning to Berendell.

CHAPTER TWENTY-ONE

Bahomet was clean from his bath, with his sides bandaged. He was wearing a new gown Trin had given him, black, with much embroidery on the edges. The gown had the insignia of Zazzamin stitched onto the left breast. Inside the right sleeve was a small pocket with his mantirakolai. He wore the traditional embroidered peaked turban of a Bilurian valikatti. A silver medallion of the snarling face of Zazzamin, the insigna of a valikatti, was on the front of the turban. His left hand was encased in the black glove Bilanguree had made for him, suspended by a small strap. He made no attempt to hide it now.

As he left the temple of Balangupong, people gasped and moved out of his way, whispering to one another.

"Bahomet the Zutherian. Karpukkai. It is Karpukkai. He is a valikatti," many said.

Everyone knew the myanpur was looking for him and that there was a huge reward for his capture. But no one would dare approach a valikatti with hostile intentions no matter how much the reward.

"Come, Darabindoo. We must go to the Black Leopard's Lair, the Karuppsertai Poyum, to see my friend Boroneeloman Dran. We have much to talk about," said Bahomet.

Darabindoo put on his towing strap and grabbed the handles of his vanti as Bahomet clambered in. The crowd of curious onlookers parted in front of him as he rolled down the hill into the town of Trangolangopan.

As they neared the bottom of the hill, a knot of the myanpur's soldiers stood uncertainly blocking the road. Word of Bahomet's presence had spread quickly. Darabindoo stopped, unsure of what to do.

"Soldiers, uravinam. They won't let us through," he said nervously.

Bahomet looked out the side curtain at the small detachment of soldiers. A crowd was gathering behind the vanti, waiting to see what would happen. As the stand-off paused, a goat wandered into the space between the vanti and the detachment of soldiers.

Bahomet did not even get out of the vanti. He pointed his mantirakolai out from behind the side curtain, and in a loud voice said, "*Ti Marrum Minnal*" (fire and lightning).

A bolt of blue lightning arced across the square striking the goat and leaving it smoking on the ground with a huge black hole in its side.

"Tell the myanpur I am going to the Karuppsertai Poyum. He can find me there if he wants me," he said to the slack-jawed captain of the guards.

"Carry on, uravinam," he said to Darabindoo.

Darabindoo picked up the poles of his vanti and moved towards the soldiers who melted like butter in front of him. The crowd continued to follow him at a respectful distance until Bahomet pointed his mantirakolai at a large willow tree. An arc of blue light blasted the trunk causing it to fall across the road. The crowd got the message that they should stop following. They milled about talking excitedly to one another about all that they had seen.

Darabindoo took the fork on the outskirts of Trangolangopan, a much less travelled pathway leading towards the Karuppsertai Poyum. The Bilurian assassins were known as the Black Leopards, the Karuppsertai, as they always dressed in black and were extremely lethal. They almost never failed in ending the life of their target.

The training regimen at the poyum was severe and demanding. All the Karuppsertais had to prove expertise in the ninety-nine ways to kill. The patolukai kumpal then rented out their expertise to whoever could pay his high fees. His fee came with a money-back guarantee of success—and he almost never had to return any money.

His customers were varied. The sasag darga in Mythrycia had used his services, as had a number of previous Zutherian dukes. Past myanpurs, their viziers, as well as a few wealthy Bilurian businessmen with troublesome enemies had asked for his help. Bahomet had been an excellent customer over the years. The loss of all four of the Karuppsertais he had contracted prior to his downfall was extremely unusual, though.

Darabindoo pulled the cart slowly towards the gated compound. The pathway was very narrow, with steep cliffsides framing the only way in. Darabindoo caught a glimpse of a black-garbed figure on the edge of the cliff to the left and prayed he wouldn't be targeted by an arrow.

Darabindoo rolled the vanti to a stop in front a large gate. On top of the gate was the head of a snarling black leopard. There was no guard in sight, although Bahomet knew his approach was noted and likely reported already to the patolukai kumpal.

Bahomet got out of the vanti and approached the gate.

"Amadel," he shouted in Zutherian, the agreed upon password if he should ever return. The gate creaked open and Bahomet returned to the vanti.

Darabindoo looked left and right as he pulled the vanti towards the main building of the Karuppsertai Poyum. There were knots of men in black trousers, many shirtless, sparring with weapons, firing arrows at targets, blowing dart guns, and grappling with one another. No one looked towards them, obviously warned by their drill masters to stay focused on their training.

Darabindoo dropped the handles of the vanti in front of the main entrance of the training centre. It was made of dark brick, two stories high, with a long veranda the whole length of the front. There were two huge doors plated with bronze, each with a leopard's head in the centre. Two windows flanked the doors, but there were no others on the front of the building at ground level. The upper level had no windows but did have narrow firing slits evenly spaced.

Bahomet alit, and seemingly out of nowhere, two Karuppsertais dropped down beside him, and another two beside Darabindoo.

"Go with them. Don't be afraid. Take the money chest from the vanti and leave it on the ground. I will send for you when I need you," said Bahomet.

They both turned their heads as the bronze doors creaked open. A small dark man of uncertain age, arms behind his back, and dressed in the simple black Karuppsertai uniform, stepped through.

"Welcome Bahomet—or should I say, Karpukkai. You've been expected," said Boroneeloman Dran.

Chapter Twenty-Two

Amathea gasped and screamed aloud, waking Baragin.

"Ammy! Ammy! What is it?" asked Baragin worriedly, but he knew he wouldn't like the answer. It was only her prescient dreams that woke her like this.

"It was him. He was standing on a big pile of rubble, smiling. He was wearing two crowns," said Amathea, biting her fingernail as she always did when she was very nervous or worried.

"Two crowns? Strange. Which two crowns? Do you remember?" asked Baragin.

"One was yours. The other I didn't recognize, but it had many tines and three colours of stones—green, white and red. I hate these dreams!"

She put both her hands to her face, and sucked in her breath, trying to keep from crying.

"What does it mean, Baragin? How could he have two crowns? He is just an escaped prisoner with only one good arm. I don't understand, I don't understand," said Amathea, burying her face in Baragin's chest.

Baragin held her in his arms.

"Ssssh. Hush now. You're safe with me. I don't understand, either. But we can't let a bad dream interfere with Midsummer's Day festivities. We have the ball tonight, and your sister has to leave tomorrow for

Mythrycia. Come, sweetheart. Let's focus on enjoying our day. We didn't really have a chance against Bahomet before but look where we are now. We can't let a washed-up wizard ruin our special day," said Baragin, giving her a kiss on the forehead.

Amathea snuggled in closer to him, sighing.

"I always feel safe when I'm with you."

Baragin was in his private work office with Berendell and Chancellor Berenfromm. The father-son duo were his closest advisors, and the ones he trusted the most.

Baragin was frowning at the pigeon message Berenfromm had handed to him. It was from Ambassador Erenbil in Biluria. Baragin's face clouded. Amathea's dream roiled his thoughts, but he chose not to share it with Berenfromm just yet.

"He put on quite a show it seems, roasting a goat with his valikatti wand, and daring the soldiers to take him into custody. He's currently at the compound of that Bilurian assassin training master near Trangolangopan. The two would know each other as Bahomet was a regular customer during his time as Regent of Evenshorn, as you well know," commented Berenfromm.

Baragin frowned again.

"Damnation! It just keeps getting worse," he shouted, crumpling the pigeon message and tossing it against the wall.

"He's not just a one-armed escaped prisoner anymore. He's acquired a valikatti's wand, and obviously all the power that goes with it. Even if the myanpur wanted to comply with our request to capture him he will find it almost impossible to do so with a full-fledged valikatti. They have the same power as a Laguntzailea, don't they?" asked Baragin.

"Damagal would probably be a better one to answer that question," noted Berendell. "Should I send for him?"

Baragin sighed.

"They're all at Elberon for their Midsummer's Council of Five Meeting. We'll have to wait until he gets back to consult with him. Let him know I need to see him as soon as he returns."

Turning to Berendell, Baragin said, "Let's do our Midsummer's Day festivities justice. Amathea's sister will need an escort for the ball. Have you taken care of that?"

"Ah...," said Berendell, wincing noticeably. "Your sister-in-law is...a bit stubborn. She insists she wants to walk in by herself. Doesn't want to be on any man's arm."

"Blast her hide! I like her spunk, but frankly, it'll be a relief to see her tormenting the Mythrycians or the Gotkurgans or—what were those women warriors called?" asked Baragin

"Khokhguis," answered Berendell.

"I pity them," said Baragin with a laugh. "I'm sure her mother and her sister will change her tune."

Pausing, Baragin said, "Berenfromm, tell the Bilurian ambassador I need to see him for a short meeting."

Berenfromm asked, "Should I be at that meeting?"

"No, no. It's a minor thing. We'll have a more in-depth meeting after the Midsummer's activities to discuss the Bahomet situation."

It was after lunch when Berendell ushered Ambassador Gandrapreen Oban into Baragin's formal reception office. Berendell hovered expectantly, but

Baragin sent him off to go over the arrangements for the ball with the protocol officer.

Ambassador Oban waited respectfully.

"This won't take long. I have a question for you, Ambassador Oban," began Baragin.

"Surely, I will do my best to answer it, Majesty," said Oban with a bow.

"Describe the myanpur's crown to me," said Baragin.

Adan raised his eyebrows in surprise. He had not expected this question at all.

"Well, Majesty. It is made of gold, like yours, with nine tines representing the nine founding tribes of Biluria," said Oban.

"Are there precious stones on it?" asked Baragin.

"Yes, Majesty. There are three diamonds, three emeralds and three rubies. All from the mines near Brobabil if I recall," said Oban with a smile.

Baragin frowned.

"Thank you. That will be all. I expect I will see you and your wife at the ball tonight?"

"Yes, Majesty," said Oban.

Baragin stood and Oban recognized the audience was over. He bowed and left with a puzzled look on his face.

Baragin was lost in thought. Two crowns. One with green, white and red stones. His and the myanpur's. On Bahomet's head. Impossible. He left for his chambers to get dressed for the Midsummer's Day ball.

CHAPTER TWENTY-THREE

Boroneeloman Dran lounged on his side on a settee. He was smoking a water pipe. A half-eaten sherbet rested on the table beside him. He eyed Bahomet through half-lidded eyes. He was not a physically impressive man, but his reptilian eyes chilled anyone who came close to him. They spoke of barely restrained evil, as if death were only a glance away.

Bahomet met his gaze. He was a kindred spirit— and a formidable ally.

"I left a contribution at the door—for the four Karuppsertais who lost their lives in my service," began Bahomet.

They had just finished a meal, the finest one Bahomet had had since the debacle at Amadel.

"It is generous. Although I understand your cousin Bahnuran was the main contributor," said Dran with a smile.

"Yes. But I left a fragrant deposit to remind him of who it was who relieved him of his gold," said Bahomet, smiling at the memory.

"It is I who should be returning your gold, though. Our arrangement was somewhat different than most of my clients, as it was a long-term one. Nevertheless, all four failed to complete their assignments. And that grieves me, my friend," said Dran, more seriously.

"Risks of the trade, as they say. Don't trouble yourself about reimbursement—what's past is past. Perhaps the funds I brought could ease the pain of their families," said Bahomet.

"I think not. I do not reward failure. I am sure we can find a mutually agreeable use for those coins."

Dran paused.

"Your vanti puller. A cousin, yes?" asked Dran.

"Your information, as always, is accurate. Darabindoo is my attam's grandnephew. A second cousin I suppose," said Bahomet.

"You have met your other second cousin," said Dran, blowing a puff of smoke into the ceiling fan.

Bahomet looked at him, questioningly.

"At Amadel, seven years ago now," said Dran.

Bahomet was genuinely confused.

"I cannot think of whom you refer. At Amadel?"

Dran smiled.

"The crown prince, the kiritam ilavaracar. He was at Amadel square for your 'near' coronation, yes?"

"The kiritam ilavaracar is my cousin? How can this be?" asked Bahomet, bewildered.

Dran leaned forward.

"Who was your grandfather?" he asked.

"I...I don't know. My pattam never talked about him. If I asked, she would change the subject. I assumed it was a sensitive topic and did not pry, out of respect," said Bahomet.

"There was a very good reason she did not talk. The myanpur made sure she didn't. Do you know how your mother died?" asked Dran.

"She died giving birth to me," said Bahomet, his brow knitting.

"Yes, that is true. But she had help," said Dran.

Bahomet's eyes widened, but words failed him. His eyes were full of questions.

"Your mother was unwise. She made it known that she intended to press the House of Saran, the Bilurian royal family, for princely status for you if you were a boy," said Dran.

"Princely status? Why would she do that?" asked Bahomet.

"Your mother was the result of a rape—your grandmother and the previous myanpur's younger brother. He was notorious for taking advantage of women of lower status who could not defend themselves. Your pattam told your mother of her origin. When she became of age, she made a request of the House of Saran to be recognized. The myanpur declined but gave her some money and made her a gift to your father, the Zutherian trader.

"But your mother was determined and began making more waves when she became pregnant with you. The myanpur lost his patience and paid the midwife to "assist" your mother into the realm of the dead if a boy was born. Then he gave your grandmother a list of all her relatives, with you at the top of it, who would die if she should ever reveal your true origins.

"So your great-grandfather, your perraya tattam, is Myanpur Dringmanan Saran. The Kiritam Ilaravacar Danputmanan Saran, has the same perraya tattam. He is your second cousin. You, my friend, are a member of the House of Saran, unofficially," concluded Dran.

Bahomet's mouth was open, and he exhaled sharply.

"That fact is a problem for you—and for me. The Kiritam Ilaravacar Danputmanan knows who you are. It is he who insisted Grand Vizier Fayan send the army to look for you. He wants you out of Biluria, dead or alive—preferably dead.

"It is not widely known that the current Myanpur Geelanguran is in his dotage. He forgets much of what he hears, and often makes no sense at all when he talks. He is not capable of ruling. His Grand Vizier Brandeeshpuran Fayan actually runs the palace and the government of Biluria. The kiritam ilaravacar is anxious to take power, though. Danputmanan knows he is just a smothering pillow away from the throne.

"Things came to a head a few weeks ago. Danputmanan is known to prefer men—and boys—to women. He and his favorite friend found a young boy, nine years old, in the palace garden. They assumed he was the child of a servant and ignored his claims that he was the grandnephew of the grand vizier. They decided to introduce him to the ways of the bedroom. Danputmanan's friend, Dareeshput Aban, was rather rough on the poor boy. His mother found him crying and bleeding. He could not walk straight for a week.

"Fayan was furious. He contacted me and requested a particularly painful and prolonged death for Aban. He is a regular customer, so I was happy to comply. I have a retired Karuppsertai, Bishnannam Brin, who is very skilled in such matters. I use him when I need to extract information from those who are reluctant or when a client requests an unpleasant death.

"Two of my Karuppsertais kidnapped Aban. Then Brin fed him the offending member for his last meal and impaled him in such a way so that he died with the taste of his own filth in his mouth. It took four days. The Grand Vizier was quite satisfied but underestimated how fond the kiritam ilavaracar was of him. The kiritam ilavaracar ordered the arrest of the grand vizier. So he has gone into hiding," said Dran.

"Do you know where he is?" asked Bahomet.

Dran motioned to a servant standing near the door. He opened the door and a distinguished looking older man, bearded and with a turban, walked into the room. He walked up to Bahomet, knelt and bowed his face low to the floor, his palms flat.

"Grand Vizier Brandeeshpuran Fayan, at your service, Your Excellency," he said.

Chapter Twenty-Four

Joya lay back in the full-length marble tub, eyes closed in pure bliss. Like Amathea before her, she had never enjoyed such a marvellous bath. A tin wash tub with tepid water and harsh soap was all she had known her entire life.

A maid cleared her throat politely. Joya opened her eyes.

"What?" she demanded.

She was enjoying luxuriating in the soothing, fragrant waters of the bath and did not want to be interrupted.

"Begging your pardon, Miss Joya. It will be time for the banquet soon. And the ball. We need to do your hair and make sure your dress is properly fitted," said the maid.

Just then Amathea entered the room with a dressmaker in tow. The dressmaker had a sky-blue dress with white lace edging and Bilurian pearls sewn in for decoration, draped over her arm.

"Come, sister. You'll turn into a wrinkled Sweetsap if you lay in that bath any longer. We need to make sure this dress fits you. Bellawin here will make any necessary adjustments," said Amathea. She was already in her formal dress and her pregnancy was quite evident beneath it.

Joya gave an exasperated sigh.

"Why do I have to go through all this fuss and nonsense? Coming out balls are for girls who want to attract a man. Why would I want to do that?" she said as she climbed out of the tub and accepted a large towel from the maid.

"Because you are the queen's sister. Because your Momma and Poppa have been waiting for this moment for sixteen years. Because you are going off to exile and we won't…"

Amathea stopped, tears welling up in her eyes.

Joya's stepped toward her and enveloped her in a soggy hug.

"Please don't cry, Ammy. Please. I said I would wear the silly dress and I will. I'll even walk into the room with that Captain Pharigon. But I won't hold his arm and I won't dance. Hush, now. You'll turn your face all red, you silly," said Joya, using her thumbs on Amathea's cheeks.

"Oh my. I've gotten water spots on your dress," she said, stepping back.

"They'll dry. Come. Let's get your hair done and get you into that dress. Momma and Poppa are dying to see you in it," said Amathea.

Joya sat beside her sister at the banquet. There were some murmurings that it was highly inappropriate to grant a convicted murderer such hospitality, but Baragin silenced them all by personally holding Joya's chair for her. He looked around the room daring anyone to say anything. Amathea broke the tension by tinkling her fork against her glass and suggesting the musikan play something while the diners had their meal.

After the banquet, people retired to the large foyer outside the Grand Ball Room of Selvenhall. Demmenbel, the protocol master, was scurrying about the foyer with his list, ensuring everyone knew who they would be following into the ball room.

Captain Pharigon was standing next to Genneset and Germilda. He was in his dress-white regimental uniform, with gold braid on the epaulets and a ceremonial saber with a gold hilt strapped to his lancer's breeches. The epaulets only exaggerated his broad shoulders, and his jacket fitted snugly to a narrow waist. With his dark hair and neatly trimmed moustache, he was a striking figure. More than one of the young ladies—and older ladies—in the foyer cast an approving eye in his direction.

Germilda had a deep purple dress on and had her hair done up in the style of the day. She looked about nervously, feeling quite out of place amidst all the finery and judgmental looks of the elite of Wreatherin.

"You are the mother-in-law of the king, my peach blossom. You outrank all of them," said Genneset, noticing her nervousness.

"I'm just not used to any of this, Genny," she whispered back.

"Oh look, here comes Joya. Oh my! Oh my!" said Germilda as Joya entered the foyer.

All eyes were on her, and not just because of her notoriety. Ignoring the current style, her long blonde hair was hanging loose, a golden cascade across her bare shoulders, except for two small side braids tied in the back. Joya moved with cat-like grace and held her chin high. Amathea had loaned her a white gold tiara and a string of pearls that matched the ones on her dress. The dress fitted her perfectly and showed off her shapely figure extremely well. Most of the men stopped their conversations with whomever they were speaking to and stared in admiration. She was without a doubt the most beautiful young lady in the room.

Ferrelaine, who had married a much older General Trillabon, the Zutherian Army's head general after Baragin tied the knot with Amathea, leaned over to her husband and whispered, "Close your mouth, you silly gob. It's pretty obvious who got all the looks in that family."

"Well, Jo-jo. What a sight you are," said Genneset, giving her a kiss on the cheek.

Germilda just put her hands to her cheeks, looking Joya up and down, then gave her a big hug.

"Oh my! You look just wonderful! It's just so terrible you have to leave tomorrow. I'm glad I won't have to wash this dress—look at all those pearls," said Germilda, running her fingers over the lace and pearls on the dress.

Pharigon stepped over, gave a nod of his head, and said, "Miss Joya, you look quite beautiful this evening."

"I'm not interested in your opinion, Captain," said Joya, frostily.

"Now, now, poppet. No need to be rude. The captain was just being polite," said Genneset.

"I see no need to be polite to my jailer, poppa. Didn't you hear the judge release me into his custody? He's my jailer and gets to kick me over the border when we get there. I'll walk into the room with him because you all insisted, but that's all I'm going to do," said Joya, pursing her lips tightly.

Pharigon gave her a bemused look, which made Joya even angrier.

Genneset sighed and shook his head. But before he could say anything else, Protocol Master Demmenbel shouted out loudly, "Places! Places, everyone! We're about to enter the ball room."

Pharigon and Joya took their places, just in front of Genneset and Germilda. Pharigon held out his arm for Joya to take, but she ignored it, looking straight ahead.

Pharigon leaned over and said in a low voice, "It's a pity your sister is expecting. I hear she's a much better dancer than you and I was looking forward to seeing her do the quellel with the king," said Pharigon, tilting his head towards Joya.

Joya's eyes blazed.

"That's not true! Poppa taught both of us and told me more than once I was the better dancer," said Joya.

"Pfft! You're all talk. I dare you to prove it," prodded Pharigon.

"I said I wasn't going to dance, and even if I did, it wouldn't be with a self-important prig like you," bristled Joya.

Pharigon chuckled and smiled, which infuriated Joya even more. She let out an exasperated growl and pointedly turned her head away from him as they were introduced.

The ball wound its way through the group dances, the sandrinel and gallalel. Genneset participated and urged Joya to as well, but she refused.

The musikan announced that the quellel was next and that dancers should find their partners.

Genneset leaned over to Pharigon and said, "You should ask her. She's very good at the quellel."

"Maybe if I were the last man on earth," said Pharigon with a wry smile.

Genneset looked at Pharigon, then turned his head to look at Joya, but she was talking with Germilda and not paying attention to them.

"Tell you what. I'll get her on the floor for the quellel. Then about halfway through, I'll pretend my knees are giving out. If you're the man I think you are, you'll jump in," he said with a wink.

The music for the quellel started, and Genneset got down on one knee in front of Joya, grasping her hand.

"Just give your old Poppa one dance on your last night with us, won't you my pet?"

Joya's heart softened when she saw a tear forming in the corner of his eye.

"Oh alright, Poppa. Let's show these Wreatherin folks how it's done," said Joya.

Genneset gave Pharigon another wink, then led Joya through the graceful steps of the quellel. Joya held her head off to the side as she'd been taught, the pearls laying against her long white neck. She really was very good, and soon other dancers were remarking how marvellous Genneset and his daughter were.

Genneset maneuvered Joya close to where Pharigon was sitting, then let out a sharp, "Oh! My knee! Have to sit down. Take over, Pharigon, take over."

And before Joya could say a word, Pharigon had Joya by the waist and was spinning her into the midst of crowd. He was an accomplished dancer, but much bigger and stronger than Genneset. He whirled Joya effortlessly around and around the dance floor, not giving her a chance to withdraw. Joya had never been held that way before, and despite herself, something stirred inside her that she'd never felt before.

The music drew to a close and the two stopped. Pharigon looked down into Joya's eyes, then at her lips, slightly parted from the effort of the dance. He began moving his head a little closer, but Joya pulled her head back and swung her arm to give him a slap. Pharigon caught her wrist.

Joya glared at him.

"Take your hand off me," she snarled.

She pulled her hand out of his grasp and stomped off to her mother's side.

Pharigon watched her go. He shook his head and let out a sigh. *What a wildcat!*

CHAPTER TWENTY-FIVE

Bahomet looked at the prostrate grand vizier, then over to Dran. Dran smiled and motioned with his hand that Bahomet should give the vizier leave to stand up.

"Please stand, Vizier Fayan. I appreciate your obeisance, but I think we are being hasty. I am in no position to rule Biluria—it never once crossed my mind," said Bahomet.

"Listen to what Fayan has to say. The three of us are in a dangerous game. The kiritam ilavaracar has vowed to destroy the Karuppsertai Poyum. He knows you are here and likely suspects Fayan is here as well. We are formidable, but few in numbers. We cannot long withstand the Bilurian army, should they decide to attack. Fayan? Continue," said Dran, looking over at the vizier.

"It is true. I made a tactical error eliminating the filth who abused my grandnephew. It gave the kiritam ilavaracar the excuse to remove me from power and take action against the Karuppsertais. Dran is right. The three of us are in great peril. You are a valikatti and have a mantirakolai but you are no match for Valikatti Parandaman, the chief valikatti of the country. The kiritam ilavaracar is sure to bring him here with the army. Parandaman will deal with you, then the army will destroy this place," said Fayan.

Bahomet frowned. This was serious news, indeed. He knew of Valikatti Parandaman's reputation. He was the equivalent of Zaharbat Astaran, the most powerful of all the valikattis in Biluria. He looked over at Dran, who looked as relaxed as ever.

"You do not seem worried, Dran," noted Bahomet.

"Oh, I am worried. But I am prepared. Fayan is right. You are no match for Parandaman. You cannot defeat him with magic, at least not directly. But no valikatti is immortal. Did you not acquire your first mantirakolai due to its master being swept away in a flood? Did not your Aladrash expire at your very coronation? It is rare, but valikattis can be killed. I am taking a big gamble hosting the two of you here. I am gambling both of you will be grateful should we prevail," said Dran, with a puff on his water pipe.

"You said you were 'prepared'. What are your preparations?" asked Bahomet.

Dran puffed on his pipe again and blew a smoke ring to the ceiling before answering.

"There is only one way in to the Karuppsertai Poyum. You saw yourself the narrow steep-sided cliffs that flank the pathway. It is easily defensible, at least against conventional attackers. This is attack will not be conventional, though. Parandaman will invoke a spell of protection, and the army will shield themselves against an arrow attack then use a battering ram on the gate. The kiritam ilavaracar's weakness is that he will be over-confident with Parandaman present. The two of them will most certainly be side by side. Danputmanan will want to see, personally, the removal of our heads. I'm sure he will be happy to send yours to King Baragin," said Dran.

"Yet you seem confident, despite these odds," noted Bahomet.

"The rims of the two cliffs are lined with boulders—many, many boulders. I, and the Patolukai Kumpals who came before me, add more every year. There is one key stone for each pile. That is where you come in. Blasts from your mantirakolai, at the right moment, will release a torrent of boulders. There is no magic in the world that can stop an avalanche like that. I will show you the location of the key stones and the place where you can wait in hiding. With Parandaman and Danputmanan under a pile of rubble, you, and Vizier Fayan, will be unopposed to rule in Tricanmallokan.

"Most of the generals in the army are loyal to Fayan. They will fall into line when they see him back at the reins of power. You have the blood of the House of Saran in you, and they will overlook your Zutherian blood—besides, you won't give them a choice. You may have to remove some troublesome relatives of the myanpur, though. I will be happy to assist with that," said Dran, with a feral smile.

Bahomet looked over at Fayan, who awaited his response to the plan.

"Show me the key stones," he said.

Chapter Twenty-Six

Joya looked up into dark brown eyes, then at red lips framed by a closely trimmed moustache. He pressed his lips against hers while broad, strong hands caressed her naked back. Then, No! She woke with a start, breathing heavily. She was furious with herself. And with him. How dare he invade her dreams! Insufferable, exasperating, annoying, chauvinistic, presumptuous, self-important—she ran out of irritating adjectives.

She couldn't wait to get to Mythrycia and start training with the Khokhguis. No men around to annoy or distract her.

Joya jumped out of bed and got dressed—man's trousers this time. No more dresses for her. She was working on a braid when Amathea came in holding Baragran by the hand.

"Baragran wanted to say good-bye to his auntie. We won't be going down to the stables to see you off. I don't think my eyes have enough tears for that," said Amathea, sniffing loudly.

"Oh, Ammy. Don't get me started. I'm going to miss all of you so. I think they'll let me go to Gragnarak every once in a while to see you, though," said Joya.

"It won't be often enough. You are much less annoying now that you're older. But you do get into more trouble," said Amathea with a laugh.

"By the way, I saw how you danced with Pharigon. I thought you said you weren't going to dance at all," said Amathea with a bemused smile.

"Poppa tricked me! He said his knees hurt, then Pharigon ambushed me, the lout. But I warned him to keep his hands to himself," said Joya, frowning and making a fist.

"You're too funny. I'll bet you were dreaming about his kiss," said Amathea, teasingly.

"Was not!" shouted Joya, throwing a pillow at her head.

Amathea ducked away from the pillow, laughing, but it hit Baragran in the face.

"Auntie threw a pillow! Auntie threw a pillow!" he shouted.

He grabbed the pillow and began swinging it at Joya. She responded with mock ferocity with another pillow and soon they were all giggling.

Amathea sighed, suddenly serious.

"I'm worried for you, sister. What if they mistreat you, make you do horrible things? I haven't had a dream about you, but I still worry."

"This nose-puncher can take care of herself," said Joya, holding a squirming, giggling Baragran on her lap.

"Just the same, I have something for you," said Amathea.

She pulled out two small leather pouches.

"What is it?" asked Joya.

"These are some coins. Baragin said to give it you," said Amathea.

"What's in the other pouch?" asked Joya.

"It's my spider blanket. You hide under it when danger is near. No one can see you. Look!" Amathea pulled it out and draped it over Baragran, who disappeared completely from view.

"Holy Elbron!" shouted Joya. "How come you never showed me this before? Did you have it at Blessingport?"

"Yes, but you are so impulsive, you would have just wanted to play with it. It's only for dire emergencies. Keep it in your hip pouch. There will come a time when you'll be glad you have it. I can always get another one from Damagal," said Amathea.

"Thank you, Ammy. I hope I never have to use it," said Joya.

She tucked it in her hip pouch.

"I guess it's time to go. My jailer awaits me."

"You mean your dance partner?" said Amathea, teasing again.

"Oooh! You're so annoying!" said Joya, giving her a punch on the shoulder.

Amathea laughed and said, "Hey! Take it easy on the pregnant lady."

Joya sighed and picked up Baragran in her arms.

"I'm going to miss being here for the new one. I'm kind of liking the auntie thing. You'll be such a big boy when auntie gets back."

She gave Baragran a kiss and tousled his hair.

They made their way downstairs. Amathea gave her a hug and a kiss at the doorway.

"Be well, Joya. Send us a pigeon when you can. I know Baragin has told Pharigon to look out for you. Try not to be such a bearcat to him—I think he likes you," she whispered.

"Well, that's his tough luck. I don't need any man to babysit me. Take care, Ammy," said Joya.

She turned and walked toward Pharigon, who was chatting with Baragin and her parents while he held her horse.

After hugs and tears all around, Joya mounted her horse. Pharigon gave the order to the twelve troopers to mount up. They were to be her escort to the border with Mythrycia.

Genneset put his hand on Joya's leg and looked up at her.

"Oh! I almost forgot!"

He pulled a fine Bilurian dagger out of his side pouch and a whetstone to go with it.

"Here. You're probably going to need these," he said.

"Thank you, Poppa."

She slipped the dagger into her right boot top.

"Good-bye. Good-bye, Momma. Brother—don't let anybody punch you in the nose," she said to Baragin.

Then she gave her horse a kick and the group headed out the gates of Selvenhall and turned north to Drabbadentown.

Baragin looked after her.

"Highest One, have mercy on the Gotkurgans," he said under his breath.

CHAPTER TWENTY-SEVEN

It took Bahomet some time to clamber down the cliff-side. There was still dust rising from the huge avalanche he had caused. The side of his face was seared—a very close call from Parandaman's mantirakolai. He had managed to get off a blast before a mountain of boulders collapsed on top of him, the Kiritam Ilavaracar Danputmanan, and several dozen soldiers of the Bilurian army.

The remaining soldiers of the rear guard stood in stunned silence at the far end of the rubble field. Bahomet climbed to the top of the highest boulder. Behind him stood Dran and Fayan with a troop of Karuppsertais clad in black.

"I am Valikatti Karpukkai, great-grandson of the Myanpur Dringmanan Saran. Behind me is Grand Vizier Brandeeshpuran Fayan. We now rule Biluria. If any of you wish to object, step forward now," said Bahomet in a loud voice.

The soldiers stared in wonder at the Zutherian speaking fluent Bilurian. They looked around at one another, then at the remaining surviving commander, Dormandesh Kiran. Kiran returned Bahomet's gaze. He drew his sword and knelt to one knee. He bowed his head and held the sword horizontally with both hands.

"Commander Dormandesh Kiran is at your service, Valikatti Karpukkai—I and all my soldiers. We are yours to command," said Kiran.

All of the other soldiers followed his lead and dropped to one knee.

"You have chosen wisely, Commander Kiran. You are now General Kiran. Send a detachment from your unit to Trangolangopan. The grand vizier and I will need suitable transportation to Tricanmallokan. Bring two of your most trusted officers here. We have much to talk about," said Bahomet.

Then he turned to Dran and Fayan.

"Let's go back to the Karuppsertai Poyum. Your plan has worked very well, Dran. Fayan, when Kiran joins us, you will tell me all that I need to know to take the palace at Tricanmallokan and ensure the other leaders of the army follow Kiran's example," said Bahomet.

The procession to the myanpur's palace at Tricanmallokan, the aranmanai, grew in length the closer they got to the city, swelled by curious onlookers. Bahomet's carriage, borrowed from one of the leading merchants in Trangolangopan, held him, Grand Vizier Fayan, and Darabindoo. A detachment of black-clad Karuppsertais followed, a chilling reminder to any onlooker that a "house-cleaning" was imminent. The newly minted General Kiran led a large detachment of Bilurian soldiers.

When the procession arrived at the city gates, they were closed. Kiran spurred his horse to the front of the procession.

"Soldiers! Open the gates for Valikatti Karpukkai!" ordered Kiran.

"Our orders are to keep the gates shut. Governor Besh has ordered it," said the guard.

"Besh governs the province of Tricanmallokan. He is loyal to Danputmanan. He will not open the gates to you," said Fayan to Bahomet.

A face appeared on the parapet next to the gate.

"It's Besh," said Fayan.

Bahomet nodded towards the Karuppsertai commander, then at Besh. With lightning speed, two archers unleashed their arrows. One pierced Besh's neck, the other his heart. He fell forward over the parapet to the ground below, next to Kiran's horse, which reared in fright.

When he had regained control, Kiran said to the guard, "It appears Governor Besh no longer rules here. Open the gate."

The guard looked at Besh's body, then up at Kiran.

"Open the gates, open the gates!" he shouted at the guards inside.

Bahomet rolled through the city streets towards the myanpur's aranmanai. The side streets were crowded with people trying to get a glimpse of their new ruler. One of them was Zutherian Ambassador Erenbil. He watched as the black-gloved Bahomet wearing the raiment of a valikatti, accompanied by Grand Vizier Fayan and a substantial detachment of Bilurian soldiers headed for the aranmanai gates. He groaned. King Baragin was not going to like the pigeon he was about to send.

CHAPTER TWENTY-EIGHT

$\textbf{P}$harigon looked over at Joya.

"You handle your horse well," he commented.

"Hmph," was her only response.

"I'm not sure I should let you keep that dagger your father gave you. Technically, you're still a prisoner until you reach the border," he said, nodding at the sheath in her boot top.

"As long as you and soldiers keep your hands off me, none of you have anything to worry about," snipped Joya.

Pharigon looked over at her and smiled.

"What are you smiling at?" demanded Joya.

"You think you're tough. You have no idea what you're getting into. Berendell told me a bit about those Khokhguis. You think it's going to be easy spending five years living in a tent, summer and winter. They are real soldiers and I know what it takes to be a soldier. You don't even speak the language. I think you'll be begging your brother-in-law for a pardon after the first month," said Pharigon.

"Leave me alone, you squidhead!" shouted Joya, using one the epithets thrown about the Silver Dolphin. She wheeled her horse around and joined the end of the column.

Pharigon turned in his saddle, smiling. He gave a nod to the sergeant of the rear guard letting him know it was alright for Joya to ride there.

It took the trooper column several days to reach Brobabil. On the outskirts of town, the column was met by a detachment of dwarvish soldiers. True to his word to Zerribil, the Dashgran of the Andragon Dwarves, Baragin had authorized the formation of four dwarvish regiments as part of the Zutherian army, led by their own general. Zerribil had appointed Grodminan, the Dordran of the Miners' Guild, as the first general. They actually handled all the security matters in Brobabil, Tribadon, the various mines, and the other smaller dwarvish communities in the Andragon Mountains.

Joya was fascinated by the dwarves. They were short, of course, with massive arms and shoulders, and beards down to their belts. They carried either nail-studded maces with huge heads, crossbows, or large battle-axes. The dwarf captain met Pharigon in the middle of the road.

"Captain Gernzedden here. You must be Pharigon. General Grodminan told me you would be bringing the lassie through," said the dwarf.

Pharigon dismounted.

"It's been a long ride so far. And that 'lassie' is meaner than a Zutherian mastiff. I understand you'll be providing an escort through Tribadon onto the Gemmerhorn Trail to the border at Dysteria," said Pharigon.

"Aye, those are my orders. You'll be sending some of your escort back?" asked Gernzedden.

"Yes. Eight will return. I'm only authorized to bring four with me into Mythrycia. The Sasag Darga has promised their own escort from the border to Gragnarak," replied Pharigon.

"Hanh," grunted Gernzedden. "Banishment, eh? Heard she knifed a drunken lout pawing her. Wouldn't mind putting a paw on her myself," he said with a leer.

Pharigon bristled.

"No need for that kind of talk, Captain. Don't forget she is the queen's sister. She'd be sure to cut that paw off with that Bilurian dagger in her boot," warned Pharigon.

"Hanh," grunted Gernzedden again, running his eyes over Joya. Then he turned to speak with his troop.

Pharigon and Joya were being hosted at the home of Linkman Ganabir, the bookseller. The rest of the trooper escort was being housed in the dwarvish barracks, which had stables for their horses. Ganabir was quite excited, talking effusively about his time with Genneset and Baragin. Joya listened intently, often interrupting with questions. Her father had told her a few stories of his adventures in Brobabil and Tribadon, but Ganabir filled in many gaps in the narrative—and he was a much better storyteller.

"Your father went head-to-head in mortal combat with two Bilurian assassins with that magic stick of his. And Baragin managed to run his sword through one of them. I wasn't there but Captain Nevelgren told me all about it over a few tankards at the Boar's Tusk Inn. He lost three fingers to one of them while he was squirming on the end of his lance. And you should have seen your father and that massive Yakat take on the Mythrycians at Amadel square. He sent that Blood Hammer stick after that horrible Bahomet and gave him a proper thrashing. It was an epic battle," said Ganabir, relishing the memory.

"I had no idea. Poppa didn't give me many details of his adventures here. I guess he thought I was too young for all that blood and gore," said Joya.

Ganabir eyed her with an appraising glance.

"So, I understand you are in for quite an adventure—with the Gotkurgans. They are a tough people, very proud. And those women warriors, the Khokhguis…"

Ganabir shook his head and clucked his tongue.

"What do you know about them?" asked Joya, a little concerned.

"Hmm, let's see. I'm sure I have a book somewhere here about the history of Mythrycia. I think there's a chapter on the war with the Gotkurgans," said Ganabir, scanning his floor-to-ceiling bookshelves.

"Ah! Here it is."

He pulled down a large leather-bound tome and blew the dust off. He flipped through the pages until he found a pen-and-ink drawing.

"Here," he said, handing the book to Joya. "Have a look."

Joya cradled the book in her lap and looked at the drawing. It was an illustration of a Khokhgui commander. She had breast-plate armor, but the right side was flattened. She was wearing a bronze helmet with a red and black horse-hair ridge down the centre. In one hand was a small-bladed battle axe, with a pyramid-shaped hammer head opposite the blade. In the right hand was a horn bow. A quiver full of arrows showed over her right shoulder. The warrior was wearing leather leggings, and a leather apron embossed with metal studs was hanging at her waist.

She had a broad flat face, with narrow eyes with an extra eyelid fold. In the illustration, the eyes stared straight out at the reader—Joya felt as though they were boring right through her.

"Who is this?" asked Joya.

Ganabir took the book back and ran his finger down the text.

"Tomira, Queen of the Gotkurgans. She won a major battle against the Mythrycians and they were independent for quite some time. But they've been under the rule of the Sasag Dargas of Mythrycia for a few hundred years now," said Ganabir.

"What does it say about the Gotkurgans?" asked Joya.

"They don't live in towns or villages. They are nomadic, living in large circular tents. They have herds of goats and sheep and move from pasture to pasture throughout the year. They are very tough, and excellent horsemen. Most of the Gotkurgan women are what you would expect. But the Khokhguis are something special. I've spoken with a few Mythrycian soldiers who told me they are absolutely ferocious in battle—tough as nails," said Ganabir.

Joya frowned.

"I can hold my own. But I wish I could speak the language," she said.

"I just may have something that could help," Ganbir said.

He replaced the history book on the shelf, then rummaged through some loose books in a box on the floor.

"Ah, here it is. This might be useful for you. It's a word dictionary—Mythrycian and Zutherian side by side. You would be well advised to learn as much as you can. Gotkurgan is similar, but the Mythrycians tell me they have a hard time understanding them. It's better than nothing, though," said Ganabir.

"Here, I have money," said Joya, pulling out the purse Baragin had given her.

"Nonsense! You are my guest. And the daughter of an old friend. It's my gift. Tell you what, though. If you ever run into a scroll of the Gotkurgan Myth of Origins, bring it back for me. They're very rare and I've never been able to get my hands on one," said Ganabir with a smile.

"Thank you, Ganabir. You've been very kind," said Joya.

She leaned over and gave him a kiss on the cheek.

Pharigon looked at her with raised eyebrows. That girl was just full of surprises.

Chapter Twenty-Nine

Bahomet was led into the private chambers of the Myanpur Geelanguran —his older cousin actually. The Myanpur was eating some grapes but was dropping quite a few of them on the floor. He didn't notice any of them.

"Who is this disturbing my lunch?" he demanded.

Grand Vizier Fayan said, "This is the Valikatti Karpukkai, Excellency. Your Valikatti Parandaman has had an unfortunate accident. Karpukkai will be his replacement."

"Tell Parandaman I want to see him! He did not have my leave to go anywhere," said the myanpur, obviously forgetting what Fayan had just told him.

"I will send for him at once, Excellency," said Fayan with a bow, exchanging glances with Bahomet.

On the way out the door, Fayan said, "He won't remember what he just asked by the time he's finished those grapes. He's no threat at all to you or anyone. But his younger brother, Gampreeshdalan, Danputmanan's uncle, is sure to be a problem."

"Send the Karuppsertais after him. I want everyone in Biluria to know the only member of the House of Saran who matters is me," said Bahomet.

After reaching the formal office of the myanpur, Bahomet surveyed the room and took his place behind the ornate desk.

"Where is your office?" he asked Fayan.

"Just through that doorway, Karpukkai. I am available whenever you call," said Fayan.

Bahomet walked over to the door and looked into Fayan's office. Turning, he said, "Bring me the commander of the palace guard. What is his name?"

"Bansundalang Boyan, Karpukkai," said Fayan.

"Bansundalang Boyan," repeated Bahomet. "Bring him at once."

While he was waiting, Bahomet opened several of the drawers of the desk. The seal of the myanpur, which validated any formal order or law, was there. Another drawer held a sheaf of blank paper with the coat of arms of Biluria embossed on the upper edge. There was a bowl of green-fleshed nuts—gallabindoos. Bahomet popped one into his mouth, and fondly remembered the flavour from his childhood. Another bowl held Mythrycian nougat. Bahomet smiled, remembering their role in his wooing of the fat Elomir. There was a knock at the door.

"Enter," said Bahomet.

Fayan entered with a tall officer in the livery of the house of Saran behind him. Two guards were following him, holding Darabindoo between them.

"Excellency. Captain Bansundalang Boyan at your service. We found this vanti-puller in the hallway. He claims he knows you," said Bansundalang.

"I've never seen him before in my life. Take him away!" ordered Bahomet.

Darabindoo's eyes widened in fright.

"Uravinam! Uravinam! It's me! Darabindoo," he said over his shoulder as the guards dragged him back to the door.

"Stop!" ordered Bahomet. "Come, uravinam. I was just having a little joke on you. Captain—this is my uravinam, Darabindoo. He has full run of the palace. Assign six of your guards to go with him to Olumadu to pick up my attam Bilanguree and Daranbindoo's wife Arashbilan. Bring them back here and assign them rooms. They are to live here with me," ordered Bahomet.

"As you wish, Excellency," said the captain.

"Now, you will show me the whole aranmanai," said Bahomet.

To Fayan, he said, "Tell the Mythrycian and Zutherian ambassadors to meet me in my office this afternoon."

"As you command, Karpukkai," said Fayan with a bow.

Bahomet nodded to Boyan, who said, "Right this way, Excellency."

Ambassador Erenbil looked uneasily at his Mythrycian counterpart Muunokhoi. They were both waiting in the antechamber of the Myanpur's office—the office now occupied by Bahomet.

Grand Vizier Fayan opened the door and bade them enter. Both stopped in front of Bahomet's desk. Bahomet looked at them expectantly. Muunokhoi took the hint and prostrated himself flat on the floor. Erenbil looked down at Muunokhoi, then back at Bahomet. Pursing his lips, he followed suit. Bahomet left them like that for some time.

Finally, he said, "Rise."

The two ambassadors waited for Bahomet to speak. He said nothing.

"May I congrat…" began Muunokhoi.

Bahomet stopped him with a raised hand, fixing his gaze on Erenbil.

"Ambassador Erenbil. I believe I met you at Wreatherin a few years back," said Bahomet.

"Yes, Bah…Excellency," said Erenbil correcting himself.

"I've been enjoying the hospitality of your King Baragin at Dabranen Island these past few years. And now I am here," he said with a wave of his hand, clearly enjoying himself.

Erenbil gritted his teeth. The man had lost none of his unpleasantness.

"I recently learned that I am actually a member of the House of Saran. My great-grandfather was the Myanpur Dringmanan Saran. Apparently the kiritam ilavaracar was rather unhappy to find such a close relative resurfacing when he was just a heartbeat away from being myanpur himself. He took it upon himself to bring the Valikatti Parandaman and a rather large contingent of soldiers to Trangolangopan to eliminate me. As you can see, he failed. Please tell your masters in Wreatherin and Gragnarak that Valikatti Karpukkai is now the kiritam ilavaracar in Tricanmallokan."

And he waved them out of the room.

CHAPTER THIRTY

"**H**im? The new kiritam ilavaracar? How could this happen?" raged Baragin.

Chancellor Berenfrom and Berendell were in his office, digesting the latest pigeon from Ambassador Erenbil in Tricanmallokan. There was a knock at door and Laguntzailea Damagal was ushered into the room. He nodded to the others.

"It seems that our nemesis has acquired a mantirakolai and has gone through the binding ceremony with it at Trangolangopan. And he has used it to eliminate the most senior valikatti in Biluria. Parandaman, was it?" asked Baragin.

"Yes. He would have been the equivalent of Zaharbat Astaran. It is quite astounding, actually. Apparently, he crushed him under an avalanche of stone in the narrow way leading to the lair of the assassins' guild," said Damagal.

"And not only Parandaman but the crown prince as well. Now he sits in the palace at Tricanmallokan thumbing his nose at all of us. Damnation!" shouted Baragin.

The three waited as it was clear Baragin wanted to speak more.

More quietly he said, "I haven't told any of you this before. Amathea had another dream, well before any of this happened. She dreamed of Bahomet standing on a pile of rubble, smiling. He was wearing two crowns. The myanpur's crown. And mine."

Berendell's eyes widened. Berenfromm frowned deeply.

"He doesn't have either. But we have learned that Myanpur Geelanguran is incapable of ruling—no memory for anything. Bahomet could eliminate him at any time. The crown of Biluria is his for the taking," said Berenfromm.

"Well, mine isn't!" shouted Baragin, sending papers flying as he stood suddenly and slammed his fist on the desk.

The three waited for Baragin's rage to subside.

"He's one man, one valikatti. To be sure, he does have a mantirakolai and that is nothing to sneeze at. But it is no match for the Staff of Elbron or the combined power of the Council of Five. Calm yourself, Baragin. I will consult with Astaran, and we will come up with a plan of defense should he be unwise enough to try anything. The power of Elbron is superior to anything that a valikatti of Zazzamin could conjure up," said Damagal reassuringly.

"Our army is smaller but better trained. And our navy is bigger than theirs, too. Not only that, Biluria is our biggest trading partner. They need us and we need them. Bahomet will not commit economic suicide by doing something foolish. Like Damagal said, the power of Elbron protects us all," added Berenfromm.

Baragin looked from one to the other.

"Your words should make me feel better. But they don't. Just a few weeks ago, that snake was a one-armed, black-handed prisoner on an inaccessible island. Now he is one step away from being the Myanpur of Biluria, and a full-fledged valikatti to boot. We cannot underestimate how vile and conniving he is. Did he not just bankrupt his cousin Bahnuran with his brazen theft? You think he will stop once he is the myanpur? He wants the crown of Zuth. He wants it all!" shouted Baragin getting worked up again.

Berenfromm looked over at Berendell, a silent plea to find some way to distract his good friend Baragin.

"Well, I think I need a drink. Something strong. Join me, Baragin?" said Berendell.

"Great Zuth, yes," said Baragin.

Then, looking at Berenfromm, he said, "Double Ambassador Erenbil's budget for spies and informants. I want to know every move Bahomet makes. And keep the border guards and port officers at Iblingport on high alert. Let me know immediately whenever Erenbil sends a pigeon. Tell General Trillabon I want training exercises near the Bilurian border. Damnation!" shouted Baragin.

Damagal and Berenfromm left the room while Berendell poured them both a tall glass of Bradden liquor. He held up the glass to the light admiring the amber colour. He handed Baragin a glass and took a sip himself.

"You're letting him get under your skin, my friend," said Berendell.

"Don't you see, Berendell? Amathea has never been wrong about her dreams. Never. Now half of her dream has already come true," said Baragin, taking a long sip of liquor, wincing as it burned on the way down.

"I have a special mission for you. I want you to take the crown of Zuth to Zerribil, the Dashgran of the Andragon Dwarves. Tell him to keep it in a safe place. Somewhere where Bahomet will never find it," said Baragin.

"Seriously? The Crown of Zuth? Are you sure, Baragin?" asked Berendell.

"Yes. This is one dream of Amathea's that will never come true. When you get to Brobabil, commission Grand Master Graznibur to make a duplicate crown, under the greatest secrecy. He is to put his own maker's mark on it, though. Take only Zerribil and Graznibur into your confidence," said Baragin firmly.

Berendell, paused, looking at Baragin intently. Finally, he said, "Well, each day has enough worries on its own. Let's take the horses out for a ride to clear our heads."

Berendell emptied his glass and placed it on the side table. Baragin tossed down the remainder of his glass and coughed loudly.

"Good idea. Let's have another glass first, though," said Baragin, with a slight smile.

CHAPTER THIRTY-ONE

Joya awoke from an uncomfortable sleep in the small inn at Dysteria. The bed was lumpy and the room smelled musty. She had flea bites on her shins and let out a bellow of exasperation as she scratched.

She looked out the second-floor window and gazed at the sea of wind-blown grass, the vast steppe-lands of Mythrycia stretching to the east under the rising sun. It was so different from the forests, meadows and the white-capped waves of the Western Sea at Blessingport. Preneport now, she remembered.

Joya looked down into the courtyard of the inn. Captain Gernzedden and the troop of dwarvish soldiers who had delivered them to Dysteria were readying their ponies for the return trip down the Gemmerhorn Trail to Tribadon. Captain Pharigon was up already and speaking with his four troopers. They were going to Gragnarak to replace four embassy guards whose term of service there was at an end.

The new Ambassador Zythramin was also in Dysteria, on his way to Wreatherin for his new assignment. Pharigon knew of his vile reputation and stiffened as Zythramin walked up to him.

"Aren't you going to introduce me to the king's sister-in-law? I hear she's quite a beauty," he said with an oily smile in his accented Zutherian.

"Not up yet, I believe," responded Pharigon, wincing at his tastelessness.

He would be disastrous as an ambassador.

Changing the subject, Pharigon said, "I understand you have a letter of safe passage from Sasag Darga Batzorig for me."

"Yes," said Zythramin, pulling a small scroll tied with a red ribbon out of his side pouch.

"You will be met at the border by Captain Onghul and a troop of lancers. He has been assigned with escorting the girl to Gragnarak. After a few days there, Onghul will take her south to the Gotkurgans. The sasag darga has received the personal guarantee of the Gotkurgan aklach, Saaral Chono, that the king's sister-in-law will be well cared for. But even he can't help her if she offends the Khokhgui mongomaa, Oyunchumai. Mongomaa means "Silver Mother" in your language. Oyunchumai runs the Khokhgui the way she wants to," said Zythramin.

Just then, Joya walked up to the pair, her pack of belongings slung over her shoulder.

"Joya, may I present Zythramin, the new Mythrycian ambassador to Zutheria," said Pharigon.

"Ooglooni mendi," said Joya, using the Mythrycian greeting for good morning.

She had been studying the Zutherian-Mythrycian word book Ganabir had given her diligently for the past several days.

"Did I say that right?" she asked.

Zythramin laughed out loud, clearly pleased.

"Oglooni mendi," he corrected. "You speak some Mythrycian?" he asked, smiling broadly.

"No. Only a few words. I have a word book and I've been studying. How do I address the sasag darga?" asked Joya.

"An excellent question. Clearly, you've been taught good manners by your parents," said Zythramin.

"I don't think they would agree with you. Or King Baragin, either," said Joya.

Zythramin laughed again. A spunky girl, and so pretty.

"You may say, 'Mendchigli, Tani Erkhamdi'. It means, 'Greetings, Your Highness'. He will be pleased to hear you say it," said Zythramin, still chuckling.

"Mendchigli, Tani Erkhamdi," repeated Joya, mimicking his accent.

Zythramin clapped his hands together.

"Excellent! What a charming young lady! You must have had a very enjoyable trip here, escorting this treasure," said Zythramin to Pharigon.

"You have no idea," said Pharigon, with a sidelong glance at Joya.

She put her chin up and smiled.

It was less than an hour's ride to the border. Pharigon stood up in his stirrups to catch a glimpse of the gate marking the frontier between Zutheria and Mythrycia. The gate was atop a steep gully and was flanked by barricades extending to two impassible rock outcroppings. It could be readily defended against attackers if necessary. As they neared the border gate, Pharigon could see a troop of Mythrycian calvary troopers on the far bank, white and black pennants flying from the tips of their lances. Another smaller group looked like archers, as they carried no lances but had horn bows on their backs.

"Looks like they're ready for us," said Pharigon.

They stopped at the border as Pharigon exchanged greetings with the border guards. One of them waved the blue and white Zutherian flag back and forth in the direction of the Mythrycians on the other side of the gully. Three horses broke away from the rest of the troop and trotted down the roadway to the bottom of the gully and back up the other side.

"It's time to say farewell to Zutheria, Joya," said Pharigon.

Joya felt her heart leap into her throat as she looked back towards the forested hills to the east of Amadel.

She let out a deep sigh, then said, "Let's go."

The border guard opened the gate, and the three Mythrycian riders cantered through. The one in the lead was obviously Captain Onghul. All three riders were wearing the distinctive sheepskin caps of the Mythrycian cavalry. Onghul had the captain's three-barred gold epaulets on the shoulders of his uniform and a richly decorated saber scabbard.

Onghul reined in his horse opposite Pharigon and looked him coldly up and down. Pharigon returned the look impassively.

"Onghul," said the Mythrycian captain tersely.

"Pharigon. This is Joya, sister of the queen of Zutheria," said Pharigon.

Joya pulled up her horse facing Onghul.

"Mendchigli, Captain Onghul," she said, using the greeting she had just learned from Zythramin.

Onghul raised his eyebrows, but otherwise didn't respond.

"We ride. Many hours to our camp tonight," he said in broken Zutherian to Pharigon, ignoring Joya.

Then he wheeled his horse around and pointed it down into the gully.

Pharigon and Joya exchanged glances. Pharigon turned in his saddle, shouting at the four troopers.

"Mount up, men."

"Well, this should be fun," he said to Joya.

She bit her lip and didn't respond.

Chapter Thirty-Two

Boroneeloman Dran sipped from the edge of his goblet, savoring the potent arickmatu. Bahomet sat opposite him. A trio of musicians were playing, while four shapely dancers in semi-transparent veils danced sensuously before them.

The dance came to an end and the dancers all bowed, hands together.

"The tall one on the end. Make sure she is waiting in my bedroom tonight," said Bahomet to a chamberlain standing nearby.

"Yes, Karpukkai," he said with a bow.

Bahomet had almost forgotten the pleasures of the bedroom. It had been close to seven long years of his own company.

"Would you like one of the dancers to keep you company tonight?" asked Bahomet of Dran.

"A kind offer, but no. I have much pressing business to attend to. Your uravinam, the myanpur's brother Gampreeshdalan, is proving more elusive than we expected. But we will find him. We have already relieved two of the more troublesome generals of their attachment to life. One would have hoped they would see which way the wind was blowing. All of the other ones have pledged their allegiance," said Dran.

He paused, taking another sip of arickmatu.

"There is one other matter I should apprise you of," said Dran.

"What is that?" asked Bahomet.

"As you know, I place a very high value on information. It is essential for what we do at the Karuppsertai Poyum. One of my Karuppsertais has an older brother, a stonemason. He is an excellent stone carver. He has been working at the quarry in Elberon for many years now. In fact, he was there when you were just an apprentice," said Dran.

"Elberon? I know it well—at least Elberon Castle. The quarry and the village are nearby," said Bahomet.

"The old duke, your father-in-law, has a villa not far from the quarry. Your wife Elomir is there as well," said Dran.

"True. I've never been there, though. And I haven't even thought of that silly giggler for years. Why do you bring this up?" asked Bahomet.

"The duke wanted a new fountain made for his garden. My Karuppsertai's brother was asked to do the carving. Obviously, he had to go in person to survey the site to make sure everything was suitable for what the duke had in mind. When he was visiting the site, he was shown to the work area by someone you might remember—Filden?"

"Filden? Filden is at Elberon?"

"Yes. He followed the duke there after Baragin became king and the duke retired to his villa," said Dran.

"While that is interesting, it's been a very long time since he was my best agent in Zutheria. Why is this important?" asked Bahomet.

"While chatting with my Karuppsertai's brother, Filden mentioned you, and wondered if you knew about your son," said Dran.

Bahomet had a grape halfway to his mouth. He stopped, mouth open, and stared at Dran.

"My son? He said, 'my son'?" asked Bahomet, dumbfounded.

"Apparently six summers old. Named Robduran," said Dran, with a smile, enjoying Bahomet's amazement. Bahomet sat back against the cushions on the settee, stunned. *A son. His son. But a son with the blood of Zuth in him. A son with the blood of the House of Saran in him as well. A scion of two countries!* Bahomet's mind raced. He couldn't leave his only son at Elberon to be raised by that obese nitwit. He should be in Tricanmallokan, with his father. Somewhere where his education and training for greatness, for becoming the ruler of two countries could be managed and guided.

In Zutheria he would be a nothing. Baragin already had a son and heir, with another on the way. There would be no place in Zutheria for the son of Bahomet.

"No one must know this. No one. If Baragin suspects I have learned about Robduran he will prevent me from ever seeing him," said Bahomet.

"It is plain you would like him by your side. A myanpur must have a kiritam ilavaracar to carry on his reign," said Dran.

"But how can I bring him here? Baragin must be beside himself knowing that I now rule in Tricanmallokan. I know he has strengthened the border controls and directed his armies to carry out mock battle exercises close to the border. How can I see my son?" demanded Bahomet.

Dran smiled. "Perhaps your old friend Filden could be helpful in providing information," mused Dran.

Bahomet smiled and nodded. That night, the tall dancer found Bahomet in an excellent mood.

Chapter Thirty-Three

Danaquill, the son of the former mayor of Blessingport—Preneport now—stepped onto the dock at Iblingport. He had a scowl on his face. He had spent the entire sea trip brooding.

Joya had murdered his best friend Futtsam. Then King Baragin had stripped his father of the mayorship, changed the town's name, and ruined the Futt family by giving the harbourmaster's job to Ibbingrin. His own father was devastated. He had relished the mayor's job. And his friendship with the harbourmaster had led to some very lucrative financial deals. His father rarely went out of the house now and spent a good deal of his time getting drunk.

Danaquill had been sweet on the younger of Futtsam's sisters, Ambera. But Futt had to divert a good portion of her dowry funds to surviving after he lost his post. Ambera had come to him in tears, begging him to find someone else, someone with a suitable dowry. Danaquill was devastated. All his dreams were dashed. All that he had was gone now.

Joya was out of reach in Mythrycia. But her father wasn't. He would teach her the meaning of losing someone close. Genneset had to die. And after he was finished with Genneset—Baragin.

Danaquill shouldered his pack and started walking. He had no money for a barge berth. He'd heard a rumor that the king had bought another pub for the murderer's father in Braddenlocks. Danaquill turned his face to the east and started trudging.

———••◦❘◦••———

Genneset polished another glass and put it on the shelf. It was good to be back running a pub again. He and Germilda had returned to Braddenlocks after seeing Joya off. Germilda had swept into the Prenadon Inn like a whirlwind, taking faded old paintings off the wall, clucking her tongue over the books and terrorizing head bartender Bobbingran with multiple commands and orders.

Genneset let her do what she did best. She'd always been a very hardworking woman and was happiest with plenty to do. Genneset spent much of his time behind the bar, chatting up the regulars and getting to know the feel of his new town. The pub had spacious living quarters on the second floor directly above the rear storerooms, and Germilda was busy with remodeling ideas.

Blood Hammer leaned against the corner just behind the bar. Genneset had not had occasion to use it yet. Umbraset had decided to join them in Braddenlocks, and along with Bobbingran, took care of any bouncing of rowdy drunks and brawlers that was necessary. Some of those polemen from the barges were a tough lot, but Umbraset had developed a massive physique and rarely had difficulty dealing with troublemakers.

It was a typical night, busy, but not overly crowded. Genneset didn't pay attention to a single man, his face partially covered with a hood, who parked himself at a dark corner table. Bobbingran brought him a tankard of ale.

Danaquill sipped his ale with one hand. With the other he fingered the long boar-hunting dagger on his hip. When the time was right, he would slip that knife into Genneset's ribs. His only regret was that Joya wouldn't be here to see it.

Two figures appeared in the doorway. As the regulars glanced to see who it might be, a hush fell over the pub.

"It's the king. It's King Baragin," said a low voice.

Cranadan, the Linkman of Braddenlocks and a Prenadon Inn regular, was the first to react.

"Take a knee, gentlemen. Show respect for the king!" he shouted.

Everyone knelt as Baragin and Berendell walked up to the bar.

Baragin turned and said in loud voice, "As you were, goodfellows of Braddenlocks. The next round's on me."

The pub erupted into a cheer, and soon Bobbingran and Umbraset were pulling taps as fast as they could.

"What are you doing here?" asked Genneset.

He had been in the back room talking with Germilda when Baragin entered.

"Well, I just wanted to see what you two have done with place. Besides, General Trillabon is conducting exercises close by and I wanted to personally inspect the troops," said Baragin.

Baragin had had an argument with Amathea. She'd had a dream about a Blessingport man whose face she couldn't see, threatening and screaming 'I hate you!'. She begged him not to go. He had tried to calm her down by saying he still had a kingdom to run and that he wanted to check on her parents. She had begged him to be extra careful.

Umbraset brought the three of them some ales and they sat at a nearby table to talk.

In the corner, Danaquill could not believe his luck. The author of all his misfortunes, King Baragin himself was here! His back was towards Danaquill.

Screwing up his courage, he pulled out his dagger and launched himself across the room, shouting, "You ruined my life!"

Berendell glanced up and saw the enraged Danaquill hurtling towards the king, knife raised to strike. He sprang to his feet and made a flying tackle at Danaquill's waist.

Baragin stood up in shock and stumbled against Genneset, falling on top of him. Danaquill twisted himself out of Berendell's grasp and made another attempt to stab the king. The point pressed against Baragin's shirt but did not penetrate—Damagal's protection amulet did its job.

Genneset, lying under Baragin, pointed his free arm at Danaquill and shouted, "*Odol Mailua Hegen!*"

Blood Hammer flew across the bar and delivered a huge whack to Danaquill's upraised knife arm as he was trying his best to overcome the protective force of the amulet. The dagger flew out of his grasp and Blood Hammer proceeded to deliver a series of stunning blows to Danquill's head and back.

Genneset finally squirmed out from underneath Baragin and seeing that Danaquill was down and unarmed, yelled, "*Odol Mailua Hegen!*" Blood Hammer flew back to his grasp.

Cranadan and Umbraset were holding Danaquill down. Two troopers standing guard outside the doorway had rushed in, weapons at the ready.

Berendell, breathing heavily, asked, "Who is this madman?"

Genneset walked over.

"It's Danaquill, son of the former mayor of Preneport," said Genneset, breathing heavily.

"It's Blessingport! Blessingport!" shouted Danaquill.

Baragin stood over Danaquill and looked into his bloodied face.

"Why, boy? Why?" asked Baragin.

"You ruined my life! You ruined my father's life! I can't even marry Futt's daughter because he had to use her dowry to live on after you took his job. I hate you!" he screamed.

Cranadan balled up his fist and smashed Danaquill in the face, knocking him out cold.

"Shut yer gob, ya murderin' bastard!" he yelled.

Baragin looked down at the unconscious Danaquill and sighed. "Berendell. Get these troopers to take him down to the jail in Iblingport. And thanks for that tackle," said Baragin, putting a hand on his shoulder.

Berendell just nodded.

Baragin looked over at Genneset. "Thank you."

Genneset shrugged. "It was Blood Hammer."

Baragin looked at the stick in Genneset's hand.

"I have a feeling this isn't going to be the last time, either."

CHAPTER THIRTY-FOUR

The Mythrycian escort of horse cavalry paused at the small village of Yaruu for the evening, halfway to the capital of Gragnarak. There was about an hour of daylight left. Captain Onghul, after showing Joya where she would sleep for the night, ignored her. Pharigon was speaking with two of his troopers. Joya took the Zutherian-Mythrycian word book out of her side pouch. She looked up and saw two of the archers standing nearby.

She looked in her book for the word archery, but it wasn't listed. She looked up 'bow' but wasn't certain if it was the weapon or bending at the waist. 'Hymcym,' it said.

She walked over to the two archers, who stopped talking and stared at her.

"Hymcym?" she asked, pointing to their bows.

The archers looked at one another and burst out laughing.

"Ti-imhee, ti-imhee," one said.

Joya knew that meant 'yes'.

The one speaking took his bow off his shoulder.

"Hym," he said.

Then he pulled an arrow from his quiver and handed it to Joya.

"Cym," he said.

"Cym," repeated Joya, smiling.

She looked down the arrow appraising its straightness and felt the armor-piercing point with her finger. The fletching was very well done, with alternating black and white feathers. All of the arrows in the quiver had the same fletching so Joya assumed that was the distinguishing standard for Mythrycian army arrows.

Joya pointed at the bow, indicating she wanted to hold it. The archer looked at his mate and laughed, then handed her the horn bow.

Joya looked at it closely. It was different from any bow she had ever used before, much shorter than the Zutherian ones. The wooden core had a layer of horn on the inside facing the archer, secured by tightly wound sinew. It was lighter than the bows she was used to. She tugged on the bowstring—the resistance was very strong.

The archer grinned and motioned that she should fit the arrow to the string. He pointed over to a straw-stuffed canvas target affixed to the side of the horse stables. Obviously, it was a place for the archers to practice during their overnight stays.

Joya walked over to the firing line, notched her arrow, and pulled the bowstring back. She sighted down the arrow towards the target, exhaled through her mouth, and released the string.

The arrow landed with a thunk on the outside left edge of the target. Joya frowned. Not her best shot, but it was an unfamiliar bow.

She looked over at the archer, who was smiling and nodding. She motioned for two more arrows, saying 'cym' and holding up two fingers. The archer handed her two arrows with a grin.

Joya jammed the extra arrow into the turf and notched the second arrow. She sighted the target again and let it fly. The arrow landed to the left side again, but closer to the centre.

"Sahn! Sahn!" said the archer, smiling and nodding.

Joya wracked her brain. She thought that meant 'good' but wasn't positive.

She notched the third arrow. She was getting used to the drawstring resistance now. She drew back the string, sighted the point on the centre of the target and let loose. The arrow landed just a finger's width off the centre of the target.

"Mash sahn! Mash sahn!" said the archer, grinning from ear to ear. Joya assumed that probably meant 'very good'. She smiled back at him. Just then Captain Onghul walked up with a scowl on his face. He let loose a torrent of harsh words at the archer. He quickly retrieved his bow from Joya, head hanging like a beaten dog, and scurried off to where the rest of the archers were resting.

"No woman touch weapon," he said with a disgusted look on his face.

Joya put her hand on her Bilurian dagger, now on her hip, and glared back at him.

The Mythrycian captain glanced at the hand on her dagger and gave her a derisive sneer. He spun on his heel and walked away.

Pharigon walked up to where she was standing.

"Making new friends, I see," he commented.

"I'll be happy to see the last of that bastard," said Joya through her teeth.

"Well, you're stuck with him until he hands you off to the Gotkurgans. Try not to annoy him, please, Joya," said Pharigon.

"Hmph!" grunted Joya, as she stomped off to her quarters for the night.

CHAPTER THIRTY-FIVE

Bahomet was sitting behind his desk in his formal reception office, Grand Vizier Fayan at his shoulder. Zutherian Ambassador Erenbil was on his knees, hands flat on the floor above his head, prostrate before them.

How long was he going to keep me like this, he wondered, his knees aching.

Finally, Bahomet gave a nod to Fayan who said, "You may rise, Ambassador Erenbil."

Erenbil got to his feet slowly, stumbling slightly as his left knee had seized up from his lengthy wait.

Bahomet eyed him closely, fingers pressed together.

"I presume you have informed your king and Chancellor Berenfromm of the situation here in Biluria," began Bahomet.

"Yes, Excellency," said Erenbil tersely.

"There are two issues I wish for you to inform them of. There are fourteen of my countrymen working at the marble quarry in Elberon. We have heard they are not being treated well," said Bahomet.

Erenbil raised his eyebrows in surprise.

"Not being treated well, Excellency? That surprises me greatly. The quarry masters respect the skills of the Bilurian stonecutters highly. I can't imagine what kind of mistreatment could be occurring," said Erenbil.

"Nevertheless, it is my duty as ruler of Biluria to ensure the well-being of all my citizens, no matter where they may be. I would like a full report from Ambassador Gandrapreen Oban. He is the one who had received the complaint and I will be directing him to investigate the allegations. That should not be a problem for King Baragin, will it?"

Any request from Bahomet would be a problem, thought Erenbil. But he could hardly refuse. There were hundreds of Zutherians working in various trading positions in Biluria and many more general travellers. He knew Bahomet could make life very difficult for the Zutherian merchants in Biluria should he wish to. He would have to recommend that the request to inspect the Bilurian quarry workers be approved. It was also possible that it was some kind of ruse. On the surface it seemed like a reasonable diplomatic request.

"I will be sure to recommend to Chancellor Berenfromm that Ambassador Oban be granted access to the Bilurian workers at the quarry, Excellency. You said there were two issues?" asked Erenbil.

"Yes. I would like to see my wife, Elomir. I wish her to join me here in Tricanmallokan, now that my situation has...improved," said Bahomet with a wry smile.

He popped a gallabindoo nut into his mouth and chewed thoughtfully, watching Erenbil's reaction.

Erenbil gulped. He knew that was never going to happen. Elomir's brief marital relationship with Bahomet had traumatized her severely. She had only marginally recovered and was still emotionally quite fragile. The old duke would explode in rage if he even heard of this request.

"Ah, yes. I can assure you Elomir is in good health and living with her father Duke Robagrin at their villa near Elberon," said Erenbil, skirting the question.

"I am not asking about her health, ambassador," said Bahomet raising his voice. "I am asking that my wife be brought to Biluria. I will soon be the myanpur and I want a kiritam ilavaracar to inherit my legacy. I am childless now, but I want my heir to have the blood of Zuth in him. Tell your king that I want my wife transported to Biluria," demanded Bahomet.

Erenbil paused. *He doesn't know. He doesn't know he has a son.*

"I will be sure to pass on your request to the chancellor, along with the other request," said Erenbil, deferentially.

"Ambassador Oban will be in Elberon for his inspection visit. Perhaps he could drop in at the duke's villa to see for himself about my wife's 'good health'. I will have a letter for her that I wish him to deliver personally," said Bahomet.

He paused.

"Remind your king that there is another formal request from a Zutherian merchant to take over the facilities recently vacated by my unfortunate cousin Bahnuran. It is the largest trading company for your country in Biluria. I will be expecting an answer that makes a pleasing sound in my ears, Ambassador Erenbil," said Bahomet, his tone indicating the audience was at an end.

"A pigeon will be on its way before day's end, Excellency," said Erenbil, bowing deeply. And he backed out of the room.

"The king—and the duke—will never agree to bringing Elomir here, Karpukkai," said Fayan.

"I know. I wouldn't want her here anyway. But I want them to think I do. And I want them to believe I am unaware of my son. I think the trading house issue will be persuasive. The merchants of Iblingport and Wreatherin are clamoring for a replacement for Bahnuran. It's their most lucrative enterprise in this country. Oban has to get inside that villa. They will obviously hide any evidence that my son is there, but Filden can find a way to get him the information we need. We will insist that Oban present that letter from me to her in person. But once we have Oban's information, we'll send the Karuppsertais to retrieve my son," said Bahomet.

Bahomet chuckled.

Oh, to be a fly on the wall when they discover Robduran's empty bedroom.

Chapter Thirty-Six

"**H**e wants what?!" shouted Duke Robagrin, his faced mottled with rage.

Berenfromm, Berendell and Baragin were all in the king's office with the duke. Berenfromm had just informed him of Bahomet's request to have Elomir transported to Tricanmallokan.

"Over my dead body!" he raged. "She's barely recovered from what he put her through. Go to Biluria? That. Will. Never. Happen."

He glared at Baragin.

Baragin had asked the old duke to come to Wreatherin as he had an important matter to discuss with him. It was the kind of matter that Elomir need not be present for, at least not at this stage.

The pigeon from Ambassador Erenbil in Tricanmallokan was certainly troublesome from many perspectives. It was a formal request from the *de facto* leader of a sovereign country to have his legally wedded wife join him. From a diplomatic point of view, it was not an unreasonable demand, not to mention the common-sense argument for honouring a legal marriage. The inspection request for the quarry workers was likely a ruse, but to what end? Bahomet was up to something.

"Does he know about Robduran?" asked Robagrin, suddenly anxious.

"Apparently not. He told Erenbil the reason he wanted Elomir in Tricanmallokan was so that he could produce an heir. He expects to be myanpur soon and wants a kiritam ilavaracar—one with the blood of Zuth. Clearly, he's taking the long view and hopes to find a way to create an empire with someone who has both the blood of the House of Saran and the blood of Zuth," said Berenfromm.

"What are our options?" asked Baragin.

"The marriage needs to be dissolved," interrupted Robagrin.

"What's the law on that matter, Berenfromm?" asked Baragin.

"Well, one party must request it formally. The elbronath who performed the ceremony must consent. In this case, it was the Evenshorn Laguntzailea Zolenfan who performed the ceremony. Permissible grounds for dissolution are abandonment of seven years or more, incarceration for criminal acts, proven cruel treatment, or evidence of extramarital relations with other persons," said Berenfromm.

"Well, there you go," said Robagrin with a look of satisfaction. "That snake has done all of those things."

"But even if the marriage is dissolved, both parties have the right to a say in the care and upbringing of any children. Under the law," added Berenfromm, almost apologetically.

"He is not getting hold of my grandson. He is not to know he even exists," said Robagrin fiercely.

"How is a dissolution actually handled, Berenfromm?" asked Baragin.

"The petitioning party must come to Wreatherin, to the High Court. It's the only court in the land which can hear marriage dissolution cases. The judge will hear the arguments and render a decision. If he rules that the dissolution request meets the legal standard, the elbronath, Zolenfan in this case, signs the dissolution document, and the marriage is dissolved," said Berenfromm.

"Doesn't Bahomet have to be in the court, too?" asked Baragin.

"He certainly has the right. But he would not be the petitioner. He can appoint a representative to make his arguments on his behalf. Besides, we all know he's never going to set foot in Zutheria again," said Berenfromm with a smile.

"What about Ambassador Oban's request to visit the quarry and deliver Bahomet's letter to Elomir," asked Berendell.

"I don't want any Bilurian near my house. He would see that there is a child there," said Robagrin.

Baragin looked at Berenfromm.

"What about the trading house issue? I understand there is another businessman anxious to take over the bankrupt Bahnuran's operation."

"Yes. Donbidden of Iblingport. Bahomet is blocking the takeover until he hears our answer on these matters. Sire, we cannot afford to have that trading operation idle—it is vital to the treasury and hundreds of Zutherian merchants," said Berenfromm.

All eyes turned to Baragin, waiting for him to make a decision. He frowned. It was extremely complicated. Bahomet was sure to have a hidden agenda in all of this. But he also had to consider the economic wellbeing of the country—so many livelihoods depended on Zutherian goods being sold in Biluria.

"Duke Robagrin, I'm sure you'll want to engage a good avocatim right away for the dissolution request. Let's get that process in motion. I'm sorry, but I have to agree to Oban's request to visit the quarry workers and deliver Bahomet's letter. Elomir will have to inform him directly of her intention to seek dissolution of the marriage, otherwise Bahomet will claim we are fabricating things. The trade relationship of our country is an also a very important consideration—as you well know when you governed Bradden. The meeting doesn't have to be at your villa, though," said Baragin.

A pained looked came over Robagrin's face.

"Elomir won't leave the house. She breaks down in a panic, goes completely to pieces if I even suggest it. She feels safe in the house and in the garden, but that's it. I don't even know how I'm going to get her to the High Court here," said Robagrin.

The group sat in silence.

"What if you take Robduran to Elberon Castle for the day of Oban's visit, and remove all evidence that a child lives there, just for that day. Oban drops off his letter, Elomir tells him the marriage is over, he leaves, Robduran returns, and you put everything back the way it was," suggested Berendell.

Everyone looked at Robagrin. It was evident he was wavering.

"I guess that might work," he said reluctantly.

"Good. Thanks, everyone. Berenfromm, get a pigeon to Zolenfan apprising him of this matter. And tell Erenbil I want daily pigeons from him. That black-hearted monster is up to something, and I want him to redouble his efforts to find out what it is," said Baragin in closing.

Chapter Thirty-Seven

Joya stood up in her stirrups. She could see the reddish-brown walls of Gragnarak in the distance. The escort troop, with a blonde Zutherian girl and five Zutherian cavalry soldiers, attracted a lot of attention from those they encountered on the road. Pharigon cantered up beside Joya and pulled his horse to a matching gait.

"We'll go to the Zutherian Embassy for the night. Ambassador Danstorin will be your host. Tomorrow afternoon, there will be an audience with Batzorig, the sasag darga. A representative from the Gotkurgans will be in attendance but I don't know who. Then there will be some sort of dinner reception—you are the king's sister-in-law after all, even if you are technically an exile. The next day, Onghul will take you to Gotkurga—it's two days' ride southeast," related Pharigon.

"You're coming, too? To Gotkurga, I mean?" asked Joya, a little anxiously.

Pharigon glanced over at her and smiled. Despite all her bluster she was still a young girl.

"My instructions were to escort you to Gragnarak. I'm the new military attache and am at the command of the ambassador. I'm not certain what my next assignment will be," said Pharigon, rather enjoying her discomfort.

He knew she did not want to be alone for two days with Onghul. Joya bit her lip but said nothing. She did not want to let Pharigon know that she wanted him to be with her, at least until she got to Gotkurga.

The group made their way through the crowded streets of the Mythrycian capital city. Joya pointed excitedly at a large, two-humped creature the size of a Zutherian black elk, but with no horns. It had a huge mound of boxes strapped to it.

"I believe they are called camels. The Mythrycians don't use them but traders from the far east have them. They can pack more than horses and apparently go days without having to drink water," said Pharigon.

Almost all the men were wearing the traditional Mythrycian sheepskin cap which came to a soft point at both ends. The women had colourful headscarves and what looked like coins dangling from chains as decorations around their waists.

There was another group of men who were wearing conical leather caps, with sheepskin earflaps. They had slightly darker skins than the Mythrycians and narrow eyes with an extra eyelid fold. They all had large broad curved sabres strapped to their sides.

"Gotkurgans," said Onghul, pointing.

He had ridden up beside Joya and Pharigon. Then he pointed at a large, gated building at the end of the street.

"Embassy," he grunted as he spurred his horse ahead to the gate.

He dismounted and waited for Joya and Pharigon to ride up. Pharigon rode up to the gatekeeping guard and handed a scroll to him. The guard opened it and scanned it briefly. He shouted a command to someone unseen behind the gate and it opened. Pharigon offered his hand to Onghul but he ignored it. He barked a command to his lancers and archers and the group of them trotted off. Pharigon shrugged.

"Nice to travel with you, too," he shouted after them.

Joya giggled, but stifled it behind her hand.

"To your quarters, men," Pharigon ordered the four replacement guards as the six of them walked their horses through the embassy gate.

Ambassador Danstorin was grey haired but cleanshaven, taller than most. He was starting to get paunchy, but otherwise his posture reflected his ex-military role. He didn't smile much, as though there was a great deal to worry about. Nevertheless, he welcomed Joya politely and had an aide show her to her quarters.

"I confess I'm not sure that your plan to serve your banishment with the Gotkurgans is a wise one. They are a wild people, nomads, living in tents year-round. They call them kezoys. And those Khokhguis are..." Danstorin paused.

"I just don't know what to make of them. I hope you and the king know what you're doing," he concluded.

"It's better than jail. I'd go completely crazy if I were locked up. I'm really going to miss my family, though," said Joya.

She paused.

"I was wondering if Captain Pharigon would be accompanying me to Gotkurga."

"That's going to be his first assignment, although the main reason is not to escort you. A Mythrycian trader by the name of Ulugan who dealt in tin goods was attacked and killed by bandits. The Gotkurgans managed to chase them off and have his possessions at their kezoy camp. The goods actually belong to your uncles' business—the trader was selling them on commission. I need to send someone to Gotkurga to arrange for their return to the embassy here. Your uncle Timbraset will advise me what to do with the goods. I've tasked Pharigon with dealing with the Gotkurgans so, yes, he will be going with you," said Danstorin.

Joya smiled and nodded.

"I've arranged for a Mythrycian dress shop owner to provide you with something to wear to your audience with the sasag darga this afternoon—and the dinner afterwards. He seems anxious to meet you," said Danstorin.

"To meet me? Why?" asked Joya.

"He probably wants to add you to his harem," said Pharigon, who had just walked up.

"What's a harem?" asked Joya.

Danstorin burst into laughter while Pharigon grinned.

CHAPTER THIRTY-EIGHT

Ambassador Oban sat in the main room of Duke Robagrin's villa. It was very spacious and had spectacular views to the coast. The villa sat below Elberon Castle on the western slope of the Prenadons. It was nestled in a secluded glen and had a large ornamental garden with a fountain. A servants' cottage sat in the far end of the gardens. Stables and other outbuildings completed the complex. The view from the window included sights of the Murranen River below and the fishing village of Murranenmouth at the outlet of the river. The Western Sea glittered like diamonds in the mid-afternoon sun. Oban could see why the duke had selected this place for his genteel retirement.

Oban had come with an escort of four personal guards from the embassy. Two of them were Dran's Karuppsertais. Gandaman Abin and Sriwalloban Ohn scrutinized the layout of the villa intently. Abin pointed to the far corner of the garden. Two huge Zutherian mastiffs were barking and pawing at a high-fenced enclosure, smelling the intruders. They were sure to be let loose at night to patrol the grounds.

Robagrin had had his servants remove all evidence that a child lived in the house. He even had a wooden playhouse removed from its block foundation and stored in a locked shed.

Ohn scanned the windows of the villa. It was a two-story structure. His sharp eyes focused on the third window of the second floor. There was something visible on the sill. The window was covered with a curtain on the inside, so someone checking the room would have missed it. It was a toy boat—just the kind a little boy would have in his bedroom. Filden had been useful indeed.

Ohn gave a nod of his head to Abin in the direction of the window. Abin smiled. He was already checking out handholds. They would have to deal with the dogs first though.

Abin walked to the edge of the driveway and peered over the side to the ravine below. The beginnings of the Murranen River chuckled and splashed through dense forest. It looked like a narrow hiking trail followed the south bank.

Abin motioned to one of the duke's personal guards that he had to relieve himself.

The guard said gruffly, "We don't want no Bilurians using our privy. Go in the bushes."

He pointed Abin in the direction of a trail leading over the bank from the roadway, then turned back to continue his conversation with his partner.

Abin clicked his tongue at Ohn and told the other two embassy guards they were going for a walk down the trail. The pathway was fairly steep at first, but then levelled out. It led to a tall waterfall, about the height of seven men. The stream splashed onto a jumble of moss-covered rocks below.

Abin stood on the viewpoint next to the torrent. It was a stunning vista. The spray from the waterfall beaded the skin of his face. He could see where the stream broadened to the Murranen River, but just below him it bubbled over rocks and boulders. The trail continued steeply past the waterfall. It looked like it was a quarter hour hike to a navigable section of the river. There were plenty of overhanging trees to hide a Bilurian canoe. Furthermore, there were no farms or houses anywhere nearby. This area was obviously part of the duke's large estate.

"We'll take him out this way," he said to Ohn.

Ohn nodded.

Oban stood as Robagrin entered the room. An older man with a ring of white hair followed him. Elomir plodded behind him, face to the ground. She didn't make eye contact when Robagrin began his introductions.

"This our avocatim, Durrenbar. My daughter, the Marquesa Elomir. Let's get this over with, Oban," said Robagrin curtly.

"Yes. So sorry to intrude on your privacy. This really is a most lovely retreat, Duke Robagrin..." began Oban.

"Just present your letter and leave," said Robagrin, interrupting.

Oban smiled diplomatically.

"Marquesa Elomir. Your husband Bahomet requests..."

"Aaaah-aaaah-aaaah-aaaah-aaaaaaaaaaah!" Elomir began wailing, pounding the sides of her head with her hands.

All three men looked stunned and Robagrin rushed to her side.

"Darling, darling! It's okay. You don't have to read the letter. You don't have to read the letter. Hush, sweetheart, hush," he said cradling her in her arms, glaring at Oban.

"I'm taking her back to her room. You can see the very mention of his name is too upsetting for her. Avocatim Durrenbar will receive your letter," said Robagrin as he walked the wailing Elomir back to her room, arm tightly around her.

"Ahem, well...I did not expect that," began Durrenbar awkwardly.

Oban didn't respond. He was looking at the retreating duke, arm tight on Elomir's shoulder. Her wails continued all the way down the hallway.

"I am authorized to tell you that the Marquesa Elomir will be seeking dissolution of the marriage, on multiple grounds. She is in no condition to respond to whatever is in that letter personally, but it matters not. Please tell your Kiritam Ilavaracar Bahomet that as far as Marquesa Elomir is concerned, the marriage is over. We will be petitioning the High Court in Wreatherin for dissolution, and we will let you know the date of the hearing. The kiritam ilavaracar is welcome to be present, obviously, or have a representative appear for him. I have already secured Laguntzailea Zolenfan's agreement to sign the dissolution document, should the judge so rule," concluded Durrenbar.

Oban looked around, not sure where to place the letter.

"I can take that," said Durrenbar, holding out his hand. "Have a nice trip back to Wreatherin. Filden will see you out."

And he turned and left Oban standing by himself in the great room.

Filden entered and bowed to Oban.

"This way sir," he said.

At the main entranceway, Filden put a hand on his arm, and whispered, "He looks just like him. Tell him that."

Oban smiled and looked around for listening ears.

"See stonecutter Agan at the Bilurian food stall in the marketplace two days from now for your reward," said Oban.

Bahomet was going to be very pleased with the pigeon news.

Chapter Thirty-Nine

Pharigon gave Joya an appraising look as she stood in the doorway of her quarters. He had come to escort her to the sasag darga's audience.

"Well, do I look like a Mythrycian?" asked Joya with a spin and a smile.

Her red Mythrycian dress swirled around her and the coin belt circling her waist tinkled slightly. She was wearing dark red Mythrycian riding boots, a gift from Ambassador Danstorin. She had the required multi-coloured head scarf around her neck. She looked good whatever she was wearing, thought Pharigon.

"You'll have to put that scarf on when you have the audience. It's expected that women wear a head scarf here," said Pharigon.

"I'll put it on when I get there. Mendchigli, Tani Erkhamdi. Mendchigli, Tani Erkhamdi," practiced Joya.

"What are you saying?"

"Greetings, Your Excellency," said Ambassador Danstorin walking up. "Where did you learn that?" asked Pharigon.

"Ambassador Zythramin taught me," said Joya.

Danstorin frowned.

"Maybe I shouldn't say this, but your brother-in-law the king paid a steep price to have you here on your Khokhgui adventure. He had to accept Zythramin as an ambassador as a condition of the deal."

"Why is that a problem? He seemed nice enough," said Joya.

"Zythramin was the head of Bahomet's Mythrycian guards years ago. He personally ordered the torture and burning alive of Dellabur, the mute chamberlain at Amadel who saved your sister and Baragin—he and the wife of the Linkman of Tribadon. He is not 'nice'," said Danstorin grimly.

Joya was stunned.

"I...I had no idea. Baragin never told me," she faltered, biting her lip.

"Not only that, we'll be delivering some substantial gold 'gifts' to the sasag darga, the aklach of the Gotkurgans, and the mongomaa of the Khokhguis to ensure your stay with them goes well. And that's just for this year," said Danstorin.

"I...I don't know what to say," said a crestfallen Joya.

"Listen to me young lady. You are going to do nothing to cause problems for your king—or for me. Do you hear me? And when you get through this, you are going to find a way to make it up to him. Do I have your word on that?" asked Danstorin sternly.

Joya paused, frowning, then looked up determinedly.

"You have my word, Ambassador Danstorin. And thank you for the boots," said Joya.

Danstorin eyed her for a moment, measuring the sincerity of her response, then glanced at Pharigon.

"Let's go. The carriage is waiting."

Sasag Darga Batzorig looked Joya up and down, then fixed his gaze on her face. Joya knew that look—the 'undressing with the eyes' look. She'd seen it often enough while working in the Silver Dolphin.

He was a short man, about Baragin's age. He had a large bulbous nose and close-set eyes. A scraggly beard decorated his chin. No one would call him handsome and in a different set of clothes he could pass for a homeless drunkard.

When Pharigon had told her what a harem was she had punched him hard on shoulder. He said, 'Zuth, that hurt!' and Joya had responded, 'Good. I hope it leaves a big bruise.'

Batzorig was flanked by two huge bodyguards who definitely were not Mythrycians. They were beardless and carried narwhal tusk lances. They looked a lot like the Yakats Joya had occasionally encountered on the wharves at Preneport.

"Are those two Yakats?" she whispered to Pharigon.

"Jalags, from the far north. Batzorig likes them for show," answered Pharigon.

"May I present Joya, Your Excellency. Sister-in-law of King Baragin of the Zutherians," said Ambassador Danstorin.

He gave Joya a nod.

She stepped forward and said, "Mendchigli, Tani Erkhamdi."

Then she bowed respectfully.

Batzorig clapped his hands and looked at his attendants with a grin.

"Such good manners to go along with great beauty. Are you sure I cannot convince you to extend your stay in Gragnarak?" he asked, smiling broadly. "I assure you that you would be well accommodated here for the duration of your exile."

When Danstorin translated, she thought, *'Accommodated'. In your harem, you mean.*

"Your Excellency is very kind. But I must respectfully decline. I am anxious to continue my journey to Gotkurga," said Joya.

Danstorin gave her a brief smile before he translated, acknowledging that she was demonstrating the best behaviour she had promised.

"A pity. Such beauty is wasted on the Gotkurgans," said Batzorig, noticeably disappointed.

He looked to the side. A woman was standing in the shadow of a column. She was tall, about Joya's height, and looked like the Jalags guarding the sasag darga. She was wearing a leather cuirass, but the right side was flat, while the other allowed room for the left breast. A studded leather apron hung down in front, almost to her knees. Mythrycian riding boots were below leather leggings.

She had short hair and was wearing the same conical leather cap Joya had seen on the Gotkurgan men the day before. There was a long-healed scar running from her chin, across her cheek and up into her hairline. She had a long straight dagger on one hip and a small-bladed battle axe on the other. A young girl, a Mythrycian about Joya's age, stood beside her.

"Kaskir Ana Booshchoo, meet your new rookie," said Batzorig, gesturing towards Joya.

"I believe kaskir ana means 'wolf mother'. It's a Gotkurgan title. She is the training master of the Khokhguis. I guess she'll be the one to escort you to Gotkurga," whispered Danstorin.

Booshchoo stepped forward and met Joya's gaze. She scowled and said nothing. Then she stepped back.

"Looks like you're in good hands," whispered Pharigon sarcastically.

Joya wanted to punch him again.

CHAPTER FORTY

Two momentous things happened on the same day in Tricanmallokan. The first was almost expected by most in the myanpur's household. His chamberlain found him slumped over and drooling on his night soil stool, unable to stand. His entire right side was paralyzed, and his face looked lopsided. His personal physician was called immediately. He bled him and counselled bed rest but did not leave his side. Shortly after noon, the myanpur suffered another massive stroke and died of natural causes.

Bahomet was informed immediately, of course. He ordered Grand Vizier Fayan to send runners and pigeons to every corner of Biluria proclaiming ten days of mourning. Ambassador Erenbil and the Mythrycian ambassador both sent out messenger pigeons, alerting their respective leaders that the myanpur had passed and that Bahomet would likely be wearing the nine-tined crown of Biluria once the official mourning period was over.

While Bahomet and Fayan were digesting the news and making plans for his succession, a messenger arrived with an urgent message.

"It's from the harbourmaster," said Fayan. "A ship, apparently from Bulankaya, has arrived."

"From where?" asked Bahomet.

"Bulankaya. From the other side of the Western Sea. The harbormaster says they look like Bilurians and even speak something that sounds like Bilurian. People are already saying it's the lost ninth tribe of Biluria, the Bulankais," said Fayan.

"This is all new to me. Explain," said Bahomet.

"Well, I'm no expert on ancient Bilurian history. The uyam pucari, Dassalimpanong Trin at Trangolangopan, is actually the one who knows most about the history of the nine tribes. Apparently, there were nine brothers. The second oldest, Bulankai, had a serious argument with the oldest, Bilur, about how the kingdom should be run and who could be myanpur. It came to a confrontation and blood was shed. The other seven brothers sided with Bilur. Bilur then banished Bulankai forever. He left the country with his entire clan—seven ships in all—and was never heard from again. There was a prophecy, though, that the Bulankai would return someday when a valikatti comes to sit on the throne," said Fayan.

Bahomet looked at Fayan with a bemused smile, then burst into laughter.

When he regained his composure he said, "It seems Baragin isn't the only one to fulfill a prophecy."

And he burst into laughter once again.

"I want to see the captain of that ship. It can't be too formal as we are in mourning. Make the arrangements. And ask the uyam pucari to come to Tricanmallokan. I'd like to know more about the nine brothers and the prophecy. Of course, we will need him for the funeral for the myanpur—and my coronation," concluded Bahomet.

The myanpur's funeral was an immense affair. Representatives from every town and village in Biluria were in the city. Bahomet made sure that the story of the prophecy was spread far and wide. Soon every tea shop and arickmatu pub was agog with talk of the prophecy.

The sasag darga delegated Zythramin as his special envoy to the funeral in addition to Ambassador Muunokoi. Baragin sent his condolences through Erenbil, and appointed Governor Drezzerell and Berendell to represent Zutheria.

Bahomet had lengthy conversations with the Bulankai captain, Bandeenmanash Asan. Dassalimpanong Trin was able to help with communicating as he was familiar with the ancient dialect of Bilurian that Captain Asan seemed to be using.

The captain had brought a number of trade items unique to Bulankaya, including what Trin translated as 'celebration powder'.

Captain Asan brought along an arm's length tube, pointed at the end, with a paper 'tail' hanging from the bottom beside a thick wooden dowel.

"When there is a very important occasion in Bulankaya, we light the tail with fire. The tube flies into the air and explodes with a huge noise. We can use different powders to make different colours, although we prefer red. It's not magic at all, but it looks like magic. The celebration powder makers keep the ingredients a closely guarded secret. Would you like a small demonstration?" he asked.

He pulled out a small red paper tube, held the string-like fuse to a candle and threw it on the floor.

It exploded with a bang, sending Vizier Fayan back against the wall.

"It's harmless. Children use them in Bulankaya. I've brought much larger ones, though," said Asan.

Bahomet was intrigued.

"Bring your largest one to the myanpur's funeral. But I want you to explain to me exactly how it works," he said.

The final day of mourning saw thousands of people crammed into the main square of Tricanmallokan. All of the foreign dignitaries, including Ambassador Muunokoi and Zythramin of Mythrycia, Governor Drezzerell and Baragin's personal envoy Berendell, occupied placces of honour on the dais. Next to Bahomet sat Grand Vizier Fayan, members of the House of Saran who wisely decided to support Bahomet, Captain Bandeenmanash Asan of the Bulankaya—and Uyam Pucari Dassalimpanong Trin, the High Priest of Balangupong.

The myanpur's body lay in state on a high bier, awaiting the funeral procession to the mausoleum of the House of Saran.

Uyam Pucari Trin took his place in front of the crowd. Criers were positioned at measured distances to the ends of the crowd to ensure his message was heard by all. Trin raised his hands to silence the crowd.

"People of Biluria!" began Trin.

He waited until all the criers repeated his message.

"People of Biluria. Today we send our beloved Myanpur Geelanguran to the arms of Balangupong."

Again, he paused for the criers.

"We also welcome back to Biluria the lost tribe of Bulankai."

And he gestured towards Captain Asan, who stood and waved to the crowd. A huge cheer erupted from all those assembled. Trin waited for the hubbub to abate somewhat before raising both arms again.

"You know the prophecy. When a valikatti sits on the throne the Bulankais will return. I will now ask the red eye of Balangupong to give us a sign that the prophecy is truly fulfilled. Valikatti Karpukkai, kiritam ilavaracar of the House of Saran, stand!"

Bahomet stood and looked heavenward. The whole crowd waited with bated breath for the sign of Balangupong.

Pulling out his mantirakolai, Bahomet shouted with a loud voice, "Balangupong, hear my cry. Do you want this valikatti on the throne of Biluria?"

He waited for the criers, then shouted, "*Ti Marrum Minnal!*"

An arc of blue light sprang from the tip of the mantirakolai, backward over the bier of the Myanpur's body to the tip of the fuse hanging down from the Bulankai celebration powder tube. The rocket ignited and flew directly over the heads of the entire crowd. It exploded with a thunderous bang and a corona of red and white light.

The crowd shrieked in terror, and many tried to flee the square. Dozens were trampled. Berendell and Drezzerell gaped at the sight. Zythramin abandoned his seat and headed for somewhere safe.

Bahomet looked directly at Berendell and gave him the slightest of smiles.

CHAPTER FORTY-ONE

Berendell and Governor Drezzerell stayed in Tricanmallokan for the coronation of Myanpur Karpukkai Saran. It was a sumptuous affair. Bahomet spared no expense and made sure every town and village in Biluria had a gift to help them celebrate the rule of the new myanpur. He didn't use Bahomet anymore as a Zutherian name would not sit well with the people.

On his return to Wreatherin, Berendell went immediately to Baragin's office. He was surprised to see both Astaran and Damagal there. Astaran almost never travelled outside Elberon. General Trillabon and his father the chancellor were also in the room.

"Your report from the funeral disturbed me greatly. I sent word to Astaran who decided he would honour us with his presence. Thank you, Zaharbat," said Baragin respectfully.

Astaran nodded in response grasping his dragon staff.

"I was aware of the Bilurian prophecy. Bahomet is either extraordinarily lucky having a ship from his long-lost tribe show up on the day of the myanpur's death—or he is the fulfillment of an actual prophecy. As you were, King Baragin of the cicatrix," he added.

Baragin shook his head ruefully and ran his finger across his cheek scar.

"But what of that explosion, the 'Red Eye of Balangupong', giving his blessing to Bahomet? Is this some sort of powerful sorcery that the Council of Five will now have to combat? Should I be worried for the kingdom?" asked Baragin with a worried expression.

Astaran paused.

"I received a rather mysterious message from Suberon the day that miraculous sign occurred. He said he had dreamed of an explosion, but that it was not magic. He said there was some peril for us, but it was not clear how. I suspect there is a connection between that Bulankayan ship that arrived the day of the myanpur's death. It is possible they brought some sort of device with them that produced the display everyone saw. Of course, Bahomet would want to keep that secret for dramatic effect. And if it is not magic, then it must bow to magic. We are quite safe as long as the Staff of Elbron protects us," concluded Astaran.

"It's so galling! He just keeps getting stronger and stronger. And now he is the legitimate ruler of the next country. There is no way we can avoid him. And no way we can underestimate him," said Baragin, fuming.

"The date for his marriage dissolution hearing has been set—twenty days from now," said Berenfromm, changing the subject slightly.

"But I understand he had been having difficulty finding an avocatim to take his case at the hearing. None of them want to be the avocatim who represents Bahomet," commented Berenfromm.

"Well, he isn't going to come here himself. What can be done about this? We can't put this issue to rest until he is properly represented," said Baragin.

"Ambassador Oban was an avocatim in Biluria before his appointment as ambassador here. Why don't we ask the High Court to give him temporary credentials here in Zutheria, just for the hearing?" suggested Berenfromm.

"Fine. Take care of that. Something else troubles me, though. Erenbil's spies report that Bahomet is building up troops close to the Dalanen River near Dalanbur Island. General Trillabon?"

"Yes, we took Dalanbur Island, which used to have a Bilurian village on it, in our last major border skirmish with the Bilurians. We use the village houses to accommodate our detachment there now. The Dalanen flows into the Bradden near Braddenlocks and forms the border between Zutheria and Biluria. The island has a tall hill at its centre commanding both sides of the river. The reason we took it is because the Bilurians who wanted to push the border northwards to where it was in the old days, set up catapults and trebuchets on its summit and pounded our positions on the north bank. We took it, but it cost us many casualties. It's where Captain Nevelgren, the former border commander at Brobabil you know well, lost his leg. They've always wanted it back. I suspect now that Bahomet has consolidated his power, he'll want to make an issue of Dalanbur Island," concluded Trillabon.

"Move reinforcements to the island and place a regiment in reserve on the north bank of the Dalanen," ordered Baragin.

"Yes, Your Majesty," said Trillabon with a nod of his head.

"Astaran, Elomir will have to come to Wreatherin for the hearing. She completely broke down when Oban brought Bahomet's letter. Could you provide the duke with something that would calm her enough to get her to Wreatherin and deal with the hearing? We really need to have all of Bahomet's connections to Zutheria severed, and the sooner the better," said Baragin.

"I'm sure there is something in the castle's herb pantry that could help. I'll send my apprentice Saragon over to the duke's villa with it," said Astaran.

Ambassador Oban regretted he would not be able to attend the High Court hearing on the day that was set, as he had been recalled to Tricanmallokan for consultations with the myanpur, his client now. He humbly requested a one-week extension. The High Court consented to the slight delay. The new date was the first day of the new moon.

Chapter Forty–Two

Joya reined in her horse and dismounted. The Mythrycian girl who had been riding beside her on her smaller steppe pony did the same. She was the same girl who had been standing beside Kaskir Ana Booshchoo at the audience with the sasag darga the previous day. She had told Joya her name was Aruzhan, but didn't offer much else, and seemed quite shy about talking to the tall, blonde Zutherian. She spoke fluent Zutherian and it was obvious that her role was going to be one of translator.

The escort troop had stopped to rest the horses near a small stream. The horses drank their fill and began pulling out bunches of steppe grass. Captain Onghul ignored her as usual. Kaskir Ana Booshchoo had yet to speak a word to Joya. It was as if she was biding her time before dropping a hammer of discipline on her. Pharigon looked like he wanted to talk to her but wandered off when he saw her with Aruzhan.

Aruzhan was small, almost petite, but had a wiry frame. Her hair was bobbed short like Booshchoo's. She wore leather leggings like the kaskir ana rather than a dress, but did not have the weapons or leather cuirass the training master wore.

Joya glanced over at her.

"I won't bite, you know. You can talk to me," said Joya.

Aruzhan smiled shyly.

"I've never met anyone like you before. They say you killed a man and you've been banished here."

"Yes, that true. I didn't mean to, even though he was very rude. I just wanted to teach him a lesson. But my dagger caught his throat instead of his cheek and he died. He was the son of an important man in our town. The king obeys the law in our country, even though my sister is his wife. So I had to choose between prison and banishment. I chose banishment," said Joya.

Aruzhan nodded, seeming at a loss for what the correct response might be to such a story.

"How do you know Zutherian? You speak it very well," said Joya.

"My mother was Zutherian. She was captured as a girl in a border raid near Lake Frennelen many years ago. My father—his name was Ulugan—purchased her as a slave. But he loved her and treated her well. I grew up speaking both Zutherian and Mythrycian.

"But then my mother died of an illness, a tumor. My father was a trader and on the road much of the year. He was very good friends with the aklach of the Gotkurgans and he put me with them while he was travelling on business. So I know the Gotkurgan dialect, too," said Aruzhan.

"You said 'was' when you mentioned your father. Where is your father now?" asked Joya.

Aruzhan looked down at the ground and didn't speak. Joya saw tears beginning to run down her cheeks.

"Aruzhan, Aruzhan! What's wrong?" asked Joya putting an arm around her.

Aruzhan buried her face in Joya's shoulder and sobbed. Joya held her until she finally calmed down.

"Last month. Bandits. They killed him and took everything. Not far from here. He was bringing a dowry for me so I could marry. I'm an orphan," said Aruzhan sadly.

Joya held for a while longer. Then she asked, "Is that why you're dressed like a Khokhgui instead of a Gotkurgan girl?"

"Yes. I have no dowry, no father. The aklach asked the mongomaa to take me on as a jana oyinsi Khokhgui, a rookie, a trainee. So they cut my hair and put me in the jana oyinsi kezoy with ten other girls. Then I was told to go with the kaskir ana to Gragnarak to get you. I'm your translator. I have to teach you Mythrycian and Gotkurgan," said Aruzhan.

"What's the Gotkurgan word for pig?" asked Joya.

"Soska," said Aruzhan.

"I think the sasag darga looks like a soska and a dwarf had a baby," said Joya.

Aruzhan's mouth dropped open and she broke into peals of infectious laughter. When she finally recovered, she said, "You're bad!"

Booshchoo looked over at the two giggling girls, frowning. Joya returned the look.

"The kaskir ana isn't Mythrycian. She looks like a Jalag," said Joya.

"She is. Her mother was pregnant with her when she was captured in the far north. She was traded to the Gotkurgans. She grew up with us, but also speaks Jalag. Her name is Jalag but I don't know what it means," said Aruzhan.

"She looks mean. And she has that big scar on her face," said Joya.

"She is very tough. She was as wild as a snow leopard as a little girl and because she's Jalag, no Gotkurgan man would want her. It's like she was always meant to be a Khokhgui. She's been in actual battle, and they say she's killed seven men altogether. She got that sword cut on her face in a battle with the Zerdagans," said Aruzhan.

"Zerdagans? Who are they?" asked Joya.

"A tribe from the Undurus Mountains to the south. They are probably the bandits who killed my father. They hate Gotkurgans. If they know the men are away hunting or fighting, they will attack our kezoy camp— it's called Birgulyuk. That's why the Khokhguis are so important to the Gotkurgans. We keep the women and children and old people safe when the men are away," said Aruzhan.

Joya mulled over what Aruzhan had said. The Khokhguis were the protectors. She was determined to do whatever she had to do to become one.

Captain Onghul walked over to them.

"Time to go," he said tersely.

CHAPTER FORTY–THREE

General Dormandesh Kiran looked troubled. He was in Myanpur Karpukkai's office with Grand Vizier Fayan and Patolukai Kumpal Dran, leader of the Karuppsertais.

"But I cannot take Dalanbur Island with only one regiment, Excellency. I would need at least three and four would be best. It's very heavily defended. Not only that, they have learned of your intentions and have brought in reinforcements. They have even moved in a reserve regiment on the north bank of the Dalanen River," said Kiran.

"They learned of our preparations because I wanted them to learn of our preparations. Do you think I do not know Ambassador Erenbil has his spies watching our every move? I am not ordering you to take Dalanbur Island, General. I am ordering you to attack it. If I wanted you to take it, I would give you what you need to do it. I have my reasons. All you need to know is that I need a diversion at Dalanbur Island, and you are the one who will be creating it. You may have one extra regiment so it looks like we are preparing for a serious attack, but you will hold them in reserve. Now go and make your preparations. Your attack will commence early in the morning on the day of the new moon," said Bahomet.

Kiran saw that he was part of a much larger game and nodded.

"Yes, Myanpur Karpukkai. You will have a most excellent diversion at Dalanbur Island," he said.

He back to the doorway, saluted, then turned and left the room.

"You play an excellent game, Karpukkai," said Dran, taking a draw on the water pipe sitting beside him. He blew a smoke ring towards the ceiling.

"That scar-cheeked whelp in Wreatherin will be spinning in circles when I'm done with him. Are your Karpukkais prepared?" asked Bahomet.

"Yes. The duke and Elomir will be heading to Wreatherin for the marriage dissolution hearing. They most certainly will not take the boy, as they do not want to risk his being seen. He will be cared for at the villa with the duke's trusted staff.

"I have assigned two of my best men, Gandaman Abin and Sriwalloban Ohn, for the kidnapping. They will travel by fishboat to Murranenmouth and put into harbour for 'supplies'. At night they will drop a Bilurian canoe over the side and paddle up the Murranen to a hidden landing below the villa. There is a pathway from there to the waterfall and the villa. They know the room where the boy sleeps," said Dran.

"How will they get past the mastiffs? I used to have two of them myself. They are very formidable," said Bahomet.

Dran smiled.

"Dogs are always hungry. A sling and a few chunks of galladerian powdered meat will take care of them."

"I don't want galladerian used on my son. What will you use to ensure he doesn't awaken while you are removing him from the villa?" asked Bahomet.

"Oil of calamang. A rag soaked with it will put anyone to sleep for several hours. There is a slight headache when the person awakens, but it's quite harmless, even for children. Healers in Biluria use it often for setting bones or treating burn victims," said Dran.

"What about the Zutherian navy at Iblingport? When the boy is discovered missing, they will assume he's been taken by boat and set sail immediately to intercept any Bilurian vessel," said Fayan.

Bahomet looked over at Fayan.

"Tell him, Dran."

"Yes, we've thought of that. I have a team of four Karuppsertais that have been smuggled into our trading house in Iblingport. We know one of the navy ships is in drydock for repairs and another is on patrol on the fishing grounds in Pendragon. A fourth is quite old, too old and slow for interception duties. That leaves the *Ferrelaine*. She's very fast under sail and would certainly be ordered to sea once Robduran's absence is discovered.

"The four Karuppsertais will board the *Ferrelaine*, take out the night guards with sea snake venom, then partially cut through all the rigging lines and rudder control lines. It will have to be totally refitted before it will be able to sail at all. That will take at least a day, maybe two. By that time, little Robduran will be playing with his toys in the myanpur's aranmanai. Having your marriage dissolution hearing on the first day of the new moon was an excellent idea, Karpukkai," said

Dran with a smile. He took another long puff on his water pipe.

Bahomet smiled. *His son.*

The kiritam ilavaracar will be where he belonged, in the aranmanai of his father the myanpur of Biluria. And there wasn't a thing Baragin could do about it, legally or diplomatically, especially since they intentionally kept the existence of the boy a secret.

He was the boy's father, and the marriage dissolution petitioner, Elomir, had wilfully violated Zutherian law by denying him access to him. She clearly intended to hide his existence from the High Court and deny Bahomet's right to have a say in his upbringing in the dissolution hearing—a very serious omission. Besides, did he not find him abandoned by his mentally ill mother and grandfather in a lonely, poorly defended villa?

Bahomet stifled an urge to giggle.

Chapter Forty-Four

Pharigon was riding next to Joya.

"It was Aruzhan's father Ulugan who was robbed and murdered by the bandits. She's an orphan now," said Joya.

"I didn't know that. That's very sad. But you two seem to be getting along well," said Pharigon.

"It helps that she's fluent in Zutherian. She'll be my translator and teach me Gotkurgan and Mythrycian as well. We'll also be together in the rookie tent. She's a jana oyinsi, too," said Joya.

"Well, I hope it all works out. But if it doesn't, I'm sure the sasag darga would love to extend his hospitality to you," said Pharigon.

Joya punched him hard.

"Ow! Quit doing that!" said Pharigon.

"I hope you get a matching bruise for the other one I gave you. Serves you right for teasing me. I wouldn't go into that little troll's harem for all the money in Zutheria," said Joya.

Pharigon grinned. It was rather fun teasing her, if a little painful.

Captain Onghul called a halt. They were nearing a cairn of rocks beside the rutted pathway they were on. Ten Gotkurgan horsemen waited in front of them. They all looked intently at Joya.

Onghul trotted his horse up to the Gotkurgans and spoke briefly. Then he wheeled his horse and returned. He spoke to his lancers and half of them turned their horses and began returning by the way they'd come.

He rode up to Joya and Pharigon.

"Escort from Aklach Saaral Chono. We ride with them to Birgulyuk," said Onghul.

"Our kezoy camp," reminded Aruzhan.

Birgulyuk was situated in a very broad valley. Joya could see a river sparkling in the distance. The tall grass of steppe land spread out as far as she could see. At the very end of her vision, she could see a faint outline of mountains. She assumed they were the Undurus Mountains where the dreaded Zerdagans lived. As she paused her horse, she could see several dozen large kezoys, a corral for horses, an enclosure for sheep and another for goats. Smoke was rising from the centre vent hole of most of the kezoys. The place was bustling with people.

As the escort neared, a man with a large kettle drum on a raised stand next to the entrance gate began pounding out a slow rhythm, alerting the camp to the arrival of horsemen. Everyone stopped what they were doing and looked to the hillside.

As they rode into the centre of the village, children, boys and girls, laughed and pointed at Joya. Many touched her boots and chattered animatedly. Joya smiled down at them. Both men and women stared at her and Pharigon, but mostly at her. She hadn't bothered to put the Mythrycian head scarf back on and her golden hair shone in the sunlight.

They stopped in front of a kezoy that obviously belonged to the aklach. It had a raised wooden platform attached to the front of it with two large triangular flags with a red and black pattern fluttering from poles. Two soldiers with the large Gotkurgan broad bladed swords on their hips, and holding tall lances, stood guard on either side of the entranceway. Joya didn't see any Khokhguis.

The group entered the tent. Onghul's soldiers stayed outside. Two soldiers of the escort group followed them inside as did Booshchoo. Aruzhan took her place beside Joya, ready to translate.

Aklach Saaral Chono sat cross-legged on a raised dais at the back of the kezoy. The entire tent was richly carpcted. Aruzhan had told Joya the Gotkurgan women were famous for their ornately designed carpets.

Chono was a middle-aged man with a wispy beard, a little heavy-set. His eyes were narrow and hard from the burden of leading. He had one hand on his crossed knees while the other held a sceptre with a brass eagle's head on it. On his right was another man, which Joya assumed was his second-in-command. On his left was an older woman, gray haired.

Probably the head of the Khokhguis, Mongomaa Oyunchumai, Joya guessed.

"Phar-i-gon. Jo-ya," said Onghul, as usual the very model of brevity. It was clear he was uncomfortable and wished to be on his way as soon as possible.

Chono looked at both of them intently. Everyone waited for him to speak.

"Welcome to Birgulyuk. Your king has been generous. He asks for you to stay with the Khokhguis. A very unusual request. I have said yes, but I do not speak for the mongomaa," said Chono gesturing toward Oyunchumai. "She will decide."

He waited for Aruzhan to translate.

Oyunchumai spoke, gesturing with her hand.

"Stand, blonde girl. Let me look at you."

Joya stood, her chin up, and returned the mongomaa's gaze.

"You will cut your hair," she said.

When Aruzhan translated, she frowned and shook her head no. She'd always had her hair long. Having it in a braid kept it out of the way just fine.

Oyunchumai raised her eyebrows, then said something to Booshchoo, who moved in behind Joya.

"Booshchoo, show the Zutherian girl why Khokhguis have short hair," said Oyunchumai.

But before Aruzhan could translate, Booshchoo had grabbed Joya by the braid and flung her to the carpet. She pinned her to the floor with her knee on Joya's shoulders, still grasping her braid. With her other hand she held a dagger to Joya's throat.

Pharigon leapt up to defend her, but the two guards jumped in front of him with their swords to his chest.

Oyunchumai gave a nod to Booshchoo, who sliced through Joya's long braid and threw it into the nearby smoking brazier where it sizzled and burst into flames. Booshchoo released Joya, who stood shaking.

"You still want to be a Khokhgui, blonde girl?" asked Oyunchumai.

As Aruzhan translated, Joya looked at the aklach who was witnessing the scene impassively. It was clear he would take no part on how Oyunchumai dealt with Joya. Joya glanced at Pharigon who gave her the 'I told you so' look. The soldiers were still holding their swords at his throat. She knew this was a pivotal moment. But there was no going back now.

"Eeyah, Mongomaa," she said, using the Gotkurgan word for 'yes' Aruzhan had taught her earlier that day.

Oyunchumai fixed her with a steely gaze, weighing Joya's mettle.

"Take her to the jana oyinsi kezoy," she directed Booshchoo.

CHAPTER FORTY–FIVE

Elomir sat in her chair in the hearing room of the High Court in Wreatherin, staring woodenly at the back of Durrenbar's chair. She was still groggy from the sedation her father had administered. Duke Robagrin had given her a large dose at the villa two days before, then four strong guards had trundled her into a makeshift bed in the duke's carriage. When she awoke in the mayor's manor house in Bidrudden, she was absolutely frantic at the unfamiliar surroundings.

Duke Robagrin explained patiently and persistently that the trip to Wreatherin was the only way to get Bahomet permanently out of their lives. The ten guards and two mastiffs at the villa, along with the housekeeper Gella whom Robduran adored, would keep him perfectly safe during their absence.

Ambassador Oban, in the unfamiliar robes of a Zutherian avocatim, argued forcefully against the dissolution of marriage. As a sovereign head of state, Myanpur Karpukkai had every right to ask that his wife join him at his side and help to produce an heir for the kingdom of Biluria. Interfering with that right was an egregious infringement and would be construed as a personal insult that could seriously damage the harmonious relationship between the two countries.

Avocatim Durrenbar related all the material grounds for dissolution of the marriage: incarceration for criminal acts, seven years of separation, physical and mental cruelty, and evidence of extra-marital relations (a bribe from one of Erenbil's agents to the tall Bilurian dancer had supplied that information).

Judge Ringforin weighed all the evidence presented. In his closing statement he strongly urged the government to make every effort to mitigate the diplomatic complications of his ruling. Nevertheless, the law was clear—Bahomet had committed multiple acts of conduct injurious to the marriage backed by ample evidence. Judge Ringforin granted the petitioner's request and referred the dissolution document to Laguntzailea Zolenfan for his signature.

Duke Robagrin breathed a huge sigh of relief. Elomir let out a very rare giggle and even smiled a little. She urged her father to take her back to Elberon immediately so she could see her son.

⸱⸱◦❧◦⸱⸱

It was the middle of a dark, moonless night when Gandaman Abin and Sriwalloban Ohn reached the villa after paddling up the Murranen River. Abin swung his sling around his head and launched a large chunk of galladerian-laced meat over the villa fence. It wasn't long before one of the mastiffs came sniffing around and gobbled it up in one gulp. His kennel mate pawed jealously at him but pounced immediately when a second ball of meat landed next to him. Abin and Ohn waited.

The two dogs began staggering and soon flopped over on their sides. Ohn and Abin vaulted the compound wall and made their way towards the villa. One night guard had fallen asleep at his post. Ohn slit his throat silently. The other guard was awake. He slapped at the snake venom blow dart that Abin delivered to his neck, then slumped over, unconscious.

Ohn threw a padded grappling hook to the roof edge and pulled the line taut. Abin pulled himself hand over hand to the second-floor window—the one with the wooden boat on the sill. He pried open the latch and slipped silently into the room.

A small candle guttered on a side table next to the boy's bed. He was sound asleep. Abin pulled out his vial of calamang oil and doused a small rag with it. He covered the boy's mouth and nose and held it firmly. The boy's eyes opened wide in fright, but soon they rolled into the back of his head.

Abin trussed the boy's arms and legs, then unfolded a large canvas bag from his backpack. He stuffed the boy in, fastened the leather closing straps, and slung the bag over his shoulder. He paused, remembering something. He pulled a small box of Mythrycian nougat out of his pack and left it in the middle of Robduran's bed—a little parting gift from Bahomet to his ex-wife. On impulse, Abin took one from the box and popped it into his mouth.

Abin slipped out the window with his burden slung over his shoulder and landed lightly next to Ohn.

"To the canoe," was all he said.

Baragin stood next to General Trillabon on the north bank of the Dalanen River. General Kiran had launched his attack on Dalanbur Island the previous morning. General Trillabon's troops had repulsed the Bilurian attack, inflicting considerable casualties on the attackers. They had only lost three defenders in the skirmish. The general was mopping up now and removing the bodies of the Bilurian soldiers who littered the shore of Dalanbur Island.

Baragin had ridden down from Wreatherin the day after Elomir's successful High Court hearing.

"Excellent work, general. It feels pretty good to give that Bahomet a thrashing. He seriously underestimated our resolve," said Baragin.

"Thank you, Majesty. The troops did well. I'm sure they would like to hear it personally from their king, though," said Trillabon.

"Lead on," said Baragin as he walked with the general to the river front.

In Wreatherin, a pigeon with a frantic message from Duke Robagrin at Elberon fluttered into the dovecote at Selvenhall. Berenfromm's face blanched when he read it. There was no way to get a pigeon to Baragin at the battlefield. He dispatched a messenger on the fastest horse in the stable to head to the border on the Dalancn River.

Berenfromm also sent a pigeon to Governor Drezzerell in Iblingport ordering the *Ferrelaine* to sea to intercept any Bilurian vessel sailing south from Murranenmouth. The Bilurian fishing boat was rolling through white-tipped swells off the mouth of the Bradden River at Iblingport when the captain of the *Ferrelaine* discovered his ship was totally disabled.

Robduran awoke, groggy and with a headache, when the fishing boat sailed into Tricanmallokan harbour.

CHAPTER FORTY-SIX

Joya ducked her head as she entered the kezoy, following Booshchoo and Aruzhan. Ten sets of eyes stared at her.

"You and Aruzhan sleep there," said Booshchoo pointing to a double wide set of bedding on the edge of the kezoy. Six identical sleeping platforms lined the wall of the tent. A brazier stood in the middle just beside the support pole, sending wisps of smoke lazily upward through the vent hole.

"Aruzhan. Tell her everyone's names, then eat. I will be back after lunch for your first lesson," said Booshchoo.

She gave a last glowering look at all the girls and rested on Joya last. She lifted the tent flap and ducked through the opening.

"I'm sorry about your hair. It was beautiful. But a Khokhgui cannot have long hair. It gives a handhold to the enemy, as Booshchoo showed you," began Aruzhan.

Joya looked around at all the bobbed hair of her tent-mates.

"I guess I have a lot of lessons to learn. Please introduce me."

Aruzhan began with Kashkara. It seemed clear that the rest of the girls deferred to her as a natural leader. Kashkara eyed Joya coolly but nodded slightly to her when Aruzhan said her name. Aruzhan added that Kashkara's uncle was the aklach.

Aruzhan then followed with the rest of the jana oyinsi: Inkar, Ayzera, Bergara, Ayana, Inzhu, Aylin, Medara, Arayu, and Ayaulym.

They all nodded and some of them giggled when Joya tried to pronounce their names.

After Aruzhan was done, there was an awkward silence. A couple of the girls looked at Kashkara. She walked up to Joya and put her nose close to Joya's face.

"Why are you here, Zuth girl?" she asked.

After Aruzhan translated, Joya said, "Tell her I am here to become a Khokhgui, that I am banished because I killed a man. Tell her I will do nothing to dishonour the Khokhgui."

Kashkara digested Aruzhan's translation, not looking convinced.

"Everyone eat," she said as she sat down in front of the communal stew pot hanging over the brazier. She handed a wooden spoon and bowl to Joya. All of the others brought their own bowls to the pot and served themselves.

Since Joya still had only a few words of Gotkurgan, she and Aruzhan chatted in Zutherian.

"You know, my father was a merchant selling tin pots and cups to the various kezoy camps in Gotkurga. Once a year he had to go far into Zutheria, all the way to the ocean. I forget the name of the place where he got his tinware from," said Aruzhan.

Joya's eyes widened.

"Did he say Blessingport?" she asked.

"Yes! Yes! That was the name. That's where he got his pots. He told me a funny story once. He was in a pub having a drink. The waitress, a pretty blonde girl, asked him all kinds of questions about the Khokhgui. And when he told her, she kissed him! He was...." Aruzhan stopped, looking at Joya, who was blushing furiously.

"Oh! Oh! Was that you? Was that you, Joya?" and she burst into hilarious laughter and could not stop. She fell over onto her side, laughing uproariously. The other girls stopped eating and looked over in surprise. Aruzhan's laugh was so infectious that some of them started laughing too. Joya looked down at her bowl and kept spooning in her stew, not making eye contact with anyone.

"You kissed my poppa!" said Aruzhan breathlessly, then broke into another round of hilarious laughter.

When she finally regained control, she let out a rapid-fire torrent of Gotkurgan to the other girls who listened with rapt attention. When she got to the last line, the whole tent erupted into gales of laughter. Joya wanted to crawl under the edge of the kezoy in her humiliation.

Kashkara looked at her, enjoying her discomfort.

"Kissed a Mythrycian, eh? You have poor taste in men, Zuth girl."

And the whole tent erupted into laughter again—except Aruzhan.

CHAPTER FORTY-SEVEN

It was Filden who found Elomir's body at the base of the waterfall, her bloodied face lying against a moss-covered rock. The duke was absolutely devastated. First, his precious grandson was kidnapped. Then his fragile daughter was so crushed that she took advantage of his drinking himself insensible to end her misery. He was the one who had found the Mythrycian nougat box, with one candy missing, and realized Bahomet had known about Robduran all along.

His wife, his only son, his silly but loving daughter, and his grandson—all gone. He was a crushed and defeated man. Filden sent a message to Astaran at Elberon Castle asking for help after he found Robagrin in his bedroom, rocking and talking to himself. He was unshaven and dirty, and called repeatedly for more wine. He cried frequently, moaning, "Elomir, I'm so sorry, Elomir. Please forgive me. Elomir, tell your old poppa you forgive him. I couldn't save precious Robduran. Elomir! I'm sorry! I'm sorry!"

Astaran came to the old duke's side and saw immediately he would never be able to care for himself properly. He arranged for Filden to attend to the duke's care at the castle, but it seemed clear he was virtually at the end of his days. The villa sat empty and unused.

—••◦|◉|◦••—

Baragin was furious. He quickly realized that the failed attack on Dalanbur Island was intentional—a diversion from Bahomet's true goal of kidnapping his son from Duke Robagrin's villa. It removed Baragin from Wreatherin so that it would take hours for him to know what had occurred. Even the slight postponement of the High Court hearing was a ruse to allow the kidnapping to occur when there was no moon. The sabotage of the *Ferrelaine* was all part of Bahomet's overall strategy to ensure the boat used in the plot could slip past Iblingport to safe harbour in Tricanmallokan. He was outmaneuvered at every turn. How did he even find out about Robduran?

He needed someone to direct his anger at and that was Damagal and Governor Drezzerell. The old Laguntzailea sat impassively as Baragin raged, but the governor looked at the floor, twisting his cap in his hands.

"What good are you Laguntzaileas when Bahomet can kidnap a boy out from under the very shadows of Elberon Castle? Aren't you supposed to be protecting us from foreign wizards? Where was Astaran in all of this? Asleep? Playing with potions? His castle overlooks the villa where Bahomet's Karuppsertais obviously roam at will! Absolutely unacceptable!" he fumed.

"How did Bahomet find out about Robduran? Do you even know that?" asked Baragin.

"It seems the duke was a little careless. He had a Bilurian stonecarver from the quarry come to the villa to install a fountain. He must have seen evidence a boy lived there, or chatted with a villa servant and put two and two together. The man is almost certainly a spy for Bahomet. He has been dealt with," said Damagal.

Baragin shook his head in disgust, then turned to Governor Drezzerell.

"And you! Governor! How is it possible that the fastest ship in our navy could be sabotaged by a crew of Bahomet's henchmen under your very nose? I want that captain transferred to a barge. Unbelievable! Can't even guard his own ship. And you have no idea a crew of Bilurian Karuppssertais is running around Iblingport, wrecking my ship and killing two sailors. Did I not ask that all Bilurians in Prene be monitored? Get out of my sight!" roared Baragin.

Governor Drezzerell scurried out of the office, glancing worriedly at Berendell as he left.

"I suppose I'll be going as well," said Damagal.

"You do that, Laguntzailea. Astaran does not answer to me. But if he did, he'd be looking for another job," said Baragin through clenched teeth.

Damagal raised his eyebrows but said nothing. He left the room without a glance at Berendell.

Berendell waited for Baragin's ire to ease, then poured two glasses of Bradden liquor. He handed one to Baragin who gulped the whole glass down in two swallows. Berendell refilled his glass.

"What next?" asked Berendell.

"I don't know. I just want to get drunk," said Baragin.

Robduran looked wonderingly around the myanpur's aranmanai. It was sumptuously decorated, with high ceilings and gold-plated torch sconces fitted to the walls. Two Karuppsertais, Abin and Ohn, walked on either side of him.

"Where am I? Where are you taking me? Where is my momma? Where is poppa?" he asked in Zutherian.

The Karuppsertais didn't answer but gave him little pushes on the shoulder to steer him down the correct corridors.

They stopped at a set of high, ornately decorated doors, guarded by two soldiers in the livery of the House of Saran. They opened the doors and Abin and Ohn walked the boy through.

Bahomet's face lit up when he saw him. He walked quickly towards him and knelt in front of him, wrapping him in his arms.

"Robduran, Robduran! My son! My son! Oh, how handsome you are! Let your poppa have a look at you," said Bahomet, pulling back to take him all in.

Robduran stood stiffly with a frown on his face.

"I don't know you. And you're not my poppa. My poppa is old. He's a duke. I want to go home. I want my momma. I want Gella," said Robduran, using his housekeeper's name.

Bahomet stood, glancing at Abin and Ohn.

"See Grand Vizier Fayan for your reward. I am very, very pleased." The pair bowed, backed to the doorway, and left.

"Yes, your 'poppa' is a duke. He is your grandfather, your momma's father. I am your father. I married your momma and we had you together. I had to go away on a long journey, though, before you were born. I just came back, and I wanted to see you. So I had those two men bring you here," said Bahomet.

Robduran said nothing, still frowning.

"Here, come with me to this mirror, Robduran," said Bahomet, pulling Robduran by the hand to a full-length mirror on the wall.

"Look at the two of us. We look alike. You have my nose. And my eyes. See? I am your father. This is your new home," said Bahomet.

"I don't look like you. You're bald. I don't want to live here. I want to go home to Elberon. I want my toys. I want Gella," said Robduran.

It seemed apparent his relationship with the housekeeper was much stronger than the one with his mother.

Bahomet sighed.

"Let's go see your pattam, your great-aunt Bilanguree. And your two cousins Darabindoo and Arashbilan. They live here, too. Then we'll find something to eat. Are you hungry?" asked Bahomet.

"Yes. Do you have candy here?"

"Oh yes! Lots of candy! Come," said a beaming Bahomet.

"What's wrong with your arm?" asked Robduran as they walked out the doorway.

CHAPTER FORTY-EIGHT

Joya stood in a line with the eleven other Khokhgui trainees. They were in the jana oyinsi kezoy, the Khokhgui 'rookie tent'. She was head and shoulders taller than most of the other girls. Kaskir Ana Booshchoo, the 'Wolf Mother' training master of the Khokhguis, was walking up and down in front the line, saying nothing but looking each one in the eye. She had a bit of swagger to her walk. She stopped in the middle of the line and looked from left to right. Aruzhan whispered the Gotkurgan translation into Joya's ear as she began.

"Well, my little maggots. You're mine now—for four months. What a sorry looking lot you are. What am I supposed to do with you? The mongomaa has asked me how many I think will make it to the initiation ceremony four months from now. Maybe none of you. You think you got here because you're tough. Hah! When I get through with you, you'll be crying for your momma's titty. Or…"

Booshchoo stopped in the front of them.

"Or you'll be the best new Khokhgui recruits ever."

She bent down to the much shorter Aruzhan and put her nose in her face and yelled at the top of her lungs.

"Are you going to make me proud?"

Aruzhan, with a terrified look on her face, said, "Eeyah, Kaskir Ana."

"Louder!"

"Eeyah, Kaskir Ana!"

"All of you! Are you going to make me proud?"

"Eeyah, Kaskir Ana!

"Louder!"

"EEYAH, KASKIR ANA!!" they all screamed.

"Good. Now take off your shirts. It's time for you to start your change from little girls to Khokhgui warriors," said Booshchoo.

All of the girls took off their shirts. Joya didn't move. All the rest were looking at her as they held their shirts in front of themselves.

Booshchoo walked over to Aruzhan.

"Did you translate what I said?" demanded Booshchoo.

"Eeyah, Kaskir Ana," said a worried Aruzhan.

Booshchoo walked in front of Joya and put her nose an inch away from her nose. Joya met her gaze. She was stilling simmering with anger over the loss of her hair under Booshchoo's knife.

"Shirt. Off," said Booschoo, drilling her eyes into Joya's as she pinched the shoulder of Joya's shirt and tugged. They were exactly the same height. Aruzhan didn't translate. It was clear what she was saying.

"Jok," said Joya firmly, using the Gotkurgan word for 'no'. She didn't move.

The rest of the girls bent their heads around to see what would happen next, eyes wide.

Booshchoo kept staring. Suddenly she took off her own shirt revealing the patterned red and black breast strap of an initiated Khokhgui. There were seven black

'X's' stitched into the red edge of the strap. She had a large, puckered scar from an arrow puncture just above her bare left breast. Another broad scar from a sabre slash was on her left shoulder. With a lightning move she pulled out her dagger and slit the front of Joya's shirt from hem to neckline. She put the blade under Joya's right breast.

"Maybe we won't need a breast strap for you," she hissed slowly.

Aruzhan's mouth was open, as were all the other girls'.

"Translate!" she yelled at Aruzhan without taking her eyes off Joya. Aruzhan complied.

Joya set her mouth to a firm line, then pulled off her shirt and tossed it to the side. Booshchoo reshcathed her dagger. She locked Joya's eyes with a steely gaze and held it. Joya returned the look. Finally, Booshchoo raised her chin slightly and turned to the others.

"In the box over there. Jana oyinsi benbays," said Booshchoo.

"Rookie straps," whispered Aruzhan.

"Take one, help each other wrap. It must be tight! You think it feels good to have a bow string take off the side of your boob? It must be tight. You must wear it all the time. You want to be Khokhgui warriors? You wear the benbay. It's what makes us who we are," said Booshchoo as the girls scrambled to get their jana oyinsi benbays from the wooden box.

There was much chattering and a little giggling as the girls helped each other put their benbays on. They were all a dull white colour, two hand widths wide, made with a soft cotton fabric. Joya helped Aruzhan with hers and tucked in the end.

"Feel okay?" she asked.

"Yes. It's tight but I can still breathe. Let me do yours," Aruzhan said.

After they were done, Booshchoo ordered them back into line.

"Shirts on!" she yelled. "You too," she said to Joya.

Joya put her sliced top back on.

"Now. We have a Zutherian with us. Jo-ya. Such a girly name. Khokhguis don't have girly names. I am Booshchoo. Do you know what that means?" she asked scanning the line.

No one answered.

"Big cat," said Joya, in Zutherian.

"What did she say?" said Booshchoo to Aruzhan.

"'Big cat'," said Aruzhan in Gotkurgan.

Booshchoo walked in front of Joya.

"And how do you know what a Jalag name means, white girl?"

"It sounds like booscho. It's Yakat for 'big cat'," said Joya.

Booshchoo made a face and spat on the ground, in inch from Joya's toe.

"Yakats! Enemies of my people. How do you know Yakat?" demanded Booshchoo.

"My sister's husband, the king, speaks Yakat. He lived in Yakatan for two years. He taught me some words," said Joya.

"Klooshkoosh. That's a good name for you, white girl. Klooshkoosh belly," said Booshchoo.

"She said, 'belly'. I don't know the other word. It's Jalag," whispered Aruzhan.

"I will not be called 'Whitefish Belly'," said Joya firmly, recognizing the slight difference between the Yakat and Jalag words for whitefish.

Aruzhan looked at her with a worried expression.

"Tell her!" she ordered.

Aruzhan translated.

"So. You don't like 'Whitefish Belly', eh? What name would you like, Jo-ya?" asked Booshchoo with a sneer, hands on her hips.

Joya thought for a moment, remembering what Futtsam had called her just before she slit his throat.

"Noostel," she said. "It means 'bearcat' or 'wolverine'," she said to Aruzhan.

Booshchoo held out her hand to Aruzhan, indicating she already knew what Joya had said.

"Nooshtal. That's how we say it. It's a good name— for a tough girl, for a warrior. Tell you what, Jo-ya. If you can pin Enkhara, you can have Nooshtal for your name. If Enkhara pins you, you will be Klooshkoosh Belly. Deal?" posed Booshchoo.

Joya bit her lip. She knew quite a few wrestling holds and pins from sparring with her cousin Umbraset, who was much bigger than her. She didn't know how big or how tough this Enkhara was, though.

She gave a quick nod of her head.

"Eeyah," she said.

Booshchoo smiled and called over her shoulder, "Enkhara! In here."

Joya recognized her as the guard at the entrance to the kezoy when they came in. She wasn't as tall as Joya, but stocky and tough looking.

"Whitefish Belly wants to wrestle you. Give me your weapons," said Booshchoo.

Enkhara grinned as she handed her bow and battle axe to Booshchoo. She undid her dagger belt and slipped off her studded apron, then the one-breasted cuirass of the Khokhgui. She stripped off her shirt exposing the red and black benbay of a veteran Khokhgui.

Joya undid the belt holding her dagger and side pouch and handed them to Aruzhan. She threw her own sliced shirt off to the side again. The girls cleared a circle in the middle of the kezoy.

Enkhara was already in a crouch, arms out, crooking her fingers at Joya for her to come and get her. Joya crouched low, legs spread far apart. They circled one another, grabbing at each other's hands. Suddenly Enkhara snatched Joya's arm, spun into her and threw her over her back.

Joya landed with a thud but quickly rolled to her feet before Enkhara could jump on top of her for the pin.

Booshchoo was smiling and nodding while the girls shouted, "Pin her Jo-ya!" or "Get her Enkhara!".

Joya used her longer arms to her advantage. She grabbed Enkhara's left wrist with her right hand, put her left hand around the back of her neck and pulled hard. Simultaneously she kicked up her right leg to Enkhara's waist and threw her left leg around the back of her knees in a scissor hold. With her superior weight, Joya slammed Enkhara hard to the ground and put a painful wristlock on her right hand. Enkhara struggled fiercely but Joya had her squeezed between her legs. She applied a little more pressure to the wristlock until Enkhara cried out in pain.

"Stop!" shouted Booshchoo.

"Stop!" echoed Aruzhan in Zutherian.

Joya released Enkhara. She grabbed her shirt off the ground and tied the loose ends in a double knot. She brushed the hair out of her eyes and looked at Booshchoo, her chin held high. Enkhara stood as well, holding her wrist but not daring to look at Booshchoo.

Booshchoo locked eyes with Joya, glowering. Then she said to the tent, still looking at Joya, "Jana oyinsi! This is Nooshtal—Bearcat! Now get out! Run to the river and back again. Enkhara. You run with them before you get your weapons back."

And she spat on the brazier in disgust.

Joya and Aruzhan were walking back through the camp after their run. Aruzhan had gotten a stitch in her side and Joya had held back to walk with her. The other girls were already at the kezoy.

Pharigon rode up on his horse, a document box under his right arm. He reined in his horse beside the girls. Joya pulled her sliced shirt closer together with one hand.

"I've finished my business here. I have to take these documents and Ulugan's inventory back to the embassy. You'd think they would just keep all those pots and cups, but the Gotkurgans are scrupulously honest."

Pharigon paused.

"I guess this is goodbye," he said, looking down at Joya.

"Luck and speed. Tell momma and Ammy I'm fine. Tell Poppa..." she stopped as the words caught in her throat.

Pharigon saw the emotion welling up in her eyes.

"I'll tell them. Be safe, Joya."

He locked eyes with her for a moment. Then he cleared his throat and looked straight ahead. He gave his horse a kick and it began walking forward.

"Oh! Wait! Wait!" said Joya running after him.

Pharigon reined in his horse.

"I almost forgot. Get this message to my uncle Timbraset somehow," she said, holding up a small scrap of paper.

214

Pharigon's horse was dancing around. He had the document box under his arm, preventing him from taking the note.

"Here," said Joya.

She stood on her tiptoes, put her hand on his thigh and reached up to tuck the message into his side pocket. Their eyes met again, a little longer this time. Neither spoke.

Pharigon kicked his horse again and Joya watched him go.

Joya and Aruzhan began walking towards their kezoy again.

"Are you going to marry that handsome captain? I saw how you two looked at each other," said Aruzhan.

"Shut up!" said Joya.

Aruzhan grinned.

Some time later, Timbraset unfolded a pigeon message: Uncle Timba. I'm fine. My friend Aruzhan's father Ulugan was your agent. Bandits murdered him and stole her dowry money. Aruzhan is an orphan. Please let her have the pot money for her dowry. Love and kisses, Joya.

CHAPTER FORTY-NINE

Joya wiped the sweat off her brow. It left a streak of dirt across her forehead. She and Aruzhan had been assigned latrine digging duty. Joya had an iron pole to loosen the dirt while Aruzhan was using a flat wooden shovel to scoop the clods from the trench. It was hard work, but they kept at it determinedly.

A shadow suddenly blocked the sun. Joya looked up.

"Sunshine Hair. Hello. I love you, Sunshine Hair," said a voice.

Aruzhan stopped shovelling.

"It's Sanzhar. He's simple in the head. He says whatever comes to his mind," said Aruzhan.

"My name is Nooshta, Sanzhar. Nooshta," said Joya.

Everyone had shortened Nooshtal to Nooshta.

"I love you, Nooshta. You're pretty. We will get married."

He smiled shyly, his toe moving back and forth along the edge of the latrine trench.

Joya smiled back. Her Gotkurgan was getting a lot better.

"You know I can't get married, Sanzhar. I'm a Khokhgui. We don't get married," said Joya.

"Yes. We will get married. I will wait until you stop being a Khokhgui. Then we will get married," said Sanzhar.

Just then, a clod of dirt hit Sanzhar in the side of the head.

"Oweee!" he cried, holding his head.

A boy about Joya's age yelled at him.

"Stop bothering the jana oyinsis, stupid-head."

"He wasn't bothering us. And you're the stupid one," said Joya, climbing out of the ditch to confront him.

"It's Bakhtiar, Aklach Chono's second son," whispered Aruzhan.

"What did you say to me, Whitefish Belly?" said Bakhtiar.

Booshchoo's nickname for Joya had spread around the camp, but no one said it to her face.

Joya put her face close to Bakhtiar's.

"I said, you're the stupid one. Only a coward attacks someone who's simple-minded," said Joya with a sneer.

Bakhtiar took a swing at Joya's face, but she blocked the punch with her left arm and drove her right fist hard into his solar plexus. Bakhtiar dropped to his knees gasping for breath. The three boys who were with him all jumped on top of Joya kicking and throwing punches. Aruzhan leapt into the melee, pulling hair and biting fingers.

All of a sudden, Booshchoo and a Gotkurgan warrior were in the middle of everything, yelling and throwing bodies to the side.

After they separated everyone, the combatants stood glaring at one another breathing heavily. Booshchoo stood next to the girls, while the warrior angrily pushed the boys into a line. He sent Sanzhar across the field to his mother's kezoy.

Joya recognized him as the man who was sitting next to Aklach Chono in their first meeting. It was

Sogis Bassisi Alinur, the war chief for Birgulyuk. He led all of the Gotkurgan warriors in battle.

The boys all looked down as he glowered at them.

"Fighting? With girls? Shame on you! You will finish digging this latrine. Get to work!" Alinur ordered.

The boys sullenly picked up the tools and began digging. Bakhtiar glared daggers at Joya.

"What happened?" demanded Booshchoo as she led Joya and Aruzhan off to one side.

"Bakhtiar threw dirt at Sanzhar's head and called him names. Nooshta protected him. Bakhtiar tried to punch Nooshta but she dropped him with one punch! Then all the other boys jumped on her. Then I ran in to help Nooshta," explained Aruzhan.

Booshchoo smiled slightly, then recovered, frowning.

"Idiot girls! Can't even dig a ditch. Go to the main Khokhgui tent, gather the weapons stacked in the corner and take them to the blacksmith for sharpening. Fighting with boys," she said disgustedly, walking away.

Aruzhan and Joya looked after her. Then Aruzhan grinned at Joya. "That was a good punch you gave Bakhtiar. You'll have to be careful now, though. He will hate you for that," said Aruzhan.

Aruzhan and Joya both had an armful of battle axes, the Khokhgui main weapon. They walked to the blacksmith's kezoy, which was a suspended canopy with no sides.

"He is called Arsen. He is a very good blacksmith, always busy. He won't be happy to see us. He always says he has no time for sharpening. Usually his son Nurasyl helps, but he fell off his horse and broke his arm. He has two other sons, but they are too young," said Aruzhan as they neared the blacksmith's canopy.

Arsen was pounding away on a red-hot blade as they arrived. They waited respectfully for him to notice them.

He was a massive man with a large black beard and very broad shoulders. His huge biceps glistened with sweat. He thrust the blade into a tin vat of water and it hissed and bubbled. Joya wondered if it was a vat from her uncles' factory.

"I don't have time for sharpening Khokhgui weapons," he said, barely looking at them.

"Leave them over there against the post. I'll get to them when I can."

"Booshchoo won't be happy about that. The Khokhguis have their turn on patrol tomorrow," whispered Aruzhan.

Joya looked at the grinding wheel on the side of the shop. It was very much like her father's. He had taught her how to put an edge on every kind of blade. She was a good sharpener.

"I'll sharpen them," said Joya.

Arsen looked up, smiling.

"You? Nooshta is it? What do you know about sharpening?"

"I'll show you," she said.

She took the first battle axe, gave the grindstone a starting spin like her father had taught her, then began rhythmically pumping the treadle. Soon there were sparks flying from the blade. She flipped it over and sharpened the other side. She paused, felt the edge with her thumb, then gave it another grinding against the wheel.

Arsen watched her with growing interest. He held out his hand for the axe and ran his thumb over the edge. He smiled.

"Finish the pile. You, Aruzhan, bring more wood for the forge," said Arsen.

Sometime later Booshchoo came looking for the pair, expecting them to return long before. Joya was just about finished all the battle-axes and Aruzhan was stacking wood for the forge.

"Nooshta! Aruzhan! We have archery practice," she scolded.

Arsen stopped hammering a sword blade and doused it in the tin vat.

"All the jana oyinsi must do a chore in the camp, yes?" he asked.

"Yes, but..." started Booshchoo.

Arsen interrupted.

"I need Nooshta to help me here until Nurasyl's arm heals. She knows how to use the grinding stone. All your axes are ready. Send her here for chore time."

Booshchoo looked at the two girls busy with their chores.

"Come to the archery range when you're done. This will be your chore place from now on," said Booshchoo.

As Aruzhan and Joya walked back to the Khokhgui kezoy, Sanzhar appeared and began following them, saying, "I love you, Sunshine Hair, I love you. One day we will marry. I love you, Sunshine Hair."

Aruzhan looked at Joya and giggled.

"I love you, Sunshine Hair," she sang mockingly.

Joya punched her in the shoulder.

CHAPTER FIFTY

Bahomet was standing with Boroneeloman Dran at the rubble pile blocking the entrance trail to the Karuppsertai training centre. There were signs that labourers had been chiselling and pounding away at some of the larger boulders trying to clear a usable pathway. It was taking a long time. There was a steep walking path around the rubble field but was Dran was determined to have a cart path again.

Captain Bandeenmanash Asan from the Bulankaya ship was there. He had explained to Bahomet that "celebration powder" had other uses in large amounts. Quarry owners and road builders used it to blow large rocks into smaller pieces. It saved a lot of time and laborious work normally done by workers wielding sledgehammers. Bahomet had asked for a demonstration.

Asan directed one of the guards to roll a medium-sized keg towards one of the larger boulders. Labourers had dug a small hole directly beneath the front of the boulder. Asan directed the guard to position the keg tightly underneath it. He pulled the cork from the bung hole and held a tin container underneath it as the powder poured out. Then he used a twist auger to fashion a small hole in the centre of the cork. He pulled an arm's length wick of rolled paper from his side pouch and fitted it into the cork.

Asan began laying narrow strips of paper end to end leading away from the end of the wick which was laying on the ground. He placed small pebbles on each corner to keep any gust of wind from blowing them away. Then, using the tin container, he poured a long line of powder all the way to a large boulder on the side of the trail.

"We don't usually do it this way. The quarry blasters take the time to fashion a much longer wick with powder rolled up inside it. They sometimes do it this way if they are in a hurry and they are inside a tunnel with no wind," explained Asan.

"Why did you make the trail of powder end at that large boulder?" asked Bahomet.

Asan smiled.

"Oh, myanpur. You do not want to be anywhere near the powder keg when it blows up. There will be pieces of rock flying into the air. It is dangerous, and you must take cover. That boulder on the side of the trail is next to an overhanging rock. We will be safe there. And you must cover your ears. It is very loud."

Bahomet glanced at Dran.

"I think we need to make this demonstration more memorable."

He gestured to an officer standing behind him.

"Bring the prisoner," he ordered.

Two soldiers brought a chained man and threw him at Bahomet's feet.

He was sobbing and begging for mercy.

One of the soldiers gave him a sharp poke with the butt end of his lance. "Silence before the myanpur," he yelled.

The man stopped sobbing, but still whimpered.

"What is your name, soldier?" asked Bahomet.

"Anasamang Prin, Myanpur Karpukkai," said the man.

"You were at the battle at Dalanbur Island, yes?"

"Yes, Myanpur," said the man.

"And why are you here, in these chains, Anasamang Prin?" asked Bahomet.

Prin remained silent.

"Answer the myanpur!" yelled the guard giving him another jab with the butt end of his spear.

"I...I ran away, Myanpur. I was afraid and I ran away from the Zutherians, Myanpur. I'm sorry, Myanpur, I'm sorry! Please forgive me, Myanpur. I will never do that again, Myanpur! Please, Myanpur, please," begged Prin breaking into sobs again.

"No. You won't do that again. Because no soldier in my army runs away from the enemy. Chain him to the rock," he ordered.

The two guards dragged a crying and pleading Prin to the boulder and fastened his chains around it. Prin sobbed and begged for mercy.

Captain Asan looked dismayed. Bahomet glanced over at him.

"And what do you do with cowards in your army, Asan?" asked Bahomet.

"Well, we execute them of course, but..." he paused.

"You've never used celebration powder for an execution before," said Bahomet, finishing his sentence.

"No, Myanpur. But it will be a merciful death. Messy, but merciful," said Asan.

Bahomet spoke to the officer in charge.

"I will be delivering the sentence on this prisoner with my mantirakolai. Take the soldiers and the labourers into Trangomangopan. When you hear a very loud noise, come back with the soldiers," he ordered. Bahomet did not want any witnesses to the demonstration—but he did want them to think it was his magic at work.

The officer bowed low and went to carry out the order.

"Shall we get behind the boulder, Myanpur?" asked Captain Asan.

Dran, Asan and Bahomet took cover behind the boulder. Prin was still moaning and sobbing next to the powder keg. Asan looked at Bahomet who gave him a nod. Asan took out a flint and struck a series of sparks onto the end of the trail of powder. It took several attempts. Finally, the end of the powder ignited and began burning towards the powder keg. Dran and Bahomet covered their ears.

Suddenly, the fizzling stopped. Asan looked up, frowning. He grabbed the tin of powder and walked quickly up to the place where the powder line had stopped burning. He poured out some more powder and repeated the flint sparking procedure. The powder line ignited again, and he ran quickly back to the boulder.

"If there is not quite enough powder in the line, it will stop. It is going again. Cover your ears!" he said to the other two.

The line burned inexorably towards the keg and the moaning Prin. He saw the line of powder burning towards him and howled and strained against his chains. The line reached the wick and burned up to the corked bung hole.

A thunderous explosion rocked the narrow canyon. Chunks of rock and rubble rained down everywhere.

An arm with a manacle on the wrist landed right beside Asan's foot. Rock dust obliterated the view of everything.

When the dust cleared an incredible sight greeted the three. The boulder was split in two and there was a blackened crater where the keg had been. Prin's bloodied torso, intestines hanging out of it, lay off to the side. His left arm and leg were completely gone and what remained of his corpse was horrible mangled. His right eyeball lay against what was left of his face.

The three men looked at the sight in awe.

"How much can you bring on your next voyage here?" asked Bahomet.

Chapter Fifty-One

Astaran was sitting in Baragin's office. He had made a rare trip to Selvenhall. Damagal had reported Baragin's comments to him and he felt it was time he and Baragin had a frank conversation.

"I understand you feel that the Laguntzaileas are not doing their jobs, and that I in particular have been remiss in protecting the kingdom," said Astaran, holding his dragon staff.

"I said what I said in great anger. But I do not regret saying it, Astaran. Duke Robagrin is talking to himself in a garret in Elberon Castle. Elomir committed suicide. And Bahomet's Karuppsertais stole Viscount Robduran out from under your very nose. Am I wrong to think that the Laguntzaileas are not doing what they are supposed to be doing? Protecting us from foreign wizards?" asked Baragin.

"Yes, you are wrong, Baragin," said Astaran firmly.

"How can you…?" began Baragin.

"Silence!" said Astaran in loud voice.

The candles in the wall sconces flickered and the room darkened noticeably as Astaran lifted his dragon staff slightly.

"Now you will listen, King Baragin. You are a young ruler and still have much to learn about statecraft. Your opponent Bahomet is far more experienced as a leader, and frankly, he has outsmarted you. He also has the advantage of being a highly trained Laguntzailea and now a full-fledged valikatti. He is a very formidable opponent and you have been underestimating him.

"Bahomet had not used any magic in this kingdom. He knows not to try because he knows the power of the Council of Five and the Staff of Elbron in particular. If he does try, and I don't think he will, the Laguntzaileas will defeat him utterly.

"So why is he succeeding with his ruses? Your Governor Drezzerell has not been effective in keeping Bilurian spies and Karuppsertai saboteurs out of Prene. That does not take magic. It takes good intelligence. And it is your job—your job—to ensure whoever is governing Prene is up to the task. Why have you not replaced him?

"As for the kidnapping. You fell for his Dalanbur Island diversion. I'm sure you will find that the 'intelligence' Erenbil collected was fed intentionally to his informants.

"You assumed he did not know about the existence of Robduran when obviously he did. Why? Because his spies were effective, and your counter-spy intelligence was not. He deceived you most thoroughly with Ambassador Oban's well-acted pleas for maintenance of the marriage so he could produce an heir. Bahomet already knew he had one, so it was simply a performance for the High Court—and for you. In fact, he manipulated the dissolution request in the first place with his letter to Elomir knowing that she would have to attend the High Court in person, knowing full well she would not bring Robduran there. Quite a brilliant move.

"Duke Robagrin did not ask for my help. I would certainly have provided a spell of protection for his household had he asked. But he did not. He was overconfident and so were you. Bahomet even manipulated the High Court so the kidnapping could be undertaken on a night when there was no moon. His strategy was thorough, and his execution was meticulous.

"There was no 'magic' in any of this, Baragin. Just clever planning and very efficient espionage. And now Robduran is in Tricanmallokan and we both know he will not be coming back. Elomir and Robagrin chose to deceive the High Court about Robduran, so there will be no help from them. It is not unlike the situation with you when you were the legal ward of Bahomet on the run in this very palace when he was Regent of Evenshorn. I had to recommend to Robagrin that he turn you over to Bahomet. The law is on his side—again. He will just laugh at you if you attempt any diplomatic efforts to have Robduran returned here.

"My job is to do what I am doing now, and that is to advise you. You need to ask yourself, what intentions does Bahomet have now that he has almost everything—the power of a valikatti, his own kingdom, and now an heir to his own throne? What does he want, how could he possibly accomplish those goals, and how can you defend against whatever strategy he might employ? You must think smarter, and you must govern smarter." Astaran paused.

Baragin slumped in his chair, overwhelmed by the undisputed logic of Astaran's arguments.

"You do have one major advantage—Amathea. She has never been wrong or failed to warn you about real danger to you personally. I heard she foresaw the murder attempt on you in Braddenlocks.

"She has foreseen your crown on Bahomet's head—again. I think it's obvious he is not going to stop at Biluria. He wants it all. He wants Zutheria. And now he thinks he has the perfect rationale in the person of Robduran, a legitimate scion of Zuth, to take Zutheria. If I were him, I would find a way to eliminate you, put Robduran on the throne and have himself as regent.

"So how will you stop that? You have Amathea and you have Damagal's protection amulet. But it is not the Laguntzaileas' job, or my job, to govern Zutheria for you. If you wish to keep the Crown of Zuth on your own head, you will need to take drastic action.

"Now I and the other Laguntzaileas will do everything in our power to prevent Bahomet from using magic to accomplish these goals. It is your job to use all the powers of statecraft to keep your kingdom safe from Bahomet's non-magical strategies. You have good advisors in Berenfromm, Berendell and Trillabon. Use them, brainstorm. And for Zuth's sake, improve your counter-spy network," concluded Astaran.

CHAPTER FIFTY–TWO

Joya sat astride her horse, bow in hand. She was waiting her turn to shoot at the target while riding at a full gallop. The Gotkurgan word for target was maksat. She had done well at almost everything else Booshchoo had thrown at them: hand-to-hand combat with battle-axe and dagger, regular archery, horsemanship, field survival tactics, and bare-handed wrestling.

She and Kashkara often sparred as they were close in size and weight. Sometimes she won and sometimes Kashkara got the pin. They had a grudging respect for one another, but Kashkara did not fail to remind her who was the head girl of the jana oyinsi.

Joya wished she had Swiftfoot, her own horse. The horse she had brought from Zutheria had gone lame, and the one the Gotkurgans had provided her with was neither fast nor nimble on its feet. And it was a hand too small for her taste. Normally a jana oyinsi's family would provide their horse.

The saddle was a tattered leftover of Booshchoo's. When her horse had gone lame, they had taken her saddle as payment for the replacement horse. Her beautifully tooled Gotkurgan saddle was still back in Preneport.

Archery from horseback was the hardest thing she had ever done. As she waited her turn, she saw a group of Khokhgui ride up. They were all wearing the conical cap and one-breasted leather cuirass of the Khokhguis. Mongomaa Oyunchumai was at their head. It was clear she had come to watch the practice session.

Booshchoo rode up to her and the two talked briefly. She rode back to the jana oyinsi.

"The mongomaa wants to watch you. But first the Khokhguis will show you how it should be done," said Booshchoo.

The mongomaa nodded to the lead Khokhgui, and the group fitted an arrow to their horn bows. Then the whole line broke into a gallop. As they neared the maksat, one after another they let their arrows fly. Every one hit the target.

They stopped on the ridge just past the maksat and wheeled their horses. The lead Khokhgui shouted something at Booshchoo, who directed one of the girls to turn the maksat ninety degrees. On their return gallop, they rode past the maksat and fired at it backwards. Joya had never seen this done before, although she had heard Booshchoo talk of it. It was a rearguard strategy for covering the retreat of the main force, she had said. Only one of the Khokhguis missed the target.

The Khokhguis rode up to Oyunchumai, who dismissed them but stayed behind to watch.

The three girls ahead of Joya took their turn at the maksat. Two of them missed. Booshchoo was surprisingly patient with them. She knew what a difficult skill archery from horseback was to master. She nodded at Joya, who already had her arrow notched.

She kicked her horse into a gallop and let her arrow fly when she came opposite the maksat. It just caught the upper edge of the target. It was only the second time she had hit it, but she was happy Oyunchumai was there to see it.

The girls finished their turns and Booshchoo ordered them to rest their horses.

Oyunchumai dismounted and had the girls sit down in a semicircle in front of her.

"Booshchoo has done a good job with you. But you still have a long way to go. If you complete your initiation successfully, you will be a junior Khokhgui for two years. If you show promise, you may get to lead your own squad.

"As you know, your time with the Khokhgui is seven years. You cannot marry. And when you finish, many of the men will already be married. If you do not think you can do this, now is the time to leave. Because next week is your final test, your initiation ordeal, your bastama.

"This is why I have come to talk to you today. The Khokhgui bastama is a hard thing. It is where you prove that you have what it takes to become a Khokhgui. All of these skills you have been learning are important. But they are not as important as what is in here and what is in here."

Oyunchumai pointed first to the side of her head, then put her fist over her heart.

"You will go out to the Undurus Mountains for three days. It is dangerous there—bears, wolves, snow leopards—and Zerdagans. If they find you there, they will kill you, because they hate the Khokhguis even worse than the Gotkurgan men. Their kezoys are on the other side of the mountains, but sometimes they come to our side and steal our game.

"You must be smart and know how to survive. You will not take any food with you. You will find your own food or go hungry. This is how you will prove you are worthy to be a Khokhgui."

Oyunchumai paused.

"Look at your seykas karinda, your battle sister," said Oyunchumai.

Joya looked at Aruzhan. Booshchoo had drummed into them that they must have each other's back, especially their 'battle sister'. The Khokhguis placed a high value on the bond between seykas karindas. They slept together, ate together, practiced together, did chore time together, washed together, even went to the latrine together. They often found that their monthly flows came on at the same time. They were expected to fight together, stay with each other if one was wounded, and if necessary, sacrifice their lives to save their battle sister.

Joya had bonded closely with Aruzhan. They were both outsiders, with Aruzhan being half Mythrycian and half Zutherian. She had been an excellent language teacher and Joya was fairly fluent now in both Gotkurgan and Mythrycian. Aruzhan loved to tease, but she had such an infectious laugh it was hard for Joya to stay angry at her. Now they were going on the bastama together.

"Now I will teach you the Khokhgui battle song. The men have their own song and we have ours," said Oyunchumai.

She had a low voice, but it sounded very pleasing to Joya's ear.

By the waters of Terishkhan
Where we set our kezoys
The hearts of the Khokhgui
Are the hearts of Gotkurga

Our axes are sharp
Our arrows never miss
Our seykas karindas
Never fear the dark foe
Our seykas karindas
Never fear the dark foe

The children look to us
The old women, too
We guard all the mothers
We guard elders, too

Our axes are sharp
Our arrows never miss
Our seykas karindas
Never fear the dark foe
Our seykas karindas
Never fear the dark foe

By the waters of Terishkhan
Where we set our kezoys
The hearts of the Khokhgui
Are the hearts of Gotkurga

She sang it over several times until all the jana oyinsi could sing it by heart.

Then Oyunchumai stood.

"Your mongomaa is proud of you jana oyinsi. When I see you next, I will present you with your Khokhgui benbay."

She held the red and black Khokhgui breast strap over her head.

"When you are on the bastama, shivering, hungry, maybe afraid, remember—this is what you want. The Khokhgui benbay!"

Then Oyunchumai led them in the Khokhgui battle cry, which Joya knew meant Khokhgui Victory!: "Khokhgui Jenis! Khokhgui Jenis! Khokhgui Jenis!"

As Joya and Aruzhan watched the mongomaa ride away, Aruzhan said, "I hope I make it through the bastama."

Joya put her arm around her.

"You're my seykas karinda. We'll make it through together."

CHAPTER FIFTY-THREE

Genneset stepped onto the dock at Preneport from the ship he had booked passage on. He wanted to see his brothers and his sister, but more importantly, he wanted to see Joya. He had had a message from Pharigon in Gragnarak that Joya was doing well and was nearing the end of her four-month training period. He also said her horse had gone lame and the one the Gotkurgans had given her was a sorry replacement. Genneset had come to Preneport to arrange to bring Swiftfoot to Mythrycia.

Genneset had talked it over with Germilda. The Prenadon Inn was doing well. Germilda, Umbraset and Bobbingran would take care of business while he made the trip.

"You give that wild girl a great big hug from her momma," Germilda had said, bidding him farewell. "And give her this, to remind her of home."

She handed him the glass snow globe that Genneset had given her so many years ago. It was her most treasured possession, a sentimental reminder of her childhood.

"But honeybee, it could break," protested Genneset.

"Hush, husband. Just wrap it up inside a sock and put it in the bottom of your pack. I know my girl. She will be overjoyed to see it," insisted Germilda.

Genneset looked up at the town sign at the end of the wharf. It said, 'Preneport', but someone had scratched 'Blessingport' under it with a knife point. Genneset sighed and shook his head.

"Genneset! Hey! Genneset!" shouted a voice.

Genneset turned around and saw Ibbingrin standing on the front porch of the harbourmaster's office.

"Ibbingrin! You old sea dog. I see you're adjusting well to an office than doesn't roll and pitch," said Genneset clapping him on the back.

"Well, the governor's appointment took me by surprise, but frankly, I'm happy for it. I love the sea, but she's a hard way to make a living. I'm not sure this is easier, though. Some of those fishermen give me a hard time. But most respect that I've been where they've been. And..." he paused looking around. "...I don't shake them down for extras like the last harbourmaster did. You wouldn't believe what that rascal Futt was up to when he ran the show," said Ibbingrin.

"Oh, I know, I know. I used to hear them complain about Futt when I ran the Silver Dolphin," said Genneset.

Ibbingrin stopped and sadly shook his head.

"It was a sad day for this town when Futt put a torch to the Dolphin. Said he didn't want anybody enjoying a drink over his son's blood. But I guess he made some pretty rash statements in the courtroom that got the king's dander up. Cost him his job. And people are still getting used to calling this place Preneport," said Ibbingrin.

"Yeah. I saw the sign. You should get that fixed, Harbourmaster," said Genneset.

Ibbingrin laughed.

"You thirsty? The old Waldenflower Inn is still standing."

"Thanks, but I've got to get up to my sister's place. I'm actually heading to Mythrycia to see my girl. She needs her horse," said Genneset.

"Mythrycia! Great Zuth, that's too far from the ocean for me. Well, luck and speed, old friend," said Ibbingrin.

Genneset waved goodbye and started the walk to Amathea's place on the edge of town, Blood Hammer swinging with each step. He came up to the space where the Silver Dolphin had been. He stopped for a moment looking at the pile of burnt scraps someone had dumped into a corner of the lot, thinking of the happy times he'd had there. It was obvious that a new building was going up but only the foundation was in.

He stopped across the street from his old house, reminiscing. Two tow-headed children were playing on the stoop and a woman he didn't recognize came out to call them in for lunch. She smiled at him, wiping her hands on her apron. He and Germilda had decided to sell the place after they acquired the Prenadon Inn. He had never liked that house much anyway.

Genneset continued up the road until he was opposite his brothers' tinworks factory. He saw Timbraset through the window, talking to a worker.

He spotted Genneset and rushed out to give him a big bear hug.

"Great Zuth, you're a sight for sore eyes. We didn't know you were coming. Will you stay with us now that somebody else is living in your house?" asked Timbraset.

"Thanks, but no. I need to stay with Amathea to see about Joya's horse," said Genneset.

"Fine, fine. We'll pop over for dinner tonight. Tell Thea she'll have extras," said Timbraset.

"Where's Donny?" asked Genneset.

"Oh, you missed him by a couple of days. He had to sail up to the foundry at Pendragon to see about our next shipment of plate. He'll be back next week," said Timbraset.

"Well, that's a shame. I'm anxious to get on the road to Mythrycia. I need to take Joya her horse and saddle," said Genneset.

"I heard from her, you know," said Timbraset excitedly.

"You? How?" asked Genneset.

"She sent a message with Pharigon at the embassy who passed it on," said Timbraset.

"What did it say?" asked Genneset.

"It said she was fine, and she asked if that load of tinware that got waylaid by bandits in Mythrycia could be sold for her friend's dowry. Apparently, her good friend's father was my agent and was bringing her dowry to her. The Gotkurgans got the tinware back, but the bandits got away with the dowry money. Sad story," said Timbaset.

"So what will you do?" asked Genneset.

"Sell the pots off and donate the funds to the poor girl, of course. It's the least I can do for Ulugan. He was a good agent over the years. Besides, it's the first favor my niece has asked of me," said Timbraset with a smile.

"How's the mayor's office?" asked Genneset.

Timbraset's face darkened a little.

"Well, we did need a change around here. Futt and Doroquill had quite the lucrative arrangement between the two of them. I don't think King Baragin knew about all that, but his decision allowed me to do a lot of housecleaning. People appreciate that, but Futt's been a burr under my saddle ever since.

"Doroquill's barely hanging on, especially after his son tried to murder you and the king. That was the talk of the town for weeks, I'll tell you. And I'm rushed off my feet running the tinworks and the mayor's office."

Timbraset paused.

"But I've got a pile of work to finish here, so I'll see you tonight at Thea's," he said, clapping a big hand on Genneset's shoulder.

Genneset continued on his way, past the waldenflower meadows that lined each side of the road. When he got to Amathea's place, he hallooed, but no one answered. He guessed she was probably out gathering herbs somewhere.

He wandered over to the barn. Swiftfoot stuck his head out over the top of the half door and whinnied. Gennesset grabbed a couple of handfuls of tall grass from beside the corral and held it up for Swiftfoot to munch on.

"You up for a long journey, my boy?" he asked rubbing his nose.

Swiftfoot nickered, seeming to agree.

Chapter Fifty–Four

Kaskir Ana Booshchoo and five other Khokhguis stood in front of the twelve jana oyinsi girls. Each had their bow, quivers with the Gotkurgan black and red fletched arrows, their daggers, and a small pack with a rolled blanket and a few essential supplies. None had any food. The other Khokhguis were there to bring their horses back to Birgulyuk. There would be no backing out now.

"We will be back here on the morning of the fourth day. I expect to see all of you here. You will not camp in a group, only with your seykas karinda. Use all the skills I have taught you. Be brave, be strong. Earn your Khokhgui benbay. Khokhgui Jenis! Khokhgui Jenis! Khokhgui Jenis!" shouted Booshchoo with her fist in the air.

The girls watched as Booshchoo and the other Khokhguis rode off with their horses tethered behind.

"Let's go," said Kashkara said to Aylin, her seykas karinda.

The other pairs followed her lead and split off in different directions. Joya and Aruzhan were somewhat at a disadvantage. All the other girls had lived in the area their whole lives and were much more familiar with the mountains. Where to find springs, best areas to hunt for rabbits or ground squirrels, best places for mushrooms and other edible plants—were all better known to them.

"Let's go that way," said Joya pointing to a narrow cleft that seemed to have a pathway to a distant mesa.

They hiked for much of the morning. They had their leather water bottles but knew they would have to find a spring or a stream to make it through the three days.

Joya reached the front edge of the mesa and turned to take in the view while Aruzhan huffed and puffed up the trail below her. It was spectacular. She could see Booshchoo and other Khokhguis in the far distance, heading back to Birgulyuk. The wind tugged at the tips of the tall steppe grass reminding Joy of the waves and swells of the Western Sea. Low lying clouds scudded across the horizon and soon blocked the sun.

"Looks like rain," she said to Aruzhan, who was sitting on a rock catching her breath.

They spent several hours with their bows trying to hit rabbits and ground squirrels, but despite coming close, they hit nothing.

"I'm hungry," said Aruzhan.

Joya said nothing at first.

"Let's find some shelter. Maybe there will be mushrooms or something else as we walk."

They walked further until they came to a low cliff face. They walked along the edge of it until they encountered a shallow cave.

"Check for bears or snow leopards first," said Aruzhan.

Both of them notched an arrow and peered inside. There was a small charred firepit near the mouth of the cave indicating someone had used it in the past, but it was cold.

"Looks empty. It'll do for tonight," said Joya.

Just then she felt a drop of rain on her cheek, then another on her nose.

"Let's get inside. We can look for food tomorrow when it's drier," said Aruzhan.

They spend a hungry night in the cave, huddled together under their blankets for warmth as the rainstorm blew and raged past the mouth of the cave. They wondered how the other jana oyinsis were faring.

The next morning saw the end of the rain as the girls stretched from their uncomfortable night in the cave. They found a pool of rainwater in one of the rocky areas next to the cave and refilled their water bottles.

They spent the rest of the morning hunting. Aruzhan managed to skewer a ground squirrel with an arrow and jumped up and down with excitement. Joya missed at a rabbit but did find some wild onions. They threw them both in the tin pot they'd brought. Aruzhan started a fire with their flint sparker and tinder, and they enjoyed their meager meal. It wasn't enough, though, and both were still hungry.

On the third day, they decided to move further into the mountains to see if they could find more game to shoot at. They saw some wild goats far up the cliff side and a silver fox, but that was all.

As they moved closer to the far end of the mesa, they heard a high-pitched shriek, then another. They exchanged worried glances and broke into a run. The end of the mesa had a panoramic view of a large meadow with a small pond at the end of it. The pond was edged by a copse of trees on one end and a single large tree at the other.

There were two girls, naked in the pond. One was almost fully submerged while the other was up to her knees. The one further in was splashing the other, who was the source of the shrieks. Their clothes and weapons were hanging on the branches of the lone tree.

"It's Inzhu and Bergara," whispered Aruzhan.

Joya and Arurzhan looked at each other, mischievous smiles forming in the corners of their mouths.

"Let's steal their clothes!" they said simultaneously.

Inzhu was an incorrigible practical joker. Both Joya and Aruzhan had been victims of her pranks, although she liked to pick on Joya most. The opportunity for payback was irresistible.

"Nooshta, I think I see a way down," said Aruzhan, as she started to pick her way down a narrow cleft in the rock face of the mesa.

Joya followed and soon they were at the bottom. They paused wondering how they would get to the tree without being seen. Inzhu and Bergara were still splashing and screeching.

"We'll have to belly crawl," said Joya.

They both began to crawl as fast as they could through the tall grass of the meadow.

Suddenly, they both heard a horse whinny. Joya pulled her hat off and poked up her head.

"Men on horses. Six of them. One has a big brown bird in front of his saddle," said Joya.

Aruzhan's eyes grew wide, and a look of intense fear spread over her face.

"Zerdagans. Eagle hunters," she whispered.

"Eagle hunters?" asked Joya.

"They hunt the mountain goats with trained golden eagles. Oh, Noostha, I'm so frightened! What will they do to Inzhu and Bergara?" asked Aruzhan, eyes wide with fear.

Joya poked her head up again. Her blonde hair blended in perfectly with the long steppe grass. Just then, Bergara spotted the Zerdagans and began to scream hysterically. Inzhu made a sprint for her bow leaning against the tree. She just managed to notch an arrow and was drawing back the string, yelling at Bergara to grab her bow. Before she could loose, an arrow pierced her mouth and came out the back of her neck, the yellow and black fletching of the Zerdagans against her lips. She collapsed to the ground.

Bergara screamed in terror and started running across the meadow. One of the horsemen chased her down and grabbed her around the waist at a gallop. He tossed her kicking and screaming across his saddle and wheeled his horse back to the others.

Aruzhan was covering her ears with her hands against Bergara's screams, moaning in fear. Joya looked up again. The men had Bergara's hands tied around the tree. One of them was loosening the drawstring on his pants.

"Aruzhan! Aruzhan!" Joya hissed.

She slapped her face hard.

"Aruzhan. We have to stop them. We can't let them do that to Bergara!" said Joya in a strangled whisper.

"Nooshta, what can we do? There are six of them. They will kill us, too," said Aruzhan desperately.

"Then we'll take as many as we can with us. Notch an arrow," ordered Joya.

Aruzhan looked at her, frozen.

"Notch an arrow!" insisted Joya.

One man was thrusting hard against Bergara while the others laughed at her screams.

"I'll take the one on Bergara, you take the one next to him. When I say 'three'. Look at me! When I say 'three'," said Joya.

Aruzhan nodded, eyes wide.

"One, two, three!"

Both girls stood, drew their bow strings and let fly. Joya's arrow struck the man behind Bergara in the centre of his back, while Aruzhan's hit the other man's shoulder.

"Gotkurgans!" one shouted, seeing the red and black arrow feathers.

They left Bergara sobbing against the tree and looked for cover.

"Horses next!" yelled Joya.

They loosed two more arrows, both hitting a horse. All six stampeded, two with arrows sticking out of them, and one with an eagle bouncing and flapping on the saddle it was tethered to.

The four men yelled and pointed and began a chase towards Joya and Aruzhan. The wounded man went after the horses.

"Run! Back towards the mesa!" yelled Joya.

The two broke into a sprint with the four men in hot pursuit. Two of their pursuers saw their intent and broke off to one side to cut them off.

They reached the mesa, but the other two men were closing in on the trail they had descended on. The second duo yelled and waved directions with their arms.

"We're trapped! We're trapped!" said a panicked Aruzhan.

Joya pulled her in behind a large boulder and both crouched low. The voices were getting closer. Then Joya remembered something in her desperation. She opened her side pouch and pulled out the smaller one which contained Amathea's spider blanket. She draped it over the two of them. Aruzhan's eyes opened wide in wonder, but Joya signalled silence.

They heard footsteps and voices. Zerdagan was a completely different language to Gotkurgan so they could not understand a word. It was clear from their tone that they were confused about the girls' sudden disappearance. Joya heard three voices moving away, but one continued to make noises close by.

He stepped closer. It was obvious he was about to walk right into where they were crouched. Joya pulled out her dagger. Two leather clad feet stood right beside the edge of the spider blanket. He turned so that Joya could see his heels, then started to step backwards.

Joya reached out from under the blanket and slashed his heel tendon. He screamed in pain and fell to the ground. Joya leapt up from under the blanket and made an attempt to stab him in the chest.

He grabbed her wrist and held her off. Both struggled desperately, but with his superior weight and strength he rolled on top of Joya. With his free hand he reached for his own dagger. Joya grabbed his wrist, but her strength was not enough to resist. She dropped her own dagger and held the man's wrist with both hands. The point inched closely and closer to her neck. Suddenly he collapsed with a grunt on top of Joya.

Joya looked up and saw Aruzhan breathing heavily. The rock she had used to crush the Zerdagan's skull lay beside Joya, blood trickling from it.

"Get him off me!" shouted Joya.

They heard three men's voices shouting and moving closer. Joya notched another arrow and waited for the men to round the bluff face. She drilled the one in the lead through the chest. The other two stopped and ducked. When they saw that Joya and Aruzhan had two more arrows notched, they turned and ran back to their wounded hunting mate.

Joya and Aruzhan looked at each other. Joya had the Zerdagan's blood all over her face and neck.

"Khokhgui Jenis! Khokhgui Jenis! Khokhgui Jenis!" yelled Joya, raising her horn bow over her head.

When they got back to Bergara, Aylin and Kashkara were there comforting her. The remaining Zerdagans had all run off.

"We heard the screams and came running," said Aylin.

"You have blood all over you, Nooshta. Are you wounded?" asked Kashkara.

"Not mine. Aruzhan crushed the Zerdagan's head with a rock. I got two more with my bow. Aruzhan wounded another. I don't think they'll be back.

Kashkara raised her eyebrows in respect.

"Let's wrap Inzhu's body. We'll camp here tonight," said Kashkara.

CHAPTER FIFTY-FIVE

"**B**ah-bah! Bah-Bah! Look! Zuzu is chasing the ball!" cried Robduran.

Bahomet looked down into the centre garden from his second story office in the myanpur's aranmanai. He had gotten Robduran a small brown and white lapdog puppy. It was a delightful creature and Robduran fell in love with it immediately. They played together constantly and Zuzu even slept in the same bed.

Robduran had taken to calling him 'Bah-bah'. He had heard Bilanguree using that term of affection for him from when Bahomet was a child. Robduran would not call him 'Poppa' as he insisted that title was only for the duke, his grandfather.

Bahomet rather liked to hear him use 'Bah-bah'. Becoming an unexpected father to a boy had been the most wonderful thing that had ever happened to him. It had aroused feelings of tenderness inside him that he did not know existed. He was always on his best behaviour around Robduran. He seemed to be warming up to his 'Bah-bah'.

It helped that Robduran's old housekeeper, Gella, was in Tricanmallokan helping to look after Robduran. After Robduran's kidnapping and the duke's move to Elberon, she was at a loss. She had moved to her daughter's place in Murranenmouth, a cramped two room fisherman's shack near the waterfront. Her son-in-law was a struggling deckhand, eking a living out on someone else's boat.

She had been in Murranenmouth for a fortnight when a Bilurian approached her while she was outside tending to some flowers in the front yard. It was Ambassador Oban. He asked her if she would be interested in continuing to care for little Robduran.

At first, she was very suspicious. But Oban was skilled in the arts of persuasion. He unrolled an official looking document.

"What's this?" Gella had asked.

"It's the ownership document. For a new fishing boat, 15 elbow spans long. Your son-in-law's. It's at the wharf in Iblingport. And this...." he said dropping a large leather sack on the table with a metallic clink, "should be enough for a much better house for your daughter. I know you miss little Robduran and he misses you desperately. He asks for you all the time. Won't you come?" asked Oban.

She came, and Robduran was absolutely overjoyed. Gella had been the primary one to care for him at the Elberon villa. Elomir's emotional condition had left her withdrawn much of the time, barely able to manage the tasks of fulltime motherhood. Robduran missed his grandfather, but rarely asked about his mother anymore.

In addition, Bilanguree was a doting great-aunt, fussing and spoiling him at every turn. Bahomet had secured an excellent teacher for Robduran as well as a Bilurian playmate close in age. He was the son of the assistant head chamberlain. Robduran was soon jabbering away in Bilurian, learning the language quickly as the young often do. Gella continued to speak in Zutherian with him, though.

Robduran was destined for greatness and Bahomet was determined to see it happen. It had to be the throne of Zutheria, though. One of the characteristics of valikattis, as it was with Laguntzaileas, was very long life. Bahomet knew he would most likely outlive Robduran as the ruler of Biluria. But Robduran had every right to the throne of Zuth and Bahomet was going to make sure he got it.

He smiled and waved at Robduran as he chased the barking puppy around the garden. Then he turned and looked back at the Karuppsertai leader, Borooneeloman Dran.

"He seems very happy here, Karpukkai. You are turning into a sentimental father—Bah-bah," said Dran with a smile.

Bahomet returned the smile, but then turned serious.

"The crown of Zuth is his, by right of birth. No one can deny that. But that cannot happen as long as Baragin sits in Selvenhall. And not as long as Astaran holds the staff of Elbron," said Bahomet.

"I think you've already proven Baragin is no match for you, even if he does have Damagal's protection amulet around his neck and that clear-seeing wife of his," said Dran.

"Pfft. Baragin. It's not him that robs my sleep. It's Astaran. He knows that the Council of Five and the staff of Elbron keep them all safe. And he knows I know it. I must find a way to destroy him. And I think I've found it," said Bahomet.

"But you can't defeat him with magic, not when he holds the staff of Elbron," said Dran.

"No. But we've already seen that it doesn't take magic to defeat a more powerful valikatti," said Bahomet.

Dran eyed him intently.

"Celebration powder?" he asked.

Bahomet smiled.

"There will be a lot of celebration powder in Astaran's future. I just need to figure out how to make it happen."

CHAPTER FIFTY-SIX

The Khokhgui jana oyinsi kezoy was crowded. Ten girls stood in a line at attention. All of the Khokhgui of Birgulyuk lined the edges of the kezoy in a circle in full battle gear. Mongomaa Oyunchumai and Kaskir Ana Booshchoo stood in front of the girls. Booshchoo had a stack of Khokhgui red and black benbays in her arms.

Bergara was not there. She was severely traumatized by the death of Inzhu and her rape. 'Battle shock', Booshchoo had said. She was in her parents' kezoy and no one had seen her for days.

The aklach had sent four squads of Gotkurgan warriors under Sogis Bassisi Alinur to the Undurus Mountains to see if any other Zerdagan eagle hunters were poaching on the Gotkurgan side of the mountains. They didn't find any but did locate the three dead Zerdagans Nooshta and Aruzhan had dispatched. They threw them in a pile and burned them. All of the Gotkurgans urinated on them first.

Oyunchumai scanned the group.

"Today is a sad day. But it is also a proud day. We lost Inzhu, a brave girl, one who would have received her benbay this day. Tomorrow, we will sing our Khokhgui song at her funeral.

"Bergara is not here either. But she is still alive. We still have her with us, and she is with her family. She is with her family because of the bravery and courage of two jana oyinsis."

Oyunchumai paused and looked at both Joya and Aruzhan, then continued.

"It will take time for her to heal. And when she heals, her benbay will be here for her.

"Now we can be proud. All of you passed your initiation. Are you ready to receive your benbays?" asked Oyunchumai.

"Eeyah, Mongomaa!" they all yelled

Oyunchumai nodded to Booshchoo.

"Jana oyinsi! Shirts off! Shout 'Khokhgui Jenis' when you receive your benbay," she ordered.

All the girls doffed their shirts and threw them at their feet. Their off-white jana oyinsi benbays were somewhat tattered and soiled from their time on the mountain.

"Khokhgui! Jana oyinsi benbays!" ordered Booshchoo.

Ten senior Khokhguis stepped forward behind the girls, loosened their benbays and unwrapped them. The girls stood at attention, bare to the waist.

"Jana oyinsi! Eyes front! Chins up! Hands out!" yelled Booshchoo.

She handed her stack of benbays to another Khokhgui as the girls put their hands out in front of them, palms up, elbows tucked.

Booshchoo took one benbay from the stack and handed it to the mongomaa. Oyunchumai started with Kashkara. She placed the red and black benbay in her outstretched palms, looked her in the eye and said,

"Welcome, seykas karinda Kashkara. You are now a Khokhgui."

"Khokhgui Jenis!" shouted Kashkara.

Then Oyunchumai moved to Aylin and repeated the rite of Khokhgui membership. When Oyunchumai got to Aruzhan, she placed the benbay in her hands. As she said, 'Welcome, seykas karinda Aruzhan' she put a gnarled finger on the edge of the benbay and smiled. A black 'X' was stitched on the edge of the red section. Aruzhan knew that meant a battle honour for killing the enemy. Booshchoo's benbay had seven X's on it.

Joya was next. Oyunchumai placed the benbay in her outstretched palms.

"Welcome, seykas karinda Nooshtal."

Her finger pointed to two X's.

"You are now a Khokhgui," said Oyunchumai.

"Khokhgui Jenis!" shouted Joya at the top of her lungs, holding her benbay high over her head.

"Khokhguis! About face!" ordered Booshchoo.

All the girls turned around to face the Khokhguis standing behind them. The Khokhguis carefully wrapped the distinctive red and black benbays across the girls' right breasts, securing it snugly in the rear with their special tuck.

"Khokhguis! About face!" shouted Booshchoo as the ten senior Khokhguis stepped back.

Oyunchumai walked to the centre of the kezoy, her face very serious.

"The benbay you now wear is your most precious possession. It is the sign of the Khokhgui. But it is not only to protect your breast. There may come a time when you will use it for benbay honour death—if you are too badly wounded to carry on, or to keep from dying dishonourably at the hands of the enemy.

You will know when the time is right. "Benbay honour death is the right of every Khokhgui. It is a way to die with honour. Your seykas karinda must help you if you cannot do it. You will use it to stop your breathing, and your last breath you will give to the benbay. Death in battle, benbay honour death, or honourable completion of your seven years of service—that is how you will stop being a Khokhgui, with honour.

"But hear me well, Khokhguis, seykas karindas. If you ever—ever—bring dishonour to the Khokhguis—cowardice in battle, betrayal, theft, abandoning your post, murder—your benbay will take your last breath. There is no worse fate for a Khokhgui than benbay dishonour death. None."

Oyunchumai walked in front of each Khokhgui, stopped in front of them, and looked them directly in the eyes. She turned and walked to the centre of the kezoy, and in a voice louder than they had ever heard her use before, she screamed, "Do you understand me, Khokhguis?"

"Eeyah, Mongomaa!" they all screamed in response.

"Kaskir Ana Booshchoo, carry on," said Oyunchumai.

"Khokhguis, shirts on!" directed Booshchoo.

They all re-donned their shirts and stood at attention.

"Khokhguis! Battle armor, apron!" yelled Booshchoo.

The ten senior Khokhguis each took a metal embossed apron and secured it around the waists of their respective girls. The girls' personal daggers were already attached to the belts. When they were done, they stepped back and stood at attention.

"Khokhguis! Battle armor, cuirass!" ordered Booshchoo.

The senior Khokhguis took the leather one-breasted cuirass of the Khokhgui and draped them over the girls' heads. They fastened the four side buckles and stepped back again.

Joya looked down briefly at hers, the right side flat against her benbay-tied breast. It was made of two layers of boiled leather from the thickest part of the Undurus Mountains wild ox. It could withstand a sabre slash and would stop an arrow from penetrating too deeply.

"Khokhgui hat!" yelled Booshchoo.

The senior Khokhguis placed the conical leather cap of their unit on the heads of each girl. It had the small battle axe with the pyramid-shaped hammer that only the Khokhguis used embroidered on it.

The ten girls all stood at attention. Aruzhan could not contain a grin.

Oyunchumai surveyed the group.

"Seykas karindas. You have your bows, and you have your daggers. Now you will receive your battle axe, the one only Khokhguis carry. Do what I do when you receive it."

She nodded to Booshchoo who motioned with her head to another Khokhgui holding an armful of battle axes. Joya had seen Arsen the blacksmith making them. He had made one with a slightly longer handle on it and gave her a wink and a smile when he handed it to her for sharpening.

Booshchoo handed her the first one. Oyunchumai looked up and raised it over her head. She looked left, then looked right. Then she kissed the blade and presented it to Kashkara, saying, "Defend the honour of the Gotkurgans with this axe." Kashkara mirrored her actions, then slipped the axe into the side loop on her belt. Oyunchumai presented the battle axe to each of the new Khokhguis in turn.

There were two left when Oyunchumai got to Aruzhan. She picked the shorter handled one and presented it to her.

Booshchoo handed the mongomaa the last one. Oyunchumai looked Joya in the eye as she presented it and said, "Defend the honour of the Gotkurgans and the Zutherians with this axe."

Booshchoo's eyebrows raised at this unexpected change in the ritual but said nothing.

All the girls, and everyone else in the tent, including Booshchoo and Oyunchumai, raised their battle axes over their heads and screamed, "Khokhgui Jenis! Khokhgui Jenis! Khokhgui Jenis!"

Chapter Fifty-Seven

Avocatim Durrenbar laid a document on Chancellor Berenfromm's desk. Baragin and Berendell were also in the room.

"It's the decision from the High Court. They've declared the duke unfit to handle his own affairs. I am his official trustee as his avocatim," said Durrenbar.

"What's his situation currently?" asked Baragin.

"He is being cared for at Elberon. His old chamberlain Filden handles most things, along with a couple of housekeepers. Astaran is a most gracious host as you might expect. Robagrin rambles a lot, asking for Elomir to forgive him and calling for Robduran. It's very tragic," said Durrenbar shaking his head and clicking his tongue.

"His estate near Elberon is going to ruin. But that's not our main concern. Our main concern is that once the duke passes, Robduran will inherit it. It gives him a legal claim to property inside the kingdom. And we all know he would be eligible to sit on the throne of Zuth should...."

Berenfromm paused, not wanting to voice an awful possibility.

"He needs to stay in Biluria. Let him inherit Bahomet's crown. We need to sever all ties between him and Zutheria. What are our options, Durrenbar?" asked Baragin.

"As trustee, I have the authority to sell the estate on the duke's behalf. I would hold the proceeds of the sale in trust for Viscount Robduran until he comes of age. When that occurs, I sign over the funds," said Durrenbar, holding up both hands indicating a deal well done.

"Do it. It's not like we're stealing his money. I don't wish him ill, but I do not want that snake of a father of his using that estate as leverage for any claim on this kingdom," said Baragin with determination.

"As you wish, Your Majesty," said Durrenbar with a bow.

When Durrenbar left, Baragin asked Berenfromm, "How are we doing with our counter-Bahomet strategies?"

"Quite well, actually. Ex-Governor Drezzerell is in his retirement villa here in Wreatherin. He was not happy, but completely understands he serves at the king's pleasure. The new governor, Brandenwill, has already rounded up over a dozen confirmed Bilurian operatives. Their interrogations are sure to lead to more. We are going to break Bahomet's intelligence sources," said Berenfromm.

"What about Trillabon's special unit?" asked Baragin.

"As you requested, General Trillabon has selected an elite group of highly skilled soldiers to act as a counterfoil to the Karuppsertai. One of the operatives we captured was a member. We told him we'd release him at the border and let it be known that his information on his colleagues was most helpful. He knew of course, that would mean a long and painful death for him. So he was persuaded to stay and act as a consultant to our new unit," said Berenfromm.

"Who commands it?" asked Baragin.

"Major Gryn. You might recall him as Captain Gryn from when I first met you at Drabbadentown. He was my commander back in my young officer days," interrupted Berendell.

"Does this new unit have a name?" asked Baragin.

"Trillabon let Gryn name it. He calls them the BLK Guards officially, and the Black Guards informally," said Berenfromm.

"BLK?" asked Baragin.

"I believe it stands for 'Black Leopard Killers', sir," said Berenfromm.

Baragin and Berendell exchanged a smile.

"Good. He is to report to you once a week, Berendell. If we even get a sniff of any Karuppsertais operating anywhere in Zutheria, I want them taken out. Tell Trillabon that Gryn gets whatever he needs. If he isn't sure, pass on the request to me directly through Berendell," said Baragin.

He paused.

"Black Leopard Killers. Berendell, next time you talk to Gryn tell him to pay a visit to my goldsmith. I want a distinctive badge for them. Bahomet isn't going to be the only one with a crack unit."

The Iblingport merchant Donbidden was finally able to secure the rights to operate the Bilurian-Zutherian trading company in Tricanmallokan. The tipping point was a substantial "gift" to the governor of Tricanmallokan province. Donbidden had been fretting over the considerable size of the expected "gift", but one of his senior partners, Grandabin, upped his investment in the firm allowing Donbidden to satisfy the governor's request.

Grandabin's mother had said, "Your uncle Filden has no children, but he says the duke has been quite generous over the years, so he wanted to help you out. He also wanted you to know that as a favour to him, he'd like you to put in a bid on Duke Robagrin's estate. He actually wants to be appointed the caretaker there if you are the successful bidder, as he thinks it would be a wonderful retirement home for him when the duke eventually passes. He knows it will be expensive, but he will supply what is necessary. Obviously, it would be awkward if it was known he was behind the bid, so he asks for your discretion. Isn't he a wonderful uncle, Grandabin?"

Three months later, Durrenbar put his avocatim's stamp on the bill of sale and deed for Duke Robagrin's Elberon villa.

"I will file this with the Land Registry in Wreatherin, Grandabin, sir. I wish you well in your retirement home. It really is a wonderful piece of property.

A pigeon landed in the Grand Vizier Fayan's dovecote. The note said, "Property secured. Filden."

Chapter Fifty-Eight

Genneset wasn't much of a horseman, but he had ridden Swiftfoot as far as Brobabil. He stayed the night with his old friend Linkman Ganabir the bookseller. Ganabir showed him the picture of the Khokhgui warrior in the Mythrycian history book that he had also shown to Joya.

"Great Zuth, I hope she doesn't look like that when I see her," commented Genneset.

The next morning Genneset paid a courtesy visit to Dashgran Zerribil of the Andragon Dwarves. Zerribil received him graciously and enquired about the purpose of his journey.

"Well, sir, I'm off to visit my daughter Joya in Mythrycia. She has that banishment to serve there. She is actually spending her time with another tribe, the Gotkurgans, learning the ways of their female warriors," commented Genneset.

Zerribil raised his bushy white eyebrows a notch. Just another odd quirk about Zutherians, allowing their daughters to do military service. But he said nothing about that.

"I see you have a very fine horse there, Genneset," said Zerribil.

"Yes, my daughter's. She's completed her training period with the Khokhguis, but I heard she didn't have a good horse. So I'm bringing her the one the king gifted her, all the way from Preneport. But I tell you, I'm not much of a rider. I'd rather be walking or in a cart," he said.

Zerribil gave a low, "Hmmmmm", then added, "I think I may be able to help with that. Perhaps a dwarf cart with a mine pony to pull it. They don't move fast, but they are very strong. You can just tether your daughter's horse to the rear."

"Oh, I appreciate your kind offer, but I don't actually have the funds for that, Dashgran," said Genneset.

"Nonsense. We'll call it a loan. You can return it on your way back," said Zerribil, smiling.

Genneset had stopped for the night in Tribadon, staying at the home of Linkman Baskar, the one-eared blacksmith.

"Great Zuth, Genneset. You're not heading to Mythrycia by yourself, are you? They may take more than just an ear, you know," said Baskar, pulling his hair back to show the scar from Zythramin's dagger.

"I have Blood Hammer. Besides, no one bothers a tinker with a good grinding wheel. Could you set me up?" asked Genneset.

He and Baskar fitted a fine-grained grinding wheel and treadle to the cart. The next morning, Genneset was rolling along the Gemmerhorn Trail towards Dysteria and the Mythrycian border. Swiftfoot plodded along behind.

When he finally got to Gragnarak, Genneset headed straight for the embassy. Ambassador Danstorin received him graciously—he was the king's father-in-law after all—and assigned Captain Pharigon and a small detachment of lancers to accompany him to Birgulyuk.

"You still have that shipment of tinware of my brother's?" asked Genneset.

"Yes. It's in a storage shed. We were just waiting for word from Timbraset to deal with it," said Pharigon.

"Well, he delegated me to handle it. I'm going to set up my grinding cart in the marketplace tomorrow and sell the tinware at the same time. My brother has decided to donate the proceeds to the poor girl who was orphaned by those bandits who robbed and killed his agent Ulugan," said Genneset.

He spent the following day grinding and selling pots and mugs in the main marketplace of Gragnarak. Ambassador Danstorin had assigned an embassy staffer to translate. Genneset liquidated the whole stock by mid-afternoon. He added the funds to a fairly hefty purse Timbraset had given him. He had said the tinware money wasn't nearly enough for a proper dowry for a girl.

———◦◦◦▐◉▌◦◦◦———

Joya and her squad were resting their horses in a small copse of trees near the north pathway to Gragnarak. Their squad leader was Aizat. She had directed Aruzhan to stand guard while the others rested. Two days out of every seven, the Khokhgui had patrol duty around the perimeter of Birgulyuk. Surprise attacks on the Gotkurgans, by anyone, were almost impossible.

Aruzhan gave a low whistle, the signal for intruders approaching.

"Mount up," commanded Aizat. "How many?"

"Five horsemen, soldiers. And a pony cart," said Aruzhan scanning the approaching group.

"Notch arrows. Prepare to surround them on my order," whispered Aizat.

Joya felt a surge of adrenaline. Every day since her initiation had been fairly routine.

Genneset rolled across the broad steppe land trail that ran south to Gotkurga in a small pony cart. Pharigon was riding beside the cart and an escort of four lancers rode ahead of them.

A trooper reined in his horse to speak with Pharigon.

"We've been spotted. We'll be getting company soon. Looks like Khokhguis," he said.

Pharigon and Genneset looked over in the direction of the copse and also saw the knot of mounted guards.

"Nooshta, put an arrow in front of the lead horse," ordered Aizat.

Joya pulled back her bow string and loosed the red and black feathered Gotkurgan arrow. It landed right in front of the lead trooper, whose horse reared and whinnied at the surprise. The trooper got his horse under control with difficulty and the group stopped.

Aizat was about to issue another command, arm in the air, when Genneset suddenly stood up in his cart and started singing in a loud voice:

Too-ra-loo-ra-lay! The tinker's here today!
Bring out your knives, and broken pans
If tinker can't fix 'em, nobody can
Bring out your knives, sharp'ning wheel's here
Too-ra-loo-ra-lay! The tinker's here today!

"Poppa!" screamed Joya.

She slung her bow over her back and kicked her horse into a gallop, flying past an astonished Aizat and Aruzhan.

Chapter Fifty-Nine

Aklach Saaral Chono hosted a welcoming feast for Genneset and Pharigon. Genneset presented him, the Sogis Bassisi Alinur, Mongomaa Oyunchumai, and Kaskir Ana Booshchoo with fine Bilurian curved daggers, honed to a razor's edge. Aklach Chono's had a very ornate gold-plated sheath. He looked it over admiringly.

"A gift from King Baragin of Zutheria," said Genneset.

Joya was doing the translating.

"Your daughter Nooshta is a fierce Khokhgui, Genneset. She already has two X's on her benbay," said Chono.

Joya coughed, and looked a little uncomfortable before she translated.

Genneset wanted to ask what this 'Nooshta' was all about but figured that could wait.

"Two X's? he asked.

"We were attacked by Zerdagans. I had to take down two of them with my bow," said Joya.

Genneset raised his eyebrows. He knew he'd have to get the whole story later when they were alone.

Pharigon looked over at Joya while she was doing the translating. Though her hair was short now, she was still stunning. Aruzhan had talked her into putting on some eye make-up. She was wearing a richly embroidered dark red dress, a gift from the mother of Bergara for saving her life. The bodice had intricate embroidery accentuating her feminine softness beneath it. Apparently, formal feasts were the one place the mongomaa allowed the Khokhguis to go without their benbays.

Joya was on his mind—a lot. The memory of her hand on his thigh as she tucked the note for her uncle in his pocket warmed him every time he thought of it. And her hand in his and the other on his shoulder when they danced the quellel at the Midsummer's Day ball in Wreatherin electrified him. He even fondly remembered the bruises she left on his shoulders from her punches when he teased her.

Joya looked over and caught him staring at her. He quickly shifted his gaze to the aklach who had launched into another speech.

It could be years before he could talk to her father about…About what? She was so prickly she might never even consider him—or any other man for that matter. Pharigon took another sip of his Milredden Pink cider.

Genneset had brought a case with him from Brobabil on the pony cart. The aklach was into his second jug and professing his undying friendship for Zutheria in general and Genneset in particular. The Gotkurgans were fiercely independent, and although they were subject to Mythrycia, they had stayed out of the Mythrycian-Zutherian war years ago. The feast wound to a close and Joya walked her father and Pharigon back to the guest kezoy.

"Oh, I almost forgot. Your uncle got your note. About your friend? He's donated the money from

Ulugan's goods to her dowry. How do I get it to her?" asked Genneset.

"We have chore duty at the blacksmith's tomorrow. She'll be there with me. You'll probably like Arsen. I do all the grinding for him," said Joya.

"Good, good. I'll see you tomorrow then," said Genneset.

He looked over at Pharigon, who had his eye on Joya.

"Pharigon, be a gentleman and walk my daughter back to her tent, will you?" said Genneset.

Pharigon wanted to hug him for that. He ached to talk to Joya alone, but knew she would make that difficult.

"I guess I can report to the king that you're doing well here," said Pharigon as they walked.

Joya glanced over at him. Mixed feelings were roiling inside her. Her experience with the Zerdagans had confirmed everything she felt about men. Yet when she was near Pharigon, someone who had held her with tenderness at the dance at Selvenhall, unfamiliar feelings arose. And she couldn't forget the heat and passion of her dream about him. It annoyed her every time she remembered it. And not.

"It's been hard. The Khokhguis are very tough, and my training master Booshchoo is hard on me. On all of us. But I've learned so much from her. I can hit a target at a gallop now," Joya said.

"Impressive. I knew you could do it. I..." faltered Pharigon.

He paused momentarily, at a loss for words. Joya stayed silent.

"They call you Nooshta. Does that mean something in Gotkurgan?" resumed Pharigon.

"It's short for Nooshtal. It's actually Jalagan for bearcat. Booshchoo thought Joya was too girly and said I had to have a tough name. I picked Noostel, which is the Yakat word for it. Booshchoo wouldn't allow a Yakat name though, so I got the Jalag version," explained Joya.

"Bearcat—seems appropriate," said Pharigon with a smile.

"Watch it! Or I'll give you another bruise," said Joya with mock ferocity.

"Joya, I..." Pharigon grabbed her hand with both of his. They were at Joya's tent.

Joya pulled her hand away.

"Don't. Just don't. I'm..."

She stopped.

"Good night," she said and ducked under the flap of the kezoy.

Pharigon sighed and looked up at the stars. He was standing there when Aruzhan came up, returning from the latrine. She had been in the shadows, watching.

"Captain Pharigon, yes?" she asked.

"Oh, Aruzhan, hello. You weren't at the banquet," said Pharigon.

"No. That's for important people. Nooshta can do the translating now," said Aruzhan.

"Yes. You've obviously been a good teacher," said Pharigon.

Aruzhan smiled. There was an awkward silence.

"Well, I guess I'll be going. Good to see you again. Good night," said Pharigon.

Aruzhan leaned in close and whispered, "She likes you, you know. Don't give up hope."

And she ducked inside the tent.

CHAPTER SIXTY

"**Y**our sister sends her love. And Baragran asks about his auntie every day. Something about wanting another pillow fight?" said Genneset.

Joya laughed gaily.

"He is such a delight. I really miss him. But wait! What about the new one?"

"A girl. Three months old now. Milla, they called her, after her grandmother. But you can't call an adorable little girl Germilda—just doesn't fit," said Genneset.

"Milla. A pretty name for a pretty girl. Tell me everything," Joya said, grabbing her father's hands.

"Well, she's pink. And blonde like her auntie, with blue eyes. Ten fingers, ten toes..." Genneset waned.

"Poppa! I said everything!" demanded Joya.

"What? She's a pink baby girl. I don't know about babies. You'll just have to see for yourself," protested Genneset.

They both grew solemn. Five years banishment was a very long time.

Genneset suddenly remembered something.

"Your momma insisted I bring this," he said, rummaging around in his pack.

He pulled out a wrinkled apple with a large brown spot.

"Oh, here it is! A nice Sweetsap apple," he said teasingly.

Joya slugged him in the shoulder.

"Poppa! I'm not six anymore!"

Genneset sighed.

"I know. But I wish you were…"

He stopped talking as a lump grew in his throat and tears began welling up in his eyes.

"Oh, Poppa. Please don't cry. Look! Now you've made me cry," said Joya, wiping her eyes. She gave him a big hug.

"Now, what did Momma insist you bring?" asked Joya.

Genneset held out a thick woolen sock.

"Poppa! No more teasing. What did she send?" demanded Joya.

Genneset just handed her the sock.

Joya took it, puzzled by the weight of it. She reached in her hand and pulled out her old snow globe.

"My snow globe! My snow globe! Oh, my! Oh, my! Wait until I show Aruzhan. Oh, Poppa!" she said, eyes glowing.

She shook it vigorously, watching the silver and mica flakes inside swirl around the winter scene. Joya looked at Genneset with a delighted grin. She was his little girl again.

Just then Joya heard Aruzhan outside the tent.

"Nooshta? It's time for us to help Arsen," she called through the tent flap.

"Aruzhan! Aruzhan! Look at this! My Poppa brought it from home for me," said Joya excitedly, as she dragged Aruzhan by the hand into the guest kezoy.

Aruzhan looked at it with amazement. They chattered about it for a few moments.

"Did you tell her, poppet? About your uncle's decision?" asked Genneset.

Aruzhan looked puzzled.

"Tell me about what?" she asked.

"I felt so badly for you, Aruzhan—about your father, about having your dowry stolen. So I asked my uncle if the money from the pots could be used to replace what the bandits stole. He said yes," said Joya.

Aruzhan looked from Joya to Genneset in disbelief.

Genneset reached into his pack and handed Aruzhan a leather purse. It was quite heavy.

"Joya's Uncle Timbraset added some extra. He thought very highly of your father, Aruzhan," said Genneset.

Aruzhan couldn't speak. Tears were streaming down her face as she held the purse with both hands. Joya gave her a big hug.

"Now when you're finished your seven years with the Khokhgui, you'll be quite the prize for some handsome Gotkurgan. Or Mythrycian. Or Zutherian. You are a little of each, you know," said Joya, laughing.

Aruzhan laughed through her tears and wiped her eyes.

"Come with us, Poppa, and meet Arsen. You have a lot in common," said Joya, ducking out the entrance.

"I'm just so thrilled you brought Swiftfoot, Poppa. And my saddle. You have no idea how big a difference he will make for me," said Joya as they walked to the blacksmith's workshop.

"I love you, Sunshine Hair, I love you. I will ask your father and we will marry," said Sanzhar, intercepting the trio.

Aruzhan giggled.

"It's Sanzhar. He's 'special'," Joya whispered to her father.

"Sanzhar. Meet my father, Genneset," said Joya, stopping.

"When can Nooshta and I get married, Nooshta's father? I love her. She's so pretty. She has sunshine hair and I love her," said Sanzhar.

Joya translated, barely suppressing a laugh.

"You have excellent taste in girls, Sanzhar. But in my country, boys must ask the mother's permission, too. So I will ask her for you, and when I come back, I will tell you her answer. Alright?" said Genneset.

"You tell Nooshta's mother I love Nooshta. She's my Sunshine Hair," said Sanzhar.

Joya kissed her finger and put it on Sanzhar's cheek.

"We have to go now, Sanzhar," she said, giggling.

"Good-bye, Sunshine Hair, good-bye. I love you. When your mother says yes, we will marry," said Sanzhar, watching them walk off.

"Persistent suitor. Better at it than someone else I know," said Genneset.

"Poppa!" said Joya, slapping his shoulder.

Aruzhan giggled again, exchanging a wink with Genneset.

Joya was right in assuming her father and Arsen would get along. She could barely keep up with the translating as they traded information and talked about sharpening techniques and metal work. Genneset was a specialist in tin metal repairs and answered several of Arsen's technical questions. He had his cart brought around and showed him the fine-grained grindstone.

Arsen only had one grindstone and it was a coarser grade. Genneset's was intended for fine blades, razors, and smaller daggers. He spotted a set of wool shears and offered to put an edge on them. Arsen readily agreed.

After he was done the shears and several smaller blades as well, he said, with Joya's help, "I really don't want to haul this stone all the way back to Zutheria. I'd like you to have it," said Genneset.

Arsen beamed with pleasure.

"I do have a favour to ask, though," said Genneset.

"Anything, my friend, anything for Nooshta's father. She has been a big help to me," said Arsen.

"My brother provided a dowry for Aruzhan. Her father Ulugan was his agent and he felt very badly about what happened. Could you keep her dowry safe for her until it's time for her to marry?" asked Genneset.

Arsen was surprised by the unexpected request. He had three sons but no daughters. Aruzhan had been a big help to him as well.

"Aruzhan. Come here," said Arsen.

She was stacking wood next to the forge. She came up, looking expectantly at everyone.

"You have a dowry now. Nooshta's father asked if I could keep it safe for you. I will do that if you want. I will also be the one to say yes or no to any suitor, since you have no father. I will tell the aklach and the elders I will stand for your father. If you want," said Arsen.

Aruzhan couldn't speak but nodded her approval. Tears welled up in her eyes. She took the heavy dowry purse out of her side pouch and handed it to Arsen.

Genneset gave her a hug and said, "Thank you for saving my girl's life."

CHAPTER SIXTY-ONE

Bahomet was brooding in his office. It had been a mutual stand-off between him and Baragin in the past five years. Baragin's Black Guards had taken out four of his Karuppsertais on a recent mission in Iblingport three months before. His spy network in Zutheria was still in place, but much reduced. He had to admit Baragin was getting better, and more ruthless as he matured in leadership.

Necessary trade between the two countries still went on, as neither leader was willing to commit economic suicide out of spite. Each knew the other was waiting for the other one to slip up. But he could not make his move until he had a way to deal with Astaran and the Laguntzaileas.

There was a knock at the door.

"Enter," said Bahomet.

"A message from the harbourmaster, Myanpur. You said you wanted to know when the Bulankayas returned. The pilot is bringing two ships into the harbour now," said Grand Vizier Fayan.

"Finally! I've waited a very long time for them. Arrange a reception for the captains," ordered Bahomet.

Bahomet stood in a warehouse at the harbourfront. There were thirty-six small kegs in front of him.

"As you requested, Myanpur. This is all that the celebration powder makers would allow me to bring. I regret it took us so long to return. We tried three years ago, but both ships were lost in a storm. I and some of my crew made it to shore in a ship's boat. Then our myanpur was not sure it was worth the risk and the great expense of another attempt, but I was finally able to persuade him. Then we had to wait for favorable winds.

I have also brought the necessary long fuses. I'm sure your road builders and quarry masters will be most pleased. I brought some celebration rockets as well, for any special occasions you may wish to commemorate," said Captain Aban.

"I am most pleased, Captain Aban. Please convey my heartfelt thanks to your celebration powder makers on your return. You have no idea how much this is going to help my kingdom," said Bahomet.

Dran puffed on his water pipe.

"So now you have your celebration powder. I could use some of that you know. I still have some boulders blocking my entrance road," he said.

"I'm sure you could. But I'm going to need every last barrel," said Bahomet.

"But the powder is here and Astaran is in Elberon. You cannot use your mantirakolai or your magic in Zutheria, not with the staff of Elbron to contend with," said Dran, blowing a smoke ring to the ceiling.

Bahomet gazed at Dran, mulling over what he was about to say.

"There is only one person I trust with this information and that is you. I have to because you have been my closest friend—and I need you to make my plan work.

"As you know, I was an apprentice to Aladrash in Elberon. I spent long days in the library, studying Elbronic and all the texts of magic spells and potions. One day, I was bored with my studies. There was a mouse in the corner of the basement storage room where I was looking for a particular scroll. One of my jobs was to deal with any mice I encountered as they would chew on the scrolls.

"So I chased it, but it disappeared behind a set of shelves. I took all the scrolls off and moved the shelves to find its nest. I found a hidden door instead. The mouse had disappeared under the small crack at the bottom of the door. I was intrigued as I did not know this door existed. It had probably been covered up by those shelves for centuries. I'm sure even Aladrash himself didn't know about it.

"I went to the caretaker's workshop and got a pry tool. It took some difficult prying, but I managed to get it open. It led to a narrow passageway, a tunnel. I got a torch and went exploring. The passageway came to a junction. I followed the right fork where it ended at a set of steep stairs. I climbed them and they stopped at a trapdoor of some kind. I pushed with all my strength and finally got it open a crack. I recognized the room. It was the small room directly behind the Council Chamber where the Laguntzaileas meet every Midsummer's Day. The Zaharbat uses it to keep necessary documents for the meetings. Whoever is the apprentice is the one who uses that room most, though. I was having difficulty opening the trap door because a large wooden chest was sitting on top of it, completely covering the door opening.

"I went back to the tunnel junction and followed the left fork all the way to its end. There was a locked metal doorway. I used the pry tool on the lock, and it finally gave way. The door hinges were quite rusty, so I had some trouble getting it open.

"When I finally got it open wide enough to get through, I saw I was in the back of a shallow cave. I could see daylight ahead. I walked to the entrance way which was almost completely covered in vines and bushes. When I looked out, I was looking down onto the roof of the duke's villa, about an arrow shot away. Obviously, it was intended as an escape tunnel in the event of a siege. I chose not to tell Aladrash about my discovery," concluded Bahomet.

Dran's hand holding the mouthpiece to his water pipe stopped halfway to his mouth.

"And that would be the villa that your agent Filden is now the caretaker of," said Dran.

"Yes. It rather grieved me to have to bribe my own governor with my own money and pay Robagrin for his villa, but Filden has been most helpful. His nephew Grandabin, the current legal owner, is content to let Filden have the run of the place," said Bahomet.

"I expect you would like my help getting thirty-six kegs of celebration powder into the tunnel and under the Council Chamber," said Dran.

"You've read my mind, my friend," said Bahomet with a smile.

"But how will you get the powder inside the tunnel with Astaran in the castle? He is not so incompetent that he wouldn't notice something amiss," said Dran.

"Then he needs to be somewhere else when the kegs are placed. He will only leave Elberon if I attempt to use my magic in Zutheria. He has promised Baragin he would do that. It's what the Laguntzaileas are meant to do—protect the kingdom from valikattis like me. It must be a threat that Damagal is not strong enough to deal with, one that he must ask for Astaran's help. That will take some doing, but I think I have found a way," said Bahomet.

"Aren't you putting yourself at some risk, going against Astaran and the staff of Elbron?" asked Dran.

"Oh yes. But my son's kingdom is worth it. And Astaran and Baragin's downfall is worth it. Astaran will come if I make the threat strong enough. And when he is out of Elberon dealing with me, your Karuppsertais will move the kegs into the tunnel.

"I have made arrangements for crates of 'furniture' labelled with Grandabin's stamp of ownership to be transported by dray wagon to the villa. They will be stored in the barn on the property.

"About a week before Midsummer's Day, there will be another serious attack on Dalanbur Island, but I will be leading it personally. Damagal will be summoned to help but he won't be able to withstand my power. Dalanbur Island has a shrine to Zazzamin and the bones of several valikattis buried there, including my great-grandfather, the original owner of my mantirakolai. The power of Zazzamin himself is in that place, if you know how to tap it. It has been a stench in the nostrils of many myanpurs over the years to have Zutherians encamped on our island, so it will not be seen as unusual that another myanpur is going to try to retake it.

"Damagal will have to admit he cannot prevail over a place with the power of Zazzamin and call for Astaran's help. He will come with the staff of Elbron and secure a marvellous victory for the forces of Zutheria. I will 'slink back to Tricanmallokan licking my wounds'.

"Then all the Laguntzaileas will convene later that week at Elberon to celebrate their victory. And I will be providing the celebration powder," said Bahomet, clenching his fist.

Chapter Sixty-Two

"**A**mbassador Oban to see you, Majesty," said Chancellor Berenfromm.

"What now? It really is tiresome dealing with that man. It is never good news when he requests an audience," complained Baragin.

"Perhaps he has come to complain about the Black Guards, Majesty," said Berenfromm with a smile.

"Yes. One of the best decisions I ever made, creating that unit. Show him in. We'll see what he has to say for himself," said Baragin with a resigned sigh.

Oban entered and bowed respectfully, waiting for permission to speak.

"Well, out with it, Oban. What message does your Black Hand have for me now?" asked Baragin.

"Myanpur Karpukkai requests the Zutherian Army withdraw from Dalanbur Island," began Oban.

Baragin looked from him to Berenfromm in disbelief.

"Withdraw from Dalanbur Island? You can't be serious, Oban. You know the reason we took it in the first place. Your army was using the high point on that island to bombard Zutherian forces. And not two years ago you pretended to try to take it. That did not go well for you, although I recognize that it was merely a ploy. Is this some sort of ploy again?" asked Baragin.

"Actually, the word 'request' was not in my instructions. The word the myanpur insisted I use is 'demands'," said Oban.

"Demands! Demands! How dare he! What possible reason would Bahomet have for 'demanding' we leave Dalanbur Island?" asked Baragin, standing in his agitation.

"You are correct, sire, that the previous attack on Dalanbur Island was part of a larger plan for the myanpur to gain custody of his son. Not this time. Dalanbur Island is a sacred place for the Bilurians. It has a shrine to Zazzamin, the god of all valikattis. It has the graves of several revered valikattis, including the Myanpur Karpukkai's great-grandfather Daragoonbalai Dra. We can no longer allow your soldiers to desecrate our holy place. We demand you vacate our Dalanbur Island," said Oban with a tone of assertiveness.

"Your island? Your island? Dalanbur Island is part of Zutherian territory now and has been for decades. We captured it in war, and we will keep it. Tell your myanpur that," said Baragin, seething.

Oban stared at him steadily.

"I will certainly pass on your reply, Your Majesty. But I must warn you that the myanpur is not prepared to let this matter go," replied Oban.

He glanced over at Berenfromm and bowed deeply, indicating he had nothing more to add.

Berenfromm looked at Baragin, who gave him the slightest of nods.

"Thank you, Ambassador. I'm sure we will have occasion to talk further of this matter," said Berenfromm.

Oban bowed himself out of the room.

"He can't be serious, Berenfromm. Is he really willing to risk war with Zutheria over a shrine and a few graves? What is he really up to? What do Erenbil's spies have to say?" asked Baragin.

"It seems that Bahomet has directed General Kiran to move towards Dalanbur. Four regiments so far and others have been notified to prepare for an engagement. We need to consider he may be serious. He appears to be making this a matter of personal honour, given that his great-grandfather's grave is on that island," said Berenfromm.

"Damnation!" said Baragin.

He began pacing, fingering Damagal's protection amulet under his shirt.

"Tell General Trillabon and Damagal we need to meet. If he truly is serious, he's not going to let the conventional army do this on their own. He will be personally involved and will be using magic," said Baragin.

General Kiran stood at attention while Grand Vizier Fayan made his report to Bahomet.

"Well, how did he take it?" asked Bahomet.

"Not well. Incredulous, actually, that we would demand they voluntarily leave the island," said Fayan.

"Not really surprising. We haven't directly threatened 'their' territory before now. Kiran...at ease, Kiran. How are your preparations going?" asked Bahomet.

"Very well, Myanpur. Four regiments are within one day's march of Dalanbur Island. We know they will block or destroy the bridge on the west end of the island so landing craft are being constructed in secret upstream. Three more regiments are close to being ready to join the others," said Kiran.

"Good. This is not a diversion this time, General. I want that island. The Zutherians will not give it up easily. I need you to capture the area which has the shrine of Zazzamin. That is your highest priority. When it is secured, I will join the battle personally," said Bahomet.

"Personally, Myanpur?" said Kiran, raising his eyebrows.

"Personally. The Bradden Laguntzailea Damagal will most certainly be called in to help the Zutherian army. I do not want to have your men subjected to his magic. But I need you to secure the shrine or I will not be able to withstand him," said Bahomet.

"We should be able to do it in the first hour, Myanpur. The Zutherians have concentrated their fortifications on the top ridge. The shrine is at the east end of the island where they have no major defensive line. The old Bilurian village is at the west end, and they have their barracks there. But they have the advantage of the high ground. I can take the area around the shrine, but it will be hard to advance further. They will rain arrows and catapult rocks down on us," said Kiran.

"You get me the shrine and the graveyard and leave the rest to me, General," said Bahomet.

CHAPTER SIXTY–THREE

Naudnil Ujun, the Ghost Singer of the Yakats at Lhooskustenkut, poked the fire with a stick. Sparks flew up into the night sky. Yat'ahna followed them with his eyes. He was almost fourteen summers now. He still practiced his Zutherian whenever he was with Dzulhcho, his honour father, his ts'udelhti 'uba. He sometimes went with Dzulhcho to Noo Wheti Akoh and even Pendragon, helping with the translating.

When they were at Pendragon, Dzulhcho always took him to pay a courtesy visit to the blind wizard, the nelhjun Suberon. Sometimes he stayed for a few days with him and learned the ways of the Laguntzaileas.

But most of the time Yat'ahna was a helper to Naudnil Ujun. He thought his nedo father, his white father Baragin, would come to get him, but he never did. Dzhulhcho said he had to be patient, that when the time was right, he would go to Zutheria to be with his nedo father.

"What do you see with your sky eyes, Yat'ahna?" asked Naudnil Ujun.

"I see the stars, and the sparks flying up, like they want to be stars themselves," said Yat'ahna.

"And can they be stars?" asked Naudnil Ujun.

"Yes, if they embrace the sacred fire, the fire that all stars burn with. A spark has the same fire. If they recognize that starfire is within them, they too can become stars," said Yat'ahna.

Naudnil Ujun looked intently at the boy. He was wise beyond his years. Perhaps it was his time with him, perhaps from his days with the great blind nelhjun at Pendragon. Perhaps it was his destiny speaking out from inside his heart, the destiny that the Ghost Singer had foreseen on the day he named him.

"On the day I gave you your name, I said that one day you would become a great nelhjun. I have not told you this before. But it is time. It is time for you to fly up to the stars. The starfire is within you, Yat'ahna. But first you must go on your vision quest.

"You will find your vision quest animal. And he will speak to you. He will tell you something very important, something that you must know. Then your path will be clear," said Naudnil Ujun.

"But how will I know if the animal I see is the right one, grandfather?" asked Yat'ahna.

Ghost Singer did not answer. He poked the fire with a stick again and was silent for a long time. Yat'ahna knew never to interrupt the silence. After a long wait, he spoke.

"You will leave tomorrow at first light. You will not eat for three days. You will go to the dzulhcho, the 'big mountain' that gave your honour father his name. You will stay there alone and seek your vision quest animal. Take this pouch. Eat what is inside on the evening of the second day. You will see visions. And when you come back, we will talk again, Yat'ahna."

It was cold and wet on the mountain. Yat'ahna shivered in his sodden clothing. A fire was not permitted on the vision quest. He wrapped his wolf skin robe around him and looked out on the mountain slope below. He was in a small cave about halfway up the mountain. Dzulhcho had walked him to the base and pointed out a pair of dead trees.

"Just above those two trees, you will find a cave. It is a good place for a vision quest, but I cannot go with you beyond this point. I will be waiting for you here on the morning of the fourth day. May the Highest One guide you. Tay untay, my son."

He turned on his heel and began the wounded deer lope back towards the village.

Yat'ahna did not dream on the first night. He slept only fitfully due to the cold and damp. He awoke stiff and hungry. He made his way down to a small creek to drink. While there he saw a deer, and a noostel, the fierce Yakat wolverine, but it ignored him. It did not 'speak' to him.

That night, he took out the small pouch Naudnil Ujun had given him. It looked like dried mushrooms inside. He smelled them and put one piece on his tongue. It did not taste good.

But he knew he must eat it as Ghost Singer had directed. He popped two small pieces into his mouth and chewed them slowly. He wanted to spit the pieces out because they tasted so bad, but he forced himself to swallow them.

After a short time, he began to feel dizzy. He had to hold onto the side of the cave wall because it was spinning around him. He got onto his hands and knees hoping the cave would stop spinning, but it did not stop.

While his head was hanging between his outstretched arms, he heard a guttural croak, then another. He forced his head up and saw a raven, a datsancho, looking at him. It croaked at him again, eyeing him with his beady black eye.

"What are you saying?" shouted Yat'ahna.

The datsancho croaked again and launched himself into the air. Yat'ahna tried to stand and follow his pathway through the air, but in his dizzy state, he fell. He reached out for his wolfskin robe and pulled it around him as the cave spun around him without mercy.

He dreamed that night. He was standing on a high place. There were white stones, but not like mountain stones. They were white and had flat sides, like they were cut with a knife. There was much dust that obscured everything. He heard a croaking sound but couldn't see the bird. He knew it was a datsancho, though, by the croaking sound.

A gust of wind cleared some of the dust. He saw the datsancho, sitting on a high tree branch. It had something in its beak, a stone, but shaped like an egg, dark blue with a kind of star inside. He could not take his eyes off the stone. It was like his eye was drawn up against it even though he was far away.

As he looked into the star, many colours appeared within it. The colours swirled and roiled as if there were a great storm inside it. Then a kind of eye appeared within the colours and the pupil of the eye grew larger and larger. Yat'ahna felt a feeling of intense fear as he was drawn towards the yawning abyss in the centre of the eye. But he could not stop himself. His panic intensified as he fell into endless blackness of the dark eye.

As he was falling, his body spun around so that his gaze was directed upward. He saw an eagle, a tse'balyan, diving towards him, talons outstretched. The talons grabbed him, but he did not feel pain. Instead, he felt safe. The feelings of fear and panic evaporated. The tse'balyan flew with him and landed in a nest. But it wasn't an eagle's nest. It was the nest of a datsancho, filled with black feathers and different shiny objects. He looked around the nest. There was an egg in the nest, but not a real egg. It was the same egg the datsancho had held in its beak. The tse'balyan picked up the egg in its beak, looked Yat'ahna straight in the eye and said, "Victory".

Yat'ahna woke up breathing hard, sweating.

Naudnil Ujun listened intently to Yat'ahna's story, paying particular attention to his vision dream.

"What does it mean, grandfather? What do the white stones and the dust mean? Why did I dream of two birds? Why did the tse'balyan say 'Victory'?" asked Yat'ahna.

Naudnil Ujun remained silent for a long time while Yat'ahna waited patiently. He knew the Ghost Singer only talked when he had something to say.

"The datsancho did not talk to you. He is not your spirit animal. But he is a helper for the tse'balyan. You will know when the time comes. The white stones and the dust are part of your story. 'Victory' is in the tse'balyan's beak, Yat'ahna. Victory is in the tse'balyan's beak. It is a powerful vision. You will know when the time comes.

"You are no longer Yat'ahna. Your vision has given you a new name. You will be called Balyan, after the tse'balyan. Use only that name from this day. You will soar like your spirit bird.

"But now, Balyan, it is time for you to leave Lhooskustenkut and the land of the Yakats. It is time for you to see your nedo father. It is time for you, little spark, to join the stars, because the starfire within you is strong, like the star within the blue egg of the tse'balyan. Yakuzda will help you in all you must do— never forget to honour the Highest One with your prayers, Balyan," said Naudnil Ujun.

"How will I get to the land of the nedos, grandfather?" asked Balyan.

"The blind nelhjun will take you," answered the old duyun.

Ghost Singer poked the fire with a stick, sending small sparks flying upward. Balyan watched them rise.

CHAPTER SIXTY–FOUR

"The mongomaa wants to see you," said Booshchoo, sticking her head inside the door flap of Joya's kezoy.

Joya was sharpening her dagger with the honing stone her father had given her. It was just over four years now since she had arrived in Birgulyuk. The time of her banishment was nearing an end. Most of her duties were routine patrols and staying battle ready with sparring and weapons training. When she could, she spent time with the aklach's Zerdagan slave and his hunting eagle, learning all she could. She found it very fascinating.

She followed Booshchoo to the mongomaa's kezoy and ducked through the opening. She was surprised to see the aklach in the tent, but simply stood at attention until Oyunchumai spoke.

"Khokhgui Nooshta. How long have you been with us now?"

"Four years, Mongomaa," answered Joya, looking straight ahead.

"Booshchoo tells me you have mastered many skills and show leadership in difficult situations," said Oyunchumai.

This surprised Joya. She had no idea Booshchoo would be reporting positive information to the mongomaa. She was demanding and hard-nosed, and rarely had anything positive to say about any of the Khokhguis.

"The kaskir ana is generous in her comments, mongomaa. I do my duty, that is all," said Joya, still at attention.

Oyunchumai and Aklach Chono exchanged a glance.

"I have decided you will now be a squad leader. You will take over Enkhara's squad. She is nearing the end of her service and word has reached me..." Oyunchumai paused, glancing at Booshchoo.

Joya knew what she had heard. Some of Enkhara's squad members had complained to her about how harsh and unfair Enkhara could be.

"Well, it is not your concern. You will start immediately," continued Oyunchumai.

Joya's heart leapt within her. Squad leader! She wanted to let out a whoop of joy but restrained herself with difficulty.

"Thank you, Mongomaa. I will not let you down," said Joya, barely masking her excitement.

"The aklach has a job for you, your first assignment as squad leader. I will let him tell you," said Oyunchumai.

"My second daughter, Aikorkem, is pledged in marriage to the son of the aklach in Temirtay, two days ride to the east. You and Kashkara's squad will be part of the escort to the wedding. It is close to the border with the Zerdagans—you will defend her with your life," said the aklach.

"Eeyah, Aklach!" said Joya, saluting.

"Dismissed. Booshchoo, take Nooshta to her new squad," said Oyunchumai.

Enkhara was relaxing with her eight-member squad in their kezoy when Booshchoo and Joya entered. She sat up and looked at Joya with narrowed eyes. She had never forgiven her for the humiliation she had been subjected to by Joya on her first day as a rookie Khokhgui.

"The mongomaa wants to see you," said Booshchoo.

"What is she doing here?" demanded Enkhara.

"The mongomaa will tell you. Go," answered Booshchoo curtly.

Enkhara glared at Joya and stomped out of the tent. Eight sets of eyes looked uncertainly at Booshchoo and Joya.

Booshchoo looked at the eight Khokhguis, half of whom were in their first year.

"Nooshta is your squad leader now. The mongomaa has decided. Get your gear ready. You are escorting the aklach's daughter to Temirtay. Nooshta will tell you the rest," said Booshchoo. And with that she ducked out of the kezoy.

Joya looked at her new squad.

"Saddle gear inspection. Move it!" she ordered.

The entire squad bolted for the door and headed for the stables with Joya close behind.

Later that evening, Joya was moving her personal belongings to her new squad's kezoy. She was about to enter when Enkhara emerged, carrying her own pile of possessions. She stopped and glared daggers at Joya.

"Enkhara, I was as surprised..." began Joya.

Enkhara gave her a look of such malevolence that Joya stopped mid-sentence. She intentionally bumped her shoulder as she passed, causing Joya to drop half of what she was holding. She stared open-mouthed at the receding Enkhara.

The escort duty to and from Temirtay had gone without incident. Upon her return, Joya noticed that the hasp of her storage box was unfastened. Puzzled, she rummaged through the various items of clothing and other personal belongings. Everything was there—except her snow globe. It was obvious one of the Khokhguis had stolen it, but who would risk benbay dishonour death to take it? Joya knew only Enkhara had the motive, but she could not point a finger without proof. She decided to report the theft to Booshchoo and let her handle it.

Neither Booshchoo nor Oyunchumai had been able to get anyone to confess to the theft. Two days later, though, Sanzhar was seen walking through the village with Joya's snow globe singing, "Sanzhar is making it snow! Sanzhar is making it snow! I am the snow man! Sanzhar is the snow man!"

Booshchoo had run up to him, saying, "Give that to me, idiot. That belongs to Nooshta."

"No! It's mine! I found it! Enkhara buried it so she didn't want it. But I want it. It's mine now, mine! Sanzhar is the snow man! Sanzhar is the snow man!" shouted Sanzhar.

And he refused to give it up, wrapping both his arms around it and glaring at anyone who came near.

Joya and several of the other Khokhguis gathered around.

Kashkara said, "Sanzhar. That is Nooshta's. You should give it back."

Thievery was absolutely one of the worst offences in Gotkurgan culture. The penalties were very severe for anyone found to have stolen anything. Joya put her hand on Kashkara's arm, indicating she wanted to handle it. Kashkara stood back.

"Sanzhar. I am so happy you found my globe. I was looking everywhere for it. Will you keep it safe for me? But you must be very, very careful with it. You are the Guardian of the Snow Globe. That is a very important job in Birgulyuk. Can you do that?" asked Joya.

"Yes! I am the Guardian. I am the Guardian for Sunshine Hair's snow globe. No one can touch it but me. And Nooshta. Because one day we will marry because I love her," said Sanzhar holding the snow globe out and shaking it.

"It's snowing, it's snowing! Look! Sanzhar is the snow man! Sanzhar is the snow man!" he shouted gleefully, holding it high.

Enkhara had been out on patrol, but Booshchoo and three other Khokhguis brought her back to Mongomaa Oyunchumai's kezoy. Booshchoo forced her down on her knees in front of Oyunchumai.

"You stole Nooshta's snow globe. Sanzhar saw you bury it. We all know it is precious to her. You lied to my face when I asked you about it. Why do you bring dishonour on the Khokhguis?" demanded Oyunchumai.

Enkhara said nothing. Everyone knew her resentment against Nooshta had been festering ever since she bested her on her first day as a rookie Khokhgui. Being replaced by Nooshta as squad leader was the final humiliation.

"Tie her. We must bring this to Aklach Chono," said Oyunchumai.

Wanton thievery was punishable by death. All Gotkurgans knew this, and theft was exceedingly rare. The aklach and the elders ruled Enkhara guilty and turned her over to Oyunchumai and Booshchoo for execution.

They stripped her of her shirt and her benbay as she knelt, hands tied in front of her. Her benbay was looped around her neck and the handle of her battle axe was inserted through the knotted end. Two senior Khokhguis stood on either side of Enkhara, holding the battle axe. They looked at Oyunchumai. She nodded.

They began twisting the benbay with the battle axe handle, hand over hand, tightening the benbay around her neck. Enkhara began gagging and choking, eyes bulging from her sockets, mouth opening and closing, fighting for air. The two Khokhguis held the battle axe until Enkhara expired and slumped over sideways.

They dragged the body, with benbay and battle axe still attached, over to the women's latrine and dumped her in. Oyunchumai threw Enkhara's hat, armor, dagger, bow and quiver in on top of the body. No Khokhgui would ever touch a disgraced weapon. Every Khokhgui threw in shovelfuls of dirt until she was completely buried. It was a somber time but reinforced to everyone in Birgulyuk that the Gotkurgans' high standard of honesty could not be compromised. Joya had 'forgotten' to retrieve her snow globe from Sanzhar when she left Birgulyuk.

CHAPTER SIXTY-FIVE

Suberon cocked his head, listening to the voice of the young Yakat boy.

"Tell me about my father's lodge, grandfather Suberon. Does it have many rooms? How old is my brother now? Does my nedo father have many wives, or just one? Will you take me to the lodge of the great nelhjun Astaran?" asked Balyan.

"So many questions, Yat...I mean Balyan. It may take me a while to get used to your new name. But I understand that after a vision quest, a new name comes with the vision," said Suberon, smiling.

"Yes, I have a new name. And a new stick," said Balyan, showing off his walking staff. Dzulhcho had carved an eagle's head out of a walrus tusk and fitted it on to the top end of the staff. The beak was open but had nothing in it. He had consulted Ghost Singer before he began carving. He had said, "Carve it with the beak open, wide enough to hold an egg." He didn't say why, but Dzulhcho knew Naudnil Ujun never said anything without a reason.

"It's not like your dragon staff, but one day I will see victory with mine. That is why the beak is open. It is saying, 'Victory'. It was in my vision. Do you want to feel it?" asked Balyan.

He handed it to Suberon who ran his fingers over the eagle's head. The carving was exquisite. Dzulhcho had spent many days on it prior to beginning the journey to Pendragon.

"A fine staff, Balyan. Your brother Baragran will be eight summers old. And you have a sister, too. Milla. She is almost five summers. I'm sure they are anxious to meet you. You will stay at your father's house until after Midsummer's Day. We Laguntzaileas have our special meeting on that day. Afterwards, I believe the Zaharbat Astaran would like to meet you. Your stepmother Amathea—I guess you would call her your honour mother—is the only wife King Baragin has. Now, enough questions. I need your help to get ready for our voyage to Iblingport," said Suberon.

At noon on the third day of sailing south, the ship carrying Balyan and Suberon south tacked past Dabranen Island. When he was told of their location, Suberon asked, "Do you see a large white stone building in the far distance, on top of those mountains, Balyan?"

"Yes. What is it?" asked Balyan

"Elberon Castle. It is the home of Zaharbat Astaran. We will go there, but the road to it is on the eastern side of the Prenadon Mountains. After we land at Iblingport, my fellow Laguntzailea Stornowin and I will take a barge to Bidrudden, then go by carriage to Elberon. It will take a few days. I have to give these old bones a good long while to travel these days," said Suberon.

"I dreamed of white stones. And much dust. But there was a raven, then an eagle. I don't know what it means," said Balyan.

Suberon was silent. He knew Balyan had the gift of foresight. Sometimes visions were clouded, hard to fathom. But they were never without meaning. When they arrived at Iblingport, the wharves were bustling with stevedores, sailors, merchants, provisioners—and soldiers.

"So many people, grandfather Suberon. And many soldiers. Are there always this many soldiers at the docks?" asked Balyan.

"I'm sure my brother Laguntzailea Stornowin will fill us in," said Suberon.

They were to stay the night with Stornowin, then travel together by barge to Wreatherin where they would join Damagal for the rest of the journey to Bidrudden.

"The king has mobilized much of the army. It seems that Bahomet is going to make a serious attempt at retaking Dalanbur Island. It could be a diversion for elsewhere along the border, so the units here in Iblingport are on high alert as well," said Stornowin.

"Hmmm," mused Suberon. "I expect that Damagal may be called into action as well. Bahomet is a full-fledged valikatti and may be tempted to use his power to help his army secure a victory. But he would be unwise to take on Damagal. He is now the most senior Laguntzailea after Astaran and not one to trifle with," said Suberon, mainly for Balyan's benefit.

Balyan listened wide-eyed at as the two wizards talked of the affairs of the kingdom, their particular bailiwicks, and the likely agenda of the Midsummer's Day Council of Five meeting at Elberon.

At the end of their chat, Stornowin set his gaze on Balyan, and gave him a kindly smile.

"So, are you hoping to become Astaran's new apprentice? The one he has now, Saragon, is nearing the end of his training. I was the last one before Saragon, but the Zaharbat does not take a new one on unless he shows great promise," said Stornowin.

"I do not know. I am here to meet my nedo father, Baragin. He is the dunecho of all the nedos. Grandfather Suberon says I can go to your white castle after Midsummer's Day. I want to meet Zaharbat Astaran. He is the greatest nelhjun of them all," said Balyan.

Both Stornowin and Suberon smiled at his mix of Zutherian and Yakat.

"Well, Suberon tells me you have been training with the wizard of your own Yakat tribe. Ghost Singer, is it?" said Stornowin.

"Yes. That is how you say his name in nedo language. He is Naudnil Ujun. He is very old and very wise. He has told me I would be a great nelhjun one day, but I do not know the path. Perhaps Zaharbat Astaran will show me," said Balyan.

Stornowin paused, then said, "If you are to become a 'nelhjun', a Laguntzailea, you will need some of the tools of our craft. I have a gift for you, Balyan."

Stornowin went over to a wooden chest and took out a small leather pouch. He whispered, 'armiarma manta' in Elbronic to Suberon, then draped the spider blanket over him. He completely disappeared, leaving only a wispy grey form where Suberon had been sitting.

Balyan gasped in amazement.

"What is this magic thing?" he asked.

"We call it an 'armiarma manta' in our wizard's language—a spider blanket. We use the threads from the bird-catcher spider, weave them into a blanket, then place a spell of invisibility on it. It can come in very handy when you are in great danger. I'd like you to have it, Balyan—a gift in honour of your visit to us," said Stornowin.

Balyan beamed with pleasure and looked from Stornowin to Suberon as his knees disappeared from view when Stornowin draped it across his legs.

"Come lad, let's get some rest. It will be a long day tomorrow on the barge," said Suberon.

CHAPTER SIXTY–SIX

Joya paused her horse. Aruzhan and Bergara reined in behind her. They were near Drinroxen Pass on the road leading towards Preneport. Joya had completed her four years and nine months of banishment in Mythrycia with the Gotkurgans. She had finished her term as a squad leader with the Khokhgui in her last year. She still went by Nooshta with her seykas karindas.

Bergara had rejoined the Khokhgui about six months after her traumatizing incident with the Zerdagans. But there was no battle sister replacement for her after Inzhu's death. The mongomaa had assigned her to Noostha and Aruzhan's squad. She was intensely attached to Nooshta, acknowledging that she owed her life to her.

The mongomaa had granted permission for Aruzhan and Bergara to accompany Nooshta back to Zutheria. They would be seykas karindas upon their return. Joya had refused an escort from Ambassador Danstorin in Gragnarak. Pharigon had been re-assigned back to Wreatherin after it was obvious Joya was fully acclimatized in Birgulyuk.

Joya had two more X's on her benbay. One was from a skirmish with Zerdagans who attempted a raid on Birgulyuk when the men were out rounding up the sheep from the summer pastures. The other was from a battle with Mythrycian bandits. In that encounter she had used the pyramid-shaped hammer point of her battle axe to puncture the skull of a bandit whose group had unwisely decided to attack a train of Gotkurgan wagons heading to the market in Gragnarak with a load of carpets.

She was anxious to get to Braddenlocks to visit her parents, but Aruzhan wanted to thank Joya's uncle Timbraset personally for his gift of dowry money. So Joya decided to detour to Preneport first, then circle south. Besides, she was anxious to see her aunts and uncles as well. Joya knew she was still officially banned from Preneport but she didn't care—she wouldn't be staying that long.

The three young women were dressed in their Khokhgui battle armor with the traditional Gotkurgan conical caps. They got quite a bit of attention in Amadel when they came through. The three had then taken the shortcut to Drinroxen through the forest trail west of Amadel. Bandits still roamed there though Baragin had reduced their numbers.

They were on a small rise of the wagon road to Biraghir, partially obscured by trees.

"What is it, Nooshta?" asked Aruzhen.

"Two wagons. Looks like one is a trader and the other is a family moving their household—three children. Eight men have surrounded them. Probably bandits. I remember my father telling me he was ambushed near this spot years ago," said Joya.

"What will we do?" asked Bergara.

Joya fingered her battle axe. 'Defend the honour of Gotkurga and Zutheria with this axe', was what

Mongomaa Oyunchumai had said when she presented her with it.

"Notch arrows. Bergara, take the big one on the left. Aruzhan, the small one holding the sword to the trader's throat. I'll take the one holding the trader's horses. After we loose, we charge. The rest should scatter. If they don't, battle axes," ordered Joya.

All three notched their red and black Gotkurgan arrows into their horn bows. The mother in the second wagon had her arms around two small boys who were sobbing in fright. The bandit leader had grabbed the oldest child, a teen-aged girl, by the arm. He was holding his sword under the chin of the father, who was begging for his family. The trader looked grim, almost resigned to his inevitable fate as he looked at the sword at his throat.

"Loose," ordered Joya.

All three arrows hit their mark. The warriors kicked their horses to a gallop screaming "Khokhgui Jenis!" and waved their battle-axes over their heads.

The bandits looked in shock and dismay as the three female warriors charged towards them. The bandit leader, who had been shielded by his hostage from the arrow attack, yelled, "It's only women! Stand and fight!"

Joya spurred her horse and charged directly at the leader. He swung his sabre at her, but she deflected it with the handle of her axe. Bergara caught up to a fleeing bandit and took off the back of his head with the blade of her battle axe, sending him sprawling, lifeless. Aruzhan chased two others into the edge of the forest where they jumped over a steep bank to escape. All three wheeled their horses around and faced the bandit leader.

"Let's get out of here, boss," said the remaining uninjured bandit.

The leader let out a growl of frustration and said, "To the horses."

They backed towards the edge of the forest, sabres bared, then turned and vanished into the woods.

Joya trotted up and dismounted. Aruzhan and Bergara remained on their horses.

"Anyone hurt here?" she asked.

"Just that one with the arrow sticking out of his chest," said the trader, pointing at a groaning bandit next to his wagon. It was Bergara's target. The other two were dead.

Joya walked over, put her foot on his chest and pulled out the arrow with a yank. The man screamed in agony.

"Get on your feet. Tell your leader this road is off limits from now on. Tell him Nooshta the Gotkurgan guards this road. Go!"

She gave him a rough shove and the bandit stumbled off, holding his hand to the wound just under his collarbone.

Joya looked at Bergara and Aruzhan.

"One more 'X' each, seykas karindas," she said in Gotkurgan.

The trader looked from Joya to the other two, eyes full of questions. The second man walked up to Joya.

"You saved my family. I'm forever in your debt, miss. I'm Sennabin, this is my wife Ebba, my two sons Darabin and Philabin, and my daughter Sabah. We were on our way to Preneport. I've got work in Pendragon, at the iron mine. We thought we'd be safe travelling with Trinrudden here, but I guess we were wrong," said Sennabin.

Sabah looked in amazement at the three female warriors with their one-breasted cuirasses. The two young boys had dried their tears and looked up at Aruzhan and Bergara with their mouths open. They were particularly fascinated with Bergara, with her broad flat face and narrow eyes.

"I'm in your debt too, miss. Trinrudden's the name, like Sennabin said. I'm headed to Pendragon with a load of Milredden Pink cider from Braddenvale. We're booked on the same ship once we get to Preneport. But I have to drop a couple of barrels at the Silver Dolphin," said Trinrudden.

"They rebuilt it?" asked Joya.

Trinrudden raised his eyebrows.

"Yes, about four years ago. Didn't I hear you say you were from Gotkurga, wherever that is? How do you know about the Silver Dolphin?" he asked.

"My father used to own it. I'm headed to Preneport to visit my aunt and uncles with my two friends here," said Joya.

Trinrudden's jaw dropped.

"Great Zuth! You're Joya, the queen's sister!"

Sennabin and Ebba looked at each other, eyes wide, then back at Joya.

"This is Aruzhan and she's Bergara. She doesn't speak much Zutherian," said Joya by way of introduction.

"We'll ride with you to Biraghir, then be on our way. The road should be safe down into Preneport," said Joya.

Aruzhan translated for Bergara.

"Futt won't be happy to see you. Aren't you banned from Preneport for another five years?" asked Trinrudden.

"I was banned from Blessingport, not Preneport. Futt can go suck a Sweetsap," said Joya.

CHAPTER SIXTY–SEVEN

"**K**ari ayel," said Bergara, using the Gotkurgan term for old woman. She was pointing at a stooped figure at the edge of meadow near the tree line.

The trio was just outside Preneport on the flower meadows near Amathea's home. Joya would help her aunt with waldenflower and calamang flower harvesting at this time of the year when she was younger.

She spurred her horse to a gallop and thundered across the meadow. The old woman stood erect, alarmed, as the horse bore down on her. She had a broad brimmed sun hat on and had a basket of flowers on her arm.

"Auntie Thea! Auntie Thea!" yelled Joya as she reined her horse to a sudden stop and vaulted from the saddle. She grabbed her aunt in a bear hug and spun her around.

"Great Zuth, you gave me a fright. Joya? Is that you, sweetie? Oh my goodness, I barely recognize you with that short hair and…and, that armour. Stop squeezing me so tight! You'll break me in two. Let me have a look at you," said Amathea, putting both her hands on Joya's face.

"Oh, Auntie, Auntie. It's so good to see you. I missed you so, I missed you so, I…"

She stopped and buried her face in Amathea's shoulder and began sobbing, overcome with emotion.

"There, there, my darling. I missed you so much, too. Hush, my darling girl, hush. Auntie Thea's got you. Now dry your eyes and introduce me to your friends," said Amathea as Bergara and Aruzhan trotted up.

After introductions, Joya gave her horse to Aruzhan and walked with Amathea back to the house.

"I know you're not supposed to come back here for another five years, but I'm glad you did. How else would I see you? These old bones just can't travel," said Amathea.

"I know. I decided to take the chance. Aruzhan wanted to thank Uncle Timba in person. He replaced the dowry money bandits stole from Aruzhan's father. They killed him and left her an orphan. You can't imagine how much what Uncle Timba did means to her. We'll be off to Wreatherin and Braddenlocks in a couple of days and Futt probably won't be the wiser. Uncle Timba and Uncle Donny and everyone else can come to your place to visit anyway," said Joya.

"Well, if Futt hears you are here he'll probably kick up a fuss. But..." she paused looking at Joya's bow, quiver, battle axe and dagger.

"It looks like you girls know how to take care of yourselves."

"We did run into some bandits at Drinroxen. They were robbing a merchant and a young family," said Joya.

"Bandits? Really? How many? Did they attack you?" asked Amathea.

"Eight. The five that survived ran away," said Joya, matter-of-factly.

Amathea's jaw dropped. She said nothing for a while, then put her hand on Joya's shoulder.

"Those Khokhguis have turned you into a warrior. We may need tough fighters like you. Storm clouds are brewing with Biluria," said Amathea.

"What's happening? Is there going to be a war?" asked Joya, brows furrowing.

"I don't know. Nothing is certain, but that Bahomet has turned things upside down. He and your brother-in-law have been sparring like Zutherian black elk in rutting season for years now. But for some reason, Bahomet wants to make an issue of some little island on the Dalanen River. Wreatherin and Iblingport are like anthills with soldiers running around, Ammy says. She says your Pharigon is in the thick of it," commented Amathea.

Joya's eyes widened with the briefest look of concern, then she frowned.

"He's not 'my Pharigon'. But I hope he stays safe," she said, looking straight ahead.

Amathea gave her a sidelong glance and smiled to herself.

"Besides, we have Astaran and the Staff of Elbron and all the Laguntzaileas to keep us safe. It's all huff and puff between two men comparing the length of their..." said Joya.

"I think that's enough speculating, young lady," said Amathea, interrupting.

"Come. I'll bet you three need some good food and a bath."

Timbraset and Donneset came over with the families for dinner that evening, and they stayed up late into the night sharing stories. Donneset's two daughters, Bilanna and Doralee, pestered their cousin with questions about the Khokhgui until their father finally said, "Now don't you two go getting any silly ideas."

Joya grinned and winked at her two cousins.

Aruzhan shyly knelt before Timbraset in a gesture of respect, giving him a beautifully embroidered Gotkurgan winter cap.

He thanked her, and said, "I don't have a daughter, but if I did, I would want her to be as beautiful and brave as you. Any man would be truly lucky to have you as his wife."

Aruzhan gave him a big hug.

On the afternoon of the third day after their arrival, Bergara came into the pantry where Joya was helping Amathea with some herb drying.

"Nooshta. Men approaching. Soldiers, too," she said in Gotkurgan.

"Armour and bows. Now. Tell Aruzhan," ordered Joya.

A small knot of men was coming down the rutted track to Amathea's house. It was Futt and Doroquill, flanked by a lieutenant and two soldiers, plus a motley crew of barflies Joya recognized from her days at the Silver Dolphin. Some of them still had bottles in their hands. She recognized the merchant Trinrudden. He'd obviously been regaling the patrons of the Silver Dolphin with Joya's exploits at Drinroxen Pass.

They stopped just in front of the high-sided hay wagon Amathea had parked in the yard.

"Joya, daughter of Genneset. We have received a complaint. You are here in violation of Judge Drellabin's order to stay out of this community for ten years. Surrender yourself," shouted the lieutenant.

He was the same one who had arrested Joya five years before.

Joya had quickly put on her armour and grabbed her bow and battle axe. Amathea put her hand on her arm and shook her head.

"Don't worry, Auntie. No one's getting hurt today. I hope."

Joya joined Aruzhan and Bergara in the kitchen and looked out the window.

"Notch arrows. Bergara, put one next to the officer's left ear. Aruzhan, put one next to his right ear. On my command. Re-notch immediately after," ordered Joya.

Joya and the other Khokhgui's walked out onto the porch, bows drawn.

"Loose!" yelled Joya.

The arrows went "Thock! Thock-thock!" creating a troika of shafts on both sides and on top of the lieutenant's head against the wood of the hay wagon. The lieutenant ducked down in shock while the two soldiers pulled their sabres but moved behind the wagon. The crowd of Silver Dolphin regulars joined them, shouting expletives.

The three re-notched.

"You should have brought more soldiers, Lieutenant," shouted Joya.

"Left corner," she said to Bergara, who let an arrow loose.

It landed right beside the face of a soldier who was peeking around the corner of the hay wagon.

"You murdering bitch! I'll see you in irons!" shouted Futt, from behind the wagon, peeking his head over the top board. He ducked with a girl-like shriek as Aruzhan sent an arrow whizzing past his head and into the barn door behind him.

Amathea came out of the front door. "Now let's all calm down here. Lieutenant...Ambrosin, isn't it?"

"Yes, ma'am," said Ambrosin. "Futt has registered a complaint alleging your Joya is violating the judge's order not to return to Blessingport." He looked nervously at the three Khokhguis with their drawn bows and battle-axes.

"Well, then that's a problem, Lieutenant. As I recall, the town sign is down the road a ways. My farm is not inside the town limits. Secondly, the judge's order was to stay out of Blessingport. As we all know, that is no longer the name of this town. Perhaps it might be wise to consult with your captain in Iblingport before you make an unlawful arrest of the queen's sister. That wouldn't look good on your record," said Amathea.

Ambrosin hesitated.

"Arrest her, arrest her, you fool!" shouted Futt.

Ambrosin looked at his two soldiers, whose expressions showed they were not at all comfortable about going after three skilled archers.

"It seems, Futt, that Joya is not currently in violation of the judge's order. Should she actually enter the town, that would be a different matter. I will, however, send a pigeon to Iblingport seeking further instructions. Men," he said, indicating he was leaving.

"You're not the only one who can send a pigeon, you incompetent! The judge will hear that you're not enforcing his order!" Futt yelled after the retreating soldiers.

Futt whirled, face mottled with rage, shaking his finger at Joya.

"If you set foot in my town..."

Joya put an arrow between his legs.

"You'll what?" asked Joya.

Futt let out a growl of frustration, turned on his heel and stomped down the driveway. His crew of supporters straggled behind him.

"Always good to get a warm welcome home," said Joya.

Amathea burst into laughter.

Joya decided to take the coastal road to Iblingport, mainly because both Aruzhan and Bergara were absolutely fascinated by the sights of the Western Sea. That meant riding through Preneport. She rather enjoyed the gapes and stares of those she passed by. She didn't encounter Futt, but they passed the walled orchard which surrounded his house. She paused and looked at the wooden name plaque next to the entrance gate.

"Let's give our friend Futt something to remember us by. Inside the 'U', ladies," said Joya, notching an arrow.

When Futt arrived home from town later that day, he found three red and black fletched arrows nicely grouped inside the 'U' of his name.

Chapter Sixty-Eight

Joya pushed through the doors of the Prenadon Inn, Aruzhan and Bergara following. Her eyes took a moment to adjust to the dim lighting. All eyes turned to look, and conversations waned into a suspicious silence.

Joya walked to the bar. No one was there, but Bobbingran, just finishing dropping a brace of steins at a table, started heading their way.

One table of three bargemen watched them. The leader nodded to his mates and headed over to where Joya was standing.

"Can I buy you ladies a drink?" he said, putting his hand on Joya's waist and the other on the bar.

"Get your hand off me," snarled Joya, putting the point of her dagger in between two of his fingers. The other two made a move to protect their friend, but Aruzhan and Bergara had their daggers at their throats before they could take two steps.

Bobbingran froze.

Just then Umbraset came out from the back room with a keg under his arm.

"Joya?" he said.

He quickly put the keg on the bar and pushing the bargeman out of the way wrapped his cousin in a huge bear hug.

"It's alright, mates! It's my cousin Joya!" he shouted and the tension in the bar evaporated.

Aruzhan and Bergara re-sheathed their daggers and stood off to the side, awaiting introductions.

"Great Zuth, look at you! What's with the armour? And the short hair?" said Umbraset giving her another big hug.

"Umbraset. This is Aruzhan and Bergara. Bergara doesn't know much Zutherian. They're my 'battle sisters'. We've been through a lot together," said Joya.

"I'll bet you have. And you're going to tell me all about it. But let me take you upstairs to your folks. Your momma has one of her headaches and your poppa is making her some tea," said Umbraset.

Umbraset led the way and opened the door to the upstairs apartment. Joya rushed in, yelling, "Momma! Poppa!"

Genneset stood up, but Germilda stayed seated, a little confused for a moment at the short-haired, armour clad female warrior that had burst into their rooms.

Joya couldn't decide which one to hug first. She put an arm awkwardly around both of them.

Then she knelt in front of Germilda, hands grasping her mother's hands in her lap. Germilda pulled her hands away and put them alongside Joya's cheeks and pulled her in for a kiss on her forehead.

"Oh, my baby girl, my baby girl," she started, but broke into weeping.

Joya enveloped her in her arms and began crying, too. Genneset moved in and put his arms around both of them, tearing dripping from his eyes.

After a few moments, Germilda said, "Well, I don't seem to have a headache anymore. Genneset. Don't just stand there! Make our guests comfortable."

"Yes, of course, my plum blossom. Joya, introduce your friends to your mother. I've already met them," said Genneset, bustling to get some refreshments for everyone.

"Momma, this is Aruzhan. And this is Bergara. I'll have to translate for her since she knows very little Zutherian. Or how about you do that Aruzhan—I have a lot of catching up to do with my parents," said Joya.

Aruzhan nodded and started translating in a low voice to Bergara.

"Look at you! Almost twenty-one summers now. And still single. We'll have to do something about that. That Pharigon is in Wreatherin now, you know," said Germilda.

"Momma! Why should I care about Pharigon? He's just the baby-sitter Baragin assigned to look after me on my exile," complained Joya.

"I'll take him if you don't want him. He's very handsome," said Aruzhan with a grin.

"You should, Aruzhan. Besides, Joya has another suitor. Sanzhar, if I recall correctly," quipped Genneset.

"Poppa!" protested Joya.

Aruzhan giggled and translated for Bergara, who started giggling, too.

"Isn't he the simple-minded one your poppa told me about?" asked Germilda.

"Yes. But he's very sweet. He calls me Sunshine Hair and insists we're going to get married," said Joya, starting to giggle as well.

Germilda broke into a big laugh.

Joya filled them in on the family in Preneport and the incident with Futt and Lieutenant Ambrosin.

"That was rather cheeky putting three arrows into his name board, poppet," said Genneset.

"I know. He's a very annoying man," said Joya, with a mischievous grin.

"So, what now my pet? You can go wherever you wish now, although it probably wouldn't be wise to stray near the border with Biluria. Things are getting tense," said Genneset.

"Yes. Auntie told me. The docks in Iblingport were swarming with soldiers and sailors. I want to go to Wreatherin to see Ammy and Baragran. And Milla. I hear she's adorable," said Joya.

"She is, she is. I never want to leave after I visit her," said Germilda.

"I think we'll visit in Wreatherin, then decide from there. Aruzhan and Bergara will need to head back to Gotkurga, perhaps after Midsummer's Day," said Joya.

"You've probably forgotten how to dance the quellel. But I'm sure Pharigon will remind you how," said Genneset.

"Poppa! Will you stop? I'm not dancing with that man. Or any man. And I still haven't forgiven you for tricking me into dancing with him last time," said Joya grumpily.

Genneset just laughed out loud at her discomfort and gave Aruzhan a wink.

Chapter Sixty-Nine

Bergara and Aruzhan gawked at the sights of Wreatherin. They got quite a few stares themselves, especially Bergara. No one had seen a Gotkurgan before. Bergara was fascinated with the occasional Bilurian she saw in the streets. She had never seen them before, either.

"They're so small. And almost black, Nooshta," she said as they rode towards Selvenhall.

"Are they the ones who want to fight the Zutherians? They look too small to fight," said Bergara.

"Don't let their size fool you. They came very close to killing my poppa and my sister," said Joya.

They stopped at the gates of the palace and dismounted. The two guards looked them up and down with skepticism.

"Tell the queen her sister is here," ordered Joya.

"You? The queen's sister?" sneered the guard.

"If you're the queen's sister, then I'm the king's brother," joked the guard.

The other guard broke into laughter.

In a lightning move, Joya swung her battle axe into the post beside the guard's head and with her other hand put her dagger to his throat. Aruzhan and

Bergara both had their daggers under the chin of the other guard.

"Perhaps I should just send your head over the gate by means of introduction then," said Joya through clenched teeth.

Captain Demmerdran, the officer in charge of the palace guard, was standing near the front door of Selvenhall talking with a sentry and noticed the commotion. He motioned to six guards and sent them running to the front gate. Soon the guards had their lances pointed at the three women. They still had their daggers out.

"What's going on here?" he demanded.

"I'm Joya, the queen's sister. Perhaps you could tell her I'm here. This imbecile doesn't seem to believe me," said Joya.

Demmerdran didn't recognize her but had been told to expect Joya and two female companions dressed like Gotkurgans.

"Stand down, men. Open the gate for the queen's sister," he ordered.

Joya nodded to Aruzhan and Bergara who sheathed their daggers.

Amathea hugged her sister for a long time. Baragran had his arms around his auntie from below, while Milla hung back shyly, finger in the corner of her mouth.

"My goodness, how you've grown! Such a big boy now," said Joya to Baragran. He grinned up at his auntie, holding her hand.

Just then, Baragin swept into the room looking rather harried—he didn't have time for a family distraction. But he softened when Milla ran up to him. He gathered her in his arms and walked over to Joya.

"Sister. You're looking well. And a little ferocious in that armour. Milla, say hello to your Auntie Joya," said Baragin.

Milla continued to stare at Joya, finger in her mouth.

"A little shy," said Amathea apologetically.

"She'll warm up to you soon. Come, sweetie. This is momma's baby sister, Joya. You're going to have so much fun together, I know," she said, taking her from Baragin's arms.

"So, I hear you tried to part my lieutenant's hair with your arrows, Joya. Or should I say, 'Nooshta'," said Baragin with a smile.

"You have good sources, brother," said Joya, smiling back.

"I know everything that goes on in my kingdom. I understand some bandits are regretting running into you as well," said Baragin.

"Bandits? Really?" asked Amathea, shocked. "I didn't have a dream about you in danger from bandits." "That's because Joya wasn't the one who was in danger," said Baragin with a laugh.

"When I completed my initiation, the mongomaa, the Silver Mother of the Khokhguis, made me promise to defend the honour of Zutheria when she gave me my battle axe. So that's what I did," said Joya.

Baragin looked at her intently.

"Have you thought about what comes next for you?" he asked.

"Not really. I'm just happy to be here, with my sister and the little ones," said Joya.

"You could stay. Your sister and the little ones could use a female bodyguard. Guards, actually. As you've heard, tensions are rising between Zutheria and Biluria. I'd feel a lot happier if you—and your two friends—would consider watching over Ammy and the children," said Baragin.

"I'm happy to stay as long as you need me. But I can't speak for Aruzhan or Bergara. They are supposed to return after I'm safely back in Zutheria. They have two years of service left," said Joya.

"Danstorin can take care of that with some appropriate 'gifts'. Buying out their two years service, I mean. Talk it over with them. They are most welcome to stay. I know how good you are, Joya. And I know how many X's you have on your benbay," said Baragin.

"How..." started Joya.

"Pharigon. He got it from Aruzhan. She's quite proud of you, you know," said Baragin.

"Why that little gossip. I'll kick her butt all the way back to Gotkurga," said Joya, clearly annoyed.

"He's here. Pharigon. In the palace. He's General Trillabon's aide-de-camp. He's meeting with Chancellor Berenfromm in the east wing. Maybe you'll bump into him," said Baragin, with the slightest of smiles.

"Are all of you conspiring to match me up? Aaargh!" said Joya with a growl of frustration.

Amathea exchanged a smile with Baragin, who winked at her. Amathea wisely decided to change the subject.

"Why don't you go find Aruzhan and Bergara and ask them if they wish to stay? I'd really feel safer with the three of you watching out for us," she said, putting her hand on Joya's arm.

Joya shook off her annoyance and walked off in the direction of the guest quarters. She wasn't thinking of Aruzhan and Bergara, though.

Both Aruzhan and Bergara said they wanted to stay. Even with a dowry, Aruzhan knew she'd be very unlikely to find a Gotkurgan willing to take a half Mythrycian-half Zutherian as a wife. Bergara's experience with the Zerdagans had turned her completely off men. She didn't see a future for herself after her term of service with the Khokhguis came to an end. Bakhtiar had cruelly reminded her that she was 'damaged goods', only suitable to be a goatherder's wife.

She said, "I will stay with you, Nooshta. I will help you protect the little ones."

Joya was walking back to the main wing when she took a wrong turn. She was annoyed with herself for not paying attention earlier. The hallway she was in did not look familiar. She turned suddenly to retrace her steps and bumped into someone.

"Lost?" asked Pharigon.

Joya was completely flustered and stuttered, "I…I… What are you doing here?" she finally asked, stepping back.

She looked him over. He was still tall, handsome, with a full beard now.

"Meeting with the chancellor. I'm on General Trillabon's staff," said Pharigon.

"I heard," said Joya.

Joya was wearing a dress of her sister's as she hadn't had time to acquire appropriate clothing for herself. It was a pale blue, tight at the waist, with lace on the bodice. It wasn't one she would have picked but it looked wonderful on her. She wasn't wearing her benbay. Joya had a belt with her side pouch and dagger on, though. She didn't feel completely dressed without it.

Pharigon eyed her silently. Joya returned his gaze. The chemistry they always had when they were alone began bubbling uncontrollably. It was something neither could suppress.

"I think I want to kiss you right now," said Pharigon.

"Maybe I should punch you in the nose. You haven't asked if you could," said Joya.

"I'm asking now," said Pharigon.

"What if I say no?" said Joya.

"Maybe I'll just push you up against the wall and do it anyway," said Pharigon, stepping in close so that Joya's back was against the wall. He grasped one hand in his and put it over her head.

"Maybe I'll just relieve you of something quite precious to you," said Joya.

Pharigon tucked in his chin and pulled back slightly, looking down. He could see the glint of Joya's dagger between his legs.

"Then what would I love you with?" he asked softly.

He looked back up into Joya's eyes, and pressed his mouth against hers. He heard the clatter of the dagger as it fell to the floor. Joya put both hands around his neck and kissed him back passionately.

His tongue found hers and they wrestled between their lips. Her tongue explored the back side of his teeth. Pharigon moved his hands down to Joya's hips and pressed his growing hardness against her. She pressed back.

"I just managed to get Milla....to sleep..." said Amathea as she suddenly rounded the corner of the hallway, espying the two in their rapturous embrace.

Joya pushed Pharigon back and slapped his face hard.

"How dare you!" she said, as she stomped off in the direction Amathea had come from.

Amathea watched Joya go past, face flushed red.

She turned back to Pharigon, who was holding his stinging cheek with a hand.

"It is worth it? She can be so aggravating," Amathea said.

"She's worth everything to me," said Pharigon.

CHAPTER SEVENTY

Balyan gawked, mouth agape, as he walked into the grand entranceway of Selvenhall. Suberon was on his arm. Suberon had planned to stay at Damagal's residence, but he was south at the Dalanen River with General Trillabon. King Baragin invited him to accompany Balyan and stay at Selvenhall where the blind wizard could be properly cared for.

"Dahoojah, 'uba," said Balyan as he greeted Baragin.

"Yat'ahna! Ye'! (son) Dahoojah! It is so good to see you finally after all these years," said Baragin in Yakat.

"S'at, Amathea," he said, introducing Amathea.

"I said 'my wife' in Yakat, Ammy. It's been so long since I spoke it, I'm not sure of the words," said Baragin.

"I am happy to meet you, honour mother Amathea. Your Yakat is very good, father. But I am not Yat'ahna anymore. I am Balyan. Naudnil Ujun gave me a new name, after the eagle, tse'balyan. He is my spirit bird," said Balyan.

"Balyan. A good name. It goes with your staff. Who carved it for you?" asked Baragin.

"Dzulhcho. He says he wishes he could be here and see his little brother again. But he said this is my journey. So, I am here with grandfather Suberon," said Balyan.

"Your son is a most charming companion, Baragin. And he has the gift, the same as Amathea. Your Ghost Singer has predicted great things for him. I think he is right," said Suberon with a smile.

"Come, Balyan. Meet your Aunt Joya and your brother and sister, Baragran and Milla. They may be a little strange with you at first, but I think they will be very happy to finally meet their Yakat brother. I will speak with you again at dinner time. I have much work to do. Suberon, perhaps you will join me," said Baragin.

Baragin led Suberon away to his office, while Amathea asked Balyan to come to the nursery where Milla and Baragran were playing.

Joya was speaking with Aruzhan and Bergara who were guarding the entrance to the nursery, asking where Amathea was.

"A Jalag is coming, Nooshta," said Bergara, nodding her head towards Balyan.

"Not a Jalag. A Yakat. I am Balyan. You must be my bearcat aunt, Joya-Noostel," said Balyan as he approached.

Joya looked intently at Balyan. He definitely had Baragin's eyes, but everything else was Yakat about him.

"They call me Nooshtal. Or Nooshta. But you can call me Joya," said Joya.

"Balyan just arrived with the Laguntzailea Suberon," said Amathea. "We're here to introduce him to his brother and sister."

Amathea introduced Balyan to Baragran and Milla, who soon were showing him all their toys.

"It's so strange to see this young man, this son of Baragin's. It's kind of surreal. He seems very pleasant, but so different from us," said Amathea.

"I had heard that the Yakats were quite warlike. Balyan is definitely not the warrior type," said Joya.

"No. But he and I do have something in common. We have visions, dreams about things to come. Did you know he knew that Baragran had been born, that he was a boy, and that he knew what colour his eyes were, before we had told anyone?" said Amathea.

Joya shook her head in wonder.

"Listen, Joya. About last night…" began Amathea.

"I don't want to talk about it," said Joya, with finality.

"Now you listen to me, little sister," said Amathea firmly. "You like Pharigon. He likes you. It's obvious to anyone who sees you two together. I see it. Poppa sees it. Aruzhan sees it. You're the only one who denies what her own heart is telling her. And you were quite horrible to Pharigon, slapping him like that, trying to pretend he was taking advantage of you. Shame on you! You owe him an apology," said Amathea sternly.

Joya just looked away, sullenly silent. Amathea put a hand on her shoulder.

"Jo-jo, Jo-jo. You are such a strong person. So fierce. So protective. Even deadly. I know what those X's on your benbay mean. But you have a loving heart. It has a shell around it, but I saw it crack last night. Don't deny what is true inside of you. Take it slowly. Let your head learn what your heart already knows—that you are in love with a wonderful man," said Amathea.

She leaned over and gave Joya a kiss on the cheek.

"I…I just don't want to be hurt the way you were hurt, Ammy. Those boys in Preneport were always so cruel to you. Those men in the Silver Dolphin. Futtsam. It made me so angry, so determined never to let anyone, any man, make me feel worthless. But maybe I took it a little too far," said Joya.

"Yes. You did. And you paid a big price. But look where you are now. Here. With me and the children. You have two friends who adore and respect you. And you have a man who is crazy in love with you—even if you did threaten to remove his manhood. Here's the dagger you dropped by the way," said Amathea, handing Joya her blade.

Joya looked at the dagger, then at Amathea. Then both of them burst into laughter and couldn't stop.

CHAPTER SEVENTY-ONE

The rice paddies in the far south of Biluria were very productive. They grew enough to feed the entire country and had a considerable amount left over for export. And they exported a lot to Zutheria.

The Bilurian-Zutherian Trading Company warehouse in Tricanmallokan was a central depot for many exports, but rice was a major one. Thirty-six barrels arrived by dray cart from the south.

"These ones look like they're for Bidrudden," said the warehouse foreman, checking the paperwork.

"Stack them next to the Wreatherin batch," he ordered.

The two batches of rice in large barrels arrived at the BZ warehouse in Iblingport two days later.

"That's a pretty large order for Bidrudden," commented one of the workers.

"I think some of it is going to be forwarded on to Elberon. Those Bilurian quarry workers up there eat a lot of rice. Plus, the wizards will be having their annual meeting, so the cooks at the castle need extra. Get them to the barge. It's the *Lazy Bee*," said the foreman.

Darrabee watched as the crew rolled the rice barrels up the gang plank and down into the hold. It was a pretty standard cargo for him. Everyone was clamouring for extra rice for all the throngs of people in Wreatherin for the weeklong Midsummer's Annual Market and all the regular celebrations.

Darrabee invited the customs inspector aboard at Braddenlocks as usual.

"What's in the hold this time, Darrabee?" he asked.

"Rice. Lots of rice. Feel free to do your checks," said Darrabee.

The inspector sighed and took out a long metal rod. The barrels for Wreatherin were on top of the smaller batch for Bidrudden. He pried open three of the barrels on top and stuck his metal probe in, feeling for the telltale signs of contraband.

"She's all good," he said, pounding down the three lids. He was supposed to inspect more as the king had insisted that all loads of goods from Biluria be thoroughly checked. But if he wanted everything checked he'd have to give the customs house more staff. He couldn't move all those barrels by himself. The barge owners were already complaining about the inspection delays.

"Have a good trip. See you on the way back," said the inspector, waving to Darrabee as he slid into the first lock.

Darrabee unloaded his large Wreatherin batch and continued up the Bradden River.

At Bidrudden, Darrabee oversaw the off-loading of the thirty-six rice barrels. They trundled down the cobblestone street to the BZ Trading Company warehouse close to the river front.

"Thirty-six? We only have an order for thirty from Elberon," complained the warehouse foreman.

"Well, I'm not taking six back," said the dray wagon driver. "You figure it out."

And he clucked his tongue to his team and drove off.

The foreman sighed.

"Roll them into the usual spot. There should be room next to that batch of furniture crates for the boss's villa in Elberon," he ordered his labourers.

Filden watched from across the street. His nephew was a senior partner of the BZ Trading Company. Sometimes he delegated his uncle Filden to deal with incoming shipments for Elberon. Filden had a key to the warehouse.

Filden walked past a non-descript house in a rundown area next to the river wharves. He glanced up at the second floor and gave his head the slightest of nods. A flash of a mirror reflecting the early afternoon sun answered him back.

Shortly after midnight, four black-clad figures slipped out of the house and moved stealthily down the back alley towards the BZ warehouse.

The door was unlocked. The leader looked around, slid open the door a crack and the four slipped through.

"Quickly!' he said.

He lit two lamps and began opening rice barrels with the other three. Soon there were thirty-six smaller kegs lifted from the bottoms of the large rice kegs.

They pried open the four furniture crates—two side tables, twelve chairs, and a large dining room table. They secured the thirty-six small kegs under the legs of the four pieces of furniture and re-nailed the crates shut. The four black garbed figures exited the warehouse, re-locked the door and left, heading west. They'd be in Elberon—at the vacant villa—before the sun was up if they rode their horses hard.

The next morning, two dray wagons of furniture and three wagons of rice barrels trundled up the road to Elberon. Filden was at the villa to receive the furniture shipment.

"Just put them in the barn for now," he told the draymen.

They complained loudly about how heavy the crates were. Four sets of eyes watched them drag the crates into the barn from an upper hay loft.

Chapter Seventy–Two

Bahomet adjusted his robe, feeling for the mantirakolai in its special pocket inside the right sleeve. He could quickly reach across and grab it with his left hand when the time came. He looked around at the masses of canoes and larger barges assembled on the shoreline of the Dalanen River just upstream from Dalanbur Island. He knew General Kiran had a large force assembled near the bridge to Zutheria behind the tree line on the shore facing the western end of the island.

This was it. The culmination of all his plans. He knew the celebration powder was awaiting its final destination in the barn of Filden's villa just below Elberon Castle. Now he just needed to get Astaran out of Elberon.

"Light the fuse," he ordered a soldier.

The aide took a small glowing branch from a nearby fire and set the fuse of the celebration powder rocket alight. The rocket took off and exploded with a thunderous bang directly over the summit of Dalanbur Island. This was Kiran's signal to attack the southern end of the island. Bahomet would have loved to have seen the faces of the soldiers, General Trillabon and Damagal as that rocket exploded in the dim light of dawn.

"Launch," ordered Bahomet, stepping into a canoe.

The flotilla began floating down the current towards Dalanbur Island.

The four paddlers in his canoe put their backs into it. The canoe sped towards the beach at the eastern end of the island.

Bahomet could see the lightening sky darken with arrows flying in both directions as Kiran's forces attacked the Zutherians holding the bridge. He saw a large rock fly through the air towards the troop formations on the shore as the ridge-top catapults started launching.

Bahomet's canoe crunched onto the beach on the eastern end of the island. His soldiers quickly dispatched the small contingent of defenders who did not expect such a large force from the east. Bahomet stepped out of the canoe and quickly strode towards the gateway marking the entrance to the old graveyard.

He paused at his great-grandfather's gravestone, put his hand on it, and whispered, "This victory is for all Biluria, payam tattam."

At the back of the graveyard was the small shrine to Zazzamin. Many valikattis of old requested to be buried on Dalanbur for this reason, as Zazzamin was the source of all their power.

A contingent of guards set up a perimeter around the shrine while Bahomet entered. One of them had brought along a trussed-up goat kid that was draped around his neck

He knelt before the small statue of Zazzamin and motioned the guard to bring the goat.

He took his dagger out of its sheath and laid it against the neck of the bleating kid.

"Oh Zazzamin, I honour you with this blood sacrifice. Restore the honour of your shrine and of all the valikattis who came before me whose bones lie here. Grant me the power to win victory," he intoned.

He quickly slit the kid's throat, dipped the end of his mantirakolai into the flowing blood and held it high.

Nothing happened for a moment. Then a small blue light, intensely bright, appeared at the end of the wand in Zazzamin's hand. It gradually became larger and larger, until it arced across the room and landed on the tip of Bahomet's mantirakolai.

The guards looked on in awe as a shimmering blue light completely enveloped Bahomet. He stood with his arm raised, chest heaving as the iridescent aura exploded in a shower of white sparks. All but two of the guards ran off in terror.

"Follow me," he ordered the commander of the landing craft troops.

The Zutherians were inflicting heavy losses on Kiran's attacking forces. Arrows and catapult boulders were continuing to rain down. The Bilurians were bogged down.

Bahomet walked at the head of his troops towards the bridge. The Zutherian commander spotted him and shouted, "Archers! To your left!"

Bahomet pointed his mantirakolai at the Zutherian defenders and said, "By the power of Zazzamin, god of this island, *TIRUMPA*!"

As Bahomet said 'return' in Bilurian, the volley of arrows launched towards him suddenly arced directly upward and began raining down on those who just fired them.

"*TIRUMPA!*" shouted Bahomet again, at the archers lining the bridge approaches and the pathways leading up to the top of the ridge.

"*TIRUMPA!*" he shouted at the Zutherians on the very top of the ridge. Every arrow fired looped back around, most striking the ones who had loosed them.

The Bilurians attacking the bridge gave a thunderous cheer and rushed their attackers with lances and swords. Their own archers began inflicting devastating casualties on the defenders.

The commander on the top of the ridge set an urgent semaphore message with flags to General Trillabon on the north bank of the Dalanen River.

"It's Bahomet. He's here personally leading the attack. He is using magic to reverse all of our arrows sent his way. We're losing ground. We're going to need your help to hold on," he said to Damagal.

Damagal grasped his dragon staff and began striding towards the riverbank directly opposite Dalanbur Island.

Bahomet used his mantirakolai to blast a pathway through to the summit of the island. Balls of fire incinerated the catapult crews. His soldiers swarmed in behind him and took over the positions. General Kiran, out of breath from climbing the pathway to the summit, stepped in beside Bahomet.

"Get your archers in place. Reverse the catapults. We'll give General Trillabon a taste of his own medicine," said Bahomet.

He turned and walked to a lookout point with a panoramic view of the river and the northern banks. He could see Trillabon's reinforcement troops assembled *en masse*. A tall, bearded figure carrying a long staff was striding towards the riverbank. Bahomet smiled. Damagal.

"Archers and catapults ready to fire, Karpukkai," said Kiran.

"Fire at will, General. Make sure one catapult is aimed at the command tent in the rear," he ordered.

Kiran nodded.

Kiran's soldiers had pushed almost all the Zutherians into the river and were slaughtering any who remained in hand-to-hand fighting. The island was in Bilurian hands.

Kiran dropped his arm, and a shower of arrows darkened the sky over the river, landing on the Zutherian reserve troops. Then one by one, the four catapults began dropping boulders on the troop formations.

An envelope of protection obviously surrounded Damagal as he stood with his dragon staff raised. It was clear he was using the same 'return' spell as Bahomet, trying to repel all the arrows being fired from the island. Bahomet raised his own mantirakolai and redirected them back.

Damagal tried to send a fireball to the summit of Dalanbur, but Bahomet repelled it with his mantirakolai. He knew Damagal's dragon staff was powerful on the soil of Elbron, but it could not overcome the power of the bones of Zazzamin's necromancers, his valikattis, on an island devoted to him. Zutheria may have captured the island in the past, but it would never be truly Zutherian territory as long as Zazzamin's shrine remained. And they could not retake it with one of Zazzamin's valikattis holding the summit.

Damagal attempted one more fireball, but Bahomet repelled it, too.

"What is happening? Why can't you destroy him?" demanded Trillabon.

"We are going to need the Staff of Elbron. He has tapped into the power of Zazzamin who has a shrine on that island. I will send a pigeon to Astaran. I suggest you move your troops back out of range, General. And send word to Baragin. This is going to be a tough fight," said Damagal.

Trillabon gestured to Pharigon.

"Send a pigeon to Selvenhall. Baragin may want to accompany Astaran," ordered Trillabon.

As Damagal turned and walked back towards the command tent, Zutherian troops began a strategic retreat away from firing range. Kiran's troops began shouting, "Verri! Verri!" Victory.

Bahomet smiled.

CHAPTER SEVENTY–THREE

Berenfromm's face was serious as he passed Pharigon's pigeon message to Baragin.

"They've taken Dalanbur. Damagal was unable to dislodge Bahomet. It seems he tapped into some infernal power lying dormant on that island. We're going to need Astaran and the Staff of Elbron to dislodge him," said Berenfromm.

"Damnation!" shouted Baragin. "What are our losses?"

"Significant. The two regiments holding the island were almost completely destroyed. A few managed to escape by swimming for it. The arrow attacks and the catapults captured by the Bilurians did more damage to the reserve units. Trillabon made a strategic retreat out of range and is awaiting further orders. Damagal has requested Astaran and the Staff of Elbron, but it will be at least three days before he can get to Dalanbur," said Berenfromm.

"You think they'll attempt to invade the north shore?" asked Baragin.

"Uncertain. They're digging in on the island at present. In the old days, before the dukes, that triangle of land between the Bradden and Dalanen Rivers was Bilurian. It's very productive farmland. He may well want to try to push us back to the old border on the Bradden," said Berenfromm.

Baragin slammed his fist down on the desk and let out a bellow of frustration.

"Do we actually know if Astaran is on his way?" he asked.

"Unknown, Majesty. The Zaharbat makes his own decisions," said Berenfromm.

"Berendell, ride out to meet him. All the way to Elberon if necessary. It may only be days until Bahomet attempts a full invasion. And Berenfromm, send a pigeon to Admiral Ambrogan in Iblingport. I want every Bilurian ship in the harbour seized and their crews interned. Put the reserve units on full alert, too," ordered Baragin.

"Which ones, Majesty?" asked Berenfromm.

"All of them!" shouted Baragin.

Berenfromm and Berendell left him stewing in his office. He fingered Damagal's protection amulet. All of this could not have come at a worse time. Midsummer's Day was only nine days away. The city was crowded with merchants and traders. Soldiers in the reserve units were not going to be happy about the prospect of being called up for active duty so close to the most important holiday of the year.

Baragin looked over at the cabinet holding the Crown of Zuth. The replica Crown of Zuth, actually. Berendell had personally travelled to Brobabil to pick up the identical copy that Graznibur had made. The real Crown was safely in Dashgran Zerribil's hands, somewhere deep in the Andragon Mountains. If the worst happened, Bahomet was not going to be placing the real Crown of Zuth on his head.

Baragin walked briskly to his personal quarters. Amathea was not there, so he went down the hallway to the nursery. He nodded to Bergara and Aruzhan standing guard outside the door and entered. Amathea was there with the children. Joya and Balyan were also in the room. They all noticed how dark his face was.

"What's wrong, Baragin, what's wrong?" asked Amathea.

"A setback. Astaran will set it aright, though. No need to worry," said Baragin, as nonchalantly as he could.

Amathea looked intently at his face, knowing full well he was minimizing the serious trouble that was occurring. She pulled him to the side.

"You're a very bad liar. Tell me what's really happening," Amathea insisted.

Baragin sighed.

"Bahomet has taken Dalanbur Island from us. He is using magic that is too strong for Damagal to overcome. We've had to call for Astaran's help," said Baragin.

Amathea's brow furrowed.

"I didn't tell you this morning. You left in a rush, and I know you have so much on your mind. But I had a dream."

"Oh, Ammy. I don't need more bad news," said Baragin.

"I don't know if it's bad news. It confused me," started Amathea.

Baragin waited for her to continue.

"I was in Amadel. I was in the same cell as when Bahomet kidnapped me. I was holding Baragran and Milla. You weren't there, but I felt strangely safe," said Amathea.

Baragin looked at her, digesting what she had just said. Then he hugged her. He knew it was so comforting for her.

"You always make me feel better, no matter how hard it gets. Don't worry. Astaran and the Staff of Elbron will get us out of this mess," said Baragin.

He caught Joya's eye and gave a nod of his head toward the doorway. She took the hint and followed him out.

"There is a carriage in the stable, second stall. Have it ready, packed, for a quick departure—clothing and food for the road for them. Make sure you and the other two have saddlebags ready for travel. You may have to take Ammy and the little ones to Amadel. Or not. I will not be unprepared, and I need the peace of mind knowing you will get them to safety if necessary. Do you understand me?" he asked.

Joya's eyed widened with alarm.

"Is it that bad?" she asked.

Baragin looked uncertain.

"Every time I have underestimated Bahomet I have regretted it. Just do as I ask."

He spun on his heel and strode down the hallway.

CHAPTER SEVENTY–FOUR

"They're digging in just out of arrow shot," said Kiran.

He and Bahomet were on the summit of Dalanbur Island, standing next to one of the catapults. Crews of soldiers had been labouring to bring more boulders to hurl. Bahomet didn't respond.

"It appears they are anticipating we'll be attacking, perhaps to push back the border to the Bradden. That entire swath of land used to be ours, Karpukkai," said Kiran.

"Prepare for an invasion, Kiran. Our goal is not the Bradden. It's Wreatherin," said Bahomet, surveying the scene below him.

"Wreatherin? But that would mean you intend to take the whole country, Myanpur," said Kiran, incredulous.

"Prepare your troops, General. That is our goal. But first we have to lose Dalanbur Island," said Bahomet.

"Lose the island? But we just took it, Karpukkai. And now you wish me to take all of Zutheria? I don't understand," said Kiran.

"The day after Midsummer, General. Be ready. I want a substantial force, eight regiments, ready to cross at Braddenlocks. They will hold the road and prevent any reinforcements from Iblingport from relieving Wreatherin. I will be with the attacking force here. That is all you need to know.

"Be prepared to retreat from this island. Probably tomorrow. Withdraw your best troops tonight and replace them with secondary units. But be sure that they put up a very determined resistance, nevertheless," said Bahomet.

Kiran left Bahomet to consult with his commanders, shaking his head. But he knew from the previous attack on Dalanbur that Bahomet's strategies were intricately planned and considered every factor for success. He still wished Karpukkai would take him into his confidence, though.

Berendell encountered Astaran riding Stellenswift just south of Drabbadentown. He had the Staff of Elbron in his hand rather than his own dragon staff.

"It seems our old friend Bahomet is proving to be quite a nuisance. He picked the one piece of Zutherian territory where he could actually have a valikatti's advantage over a Laguntzailea. But Elbron will have an answer for him," said Astaran, brandishing the Staff of Elbron.

At Selvenhall, Astaran swept into Baragin's office. Suberon and Damagal were both present, along with Berendell and Berenfromm. Both Laguntzaileas had left their dragon staffs in their rooms, as they knew the Staff of Elbron would not abide any other staff of power in the same place.

"So, what is the latest news from Dalanbur?" asked Astaran.

"Both sides are holding firm. They are dug in and so are we. It's not unthinkable that they may attempt to push us back to the old border on the Bradden. They outnumber us, but it would be very costly for them, even if you weren't here. But I am hoping you will agree it is time to teach Bahomet a lesson he will never forget," said Baragin.

"If…when we retake Dalanbur, we're going to have to destroy that shrine to Zazzamin and throw all of the old valikatti bones into the river. We need to make sure he can never tap into that power again," said Damagal.

"I think that can be arranged," said Astaran with a smile. "Bahomet knows full well the power of the Staff of Elbron. Perhaps he was hoping I wouldn't come."

"Maybe he was hoping you would," said Suberon quietly.

All eyes in the room turned to the old blind wizard.

"What do you mean, Brother?" asked Astaran.

"We all know Bahomet never does anything without a reason. We have underestimated him in the past. He deceived us most thoroughly on his last attempt to take Dalanbur, which we now know was a distraction from his true goal, kidnapping his own son. Is there a goal we haven't considered? Is this another distraction?" asked Suberon.

"That may well be, Brother. But he is going to rue the day that he forced me to bring the Staff of Elbron to a battle. I'm rather looking forward to tomorrow," said Astaran.

Suberon looked as if he still harboured doubts but said nothing more.

The following day, Astaran and Baragin rode south to the Dalanen River. They arrived in late afternoon.

The troops all cheered loudly when they saw Baragin next to Astaran and the Staff of Elbron.

"We are taking back our island! They will never threaten us again from there. Prepare for battle!" shouted Baragin.

The soldiers all cheered wildly again.

Astaran dismounted and strode by himself to the riverbank. Bahomet was not there to see him. He had conjured the strongest spell of protection he could muster and left for Trangolangopan.

The commander on the summit of Dalanbur ordered, "Catapults! Loose!"

Four boulders arced into the sky heading towards the lone wizard on the riverbank.

Astaran raised the Staff of Elbron high and uttered a short incantation in Elbronic. Four fireballs erupted from the end of the staff struck each of the boulders, turning them to sand.

He uttered another incantation, and four more fireballs spewed from the Staff of Elbron. Each scored a direct hit on the catapults, turning them into matchsticks and obliterating all the crews along with them. Astaran turned and signalled to Baragin, who leaned over to Trillabon. "Give the order to advance, General."

Astaran began striding towards the bridge on the western end of the island, Staff of Elbron out before him. Soldiers flew screaming high into the air. The lucky ones fell into the river. Astaran encountered a magical wall of resistance at the far end of the bridge but pointed the Staff of Elbron at it until it finally evaporated in a huge explosion of sparks and flames. The Bilurian troops fled in terror before him.

Zutherian troops followed in force over the bridge behind him. Astaran crossed the bridge and headed up the pathway to the eastern end of the island, incinerating any troops who dared to fire weapons at him.

He stood finally at the gate of the graveyard. He raised the Staff of Elbron over his head, then lowered it until the dragon head with the egg-shaped Eye of Elbron was pointed directly at the shrine of Zazzamin.

"*SUNTSIKETA*!" he shouted at the top of his lungs, using the Elbronic word for 'destruction!', dragging out the last syllable until he ran out of air.

A bubble-shaped sphere of fire erupted from the Eye of Elbron and enveloped the shrine of Zazzamin. It simmered and boiled, turning from dark red to white hot. Finally, it erupted into a geyser of flame. When it subsided Zazzamin's shrine was a smoldering ruin. He turned to an officer behind him.

"Get some men with shovels. Remove every single bone from this graveyard and pile them up. Burn them and dump the ashes into the river. Bahomet will not be bothering us from this island ever again," said Astaran.

CHAPTER SEVENTY–FIVE

The sun had just reached its zenith on the day that Astaran had left for the battlefront. Filden stood on the high parapet of Elberon Castle looking west to the coast at Murranenmouth. Just below him, about an arrow's shot away, stood the duke's old villa, nestled among the forested slopes of the Prenadons.

He looked around to ensure he was alone, then took a small, polished metal mirror from his pocket. He angled it towards the sun three times. Two flashes answered him from the villa.

After midnight, when all the staff were asleep, Filden made his way down to the basement storage room. Bahomet's last pigeon had included detailed instructions. He found the room and the set of dust covered shelves, laden with musty scrolls and moldering tomes of magic. He unloaded the shelves and moved the unit from against the wall.

Behind it was a doorway, just as Bahomet had indicated in his note. Filden opened the door and, with a small lantern in his hand, made his way to the T junction. He turned left and followed the dank tunnel to its end. A rusty metal door lay in front of him. He knocked lightly three times. Two knocks answered him.

He unbolted the door and pushed his weight against it. It creaked loudly. He stopped, listening for any sound that someone from inside the castle may have heard. Nothing.

He pushed the door again. It swung more easily as it was clear those on the other side were pulling at the same time.

Filden held up the lantern. Four black-garbed figures stood in front of him. Each of them had a small barrel strapped to their backs.

"Follow me," he whispered.

He led them to the T then turned left. The five of them arrived at a small room. Filden raised the lantern exposing the dim outline of a trap door directly above their head. The room continued a short way. The space was directly beneath the Council Chamber.

"Here," said Filden.

The four Karuppsertais dropped their kegs in the alcove and turned back towards the tunnel. They made eight more trips from the villa's barn to the castle tunnel.

The lead Karuppsertai removed the side cork from one of the barrels and inserted another, already fitted with a fuse end. He unrolled a small patch of cloth coated with pitch and fastened the fuse end to a much longer rolled paper fuse that he had coiled up inside his side pouch. He nodded to Filden, then the others, and began carefully backing down the tunnel to the T then towards the mountainside opening.

Filden watched them leave, then retreated to the storage room. He closed the door, moved the shelving back into place, and re-stacked the books and scrolls.

He blew out his lantern and scuttled quietly back to his room.

The Council Chamber was ready for celebration.

CHAPTER SEVENTY-SIX

Baragin rode beside Astaran down the main boulevard of Wreatherin. Crowds of cheering citizens lined both sides of the street. General Trillabon and a newly promoted Major Pharigon rode behind them, followed by a representative contingent of victorious soldiers from the battle of Dalanbur Island.

This was Baragin's first victory in a major engagement with the enemy and he felt exultant. Ambassador Erenbil's spies in Biluria had reported significant troop movements south of Braddenlocks, though, which was troubling. Nevertheless, Baragin was determined to enjoy his troops' success—and the feeling of security that came with the Staff of Elbron.

Baragin and Astaran entered the main reception room at Selvenhall. Berenfromm and Berendell were there, along with Damagal and Suberon.

"Congratulations on your great victory, Majesty," said Berenfromm with a bow.

"It seems Bahomet's mantirakolai was no match for the Staff of Elbron," commented Damagal.

"Not a surprise. The shrine of Zazzamin is no more. Neither Bahomet nor any other future valikatti will never be able to harness the power of that demon on Dalanbur Island again," said Astaran.

He glanced over at Suberon, who was sitting impassively.

"You seem unmoved by our success, Brother," said Astaran.

Suberon paused before answering.

"I did not hear that the body of Bahomet was among the fallen," he said finally.

"No, but he has obviously run back to his palace with his tail between his legs. The Staff of Elbron showed him what real power is," said Baragin.

"Some victories are not all that they seem," said Suberon, quietly.

"Blast and bother, Suberon!" said Baragin, exploding in frustration.

"Can't you let us enjoy our first victory over that wretched man?" he asked, hands spread wide.

Suberon got slowly to his feet.

"Perhaps you could call that young Balyan in for me. I'm rather tired and should head to my barge for the trip to Bidrudden," said the old wizard.

Baragin stared at him for a moment, then nodded to Berendell.

After he and Balyan left, Baragin said, "Well, I'm glad that wet blanket has taken his leave. I'm in the mood for celebrating!"

Astaran smiled but looked thoughtful.

The next day, Suberon and Balyan began the slow barge trip up the Bradden. Damagal accompanied them as he preferred to travel in comfort. Astaran and Stornowin left by horseback. The Zaharbat wished to return to Elberon as soon as possible to prepare for the

Midsummer's Day Council of Five meeting. He asked Stornowin to accompany him to give his apprentice Saragon some assistance in the preparations.

Astaran had asked Baragin if he would mind if young Balyan came along to Elberon. He had interviewed him thoroughly and thought he showed great promise.

"His time with your Ghost Singer has clearly given him a good grounding in the arts of our profession. And Suberon has indicated he does have the gift of foresight. He just may make a suitable apprentice for me. Saragon is nearing the end of his training," Astaran had said.

"I think he would like that. He's been talking nonstop about you and Elberon ever since he got here," said Baragin.

At Bidrudden, Zolenfan, Laguntzailea from the Bailiwick of Evenshorn, joined them. Damagal and Suberon rode inside the carriage, while Balyan sat beside the coach driver. Zolenfan was astride his own horse and rode beside the carriage when the road allowed. Balyan and Zolenfan chatted as they travelled, with the young wizard pointing out the sights to the Yakat boy as they travelled. Balyan peppered him with questions about Zutheria in general and the Laguntzaileas in particular.

As they neared Elberon, Balyan gasped in awe at the white stone ramparts of Elberon Castle. The village of Elberon nestled just past the castle, while the white scar of the Prenadon marble quarry glinted white in the distance.

It was the evening before Midsummer's Day when they finally arrived.

Chapter Seventy–Seven

$\mathbf{B}$alyan was in the castle library on the morning of Midsummer's Day. Astaran had given him a book of Elbronic and urged him to begin studying it. It had the main points of the language as well as a large selection of spells and incantations.

"We'll be busy with our deliberations for most of the day. Study the first part of this book and we'll talk again this evening over our meal," Astaran had said.

Balyan looked intently at the Staff of Elbron Astaran was holding. The Eye of Elbron was nestled in the mouth of the dragon head atop the staff.

Astaran followed his gaze.

"There is no power in all of Zutheria that can match what is inside this eye, young Balyan. That is why we were victorious over Bahomet and his Zazzamin power. But I must put it in its place in the Council Chamber for our meeting today. We'll talk again soon," said Astaran.

His robes flared out as he turned quickly and headed for the Council Chamber. Balyan watched him go. He looked at the empty beak of his eagle headed staff. Perhaps one day he would have a stone of great power for his eagle staff. He shrugged off the thought and began poring over the book of Elbronic.

About two hours later he was interrupted by a housekeeper.

"Beggin' your pardon, young sir, but the Laguntzailea Stornowin has asked you to come. It seems the duke has been pounding on the door of the Council Chamber looking for Filden and we can't find him. Please come with me," said the housekeeper.

Balyan put his book into his side pouch and followed her to the duke's quarters. Stornowin was standing outside the door. They could hear the old duke ranting inside the room.

"I've locked him in. It seems he wants Filden for something and interrupted our meeting with his pounding on the door. He's probably down at the villa that he is caretaker of. I need you to go there as quickly as you can and tell Filden to get back here immediately to deal with the duke. The housekeeper will point you in the right direction, but it is pretty easy to find. You just keep on following the road we came in on over the crest and down the other side of the mountain," said Stornowin.

"I'll go right away," said Balyan, following the housekeeper to the main entranceway.

Balyan was almost at the villa when a horrendous explosion knocked him flat on his face. Small rocks and other debris began raining down around him. A good-sized rock hit him in the side. The pain was intense. It felt like his rib could be broken. Blood was streaming from both of his ears. and he could not hear anything. He lay there stunned, his side aching with stabbing pains every time he breathed.

He finally got to his hands and knees and looked back at the castle. A huge cloud of dust obscured everything. He stared at it in disbelief. It was the dust of his vision.

He rose painfully to his feet and started to walk unsteadily back towards the castle. The dust cloud was slowly moving to the east as a breeze picked up. As it lifted, Balyan expected to see the castle, but it wasn't there. One end was still standing, the servants' wing, but everything else was a heap of white stones—the flat-sided white stones of his vision.

Balyan stopped and put his hands to his head, numb with shock.

Then he heard faint voices speaking an unfamiliar language, coming from the direction of the villa. There were four black clad men running towards him, brandishing daggers. Dark skins! It was clear they meant harm.

Balyan broke into a run, his side searing with pain with every step. The voices were gaining on him. He turned and saw they were closing in.

In desperation, he jumped over the side of the road and into dense brush. He pushed his way through shrubs and willows. To his left he spotted an old moss-covered fallen tree. There was a small space underneath it. He crawled beneath it, unable to run any further. The voices followed, closer and closer.

Then he remembered something—Stornowin's gift! He pulled out the spider blanket from his side pouch and draped it over himself.

The voices approached even closer. Finally, it was clear that two of them were standing on the log he was hiding under. Balyan hardly dared to breath.

Two men jumped off the log and landed directly in front of him. They scanned from left to right intently and even bent over to look under the log. They jabbered incomprehensibly to one another then hopped back up on top of the log. Balyan heard their voices fade into the distance.

He exhaled slowly and painfully.

As the dust swirling around the castle cleared, a lone raven landed on a tall fir tree next to what remained of the building. The explosion had stripped most of the boughs from the tree, but a few stout branches still remained.

The noon sun beat down steadily on the rubble. The raven espied something shiny, colourful. Like all ravens and crows, it was fascinated with anything shiny. It swooped down and landed next to it. It was a smooth, deep blue stone, egg-shaped. It was lying next to a dragon-headed staff with the jaw broken off.

The raven looked at the egg-stone, first with one eye, then with the other, cocking its head from side to side. It picked the stone up in its beak and flapped into the air. Just as it gained altitude, four black figures arrived. They started peering intently at the rubble scene, turning over rocks and slabs as they were able.

One of them found the broken-jawed dragon and excitedly called his mates over. They all began digging frantically with their hands, lifting slabs of marble in twos and threes. A dead hand protruded from underneath one massive slab. They did not find what they were looking for.

The raven flapped in a straight line, heading for its nest in a grove of firs on the downhill road to Bidrudden. It landed on the branch next to its nest and dropped the stone in. Just one more bauble to add to its collection.

CHAPTER SEVENTY–EIGHT

Captain Krindellin of the Bidrudden garrison was just putting the saddle on his horse for a regular patrol when he heard the explosion. The horse reared violently and the other troopers who were already in their saddles had great difficulty restraining their mounts.

Krindellin looked west to the huge plume of smoke and dust rising from Elberon.

"Great Zuth! Corporal Dobberan! Grab a pigeon! Troopers! We ride for Elberon," he commanded.

Even galloping as long as the horses could manage, it would take almost three hours to get there.

———◦◦◦❖◦◦◦———

Balyan stared in dismay at the ruins of Elberon Castle. A few of the survivors from the village were there as well, trying to see if there was anyone left alive under the rubble. A couple of quarry workers had brought pry bars to try to lift some of the slabs, but the only bodies they found were horribly mangled. The servants' wing was still standing but heavily damaged. The searchers found more bodies, physically intact, but violently concussed to death by the force of the blast.

No one knew what to do. There was no army garrison in Elberon. No one thought one was necessary with the Zaharbat, the most powerful wizard in all the land living there.

Everyone knew that all of the Laguntzaileas had been in the castle at the time of the blast, as well as the old duke. All were lost.

The mayor of Elberon village had tears streaming down his cheeks. He had his arm around his wife, who was sobbing openly. Two of their daughters had been servants at the castle.

Someone found the broken Staff of Elbron, with the lower jaw of the dragon missing. The Eye of Elbron was nowhere to be found.

———••◦|◦|◦••———

Baragin was putting on his dress uniform in preparation for the formal banquet and ball of Midsummer's Day when heard a distant rumble. The very walls of Selvenhall shook slightly.

"What was that loud noise, poppa?" asked Baragran, who was also getting dressed alongside his father.

"I don't know. It was a scary loud noise, wasn't it? Why don't you go down to momma's room to finish getting dressed. Poppa has to go to his office," said Baragin.

The noise had come from the northwest, from the direction of Elberon.

He nodded to the attendant who ushered Baragran out of the room.

As he entered the hallway, Amathea walked up holding Milla by the hand.

"Milla wanted to show her poppa her new party dress," said Amathea, exchanging a worried look with Baragin, eyes full of questions.

Baragin returned the look, indicating there was nothing he could tell her. But he bent down to admire Milla's dress.

"Oh my! That is so pretty, Milla! All of the other ladies at the ball will be so jealous," said Baragin.

"That loud noise scared me, Poppa," said Milla.

"Well, it scared me too, darling. Now don't you worry. Poppa will make sure everything is perfect for the party tonight. Why don't you go show Auntie Joya your new dress, alright?" said Baragin.

He exchanged another worried look with Amathea, then turned and headed towards his office.

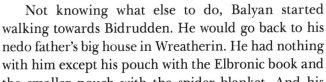

Not knowing what else to do, Balyan started walking towards Bidrudden. He would go back to his nedo father's big house in Wreatherin. He had nothing with him except his pouch with the Elbronic book and the smaller pouch with the spider blanket. And his eagle staff. He didn't even have a water bottle but knew there were a number of small creeks that crossed under the road back down the mountain to Bidrudden.

The pain in his side was throbbing with every breath. He stopped to rest in the shade of a large fir tree. There was no one else on the road at that time. People in Elberon were still in complete shock.

There were more large trees on that section of the road. Balyan heard ravens cawing and croaking behind him. He stood with difficulty and looked for the source of the sound. A large white-headed eagle was perched on a branch of a tall tree. Just below it was a nest, but it was obviously too small for an eagle's nest. Four ravens were swooping and diving towards the eagle, harassing it with high-speed dives. They came very close to its head.

Balyan had seen this sort of thing before. Ravens hated eagles and would harass any that strayed into their territory. But to have one close to one of their own nests in their rookery was absolutely infuriating. They kept up the harassment nonstop.

As Balyan stared at the drama above his head, something began to niggle inside his mind.

"The raven is the eagle's helper. He is not your spirit bird. The eagle is your spirit bird because he spoke to you," Naudnil Ujun had said.

He looked up at the eagle. In a brief respite from the diving ravens, the eagle looked directly at him, then opened its beak wide and let out its distinctive shriek.

It suddenly leapt off the branch and began to flap vigorously away, with four furious ravens in hot pursuit.

Why did the eagle look at him? Why was it near that raven's nest? Balyan stood at the base of the tree and looked up. The nearest branch was too high to reach. He looked around for something to stand on. A small partially rotted log, as big around as his thigh, lay a short distance away.

Balyan dragged it over to the base of the tree and leaned it against the trunk. With difficulty, he inched up to the top end of the log. He was still too low. He got back down and increased the angle of the log. This time he could just reach the lowest branch.

The pain in his side was excruciating. Balyan winced, but something drove him. He had to see what was in that nest. Getting onto the first branch was the worst part of the climb, but he finally managed it.

He stood gasping on the branch, one arm around the trunk of the tree. The way up to the nest was clear as there were many branches to climb on. He began ascending, hand over hand.

He heard cawing again. The ravens were returning from driving off the eagle. Finding another intruder threatening their rookery renewed their fury. They began swooping and diving towards Balyan.

"You don't like another tse'balyan, do you?" said Balyan with a wry grin.

Then he yelled in pain as one got close enough to peck him on the scalp. He felt a trickle of blood run down beside his ear. But he continued climbing. Another raven managed to get a peck on his shoulder, again drawing blood.

Balyan finally reached the nest. Four ravens were still swooping around him, but the thickness of the branches near the nest prevented them from getting too close to stab Balyan with their long, pointed beaks. Balyan's eyes broached the rim of the nest. There were feathers, moss, some sheep's wool, a metal button, a white rock with shiny flakes of mica on one side—and an egg.

Balyan's eyes widened. It was Astaran's egg-stone, the Eye of Elbron. The shiny surface glinted iridescently as a ray of sunlight struck it. The colours seemed to roil and surge inside the stone. Balyan reached in, grabbed the stone and put it in his side pouch.

He got two more pecks on the way down the tree. The pain of the last jump to the ground was almost unbearable. Balyan made his way back to the road. He was just about to step onto it when nine cavalry horses galloped past him, lathered with foam. They didn't stop.

Balyan watched them fade into a cloud of dust. He took the stone from his pouch and held it up to the light. A strange sensation ran through his hand and up his arm. Balyan put the stone up against the open beak of the eagle's head on his staff. It would be a perfect fit.

Chapter Seventy-Nine

Two pigeons flapped into the chancellor's dovecote within minutes of each other. Berenfromm's face paled. He flung open the door to his office and sprinted down the hallway, robes flying behind him.

He burst into Baragin's office without knocking and stood gasping in the doorway. Baragin and Berendell looked at him, shocked. Berendell could not remember the last time he had seen his father out of breath from running.

"Father! What's wrong? What happened?" asked Berendell.

Berenfromm was still gasping. He bent over with one hand on his knee. With the other he held up the pigeon messages.

Berendell took them out of his hands and handed them to Baragin.

He watched Baragin's face as he read the messages. His eyes widened and his jaw dropped in disbelief. His mouth started moving but no sound was coming out.

"What? What is it?" demanded Berendell.

"Elberon," said Berenfromm, finally able to speak. "Captain Krindellin from the Bidrudden detachment is in Elberon. Elberon Castle is totally destroyed, a complete ruin. There are no survivors. All the Laguntzaileas and the duke are dead."

"What did he say about Balyan? What of my son?" demanded Baragin, picking up the note again, scanning for something he had missed the first time.

"He did not say. He was at the castle. But Majesty, the Bilurians are set to attack. We need to act," said Berenfromm.

"What?!" said Berendell.

"The second pigeon is from Erenbil. Two massive armies are approaching Dalanbur Island and the border just south of Braddenlocks. It's an invasion. The destruction of Elberon means no help will be coming from the Laguntzaileas. We won't be able to hold them off for long, especially if Bahomet is using magic to help the attack," said Berenfromm.

A look of resolve came over Baragin's face.

"Get Trillabon and Pharigon here now! Send the criers around to cancel all Midsummer's Day celebrations. Close the city gates and get the governor to mobilize every unit immediately. Let those who want to leave go from the north gate. Send pigeons to the governors of Prene, Pendragon and Evenshorn. Send a pigeon to Dashgran Zerribil. He needs to prepare the Dwarvish Regiments at once. Berendell! You help him," said Baragin heading for the door.

"Where are you going Majesty?" asked Berenfromm.

"To get my family to safety," said Baragin over his shoulder.

Baragin ran down the hallway his personal quarters. Joya stood outside the door and looked in alarm at Baragin's face. She followed him into the room. Amathea was at her table with a hairdresser getting her ready for the Midsummer's Day banquet and ball.

"Out!" he shouted at the hairdresser. She hesitated, holding a warm curling iron in her hand.

"Get out! Back to your quarters," yelled Baragin.

As the frightened hairdresser scurried out of the room, Baragin pulled Amathea to her feet.

"You're going to Amadel. Now. Joya will take you. There is no time to lose. Get the children into the carriage and take enough clothes for them and you for a week," said Baragin urgently.

"But, what..." began Amathea.

"Joya. I am putting their safety in your hands. Get six palace guards from Captain Demmerdran to accompany you. I want all of you out of here within the hour," said Baragin, interrupting.

Joya dashed out of the room to inform Bergara and Aruzhan.

"Baragin, no, stop. What is going on?" asked Amathea.

"Bahomet. I don't know how, but he destroyed Elberon Castle and all the Laguntzaileas in it. He has two large armies ready to invade at Dalanbur and Braddenlocks. Without the Zaharbat and the Staff of Elbron, we can't hold them for long. You cannot stay here. Take the children to Amadel and wait for me there. Joya will take you," said Baragin.

"But when will you come? Did you say Braddenlocks? Momma, Poppa..." said Amathea beginning to cry.

Baragin enfolded her in his arms.

"Hush, darling. I need you to be strong for the children. You've had no dream about harm to me or the children, have you? I will join you as soon as I am able. My people need to see their king standing up to that monster. I must lead my armies as long as possible.

"If the Bilurians are too much, I will regroup on the other side of the Andragons at Amadel. Your father can take care of himself, especially with Blood Hammer to protect him. Now dry your tears and gather what you need for children," said Baragin.

"Oh, dear. Milla is going to be so disappointed she won't get to show off her dress at the ball."

Amathea gave a little laugh as she wiped her tears. Baragin smiled and kissed her forehead.

Amathea, her maid Bellawin, and the two children were in the carriage. Bergara and Aruzhan were already mounted. Joya was tightening the cinch strap on her saddle. She was in full Khokhgui battle armor with her bow and quiver strung over her back.

A shadow blocked the sun. She looked up shading her eyes.

"Pharigon," said Joya.

"I wanted to see you before you went. To say goodbye," said Pharigon.

Pharigon...I'm sorry. About the other night. I shouldn't have..." began Joya.

"No. You shouldn't have," interrupted Pharigon. "I'm thinking of asking Trillabon to strike a new medal—'Survivor of Nooshta Attack' medal," he said.

Aruzhan, who was within earshot, let out a barely suppressed snort, then quickly covered her mouth with her hand to keep from bursting into laughter.

Joya looked chagrined, then put her hand on his thigh, looking up to him.

"Stay safe. Our next conversation will end differently," said Joya.

Pharigon didn't answer immediately. Joya searched his face. Was he still angry with her? Was he giving up on her? She couldn't tell.

"We'll see. Luck and speed, Joya," said Pharigon as he clucked his horse into a trot.

Joya watched him go. She had never felt this way before. Shame. Longing, Confusion. Anger. Angry with herself. Angry with Pharigon for not accepting her apology. She turned and snapped at Aruzhan.

"What are you grinning at?" Joya demanded.

"Nooshta medal," said Aruzhan, looking like she was going to explode.

"Shut up!" shouted Joya.

Aruzhan burst into laughter anyway.

The day after Midsummer's Day dawned bright and hot. Bahomet surveyed the long lines of troops and mounted cavalry, each unit with its distinctive pennant flapping from the lead lance. Every horse had a leather thong with an amulet dangling from it. The second army's cavalry awaiting the order to attack the bridge at Braddenlocks also had them.

Bahomet rehearsed the horse madness incantation he had used with such effectiveness in the Mythrycian war. The Zutherian cavalry would turn in terror and the Bilurian horse units would crush any infantry in their path. No Zutherian army would be able to stand before him.

They had no Laguntzaileas to come to their rescue. A pigeon from his Karuppsertais in Elberon was bittersweet. It said, "Castle destroyed. All dead. No Eye found." He would send a larger team in later to go over every inch of that rubble pile.

"We are ready to advance on your order, Myanpur Karpukkai," said General Kiran, riding up on a splendid Mythrycian stallion.

"Good. Release the pigeon to the second army at Braddenlocks. I have a team of Karuppsertais with them to locate that tinker with the magic stick. He has a public house near the locks. Some sea snake venom should keep him from ordering that stick to attack. I want him alive. He will not enjoy his last days on earth.

"They will hold Braddenlocks and prevent any reinforcements from Iblingport from supporting Wreatherin. To the bridge, General. I want to be in Wreatherin by dinner time," said Bahomet.

CHAPTER EIGHTY

"The Bilurians! They're coming!"

Bobbingran burst in through the doors of the Prenadon Inn. It was his rest day and Genneset was behind the bar pulling drafts for the handful of patrons who usually wandered in just after he opened before noon.

"Calm down, Bob. What are you saying? The Bilurians?" asked Genneset.

"Gormanen, the Customs Chief," said Bobbingran breathlessly. "He got a pigeon from Wreatherin. Elberon and all the wizards are destroyed and Bahomet has two huge armies heading north. One for Wreatherin and one for here. They'll be here within hours."

Genneset gaped. The handful of patrons got up quickly and headed for the door, pushing Bobbingran out of the way.

"Germilda! Umbraset! Get out here!" yelled Genneset.

They came out from the back, Germilda wiping her hands on her apron.

"What is it, husband? Why are you yelling? Where are all the customers? I have three orders of food on the stove," said Germilda.

"Elberon is destroyed. The Laguntzaileas are dead. And Bahomet is headed here with an army. He doesn't remember me fondly. I am sure to be high on his list of people who need to die an unpleasant death. We need to leave. Immediately!"

Germilda's eyes grew wide with fear. She didn't move.

"Go! Go now! Gather some clothes for a journey! Go!" shouted Genneset.

Germilda scuttled to the stairs moaning in fear.

Umbraset looked with concern at Genneset.

"Where will we go, Uncle?"

Genneset thought hard for a moment.

"If they're coming here and not Iblingport, it means the army will take Braddenlocks and prevent any reinforcements from Iblingport from helping Wreatherin. They probably don't want to take on the navy at Iblingport, at least not yet. You still have that rowboat, don't you?" asked Genneset. Umbraset enjoyed rowing on his rest day.

"Yes. It's tied up at the second wharf," said Umbraset.

"We won't be able to get to Wreatherin to help Ammy and Joya. I'm sure Baragin will have the brains to send them to safety. We're going to row down to Iblingport and try to get a ship north to Preneport. It will be a while before the dust settles and that will give us time to figure out what to do. Go! Get what you need. We'll meet you at the wharf," said Genneset.

He watched Umbraset's back as he headed to his room to gather what he needed. Genneset looked over at Blood Hammer. If the Laguntzaileas were all dead, maybe that meant the magic that animated his stick was also gone.

Genneset stretched out his hand and said, *"Odol Mailua Hegen!"*

Blood Hammer rose slowly from its resting place in the back corner and flew into Genneset's outstretched hand.

"Well, at least you're still kicking," said Genneset to the empty room.

The Bilurian Second Army quickly overwhelmed any resistance at Braddenlocks. They set up defensive entrenchments on the western edge of the town and took control of the locks. A team of Karuppsertais headed for the Prenadon Inn. The found the place empty with a large padlock on the door.

Bahomet rode at the head of the Bilurian First Army. The Zutherians fought desperatedly, but all of their horses fled in terror before the power of Bahomet's horse madness spell. The volleys of arrow fired in the direction of the Bilurian all arced backwards and landed on their own men. Trillabon accepted that further resistance was a waste of men and called for a strategic retreat behind the walls of Wreatherin.

It was nearing dusk when Bahomet called a halt before the western gate of Wreatherin.

"Come, Kiran. You'll enjoy this," said Bahomet.

He trotted his horse forward with Kiran at his side.

"Baragin! You have my Crown! Now be a good boy, open the gates and bring it out to me!" shouted Bahomet.

Baragin appeared on the parapet, Berendell and Trillabon beside him.

"I should have taken your head at Amadel!" shouted Baragin in return.

"Yes. You should have. But you are too soft-hearted. You thought your little island in the Western Sea could hold me. Yet look at me now. Myanpur of Biluria. And now King of Zutheria. Well, my son Robduran will be King of Zutheria. But I will run things for now.

"First of all, I need to remove anyone who might claim they have the blood of Zuth. You. Your little Baragran. Milla," said Bahomet with an oily smile.

"Aaaargh!" roared Baragin. "Loose!" he ordered the archers.

A volley of arrows arced towards Bahomet and the Bilurian line.

Bahomet pulled out his mantirakolai and shouted, "*Tirumpa!*"

All of the arrows circled back and landed on the archers who fired them.

"Now, now, Baragin. That was not polite. You were always an impulsive boy, even at Amadel. Come, now. We were having such a nice chat. There is no need for arrows and such. Accept the inevitable. You and your line are finished. Your blue-eyed Yakat son is under tons of rubble at Elberon. Oh yes, I know about him. He and all the Laguntzaileas crushed. So sad. You know, I was thinking a shrine to Balangupong would look quite nice at Elberon, don't you?

"Oh, and by the way, a team of Karuppsertais is in hot pursuit of your homely wife and children. I've ordered that they be brought here alive. Perhaps I'll nail them to this gate so you can hear them screaming for you to help them. If you kiss my boot, I'll give them a merciful death. But first they will see their poppa's head rolling on the ground. Or maybe I'll tear the heart out of your chest so all your former subjects can see how soft-hearted you were. Oh, and I think I'll bring that very annoying father-in-law of yours to the party as well. He should be the guest of my Karuppsertais any time now. Now open the gate and let's get this over with," said Bahomet.

Baragin pulled the sword of Zuth from its sheath, held it high over his head, and shouted, "Zutheria!"

"We need to get you out of here, now, Baragin. The gates will hold for a while, even against his magic—as long as he doesn't use whatever he used at Elberon. There is a secret way under the northern wall. Pharigon is waiting outside with horses. You must go," said Berendell.

Baragin slowly lowered his sword, tears steaming down his cheeks.

"Hold them off as long as you can, Trillabon. As the Highest One is my witness, we will see Bahomet on a stake. But I need to save my family and the line of Zuth," said Baragin.

Trillabon nodded grimly.

"Let's go," said Baragin to Berendell.

The following morning, just before noon, the gates of Wreatherin gave way before the power of Bahomet's mantirakolai. The Bilurians poured in, slaughtering any troops who offered resistance. Bahomet had Berenfromm and Trillabon thrown off the highest point of the walls. He appointed Kiran as the military governor of Zutheria.

"We've found it, Karpukkai. The Crown of Zuth," said Kiran, walking up to Bahomet in the main foyer of Selvenhall. A soldier carried a wooden box with the Zutherian coat of arms.

Bahomet opened the lid of the box. The four tines of the Crown of Zuth gleamed before his eyes. The large centre ruby was flanked by the two emeralds.

Bahomet lifted it from the box, held it up high over his head and slowly lowered it onto his brow. A beatific smile crossed his face. He didn't see Graznibur's maker's mark when he put it back in the box. It was stamped into the gold behind the velvet lining.

EPILOGUE

Amathea awoke from a fitful sleep, gasping and sweating. Joya was sleeping on the floor beside them. Baragran and Milla were still sound asleep beside her.

"What is it, Ammy? A dream?" asked Joya, fully awake now.

"Dark faces. Bahomet's black assassins. They're coming, Joya. They're coming for us. We need to go now," said Amathea.

They had spent the night at Drabbadentown. The mayor had insisted on accommodating them in his spacious house.

Joya roused Bergara and Aruzhan, then went to the stables where the six palace guards had bedded down for the night. Sergeant Yanneron led the six-man protection detail.

"Yanneron. Yanneron! Time to go. Get the men up. We need to get on the road to Bidrudden. Keep two men back. There's a chance Bahomet's Karuppsertais may be on our tail," said Joya.

"How do you know...?" began Yanneron.

"Just get ready. We may see action today," said Joya.

She quickly strapped on her armour, checked the edge of her battle axe, and examined her bow string.

They were halfway to Bidrudden when one of the rear-guard soldiers came riding up.

"Four Bilurians. In black clothing. They got Hanradden with some kind of dart," shouted the soldier to Yanneron.

"Aruzhan! Stay with the carriage. Bergara, with me!" yelled Joya.

She knew some rearguard archery might be necessary. Aruzhan had never quite mastered the skill, but Bergara was the best defensive horse archer in the Khokhguis.

As the carriage rolled off at a gallop, Joya and Bergara reined in their horses at a bend in the road. They didn't have to wait long. Trooper Hanradden's empty horse was galloping down the road in front of four Karuppsertais.

"Loose. Aim for the horses!" said Joya.

Bergara's arrow hit the lead horse, while Joya's pinned the thigh of a Karrupsertai to his saddle.

"Ride!" said Joya.

They vaulted into their saddles and headed down the road.

The wounded Karuppsertai broke the arrow from his thigh and kept riding. The lead assassin goaded his horse ahead and managed to grab the reins of Hanradden's horse. The Karuppsertai with the wounded horse abandoned his and mounted the Zutherian horse, remembering to transfer his horse madness amulet. The four resumed their pursuit.

Joya and Bergara caught up to the carriage. The horses were tiring, and the carriage had slowed to a canter.

Joya looked back. The four Karuppsertais were gaining quickly, whipping their horses.

"Notch!" shouted Joya.

Bergara and Joya loosed their arrows. Bergara's hit the Karuppsertai in the lead and he tumbled from his saddle. Joya's missed.

"Again!" commanded Joya.

Two more arrows flew back. Bergara's arrow hit a horse square in the chest. It tumbled into the dirt throwing its rider. Joya's arrow skewered a Karuppsertai through the neck.

With one wounded man left and two others down, the Karuppsertai commander called a halt to the pursuit and reined in his horse.

Amathea wept with relief as they neared Bidrudden.

"I was so scared, Joya. You saved us. You saved us," said Amathea, giving Joya a huge hug.

"We need to keep going. They will likely try again," she said.

Joya had her horse at a walk beside the carriage window.

"Someone's coming. Aruzhan! With me."

Joya spurred her horse ahead to confront the traveller.

It was Balyan. He was barely recognizable. Dried blood stained his neck from his ears, and more blood was on his brow and on the shoulder of his shirt.

"Oh, my goodness! Balyan! What happened to you? We thought you were dead," asked Amathea as Joya helped him into the carriage. Baragran and Milla looked at him with wide eyes.

"The castle. It's gone. Dust and white stones. Like in my vision. Grandfather Suberon. All the others. Dead. But an eagle helped me find it. An eagle and a raven," said Balyan.

"What? An eagle? I don't understand what you're saying, Balyan. You're not making sense. What did the eagle help you find?" asked Amathea in puzzlement.

"This," said Balyan, holding up the Eye of Elbron.

ABOUT THE AUTHOR

C.S. Kempling is a retired teacher/counsellor living in Kamloops, British Columbia, Canada. He is father to three and grandfather of five. He enjoys making walking sticks in his spare time—it was the inspiration for Blood Hammer. While he has been a newspaper columnist, poet, songwriter and story author for many years, the Blood Hammer trilogy is his first novel. More information can be found on the Blood Hammer Fantasy Trilogy Facebook page.

Preview to Ghost Singer's Prophecy—Book Three of the Blood Hammer Trilogy.

A vicious army of occupation takes over most of Zutheria. The royal family become refugees in their own land in the old castle at Amadel. Will Dwarf Lord Zerribil and his Dwarvish Regiments keep the Bahomet and the Bilurians out of Evenshorn? How will Balyan harness the power of the Eye of Elbron when the evil Bahomet is doing everything in his power to acquire it? How many more X's will the Khokhgui warrior Joya add to her benbay? Find out in the dramatic conclusion to the Blood Hammer Trilogy.